GRAY VENGEANCE

Also by Alan McDermott:

Gray Justice (Tom Gray #1)

Gray Resurrection (Tom Gray #2)

Gray Redemption (Tom Gray #3)

Gray Retribution (Tom Gray #4)

ALAN McDERMOTT

GRAY VENGEANCE

THOMAS & MERCER

Published by Thomas & Mercer, Seattle

www.apub.com

ISBN-13: 978-1477830611
ISBN-10: 1477830618

Cover design by bürosüd° München, www.buerosued.de

Library of Congress Control Number: 2014959846

Printed in the United States of America

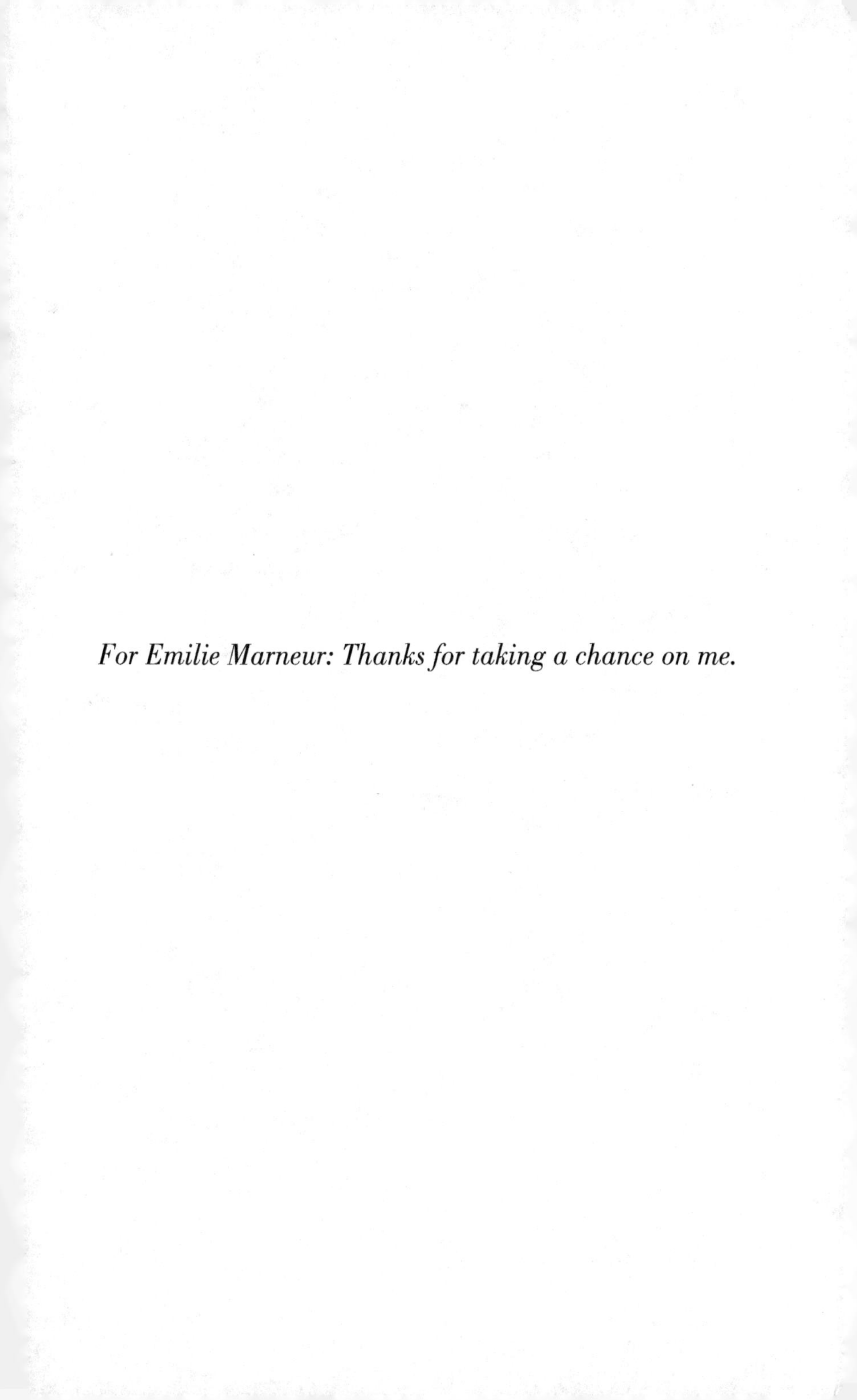

For Emilie Marneur: Thanks for taking a chance on me.

WINTER

Prologue

20 January 2014

A crescent moon watched over the ersatz motorcade as it turned off Kufar Mata Road and into a maze of side streets that led to the old city. Despite being the second most populous city in Nigeria, with more than two million inhabitants, Kano appeared deceptively quiet at eleven in the evening, which was why the new leader had chosen such a late hour for his first address to the council he now ruled.

The three battered vehicles pulled up at the compound, whose pockmarked white walls surrounded a modest residence. Armed guards were waiting and, after confirming the identity of the visitors, slowly pulled open the huge metal gates to allow them ingress.

At the front door of the house, the host welcomed his exalted guest.

'Takasa, it is a pleasure to welcome you to my humble dwelling,' the elder said, guiding the leader into the living area. Six men were waiting, and as the host barked an order, two young girls brought food in before quickly disappearing, leaving the men to their business.

Takasa took a seat on a pile of cushions and prepared himself a cup of hot tea while the other members of the council took in their new leader, most for the first time. A couple of them engaged in a hushed but animated discussion, while the others simply stared at the man who had been chosen to lead their organisation.

His selection by the three senior members of the council had come as a huge surprise to most, not least because of his skin colour, but that didn't faze Takasa in the slightest. He was prepared for any animosity, though he felt certain that once he'd addressed the men, his vision would unite them and they would accept him as one of their own.

He placed his tea on the low table and coughed loudly, grabbing everyone's attention.

'Brothers,' he began in English, 'I am honoured to have been chosen to lead you into history.'

Takasa waited for the words to sink in and realised he was facing a tough crowd. He stood and began pacing the room, the traditional local garb feeling surprisingly comfortable.

'Da Sunan Annabi, or *In the Name of the Prophet*, is a very young organisation, and I have watched your development with interest.'

In truth, he'd been looking for just such a group to establish itself in the hope of getting in at an early stage, and with the death of their leader in July of that year, he'd known the time was right to step in and fill the breach.

'Over the years,' he continued, 'many organisations have tried to take on the might of the West, but they have only succeeded in bringing fire down upon themselves. That outcome won't change while the West is capable of striking back. It is impossible to defeat their military, and for every Western soldier we kill, a hundred will rise up to replace him.'

He paused, as if trying to find the next words, even though he'd been over the speech a hundred times in preparation for this meeting.

'If your dream is for meaningless small victories and a short life, then we can continue on the current path.'

A man wearing a scowl raised a hand, but Takasa waved him off. 'If, however, you dream of a world where the West no longer has any influence, be that militarily, economically or politically, then you need my help. I promise to lead you to a victory that will be remembered for thousands of years.'

The hand went up again, and this time the man wouldn't be silenced. 'And just how will you guarantee this? What experience could you possibly have that will make any contribution to *our* cause?'

The emphasis wasn't lost on Takasa, but he'd expected this kind of reaction. Being the only white man in the room naturally made him a target for their animosity.

'To defeat your enemy, you first have to know him,' Takasa said. 'I know our enemy well. Now, you obviously know where the strengths of the West lie, but what of their weaknesses? Could you take down a whole country with just two hundred people?'

The man laughed, his derision palpable. 'That's impossible.'

'Is it?' Takasa asked. 'Imagine a baker taking his wares to town to sell in the market. He is pushing his barrow but finds the road blocked. He has no option but to return home, knowing that he won't be earning any money that day. On top of that, he has lost all the money he spent on ingredients.'

'So?' the man asked.

'So, imagine instead that he had planned to sell his bread to a shop owner. Now two people have no income for the day.'

'Can you get to the point?'

'The point is,' Takasa said slowly, refusing to be rushed, 'two people suffering financially for a short period of time isn't the end of the world, but let's say *every* merchant used the same road into town, and nobody could get in to sell their products. Now you have a whole community that is suffering. People aren't earning a living, and their customers have nothing to eat.'

The man stood, showing his annoyance. 'This is preposterous! We need a leader who is not afraid to take the fight to the West, and you bring us . . . *this*?'

He gestured at Takasa with disdain, but one of the senior members shouted him down.

'Silence, Kwano! I have heard his plans, and if you are willing to listen, you will see why he is the perfect choice to lead us.'

Kwano sat again but wasn't quite finished. 'Your story makes no sense,' he said to Takasa. 'As soon as news of the blocked road spread, everyone would help to clear it.'

'Exactly!' Takasa smiled. 'That's precisely what *you* would do. However, the British are cut from a different cloth. They would complain about the blockage and wait for someone else to clear it. And when no-one listened, the complaints would mount while the road remained obstructed.

'You see, the West takes pride in its advanced culture. It is a place where a man can sit at home and order a meal to be prepared and delivered within thirty minutes, and have someone fix his car without having to take it to the garage or, heaven forbid, do it himself; where groceries, furnishings and entertainment are brought to him rather than the man having to go out and buy them; where he can make a phone call to have a woman satisfy his needs, whatever they are. Their lifestyle has made them lazy and reliant on others, and that is their first failing. Their reliance on technology is their next.'

Kwano appeared only partially appeased. 'I was in England for a few years, and the small community I lived in doesn't sound anything like what you've described.'

'Granted, there are pockets of society that will still chip in and help each other out, but they are isolated and won't be affected by my plan. You certainly won't find villagers from Kent rushing into London once we strike.'

'So you plan to block a road?' Kwano said. 'Is that your big plan?'

Takasa smiled as he resumed his seat. 'Your problem is, you're thinking small. That's why I'm here.'

He laid out his plan, which took another thirty minutes, by which time he had almost everyone on board.

'It still sounds like fantasy to me,' Kwano said.

'Really?' Takasa asked. 'Then let me tell you how delicate the UK infrastructure is.'

He explained how tens of thousands of homes had been without power for days following a Christmas storm only a few weeks earlier; how air traffic had been severely disrupted following a glitch with the telephone wires; and the countless occasions when traffic accidents had closed major roads.

'These were random acts that brought chaos and misery, but imagine the impact if they were co-ordinated.'

As Kwano thought this over, another man asked about timescales.

'If we start immediately, we can have the groundwork done within a few weeks. After that, it is a matter of releasing the necessary funds and sourcing the materials. I expect to be ready to strike within the next six months.'

'How much will it take to bring this plan to fruition?'

'Fifty million should be enough,' Takasa said.

This drew a smirk from Kwano. 'An easy number to speak of, but how do you expect us to raise so much in half a year? It would take a lifetime of lifetimes to gather such wealth.'

'I already have half of the amount we need,' Takasa told him, 'and I can call on the rest at any time.'

At this, Kwano conceded. As Takasa had anticipated, financing the entire venture sealed the deal.

The meeting ended and Takasa was escorted back to his conveyance, the first step of his plan ratified. An auspicious start.

When he reached his temporary residence in Kano, he would make a phone call that would take the second step towards Britain's downfall.

Chapter 1

23 January 2014

Andrew Harvey brushed the hair from his forehead and made yet another mental note to visit the hairdresser before it got completely out of control, despite it being only a couple of inches in length. Work had taken up every waking moment of the last three weeks, and the news that Da Sunan Annabi, or DSA, had appointed a new leader only added to his section's workload.

Harvey walked over to Hamad Farsi's desk and asked the intelligence operative for the latest news from Nigeria. He was rewarded with a frustrated sigh.

'None of our contacts knows anything apart from the name, and they're pretty sure it's a pseudonym.'

'You think?' Harvey asked, with a touch more sarcasm than he'd intended.

It had been yet another long, unproductive shift, and three days since the announcement had come in, they still knew nothing about the mysterious Takasa except that the name meant 'purifier' in the local language.

Harvey put his hands to his temples. 'I'm sorry. I shouldn't have snapped at you. Just keep digging and see if any of our sources can get a break. This guy didn't pop up out of nowhere, so there must be some clues to his identity.'

'No worries. Hey, maybe you should ask Ellis for some time off.'

Harvey found the idea tempting, but going to Veronica Ellis wouldn't solve the problem. The director general of MI5 wasn't responsible for the heightened security alert, and with everyone in his team working above and beyond, Harvey didn't feel as if he could let the side down by slinking off to bed for a couple of days. Two new fundamentalist groups had cropped up in recent weeks, and efforts were being concentrated on establishing their structures and goals, as well as dealing with a spate of suicide bombings that had targeted British military personnel in Gibraltar and Cyprus. No group had yet claimed responsibility for the attacks, which made Harvey's job even harder.

The arrival of a new boss reinvigorating DSA was the last thing he'd needed.

'I might have a late start tomorrow,' he told Farsi, though he knew he'd be the first in the office, well before the sun came up. As usual. 'In the meantime, see what the forensics people in Gibraltar have come up with.'

Harvey walked back to his office, a small space he'd been allocated a few weeks earlier and one that he already despised. He felt out of the loop, and missed the bustle of the main office. Sure, it was noisy at times, but somehow the chaos had helped him concentrate. Still, Ellis thought it important that the section leader have his own space, and he wasn't about to argue the little things with his boss.

He found himself going through the most recent intel on DSA, even though he felt he knew the organisation inside out. They had been formed in the northern region of Nigeria less than three years earlier, and so far their activity had been limited to the surrounding region. As they grew, they had formed into separate, cell-like factions, and so their overall structure had become unclear. It seemed anyone with an axe to grind could now throw themselves under the DSA umbrella, which had begun to muddy the group's original Islamist ideals.

Their latest intel suggested the main body was planning to broaden their reach, though MI5's analysts had played down the threat level. They hadn't entirely dismissed it as pure rhetoric, the ravings of a new leader determined to make an impression on his own followers, because doing so would leave their arses hanging out if they got it wrong. Instead, they'd suggested that DSA had limited funds, so despite the chatter they were picking up from the rank and file, the chances of the group expanding beyond its own city limits remained slim to none.

Harvey's computer beeped, signalling an incoming internal message, and he opened it to find a summons from Veronica Ellis. Locking his computer, he walked to her office and gave a cursory knock before entering.

'You wanted to see me?'

Ellis nodded towards a chair and he took a seat. She remained standing, her impeccable grey pencil skirt hugging her figure as she pushed a wisp of platinum hair over her ear and leaned on the desk.

'You remember James Farrar?'

'Not a name I'm likely to forget,' Harvey said.

Farrar had once run a covert government wet team, designed to carry out foreign sanctions. When he'd turned his attention to killing British citizens, it had been Harvey's department who had shut down his operation. 'The last I heard, he was on remand, awaiting trial.'

'That was the plan, but it seems he was granted bail.'

'Who the hell authorised that?'

'His lawyers argued that by being incarcerated, he wasn't in a position to liquidate his assets in order to fund his defence, so the judge confiscated his passport before tagging him and letting him go.'

'And you're telling me this because . . . ?'

Ellis rose from her chair and straightened her pencil skirt before pacing the office, arms folded rigidly across her chest.

'He skipped town. We've been tasked with finding him.'

'Quelle surprise,' Harvey said. 'Did no-one see that coming?'

'We'll leave the recriminations for another day,' Ellis said. 'What matters is tracking him down now.'

'I thought you said he was tagged.'

'He was,' the director general said, 'and he was being monitored remotely, but somehow he managed to remove his electronic tag and put it on a substitute. Apparently he was renting a small flat after selling his house, and he paid a homeless guy a grand to stay there for a few weeks. The place was stocked with alcohol and cigarettes, so the old drunk had no reason to leave.'

'And this guy knows nothing, I assume.'

'Nada,' Ellis said. 'All we know is, Farrar left around a month ago.'

Harvey immediately thought of Tom Gray, the man Farrar had been trying to eliminate when he'd crossed paths with Harvey. If Farrar were out for revenge, Gray would surely be his first target. After all, he'd been instrumental in getting Farrar to confess his crimes live on TV.

'What do you think Farrar is planning?' he asked.

'I know what you're thinking, but I don't believe this is about your friend. More likely he just wanted to avoid prison and used a fake passport to take him to some backwater country that has no extradition treaty in place.'

That made sense, but Harvey made a mental note to give Tom Gray a heads-up anyway.

‘That doesn’t leave us much to go on, assuming he ever left the UK in the first place. How high is this on the priority list?’

‘Near the top,’ Ellis said. ‘You can imagine the political backlash if this makes the papers, so we need to be seen to be looking. I’ll need daily progress reports to pass upstairs.’

Harvey wondered exactly how his team were supposed to fit in the extra work. Needle in a haystack didn’t come close, and unless they had a trail to follow, there wasn’t much they could do apart from alert Interpol and wait for Farrar to pop up somewhere.

‘Okay, I’ll put the word out and let you know if he appears on our radar.’

Ellis resumed her seat and interlaced her fingers atop her desk, looking Harvey in the eye. ‘As I said, this is politically sensitive, so we can’t go broadcasting this to every agency in the world. If word leaks, the PM isn’t going to be happy with us. We have to do this in-house.’

‘So no Interpol and no extra-agency support. Do I get extra resources to work it up?’ Harvey asked, but he already knew the answer.

‘Not at this time. Once we have something to go on, we might be able to borrow a couple of people from Six, but that’s about it.’

Harvey stood suddenly to leave, his frustration showing. ‘I’ll get things moving and have the first report ready for you in the morning.’

Back in the main office, he returned to Farsi’s desk and delivered the bad news.

‘If he skipped the country, he won’t be anywhere friendly. Dig up a list of countries that we don’t have extradition treaties with, then get all flight departures to those destinations for the last six weeks. Once you have the passenger lists, screen each person against the passport database. Farrar was using a fake, so we’ll be looking for close matches on the photo, first-time use or anything else out of the ordinary. If that doesn't give us anything, expand it to seaports and the Channel Tunnel.'

With the orders relayed, Harvey went back to his office and locked the door, hoping to keep the world at bay lest it throw any more crap at him.

SPRING

Chapter 2

11 March 2014

Paul Roberts powered down the ancient Dell laptop and packed it into his dishevelled backpack. After ensuring all the office lights were off, he closed the door and locked it before descending the stairs to the street, passing the Chapter Nine logo plastered on the wall. The elements had taken their toll on his poster, its clenched fist with razor wire around the wrist barely distinguishable from the faded sepia background.

At the bottom of the stairs he turned into the alley and exited onto the main road. A Chinese takeaway and a small grocery store were the only businesses still open at seven in the evening, and the area had a desolate, depressing feel to it. With his shoulders hunched against the early spring breeze, he set off for the ten-minute walk to the bedsit he called home.

Twenty yards into his stroll, a black saloon pulled up beside him. The rear window glided down and Roberts found himself looking at a dark-haired man of medium complexion who looked to be in his mid-forties.

'Paul Roberts? Can I have a word with you about this?'

The man held out a leaflet, and Roberts immediately recognised it as one of his own.

He eyed the man warily. 'What about it?'

'I work for someone who would like to fund your organisation.' The man swung the door open, inviting Roberts inside, but he hesitated. The only people who had shown any interest in Chapter Nine—apart from its members—were the police, whom he loathed with a passion.

The man reached into his jacket pocket, and Roberts tensed, expecting him to pull out a weapon, but all that appeared in the gloved hand was a thick, white envelope.

'I can understand your reticence. Here's a grand in cash. All I ask is that you take a short ride while I explain the proposition.'

'What if I don't like your offer?'

The man shrugged. 'Then I'll drop you off at your place and you'll be a thousand pounds richer.'

Roberts considered the proposal. The money would be extremely helpful to his organisation, covering his latest printing costs at the very least, not to mention the arrears on the rent for the tiny office. *Risk versus reward . . . . Always the calculus* . . . . All he had planned for the evening was a trip to the laundrette, and as his clothes had been festering in a black bin liner for nearly three weeks, another half an hour wasn't going to make much of a difference.

He took the envelope, climbed into the car and closed the door, and the driver pulled away.

'Are you the police?'

The man chuckled. 'No, not the police. Nor do I have any involvement with any government department, if that was going to be your next question.'

'Have you got a name?'

'You can call me Efram.'

'And your surname?'

'I think Efram's distinctive enough.'

'So how do you know my name?'

'You ask a lot of questions for a man who's been paid a lot of money just to listen,' Efram said.

'Call me paranoid, but I trust no-one, least of all strangers.'

Efram pulled a file from his briefcase and opened it. 'Paul Roberts, born at Brighton's Royal Sussex County Hospital on June the seventh, 1980. Left school and went to Sussex University in 1998, studied philosophy and sociology before dropping out in your second year with a poor attendance record. Moved to London shortly afterwards and had a succession of poorly paid jobs for a couple of years, then were approached to join the Direct Action Movement, or DAM. After a brief spell in their ranks, you left, seeing them as too liberal for your liking. You found the same problem with the Anarchist Federation, and so you formed Chapter Nine, along with a few other disillusioned members of DAM and AF. You currently have seventeen members and just over two hundred pounds in your bank account.'

'I thought you said you weren't government,' Roberts interrupted. The conversation had taken a distinctly uncomfortable turn. 'How could you know all this about me?'

Efram chuckled. 'A decent private detective could dig up this information within a couple of hours, especially one with a disregard for privacy laws, so don't be shocked.'

Efram glanced down at the file. 'According to this, you have three convictions for criminal damage in the last two years. Tell me about them.'

Roberts briefly explained how he'd attacked a car belonging to the head of a major bank, covering it in blue paint, and how he and some fellow members of Chapter Nine had sprayed their slogans all over the walls of the buildings in Egerton Crescent, Britain's most expensive street. The final act had been to pelt the prime minister's car with paint bombs as it left Downing Street.

'I'm confused,' Efram said. 'You claim to be anarcho-syndicalists, and you state that through direct action, workers will be able to liberate themselves, yet all you've done is throw a little paint around. How exactly is that supposed to bring down the government?'

Roberts's face burned. True, his actions so far hadn't exactly caused ripples through parliament, but what was such a small group supposed to do?

'Our acts were designed to drum up support,' he said. 'As our numbers grow, our voice will be heard.'

'Is that really the case,' Efram asked, 'or are you just a whinging pussy who's using Chapter Nine as an excuse not to do a real day's work?'

The insult was too much for Roberts.

'Stop the car,' he said. 'I'm not listening to this shit, no matter how much you're paying.'

Efram put a hand on his chest and pushed him back into his seat. His demeanour instantly changed, gone the genial soul who'd made the initial offer.

'When I think of smashing the state, I'm not interested in waving a placard about, or a little vandalism: I envisage a country with no effective government where the people rise up and take what's theirs; where the rich become the poor; and where anarchy reigns. The workers determine their own conditions and answer to no-one.' He stared into Roberts's eyes as if peering into his soul. 'What do you see?'

'The same,' Roberts said, 'but there isn't much I can do with less than two dozen men and no funds.'

'You see the size of your group as a disadvantage, but that's exactly why we sought you out. The only question is, how far are you willing to go to realise your dream?'

'I'm ready for anything,' Roberts insisted.

'That's the answer I was hoping for, but let me warn you: once you accept our offer, there's no going back.'

'Yeah, red pill, blue pill. I get it.'

'I'm serious,' Efram said. 'We can help to bring about your dream, or you can carry on as you are, making no difference whatsoever. Just be aware that this will be far beyond anything you've done so far. People will die, and I mean lots of them.'

'That happens with all real revolutions,' Roberts said. 'The elite aren't just going to hand over the reins and step aside: we're going to have to take them down.'

'I agree, but I'm also thinking of the common folk who will get caught up in the violence. Do you think you could live with that?'

Roberts didn't hesitate. 'Eggs and omelettes.'

'So the end justifies the means?'

'Exactly.'

Efram closed the file and put it back in his briefcase. 'I'll call you tomorrow,' he said, as the car pulled up to the kerb. 'If you decide to accept our offer, we'll have to move fast, so have your passport handy.'

'Where will I be going?'

'If you're in, you'll find out when you get to the airport. In the meantime, find three others from your ranks that you'd like to take with you. No more, no less. And make sure they're hard-core. I don't want any tree-huggers.'

'I know the three I'd choose,' Roberts said, '*if* I agree to go along with this. It still stinks of entrapment.'

'Don't flatter yourself. Your little organisation isn't even an irritation to the authorities. They know you exist, but you're so far down the watch list that you're invisible. Like I said, exactly what we need for our operation.'

Feeling both a bruised ego and excitement at the possibility of real change, Roberts opened the door and climbed out.

'Think about it,' Efram called after him. 'This will be your one and only chance to make a difference.'

Roberts closed the door and the saloon pulled away, leaving him slightly confused, if not a little better off than he'd been for a long time. He stuffed the cash into his pocket and headed back to his bedsit for another night alone, only this time he would treat himself to a bottle of vodka while he reflected on the man's offer.

Chapter 3

12 March 2014

Despite the sun beating down on Tom Gray as he steered his daughter's pushchair into the Minotaur Logistics car park, March had served up a bone-chilling day. He pressed the intercom and was grateful when the door buzzed open, allowing him entry into the warm reception area.

'Hi, Tom,' the receptionist said, walking round to get a look at the warm bundle in the chair. 'Melissa, you're getting so big!'

'That's because she never stops eating.' Gray smiled, lifting his daughter from the conveyance. He allowed Gill to fuss over her for a couple of minutes, then asked if Len was busy.

Gill called through to the office to check, then nodded for Gray to go in.

'You can leave Melissa with me if you like,' she said, but Gray declined the offer.

'Len wants to see her, too,' he lied, carrying his daughter to the office door.

The truth was, Gray felt uncomfortable leaving his daughter with anyone, even his secretary-cum-receptionist of more than five years. The fire that had killed his wife Vick had almost claimed the life of his daughter, and having discovered that it wasn't an accident, he remained reluctant to let Melissa out of his sight. He'd been in Africa when the blaze took hold, and he still blamed himself for not having been home to save Vick.

In the office, Gray found Len Smart sitting behind the desk that had been his own for many years. Though Smart held the title of managing director, it was purely a smokescreen. Minotaur remained Gray's company, one that he'd built from the ground up after leaving the army years earlier.

Having sold the company to fund his infamous escapade, Gray had subsequently bought it back, despite his solicitor Ryan Amos's warnings that his customers wouldn't want to be seen as bedfellows with someone the newspapers called a terrorist.

Don't expect the world to return to normal after you kidnap five criminals, parade them on the internet, and hold the entire country to ransom, Amos had scolded.

Unfortunately, Amos had been right. The customers had been fine with the arrangement when no-one knew about it, but once a tenacious tabloid reporter had published a list of the blue-chip clients Gray was servicing, the clients had wanted nothing to do with Minotaur.

Gray's only option had been to resign his position to prevent the company from folding completely, though he still earned a monthly stipend for his consultancy work, which involved making all the important decisions while letting Smart act as his steel-plated mouthpiece.

'Hey.' Smart walked around the desk and greeted Melissa and Gray with a broad smile.

Gray happily handed his daughter over, watching the big man make a fuss over her.

Smart looked every inch the company director, with his balding pate and bushy moustache. Those who met him for the first time invariably saw him as a competent businessman with an affable disposition; few would have guessed that he'd served with distinction in the Special Air Service for a number of years, including in Iraq.

Smart was one of Gray's trusted employees and—more importantly—friends. They'd been through a lot together, both in the SAS and subsequently in civilian life. He'd saved Gray's life more than once, and Tom couldn't think of anyone better to represent his company.

'At least you're not skimping on her food,' Smart smiled as he lifted Melissa up above his head, earning a giggle from the nine-month-old.

'She eats more than you,' Gray said. 'I may need to ask for a raise.'

'Now would be the time,' Smart said. 'I'm working on a new contract in northern Nigeria. A petrochemical company is heading into DSA territory, and they want a four-man protection detail.'

'Da Sunan Annabi? They've been quiet for a few months now.'

'I know, but the client wants to be on the safe side.'

'Who have we got available?'

Smart returned to his desk and opened the personnel files before rattling off a dozen names. 'They've all got time on the continent, so acclimatisation shouldn't be an issue.'

'Well, you know the score,' Gray said. 'Choose a squad leader and three men, but make sure they're near the top of the detail roster.'

The list was ordered by the amount of time it had been since a contractor had been on assignment, and it was designed to ensure that roles were dealt out fairly. It meant those who had been waiting longest for a contract were at the top, and as the list was updated monthly and emailed to all staff, it eliminated any suggestion of favouritism. Of course, there were times when a certain skill was needed and the person at the top had to be skipped, but everyone understood that this could happen. It was details like this that meant Gray had a constant stream of top-class talent to choose from; no other private security firm offered such transparency to its operatives.

'There is someone who has requested the squad lead position . . . .'

Gray knew what was coming. 'It's Sonny, isn't it?'

Smart nodded. 'I hate to even suggest it, but he's been begging me for weeks.'

Simon 'Sonny' Baines was another of Gray's close friends. Sonny and Smart had long been inseparable on operations, but while Smart was happy in his new role of office manager, Sonny was itching to get back into the field. His current role of liaison officer didn't exactly offer the excitement he craved.

'I won't risk his life again,' Gray said. 'Sonny may look and act like a twenty-something, but he's about to hit forty. He's been in enough scrapes to last a lifetime.'

'Agreed,' Smart said, 'but he's a kid at heart. Screening potential recruits isn't his forte, and you know it.'

'I know, but I almost got you guys killed in Malundi. I can't go through that again.'

Just mentioning the place again brought back thoughts of Vick, and Gray closed his eyes in an attempt to banish the image of her lying unconscious while flames leapt around her . . . .

'Now, that wasn't your fault, so get over it. Not even the Foreign Office knew what was going on. I'd have made the same decision.'

Gray knew his friend was right, but it didn't detract from the fact that if he'd pulled the men out a day earlier, he wouldn't have gone in to get them, and his wife might still be alive.

Melissa began fidgeting, and a noxious odour emanated from her jumpsuit.

'Come on, you,' Gray said. 'Let's get that nappy changed.'

'Ah, Tom?'

Gray looked to Smart. 'What?'

'What about Sonny?'

'I've got something in mind that'll keep him happy,' Gray promised, then made a beeline for the bathroom.

Chapter 4

12 March 2014

'What the hell are you doing, Erik?'

Roberts watched the tall Dutchman glancing furtively around the departures lounge at Heathrow Airport, his actions more than suspicious.

'They're going to come for us,' Erik Houtman whispered. 'I can feel it. I told you this was a bad idea.'

Roberts, not for the first time that day, regretted bringing Erik along. He'd always been a belligerent shit, and his dedication to the cause was the only reason Roberts hadn't kicked him out of the organisation. That, and the fact that their numbers were already on the lean side.

Today, however, Erik had been worse than usual. He'd constantly stared out of the rear window on the taxi journey to the airport, convinced they were being tailed, and anyone who looked at them as they queued up at check-in just *had* to be an undercover police officer.

'We're doing nothing illegal,' Roberts whispered, 'so just shut the fuck up and relax.'

Easy to say, he thought. He hadn't done much relaxing since the initial meeting with Efram, despite making a big dent in the alcohol he'd bought on that first night. It had been with a sore head that he'd taken the call the following morning, and while still hesitant, he'd found himself agreeing to Efram's proposal. After taking down instructions on what to pack, he'd met with his three fellow members. As per Efram, he'd chosen a trio with no family ties, so their absence wouldn't be questioned. Roberts had told them what little he knew about the offer, and two had been keen to take part.

Erik was the exception.

The Dutchman was in his early forties and had taken part in the poll tax riots in 1990, the worst civil unrest London had seen in more than a century. He hadn't even been required to pay the new duty, but the chance to attack the government—any government—had been too hard to resist. Since then, he'd been in and out of prison in several countries for a number of violent acts, with his most recent spell ending only six months earlier.

Houtman had at first been keen on the idea of causing havoc, but as the story of the meeting progressed, he'd become increasingly uncomfortable, his hatred and distrust of authority fuelling his native paranoia.

'This Efram sounds like a plant,' Houtman had argued, and while the others agreed that it was suspicious, Roberts had pointed out that they were being asked to do nothing more than board a flight.

To Nigeria, it turned out.

'What do you think they've got planned?' Tony Eversham asked.

'They want us to play for the national football team,' Ed Conran deadpanned. 'But first, you need to get a haircut.'

'Piss off, Ed.'

Eversham was proud of his long hair, which reached well below shoulder length. Not proud enough to wash it regularly, but proud nonetheless. He tended to let his hair hang around the sides of his face, and Roberts wondered if he did so to take the focus off his acne-covered cheeks. Roberts had always thought that spots were an adolescent thing, but Eversham seemed to be producing them in abundance well into his thirties.

'Yeah, knock it off,' Roberts agreed. He found Conran annoying as well. Most days he spent his time teasing Eversham about his bountiful locks, but for Roberts, the joke was becoming stale. Conran's one redeeming attribute was his planning skills. He'd been the one to suggest giving the prime minister's car an ad hoc paint job, and while others would have just stood near the gates waiting for the vehicle to pass through the security gates, Conran had scoped out several ambush points over the course of a week, and had found the ideal place to lie in wait. What was particularly impressive about that surveillance was that he'd changed his clothes and appearance each day to avoid arousing suspicion.

Roberts had a feeling these qualities were going to be useful on this venture.

An announcement invited the passengers to begin boarding, and despite Houtman's fears, they managed to get to their cramped seats without being accosted.

Six and a half hours and one plastic meal later, they arrived in Lagos, where, as promised, someone was waiting for them. A tall Caucasian figure with military written all over him held up a sign bearing Roberts's name, and the man eyed them disapprovingly when they approached him to introduce themselves.

'I'm Dan,' he said by way of welcome. He handed out airline tickets, and they followed him to the departure area.

'We're taking another short hop,' Dan explained.

'Where to?'

'North. Kano.'

Roberts pressed for more information, but Dan simply told him they'd find out when they got there.

'That's a Yorkshire accent,' Conran said. 'What brings you over here?'

'Work,' Dan said, and resisted any further attempts at conversation.

The two-hour flight north was spent in silence, and Roberts spent his time trying to control his anxiety. Efram stank of government—current or ex, he couldn't tell—and Dan, with his buzz-cut hairdo, had to be ex-army. Had he made a mistake in trusting them? Was he leading his friends into a government-sanctioned trap—and a bullet in the brain in the middle of a jungle?

There was nothing he could do about it now, so he tried to focus on positives. As Efram had said, he wasn't that big a fish in the grand scheme of things, and there would certainly be more deserving cases if their destination were indeed a termination camp.

After landing and taxiing to the domestic terminal of Mallam Aminu Kano International Airport, Dan led them through cursory identification checks and out into the warm night. A clock mounted on the wall told them it was just after eight in the evening, and they hoped their twelve-hour journey was over, but Dan walked them to a dilapidated minibus and told them it would be another three hours until they reached their destination.

The conveyance shuddered down Airport Road and turned right into the city, where Roberts got his first real glimpse of life on the African continent. It wasn't all jungle, as he'd envisaged, but a flat expanse of low, irregularly shaped stone and concrete houses in a myriad shades of browns and whites. An occasional malnourished dog could be seen rummaging in the gutter for scraps to eat, and goats wandered the side streets.

It took an hour to navigate their way through the town and out into the countryside, where they relied completely on the vehicle's headlights to guide their way. After two bone-juddering hours, they pulled up at what Roberts imagined a 1930s holiday camp to have looked like. Dozens of small chalet-like wooden huts formed two rows off to one side, with a larger, rectangular building opposite.

Separating them was a large area of bare soil, where a few wooden tables stood empty.

The bus pulled up at the main building and Dan ordered the men out, leading them up the wooden steps and through the door. The small entrance hall led to three doors. One was marked as the mess, while the others served as offices. Dan knocked on one of the doors and opened it, ushering the party of four inside.

A Caucasian man in his fifties wearing army fatigues was sitting waiting, and Dan addressed him.

'Colonel, the latest arrivals,' he said, handing over their passports.

The officer regarded the newcomers, comparing them to their documents before dismissing Dan with a nod of the head.

'Gentlemen, so glad you could join us,' the officer said, while managing to sound far from pleased. 'My name is Colonel Mitchell. You'll be wondering what you've signed up for, so I'll keep this brief and to the point.

'We will be launching a guerrilla campaign against England at the end of the year. During the next five months, you will be given all the training you need in order to carry out your assignments, which will be many and varied. You will see other recruits here, but you will not engage with them.

'As of now, you have no names. You will be known by numbers, and that is the only way you will be addressed. Anyone caught using names will be disciplined.'

Eversham flicked his hair back and stood with his arms crossed. 'I knew this was bullshit,' he said. 'You bring us half-way around the world and tell us we're just numbers to you. I had enough of that shit back home—'

Eversham was cut off as a bullet from the colonel's pistol caught him in the centre of his forehead, and he collapsed to the ground in a heap.

'In case you were wondering,' Mitchell said, 'that is what passes for discipline around here.'

The three men looked in shock from the corpse to the colonel and back again.

'We didn't bring you here to hear your complaints; we recruited you because you want to bring Britain to its knees, and we have the resources to help you do that. However, only by treating this as a military operation can we expect it to work. If anyone else feels they don't want to be here, tell me now.'

All three looked at the pistol held at Mitchell's side and decided to hold their tongues.

'Good.' Mitchell pointed to each man and gave them a number. 'You are 134, you're 135, you're 136. Do not forget those numbers. If you fail to respond instantly to your number when called, expect to be disciplined.'

The three men stood upright, eyes front, showing their understanding.

'Sergeant!' Mitchell called, and Dan opened the door a second later.

'Colonel.'

'Have them clear this mess away, then show them to their bunks.'

Dan barked instructions, and the trio made a meal of carrying Eversham out of the office, through the main door and down the steps to the training area, where their luggage was lined up, the bus having departed.

'There are two shovels at the side of the building,' the sergeant said to Conran, who disappeared like his life depended on it. He was back in seconds, and handed one of the tools to Houtman.

'You,' Dan said, pointing to Roberts, 'get back in there and clean the colonel's floor. There's a mop and bucket in the mess.'

Roberts initially baulked at the thought, but a glance down at Eversham steeled his resolve.

He returned five minutes later and found Sergeant Dan waiting for him, another shovel in hand.

'Get round the back and give them a hand,' he said, holding it out. 'Once you're done, get back here, sharpish.'

Roberts trotted to the rear of the building, where his two sweat-covered friends laboured over a shallow pit, their fallen comrade lying nearby. Five other graves were visible, the fresh soil suggesting they had only recently been filled.

Bugs flitted around their heads as they worked the hole, their only illumination the faint light of an ancient oil lamp.

'What the fuck have you dragged us into?' Houtman hissed.

'How the hell was I supposed to know this was going to happen?'

'You're the one that sold this deal to us,' the Dutchman continued. 'I swear, if I have to dig another grave, the next one will be yours.'

Roberts looked down at Eversham's body and had to wonder whether his dead friend had got off lightly.

Chapter 5

13 March 2014

Roberts felt as if his head had barely touched the pillow when he was roused from his sleep by the banging on the door of the hut.

'Wakey, wakey! Breakfast in twenty minutes. Hit the showers!'

He looked at his watch and saw that he'd been asleep for barely three hours.

'What time is it?' Houtman yawned, as he looked out of the window into darkness.

Roberts groaned. 'Nearly six.'

He joined Houtman at the window, where they saw a stream of people silently filing past, washing kits in their hands.

'I think we'd better join them,' he said, and got another growl of disapproval from the Dutchman.

Roberts grabbed his wash bag and a towel from his suitcase and went out to join the throng, who were heading towards a structure that had been hidden from view the night before. He noted that many of them were built like him, with the same pasty expressions and hunched shoulders. Clearly Efram hadn't been looking for the typical soldier type. Inside the building they found rudimentary shower facilities, and as they queued they noticed that no man took longer than three minutes to finish his ablutions.

'Better make this quick,' he whispered to Conran, keenly aware that no-one else in the building was talking.

When it was his turn, Roberts stripped off his boxer shorts and stood under the shower head. The water was cold, but given the outside temperature even at such an early hour, it felt refreshing. He brushed his teeth quickly before shampooing and rinsing, the whole process taking just over four minutes, drawing angry looks from those still queuing.

Back at the four-man cabin, Roberts dressed in shorts and T-shirt before rolling up his sleeping bag and placing it at the foot of his camp bed. Through the window he could see people making their way to the main building, and Roberts told his companions to get a move on.

They followed the stream of men into the mess hall, where a serving station was manned by three local women. Men filed past slowly, and Roberts grabbed a tray and fell in line. The smell grew stronger as he neared his turn, and when he held out his tray he was rewarded with a dollop of yellow and a stew-like mixture. He hadn't eaten since the airline food the previous day, but despite this, he was hesitant to tackle the strange offering.

He went to find a seat, and noticed that the tables were designed for a maximum of four people. It brought the colonel's introductory speech back to mind, and he realised that even the eating arrangements were designed to discourage talking to anyone outside their own little group.

It suddenly struck him that no-one was talking at all, and he put that down to the three armed men standing in the corners of the room.

'This isn't bad,' Houtman said, licking his finger as he took a seat opposite Roberts.

'Shut it!' Roberts whispered, as Conran joined them. He looked around to see if anyone had heard, but thankfully there was no sudden rush to discipline the Dutchman. Roberts kept his head down, eating his meal as quickly as possible so that he could retreat to the cabin.

After wolfing down the food, he queued up to put his tray in the wash area and walked back to the accommodation block. Once inside, he sat on his bed with his head in his hands. Houtman and Conran arrived a few minutes later. Despite the closed door, they kept their voices low.

'This is some weird shit,' Conran said, a sentiment echoed by Houtman.

'Agreed,' Roberts said. 'So what do we do now?'

'What choice do we have?' Houtman asked. 'If we don't do exactly as they say, we end up like Tony, with a bullet in the head.'

'And we can't leave,' Conran added. 'Somehow, I don't think they'll just hand over our passports and give us tickets home. Even if we ask nicely.'

They thought about their predicament, until Roberts broke the silence.

'I say we go with the flow.'

Houtman shrugged. 'As I said, what choice do we have?'

Shouts from outside broke up the discussion, and when Roberts opened the door he saw everyone running towards Sergeant Dan, lining up in groups of three or four.

Roberts called his friends out and they followed suit, taking up a position towards the rear.

'Welcome to Camp Sunshine,' Dan said, once he'd done a head count. 'Now that you're all here, the first thing we're going to do is go over the rules one last time.'

He reiterated the no-talking rule, but explained that when they got back to England, the small groups were going to act as individual cells, each having no idea what the objectives of the others would be. That way, if anyone was caught, they couldn't compromise the larger operation.

'Ideally, we would have brought three or four of you here at any one time for training, but we have neither the time nor the resources to do that. Instead, you will all learn the same skills, but your final objectives will be known only to your own team.'

Roberts suddenly understood the reason for the rule, and why everyone was given a number as identification. Still, the colonel could have explained that in the initial meeting, rather than putting a bullet in Eversham's head. Well, Tony had been an argumentative sod, even on a good day, and he guessed it would only have been a matter of time before steel met skull.

Roberts guessed there were roughly forty groups on parade, close to two hundred men. If they were all to work in different geographical locations, it meant just about every major city would see some action towards the end of the year. The scale of the mission suddenly dawned on him. It wasn't the localised mayhem he'd envisaged in the last few days, but a nationwide campaign.

That brought a smile to his face.

'To pull this off,' Dan continued, 'you'll need to be physically fit and mentally alert. That means daily exercise and lessons in everything from explosives to counter-surveillance.'

More instructors appeared, all dressed the same way: khaki shorts, boots and green T-shirt. The small groups of men were split up, with some being told to gather around tables, while others were given warm-up exercises to do in preparation for the morning run.

Roberts and his cell, along with four other teams, were directed to a table on which lay a cream-coloured lump that resembled putty. Next to it were a few cheap mobile phones and a box marked Detonators.

Their instructor launched into the lesson without introducing himself, which Roberts took to mean No questions: just observe and learn.

As the African sun began its daily climb, Paul Roberts began the first of a hundred and fifty days of intense training, starting with Explosives 101.

SUMMER

Chapter 6

9 July 2014

'That's right, darling. It's a sheep.'

Tom Gray looked over at his daughter, who was riding in the front passenger seat of his BMW. He didn't know if Melissa was actually associating the sound with the cuddly toy she was playing with, or if 'baaaa' was just an easy sound for her to make. Either way, she was certainly expressing herself a lot more than she had even a month ago. All of the books and articles he'd read suggested the average child would start forming their first words right about now. But, then again, his one-year-old hadn't had an average first year.

Melissa had such a bubbly nature, it was hard to believe that nine months earlier she'd been lying in a medically induced coma, the result of smoke inhalation from the fire that had killed his wife. It had been a tense few days, but she didn't seem to have been affected that badly, though Gray knew it would be another couple of years before any damage would be fully known. Her brain had been starved of oxygen for a number of minutes, and that meant a fair chance that she would grow to be at least mildly impaired. Any damage had yet to be seen, however, and Gray gave thanks each day that his daughter's development remained so unremarkable.

He turned the car onto the dirt track that was signposted Broughton Farm. Another yellow sign warned trespassers to steer clear, and a locked steel gate reinforced the message. Gray used his key to open it, and followed the rutted track until he came to a two-storey house.

Half a dozen cars were parked off to one side, and Gray pulled into an empty space next to them. He carried Melissa through the front door of the building, which had been converted into a training suite.

In an office off to the left, he found Sonny Baines sitting at a desk and tapping away on a laptop.

'Morning.'

'Hi, Tom.' Sonny grinned and gave baby Melissa a wink. 'How's it going?'

Simon 'Sonny' Baines was so named because of his youthful looks. He'd looked like a school kid when he'd passed selection for the SAS, and twenty years on he could still pass for a college graduate.

It had been a while since Gray had seen a smile on Sonny's face. It was probably owing to Gray's recent decision to set up a training and evaluation programme for Sonny to run. Doing so had killed two birds: Sonny was finally doing something that enabled him to play with guns again, and Gray got to see his recruits in action, rather than having to depend on references alone. It had been four months since he'd first proposed the idea to Smart, and what followed had been plenty of hard work to get everything organised. Buying the buildings and land, and securing permits for live-fire exercises and renovations had taken a lot of effort and money, but it had been worth it. Sonny was back in his element, and now Gray could pick only the very best operatives for his clients.

'Not too bad,' Gray said. 'Just thought I'd pop in to see how the latest batch are getting on.'

'They're mostly a good bunch. One or two could be putting in a bit more effort, but I think we've got some real talent on show.

They're having lunch at the moment, and afterwards I'll get them together for some shooting practice.'

'I'll hang around for that if you don't mind. I miss the smell of cordite in the morning.'

Sonny opened a drawer and emerged with a tiny pair of ear defenders.

'I got these for Melissa. I knew you wouldn't come along without her.'

Gray's daughter grabbed for the pink, fluffy protective ear muffs, complete with Peppa Pig motif.

'Thanks, Sonny. Though I think she's more likely to eat them than wear them.'

As expected, the moment Gray put the contraption on Melissa's head, she tried to pull it off and put it in her mouth. He tried swapping the ear muffs for her toy sheep, but Melissa was having none of it.

'I think we need two pairs,' Sonny said. 'One for her ears, the other for her lunch.'

Gray agreed. 'So maybe I'll skip the range today.'

'Why not just strap her into her car seat for a few minutes?'

'No, thanks. I'm not leaving her alone, not even for a minute.'

Sonny sat in his chair and leant back. 'You know, you mollycoddle her too much.'

Gray shrugged. 'Daddy's privilege.'

'I know, but the time will come when you've got to let her go.'

'Not necessarily.'

'What about nursery?' Sonny asked. 'Or school? Are you going to sit in on her classes? Don't you think the other kids might notice the menacing six-footer in the corner?'

Gray conceded the point. It was something he thought about every day, but that all seemed so far in the future. Eventually he would have to cut her loose and let her start growing up like any other child, but it just seemed too soon. The painful memories of his wife's death still haunted his dreams, and his personal vow never to let his daughter out of his sight had quietly become an obsession.

'I'm thinking of home-schooling her.'

Gray actually had looked into the possibility, and there seemed no real barriers. He was certainly intelligent enough, and taking his daughter on educational trips wouldn't be limited to strict term timetables.

'Great, that's good. And during playtime, who will she be socialising with? Daddy?'

'What's wrong with that?'

'She needs to be around kids her own age, man. While she's supposed to be skipping and playing hopscotch, you'll have her stripping down an AK-47.'

'Don't be daft,' Gray said, but as the words left his mouth, he knew Sonny was right. Melissa needed to run and play and scream with other children, not sit with her boring old father.

'I guess one day I'll have to cut the apron strings,' Gray admitted.

'No time like the present,' Sonny smiled. 'Take her out to the car and strap her in. She'll be fine for a few minutes.'

Gray reluctantly took Sonny's advice and carried his daughter back out to the BMW. He strapped her into the child seat and gave her the sheep to keep her occupied.

'Here's some music,' he sing-songed, putting one of her CDs into the player. 'Twinkle, Twinkle, Little Star' filled the saloon, and Gray closed and locked the doors after turning on the air-conditioning. It wasn't that hot a day, but he wanted her to be comfortable.

He found it hard to tear himself away from the vehicle, but Sonny took his arm and led him back inside the house.

'Relax. The gate's locked and the car's secure. She'll be fine.'

Gray couldn't resist looking back a couple of times, but as the car was still there and wasn't being attacked by hordes of bad guys, he decided Sonny had a point. He was being over-protective, and it was time to snap out of it.

'Okay, show me what these guys can do.'

Sonny led him to the indoor range. In its previous incarnation it had been a milking shed, but the economic downturn and supermarket price wars had squeezed the farmer dry. The cows were long gone, and the walls of the twenty-metre building were now soundproofed. At one end stood a row of empty tables, while at the far end a bank of soil covered with sandbags sat behind a set of man-sized targets.

'If you don't mind setting up the targets, I'll go and get the lads.'

Gray walked downrange and replaced the bullet-ridden paper with new cut-outs. He was just setting them side-on when Sonny returned with six men in tow, two of them carrying a large, metal box between them.

Gray introduced himself and stood back while Sonny explained the purpose of the test.

'Ten rounds each using a Glock 17 at twenty metres. The targets will appear for three seconds, and you'll be drawing from a shoulder holster. Let's see what you can do.'

Sonny unlocked the box and handed out the holsters. The men put them on while Sonny checked the weapons and placed one in front of each candidate. He then put a box of ammunition next to each man and told them to load up.

While the men filled the magazines, Gray called Sonny over and pointed out a recruit named Mackenzie. At well above six feet, Mackenzie towered over most of the others, though his size didn't seem to slow him down any. Together, Gray and Sonny watched the tall recruit loading rounds into the clip, his ebony fingers deftly making short work of the exercise.

'According to his application, he spent some time in central Africa with his last employer,' Gray said quietly to Sonny. 'He'd be useful for the Benin mission. The current squad will be rotating home in a few weeks, and we need replacements who won't take too long to acclimatise.'

'He's one of the better ones,' Sonny said. 'He aced the five-mile run this morning, and his intelligence test was one of the highest scores we've seen. He's also proficient in six languages, including Hausa. His father was from Niger, which made his last mission a bit of a homecoming. What troubles me is that he left E squadron after just a few months.'

Known as the elite of the elite, E squadron was the successor to the shadowy Increment, which had been made up primarily of British soldiers who had attained the SAS rank of sergeant. As with the Increment, the role of E squadron's hand-picked soldiers was to assist MI6 operatives in the most sensitive of operations. Many aspired to join the ranks, but few made it.

'I saw that, but he said in his application that it was for personal reasons. A fiancée, wasn't it?'

'Apparently,' Sonny shrugged. 'Can't knock a guy for wanting a private life. I spoke to him earlier and he said he was looking for more of a training role close to home, though he knows he'll have to go into the field from time to time.'

Gray watched the men go through their drill, loading the magazines before stowing the weapons in their leather holsters.

'Ready!' Sonny shouted.

After a few seconds, he flicked a switch, and the targets spun ninety degrees, giving the shooters a face-on aspect. Weapons were drawn, and the shed erupted with simultaneous gunfire.

'Reset!'

The targets disappeared, and the handguns were stowed.

After four more iterations, Sonny went from man to man to ensure the pistols were empty. Satisfied that all rounds had been discharged, he walked the men downrange to inspect the targets.

The shooting had been of a very high standard. One or two rounds were a little high or wide, but as they were using the guns for the first time, it was to be expected.

Mackenzie's grouping was particularly impressive, with all ten shots clustered within two inches.

'Considering the distance, that's some damn fine shooting,' Sonny told the group. 'Okay, guys, there are cleaning kits in the box. Strip and oil the weapons, please.'

Sonny walked back over to Gray. 'Score another point for Mackenzie.'

Gray nodded. 'He'll fit the Benin contract nicely. If he baulks at that, we'll look for something closer to home. Send all the reports over to Len and copy me in when you're done, please.'

Gray left Sonny to continue the rest of the session, keen to get back to the car to see how Melissa was faring. His daughter seemed none the worse for the time alone. Gray unlocked the door to find her making gurgling noises to the toy sheep, and she gave him only a brief glance as he climbed behind the wheel.

'Nice to know you missed me,' he cooed, and Melissa offered him the goo-covered toy as a consolation.

'No thanks, sweetheart. Let's go see the doctor.'

Gray pulled away, pointing the car towards the hospital. The monthly check-ups hadn't detected any problems so far; hopefully today's would prove no different.

Chapter 7

9 July 2014

'Pardon my French, Veronica, but this is bollocks!'

Andrew Harvey was sitting in Ellis's office, and the news that he was being replaced as section lead had come out of the blue.

'I know, but my hands are tied. The orders came from the home secretary herself.'

'Since when was it her job to micro-manage the security services?' Harvey stood and thrust his hands into his pockets as he paced the room.

'It isn't,' Ellis agreed, 'but since the story broke about James Farrar absconding, she's decided to take an active role in finding out what went wrong.'

'What went wrong was that six months ago, one of *her* judges decided to grant him bail,' Harvey seethed.

'Apparently, he acted within the framework of the law. Besides, she claimed this isn't just about Farrar. The lack of progress on DSA's new leader was another point she raised, as well as the terror suspect who vanished while dressed as a woman.'

Harvey began counting off on his fingers. 'Farrar couldn't be found because we needed help from external agencies, which we weren't allowed to contact under any circumstances. DSA's new leader has been seen by just a handful of people in its upper council, and no council members are stupid enough to let intel about their beloved Takasa slip our way. And the terror suspect who fled was being monitored by a third-party private security firm, and they had orders to contact the Home Office, who then contacted the police, who then arrived too late to find him. It was their internal procedure that let him get away, not anything we did.'

'I hear you on all counts,' Ellis said, 'and I raised these arguments myself, but she isn't interested in anything but results.'

She pointed to the chair, and Harvey reluctantly took a seat.

'Andrew, you know as well as I do that this close to election time, the politicians need to be seen in a favourable light. The last thing they need is an embarrassment that could trip them up on their way to the polls.'

Harvey was well aware of the way things played out when people were preparing to choose their new leaders: broken promises were swept under the carpet as new ones were offered to a believing public; figures were massaged—or 'seasonally adjusted'—to make their time in office seem a success; and bad news was suppressed or played down until the hustings were over.

That didn't make his demotion any easier to swallow.

'So who takes over from me?'

'The home secretary is sending someone from Six,' Ellis said. 'Farrar used to work for them, so she thinks having them take the lead will produce results.'

Great. Harvey had had only a few dealings with his counterparts in MI6, and none of them had turned out well. Working under one of them wasn't going to be a cakewalk, that was for sure.

'I'm sure this is only temporary,' Ellis assured him. 'Once we have Farrar and the lowdown on Takasa, we won't need their . . . assistance.'

'And I regain my position?' Harvey pressed.

The question made Ellis squirm, confirming Harvey's suspicions.

'That remains to be seen,' she said. 'The home secretary will want a report from me as well as from your replacement. If you shine, the slot should be yours again.'

Harvey knew there wasn't much he could do except swallow his pride and get on with the job, which should be easier now that Farrar's disappearance had hit the headlines. He could now bring Interpol and other foreign agencies into the search, which would speed things along.

'When does he get here? My replacement?'

'*Sarah* will be here this afternoon,' Ellis said. 'If you could have your office cleared by lunchtime, that would be great.'

Harvey nodded and rose to leave. 'I assume we're okay to get the ball rolling on Farrar,' he said, as he headed for the door.

'No, just wait until Sarah gets here and let her co-ordinate things.'

'Sure. No problem.'

Harvey went back to his office and began clearing out his drawers. He took his time, trying to gather his emotions before having to face his colleagues. He was sure they'd sympathise, but he wanted to share the news with a level head, rather than reveal the anger that was gnawing at his insides.

Finally calm, he removed his laptop from the docking station and carried it out of the office, finding an empty desk to call home.

As he turned to address his team—former team, he reminded himself—he took small consolation from being rid of the stifling office and back in the thick of things.

Chapter 8

15 July 2014

Paul Roberts walked up to the immigration desk at Heathrow, wearing the same jeans and T-shirt he'd used on the outward journey five months earlier. This time they were pressed and clean, and the man wearing them hardly resembled the scruffy thirty-four-year-old who'd left the country in the early spring.

His hair, which had once fallen over his ears and down to the nape of his neck, was now cut in a neat side parting, and the sun had bleached it a lighter shade of brown.

'I've been on a voyage of self-discovery,' Roberts said to the immigration officer, who was clearly having a hard time matching the man in front of him with the passport he was holding.

With a grunt and a stamp, he allowed Roberts on his way. After visiting the foreign exchange booth to convert five hundred dollars into sterling, Roberts followed the signs for the Tube. Once seated and pointing towards the centre of London, he went through the counter-surveillance exercises he'd been taught. He pretended to be engrossed in a newspaper, but every time the train slowed, he looked up and scanned the carriage on the pretence of checking which station he was approaching.

None of his fellow passengers seemed interested in him, but just to be sure, he alighted at South Kensington and switched to the Circle line, which he followed to Notting Hill Gate. Here he transferred to the Central line, but by the time he got to the final switch, at Bank station, he'd seen nothing to arouse his suspicions.

Confident that he wasn't being tailed, Roberts took the Northern line to Oval, where he started looking for a bed and breakfast establishment that could accommodate him for a few nights. He found a place that was off the beaten track and paid for three nights in advance.

The room was sparse, with a small TV and basic coffee and tea-making equipment. The bathroom was functional, if in need of a good clean, though it was luxurious compared to the facilities in Africa.

After unpacking his few belongings, he lay on the bed and went through a mental checklist of his tasks over the next few days. Step one was to get hold of a cheap laptop so that he could receive orders from his handler and update him on the team's progress. He had the website address memorised, along with his username and password, and he was due to check in at one in the afternoon the following day. That gave him plenty of time to source both the laptop and a phone to act as a Wi-Fi hotspot.

He would also need to change up more of the ten thousand dollars he'd been given before he left Kano, and he heeded their warning to spread it around different change bureaus to avoid suspicion. In addition, he'd been given a pre-paid credit card loaded with another five thousand pounds sterling for those purchases that couldn't be made using cash.

With the following morning planned out, he headed to the high street in search of supper. The streets were lively as rush hour approached, and he saw the bustling people in a different light. Six months ago, he would have walked among the crowd without thinking about it, but his time in Nigeria had changed all that. He sensed their numbers, and it filled him with confidence that the plan would work.

'The people think they are powerless,' Sergeant Dan had drummed into each and every one of the recruits, *'but they hold the key to this country. We are sixty million ruled by six hundred self-serving parasites. It's time for the people of Britain to wake up and see that this is their land, not the playground of the rich and privileged.'*

Roberts scanned the faces of those he passed. Mothers, fathers, every one of them someone's child. His actions would take some of their lives, and their passing would be mourned, but one day a monument would be built to commemorate those who'd lain down their lives in the name of freedom.

Roberts was up at seven the next morning, and he showered and dressed before watching the morning news with a cup of instant coffee. At eight, he set off for a local café in search of breakfast to pass the time until the shops opened an hour later.

He found a window seat and ordered the full English with toast and a coffee, then took a seat that gave him a good view out of the window. None of the passersby seemed to take any notice of him, and there were no occupied parked cars or vans that he could see.

Which didn't mean he wasn't being followed.

Always assume they're on to you, was the warning his instructor had given him. *Stay calm, yet alert. Don't make it look like you think you're being followed.*

It was Spy-Shit 101, the kind of things people picked up from thriller novels and action films, but with all the other training they had had to undergo, there simply hadn't been the chance to elaborate and go into in-depth techniques. It was assumed that Roberts and his ilk were so far down the pecking order that the security services wouldn't give a damn about them until the brown stuff hit the swirly thing, and by then it would be far too late. Still, though, basic precautions were always prudent.

Just before nine, he headed towards the Tube station and once again took a circuitous route before ending up in Hammersmith. He knew a good place in his old stomping ground where he could get the equipment he needed at a fair price, but he'd been told to avoid the old area. He'd given up the bedsit, and the lease had lapsed on the old office, so he had no real ties with the place. The concern was that he might meet old friends who would question his absence, and his instructions were to avoid any such communications. If he did happen to stumble across anyone he knew, he would simply tell them that he had found religion and was done with the anarchist shit.

By lunchtime he was back in his room, with a new Acer, a Samsung phone and a sandwich, which he ate while charging the devices and reading the instructions. It took a while to get internet access, but once online he went straight to the website for the latest updates.

Houtman had already been in and left his phone number, and Roberts added it to his contacts list before leaving his own number for the other members of the cell. He then read the first set of instructions, which told him where to find a warehouse that had some of the resources he would need in the coming days. Roberts looked it up on the internet and worked out a route, then entered *vans for sale London* into the search engine. He was inundated with results, and it took him an hour to find a suitable second-hand Ford Transit. The owner was asking a thousand, but Roberts thought he could argue him down to nine hundred pounds, and he called the number in the advert to arrange a viewing.

With a meeting set up for three, he closed down the laptop and put it under his mattress, then pocketed the phone and headed back to the Tube station. It was a twenty-minute journey to Maida

Vale, and when he arrived at the address he saw the twelve-year-old white van sitting forlornly in a driveway. Roberts wasn't sure it would even start, let alone sustain him for the next few months, but the owner came out and assured him that she was a good runner, and he was selling up because his business had folded.

It sounded credible, but Roberts wanted a second opinion, and the seller agreed to escort him to a local garage to give it the once-over.

The van sounded fine on the way there, and the mechanic spent twenty minutes checking the electrics and engine before giving it a clean bill of health. Roberts handed over fifty pounds for the check-up, and then drove the owner home to complete the paperwork.

Once everything was signed over, Roberts parted with nine hundred and fifty pounds and called an insurance company to get cover. The last thing he needed was to be pulled over for not having the right documentation, especially once his van was fully laden. A search of the vehicle at that point would jeopardise the entire mission, so he wasn't inclined to cut corners.

He paid for the insurance with the pre-paid credit card, then drove to a petrol station to fill up before heading out of the capital in search of the warehouse. He found it on an industrial estate just outside of Oxford, and after pulling up outside, he went into the small reception area.

'I'm looking for a three-inch flange with a diaphragm base,' he said, reciting the pass code he'd been given. The man behind the counter picked up the phone and made a hushed call, then nodded and buzzed Roberts through a door, which led to the main storage area.

He was greeted by a small, elderly man, who introduced himself as Ted. Roberts was ushered down an aisle, the shelves on either side stacked to the metal rafters with an eclectic mix of items. Ted stopped at a pallet containing dozens of red fire extinguishers and handed one to Roberts.

'Looks authentic,' Roberts said. 'How does it stand up to close inspection?'

Ted released the security pin and squirted CO_2 into the air. 'It holds about forty percent of the normal volume; the rest is the explosive. If it's used on a small fire, it should be fine.'

All well and good, Roberts thought, except that he'd been told that at their intended destination, fire extinguishers were routinely replaced with full ones after even partial use.

'I'll collect these the day before I need them,' he said. 'Planting them early is just inviting trouble. If they're called into action, it could tip our hand.'

Ted agreed, and led him to another aisle, where toilets and sink units dominated the shelves.

'Okay, now I'm confused,' Roberts said, and Ted pulled back some of the cellophane covering a toilet bowl. He tapped it with his pen, and the sound was what Roberts expected to hear.

'The coating is just four millimetres thick,' Ted explained. 'The core of each unit is packed with roughly twelve kilos of C4. All you need to do is break off the outer skin of porcelain and you've got enough plastic explosive to bring down half of London.'

Roberts smiled at the ingenuity. 'Detonators?'

Ted led him to the other side of the warehouse and handed over two packs of children's colouring pens.

'Each pen contains one detonator, so you've got fifty there.'

Impressive. They would be easy to transport without raising any eyebrows.

'I was told there would be directional EMP devices.'

'There will be,' Ted said. 'They're still being manufactured, but we should take delivery within the next couple of months. We tested the government-commissioned prototypes, but the range was ineffective for some of our targets. We're working to increase that, and then we need to provide adequate shielding for the delivery vehicle and disguise it as some kind of household appliance.'

'Are you sure they'll be ready in time?'

'Absolutely,' Ted assured him.

He led Roberts around the building, pointing out the boxes of second-hand mobile phones and several other items the plan would require.

Roberts was impressed with the ordnance, but explained that he had a few things to sort out before he could take anything with him.

'I should be back in a couple of days,' he said, and gave Ted a list of items to have ready on his return.

Once in the van, Roberts drove back to his room in London and spent the rest of the day looking for more permanent lodgings, as well as a storage company that could provide a room to store his arsenal. He'd considered a lock-up garage but worried it wouldn't be secure enough.

By three in the afternoon, he'd arranged viewings on two flats in the area, and drove to Elegant Storage to see what they had available.

The manager was happy to show him around, and Roberts explained that he was going into business and was looking for a short-term arrangement while he tried to grow his brand.

'What will you be selling?'

'Money belts,' Roberts said. 'They're hand-made and personalised. I'll need room for two tables and a few large boxes of materials.'

The manager guided him to a large unit that contained a dozen spacious rooms, each with a steel door and a clasp to accommodate a padlock. Roberts went inside one and looked around, glad to see that the CCTV coverage ended outside the door. The two electrical plug sockets at the far end of the room would be more than enough for his needs.

'Perfect,' he said.

He returned to the main office and completed the registration process before handing over enough money to cover the next three months.

'We have a good range of padlocks,' the manager said, but Roberts assured him that he would provide his own.

It was almost dark by the time he arrived back at the bed and breakfast, and he went out for a burger before heading back to his room for the evening, pleased at the progress he was making.

For the first time in his life, Roberts felt a sense of belonging, of real purpose. His many years as an activist had been spent dreaming of the chance to make an impact, but those hopes had never transitioned into reality. Now, though, he was part of a huge, invisible machine that was rolling through the streets of Britain unnoticed, unhindered. It was still early days, but after months of preparation, he finally felt the exhilaration of seeing his long-held plan take shape.

After checking the website and getting Ed Conran's new contact details, he sent both cell members a text offering to meet for lunch in a pub the following day.

Both responded immediately, and he settled in for a night in front of the TV. The twenty-four hour news channel regurgitated the same stories over and over, the headline being the multi-vehicle pile-up on the M25 that had closed the northbound carriageway for over eight hours. Some commuters were being interviewed, and they bemoaned the fact that they'd missed a whole day of work after being stuck behind the carnage, though they were thankful that it hadn't resulted in any deaths.

Roberts smiled.

You ain't seen nothing yet.

WINTER

Chapter 9

12 December 2014

Ed Conran pulled into the field and killed the lights before parking the Land Rover next to the hedge. After a quick scan of the area, he climbed into the back and removed his rucksack from the hidden compartment underneath the seats before heading off into the darkness.

The grass was wet beneath his feet, and he almost slid onto his backside more than once as he descended towards the railway track. He easily navigated the small, wire fence that blocked his path, then scrambled down the embankment and onto the gravel lining the rails.

To his right, the tracks disappeared into darkness, while in the other direction the mouth of the tunnel beckoned. He pulled out a headband and secured it around his forehead, ensuring that the torches fastened to each side were facing forward.

A hundred yards later, he stopped to listen for any untoward sounds, then placed the bag on the ground. With the tracks illuminated by his torches, he began scraping the stones from underneath the closest rail until he hit soil, then brought out a trowel and began digging farther. Once he had a six-inch gap, he removed the shaped charge from the rucksack and placed it gently into the scrape. He then inserted the detonator and attached the trailing wires to a mobile phone, which was modified to run off an array of batteries. This arrangement allowed him to deploy it three days before detonation without the risk of the charge running down.

With the explosive in place, he moved over to the other side of the track and repeated the process, connecting the second charge to the same mobile to ensure both explosions happened simultaneously. He knew that hundreds of trains would pass over this point before he was ready to detonate, so he made sure the connections were tight and had no chance of coming undone.

Satisfied that the devices would withstand the repetitive vibrations, Conran carefully covered both packages with soil before replacing the stones on top, then stood back to check his handiwork.

Nothing looked out of place, and he was confident that it would escape anything but the closest scrutiny. His watch told him that it was almost three in the morning, and he yawned as he shut off the torches and took off the headband. The rucksack went over his shoulder, and he walked back to the mouth of the tunnel, scanning the area for signs of movement.

Nothing.

Ten minutes later, he was heading back to London, to the bed-sit accommodation he was renting in Wembley. After a few hours of sleep, he would meet Roberts to get the next set of packages, and the following few nights would be much the same as the last: late-night excursions into the countryside to plant his devices, then a few hours' sleep before repeating the process.

The day was finally drawing near, and all the hard work of the last nine months was about to pay off.

Chapter 10

13 December 2014

Erik Houtman adjusted the blue coveralls bearing the Chubb insignia and cursed Roberts for providing a uniform a size too small. It didn't look too bad when he stood erect or walked, but when he crouched to perform his work, the gusset cut into his groin, all too often with painful consequences.

Armed with a convincing ID badge and clipboard, he walked through the hospital, stopping to inspect every fire extinguisher he came across. No-one paid him the slightest attention as he went about his business, though he was prepared in case a member of the estates department asked why he was there. His forged worksheet was as close to the real thing as there was, and a cursory glance would satisfy anyone.

Avoiding the more sensitive areas of the hospital, he wandered the corridors until he arrived at the surgical unit. A couple of patients were waiting outside the double doors to be processed, and he offered a young girl a smile as he passed her trolley.

The extinguishers were clipped to a wall at knee level and, as expected, one was the CO_2 variant. Houtman knelt next to it and pretended to check the maintenance label, then made a sound of displeasure as he marked a comment on his sheet before heading out of the building. He returned soon after, carrying a brand new replacement, and noted the date on the label before taking the old one back to his van.

An hour later, three explosive extinguishers had been planted in the hospital, his fourth target of the day. He was thankful that he had only the A&E unit at the Royal Free Hospital still to do, then he could relax for the day and finally be free of the damned overalls.

Paul Roberts walked into the offices of NTS Couriers Limited and smiled at the twenty-something blonde behind the counter.

'Hi. I understand you do international deliveries.'

The girl flashed white teeth in response and began typing on her keypad. She asked for his personal details before enquiring about the nature of the delivery.

'I'm renovating a house in France, and want to have a toilet and sink delivered. I thought about having them flown over, or taken by ferry, but you just can't trust people not to damage them. They're custom made.'

If the girl thought tailor-made toilets were unusual, she didn't show it. Instead, she maintained her professional demeanour and asked for the pickup point and destination. Roberts gave her the address of a cottage just south of Bordeaux, something he'd found after a five-minute search on Google.

'I'd like to deliver the items here and make sure they're properly secured in your van,' he said. 'They cost over four thousand, and I don't want them getting knocked about on the journey.'

'No problem,' the girl assured him.

'I'd also like them to go via Eurostar,' he added. 'The Channel is rough at this time of year, and I don't like the idea of them being tossed back and forth for an hour.'

'We usually take them by ferry because it's cheaper.'

‘I don’t mind paying extra for the Tunnel,’ Roberts said, receiving another smile in return.

The total bill came to just short of four hundred pounds, and Roberts extracted a bundle of notes, counting off the twenties. He arranged to drop the items off at seven on Monday morning.

‘There’s a Eurostar leaving at eight thirty, and I’d like my items to be on that if possible. My plumbers will be waiting at four in the afternoon to fit them.’

‘We don’t usually open so early,’ the girl said, ‘but I can see if the driver will make an exception.’

Roberts handed over another fifty pounds, and the early start was suddenly no longer a problem.

He thanked her for her help and returned to his van.

Monday would be December 15th, the day earmarked for Britain’s collapse.

Chapter 11

14 December 2014

Takasa had two electric fans pointing at him as he sat by his laptop, surveying the messages coming in. The open windows did little to cool the room, as the hot Nigerian night offered nothing more than an infrequent gentle breeze to make life more tolerable.

Three cells had yet to report their status, but as they had last-minute arrangements to make, he wasn't panicking. The news stations hadn't mentioned anything about foiled terrorist plots in the last couple of days, and as the hours ticked down, he thought it increasingly unlikely that anything could stop his plan.

He took a sip of his gin and tonic, conscious of the fact that devout Muslims didn't imbibe alcohol. But then, he'd been an atheist since he was old enough to make that decision, and playing the role of leader of a Muslim group didn't make him a servant of Islam.

He sat back on the sofa, a smile creeping over his face as he pictured the reaction once he unleashed hell. Within hours, the country would come to a standstill.

There would be deaths, of course, but that was necessary and unavoidable. He'd long ago reconciled himself to the fact that blood would be on his hands, but with each act of aggression he'd planned, the value of life decreased, until they were nothing more than theoretical numbers. Perhaps a hundred thousand would never see Christmas but, then again, people died every day.

His laptop screen showed another incoming message:

97 ready

Good. His cell in Newcastle had completed its preparations; that left only Manchester and Coventry to report in.

He picked up his gin and stepped out onto the balcony, where the sun was painting the sky a fiery orange as it sank below the horizon. An apt omen, he thought, taking another sip of his drink.

He glanced at his watch and saw that it was almost time to place his bets. Britain was going to become a war zone in short order, and the damage he was about to cause would devastate some of the larger companies on the stock market. Their stock prices would tumble as investors bailed, which they surely would once the financial liabilities became apparent. The National Grid, for example, would have to spend close to a billion undoing his work, almost a whole year's profits. As the share price tumbled, he would reap the rewards.

Although he had offered DSA's council fifty million towards the venture, he'd kept back two million for this very moment. He would sell a vast amount of shares in NG and several other companies certain to be affected, and once the dust had settled, he would honour his investment and complete the transaction by buying the shares back at a much lower price.

He decided to sell half a million shares at 800p, knowing that once the attacks started, they would be closer to 400p, earning him a tidy profit. He called his broker in Switzerland and gave him a list of transactions with instructions to execute them as soon as the stock exchange opened the following morning.

In the next day or two, he would have more than enough to spirit himself away to a new safe haven and a comfortable retirement, which was no more than he deserved. He'd spent his master's money as requested, and soon the results of his work would be on every television screen around the world.

The cash would be a nice return for a few months of planning, but the real satisfaction would come in the next few days.

Chapter 12

15 December 2014

Andrew Harvey was the first into the meeting room, determined not to incur Sarah Thompson's wrath once more.

Since she'd arrived to take over his position as section lead five months earlier, he'd managed to rub her up the wrong way on more than one occasion, and Ellis had been clear in her warning that one more time would see him permanently demoted, at the very least.

Get with the programme, or kiss your career goodbye.

Harvey had no problem following orders, but when they came from someone who'd clearly been deskbound for their entire career, it rankled. Thompson had flounced into the office in July and given her 'I'm in charge now, so let's start doing things properly' speech, which had got more than a few backs up. Her subsequent ideas showed that she had no field experience, sending MI5's finest off on pointless errands that ultimately proved fruitless. Any attempts to challenge her orders invariably ended with a trip to Ellis's office to explain one's actions, and while it was frustrating, Harvey told himself that it was a temporary arrangement.

At least, he hoped so.

Having followed Thompson's instructions since summer, they were no closer now to finding Farrar than they had been ten months earlier, and Harvey had taken to working later and later in order to try to generate different leads that could put a swift end to her presence.

The trouble was, every time he came up with something, Sarah Thompson was there to shoot him down in flames. He'd found a source that claimed there was a sighting of Farrar in Algeria at the start of the year, but when asked for resources to follow it up, she'd denied his request.

'Algeria is a category two extradition territory,' she'd said. 'Farrar won't be hiding there.'

Harvey had agreed that it was unlikely he'd settled there, but couldn't he have been spotted there while in transit? When he asked if he could take a couple of people and see if Farrar's onward destination could be ascertained, Thompson had dismissed the idea as a waste of time, not to mention resources.

Today, his nemesis entered the room a few minutes after everyone had gathered, as was her style, and immediately focused on Harvey. It was her normal tactic, and he guessed it was designed to break his spirit before the meeting actually began. She stared at him with her olive eyes, the hint of a smile curling her ruby lips.

Harvey had to admit that Thompson was a stunner. She stood six feet in her high heels, and a lot of that was perfectly shaped leg. He'd caught himself watching her walk away a couple of times, and chided himself for it. In another time and place, he could easily have fallen for her, but this was work, and she was the most officious taskmaster he'd ever known.

'What have we got from South America?' she asked.

Harvey didn't even need to consult his notes. 'Nothing. No sightings, no transactions, nothing. Maybe we should send in a couple of resources to check things out.'

'Andrew, your answer to everything seems to be to send in some people to see what we can dig up. Need I remind you that we can't just take people off other cases simply because you can't make headway with the information at hand? Our assets are already out combing the world for Farrar. There's no-one left.'

'You're the one who asked me to check out the region,' Harvey said, 'and as you know, Interpol covers just about every South American and Caribbean country, with a couple of exceptions. Martinique is one, and it also happens to be a non-extradition country. If he's hiding down there, we need eyes on the ground.'

'Try the local banks, see if they've—'

'Not co-operating,' Harvey interrupted.

'Then speak to the law enforcement—'

'They said they've got better things to do.'

Thompson slammed her clipboard onto the desk, exasperated.

'Do you think that, one day, you could come to one of these meetings with some good news? All I ever hear is can't, won't, didn't.'

Harvey knew that protesting would only earn him another visit to Ellis's office, so he promised to push harder with the locals and left it at that.

Thompson turned to Hamad Farsi. 'What have you got for me?'

'We have word that Takasa is due in Kano, despite rumours that he rarely ventures out of his hideaway in Chad. Apparently, DSA have something big lined up. They—'

'DSA are a thing of the past,' Thompson cut in. 'I told you to forget about them and focus on finding James Farrar. Why are you still working it?'

She turned to face Harvey, and the penny dropped. 'Don't tell me: you asked him to follow it up.'

Hamad shook his head. 'No, I heard it from the Africa desk and thought it might be useful.'

'Well, I'm telling you it's not. DSA are a motley collection of unconnected criminals using the name to lend credence to their actions. They've never ventured beyond northern Nigeria, and they never will. Their biggest claim to fame is torching a Catholic school, for God's sake. For the last time, forget about them and focus on the main mission.'

Farsi nodded, contrite.

Thompson asked the two other operatives for progress reports, and while they too had nothing new to offer in Asia and the Middle East, Harvey thought she seemed to accept their answers with a lot more grace than when he'd come up empty.

The meeting broke up, and Harvey followed Farsi back to their desks.

'I think she's got the hots for you,' Farsi said.

Harvey looked towards the meeting room, just in time to see Thompson leaving, her long, blonde hair swaying with every step. Despite the animosity between them, he couldn't help but watch the way her hips moved as she strode to her office with her cell phone to her ear. He had to admit that there was something about her that intrigued him, even if it wasn't her sparkling personality.

'If she has, she's got a funny way of showing it,' he said.

He unlocked his computer and began searching for holiday homes in Martinique, in the hope that someone matching Farrar's description had rented one in the last year.

It was a long shot, but it would keep Thompson happy for a few hours. He was looking at the second page of results when Sarah Thompson suddenly appeared next to him.

'I've just spoken to the home secretary. You can have two people for Martinique, but only for a week. If they find nothing, we pull them back.'

She walked away before Harvey could even register surprise at her concession.

'Told you,' Farsi said with a smirk.

Paul Roberts was cruising at sixty-five on the M25, heading west towards the junction with the M23 that led to Gatwick Airport. As he passed the turnoff, he hit the button on his trigger and let a three-second burst hit the traffic in the oncoming lanes. Almost immediately, the cars he'd hit ground to a halt as their electrics failed and engine-management software shut down. There was no warning for the cars behind, and they powered into the stationary vehicles at speeds in excess of seventy.

As he released the button, he realised that his actions would leave many people dead. Children would go to bed without mothers or fathers, and parents would wait all evening for offspring who would never return home. A year ago, such thoughts might have consumed him, but all he felt was the heady thrill of wielding the power of life and death.

Roberts checked his wing mirror as the first explosion took place, followed by others as the concertina effect added more and more vehicles to the carnage. The flames were receding as he sped away from the scene, but his work wasn't done.

A mile up the road, he hit the trigger again, just as he saw two articulated lorries powering up the motorway. His burst stopped the vehicles in front of the trucks, and the juggernauts ploughed through the saloons and hatchbacks like they were made of paper. By the time they managed to pull to a stop, twenty vehicles were destroyed, and yet another fire had broken out.

Roberts continued down the road, creating another four accidents before the overhead signs ordered all traffic in the opposite lanes to a halt.

He wouldn't be causing any more crashes on the motorway that day, but every now and then he hit the trigger in three-second bursts, immobilising the already-stationary cars and adding to the nightmare. It would take days to clear that stretch of the motorway, and he knew Houtman and Conran would be doing the same thing on the northern sections of the London Orbital.

He arrived at the turnoff for Heathrow and pulled onto the hard shoulder, turning his hazard lights on. The exact spot had been chosen weeks earlier, and he climbed into the back to look through the letterbox-sized glass panel built into the side of the van. It gave him a view to the west, where the aircraft heading for the airport would make their final approach. Just over a kilometre away, parked in a street next to a couple of bungalows, another van waited for his command.

Roberts picked up a remote control device and turned it on. The built-in screen showed darkness, but when he pressed the first button, a panel on the van's roof opened to give him a view of the clouds. He hit another button, arming the heat-seeking surface-to-air missile that was pointing to the sky, and waited until the fish-eye lens first indicated the presence of the latest arrival.

A two-tone siren filled the small space as the indicator showed the missile had a lock on the plane, and Roberts let it loose. Through his van's glass panel, he could make out the oncoming aircraft, and a streak of smoke rising from the ground quickly converged on the right wing. As soon as the hit was confirmed, Roberts climbed back into the driver's seat and gunned the engine.

From the side window of his van, he saw the British Airways Boeing 747 yaw to the right as flames danced from the damaged engines, and he wondered whether the pilot could keep it together long enough to make the runway; the purpose of the exercise wasn't to claim lives, but to reduce the airport's capabilities.

He lost sight of the plane through the side window, but his side mirrors showed the aircraft limping over the motorway, the belly beginning to show as the plane rolled to the left, and he knew he'd achieved his aim, or as close to it as he could have hoped for.

Somewhere in the back of his mind, he knew that hundreds of people were currently screaming as the ground rushed towards them, but he didn't have time to reflect on the damage he'd done. There was still a lot to do before he could afford himself that luxury.

He continued along the M25, and at the next exit he followed the M4 towards the centre of London. Once he hit the capital, he pulled into a side street and removed the plastic licence plates that covered the real ones. He would need the van over the coming days, and no doubt the security services would use CCTV coverage to determine what had happened. Once the vehicle was pictured at the scenes of the crashes, the security services would put two and two together. Somewhere in Middlesex, an unwitting Transit van owner was in for a big shock when they ran the fake plates.

With the vehicle's identity changed, he drove to a café and ordered a couple of bacon sandwiches to go, before parking up in a nearby supermarket car park. To the passersby, he was just another workman taking a late breakfast while surfing the internet, but Roberts wasn't interested in anything other than the GPS signal he was getting, and the list of phone numbers in his contacts log. The dot on the screen told him that the toilet and sink were already aboard the Eurostar train, and would reach the Channel Tunnel within ten minutes.

That left time to make a few important phone calls.

One by one, he selected each number, waiting for the response to go to voicemail before ending the call and deleting the entry.

Each time he hit the Connect button, another device took out a significant piece of infrastructure: a giant metal pylon carrying power lines into the capital; smaller wooden poles feeding electricity to towns in the suburbs; a water distribution pipe; cable TV junction boxes—the list went on and on.

After twenty minutes, his initial targets had been destroyed or seriously damaged, and that left only the train. He checked the location and saw that it was nearing the halfway mark, its lowest point beneath the English Channel. He closed down the GPS app and returned to the phone menu, where the entry 'Chunnel' sat at the top of the queue.

Roberts called the number, and after a few seconds was told that the number was unavailable. He switched back to the GPS app, and saw that the signal was no longer being fed from the Tunnel.

With that phase of the operation over, he opened his email client and accessed a mail draft with video attachment that he'd created the day before. After sending it, he started the engine and pointed the van towards Westminster.

By the time he got to Thames House, MI5 would have had time to watch the video and know what they were facing.

The driver hit his hazard lights as he pulled onto the hard shoulder of the M27. The NATS centre—formerly the National Air Traffic Services—sat three hundred feet off to his left, and having staked out the area in the previous weeks, he knew this was as close as he was going to get. It would have been nice to have driven up to the building, but the only entrance was manned by security personnel, as would be expected of the company that provided air traffic control for the UK.

He checked his watch and saw that he was three minutes early, and he knew it was going to be the longest three minutes of his life. If a police patrol happened by, he had a cover story prepared: his wife was due to give birth and had called his mobile, which was why he'd pulled over. As had been drilled into him again and again during his training, he'd paid cash for the van and insured it immediately, so there was no need for the police to pull him over for any traffic violations. Even if they came across him now, all they'd find in the back was a washing machine that he'd claim was being delivered to a repair shop in Southampton.

The more immediate danger was that one of the big rigs heading along the south coast would plough into the back of him, a common enough scenario that would have him on edge for the remaining two and a bit minutes.

He considered firing his weapon early, but instructions had been explicit: it must be twelve minutes past ten in the morning, not a minute earlier or later. Why, he didn't know, but it had long been drilled into him to stick to the agenda.

The seconds ticked agonisingly by, until his watch indicated that it was time. He already had the trigger ready, and he pressed the red button, keeping it depressed for ten seconds, as instructed.

In the back of the van, the device sat in its makeshift housing, which made it look like any other washing machine. This one, however, was fitted with an electro-magnetic pulse weapon, which could send cone-shaped high-energy microwave bursts out to a range of five hundred feet.

Despite the shielding that had been installed within his cab, the driver felt a strange tingling sensation as he held the button down, and briefly wondered if he'd ever father children after this was all over.

When the time had elapsed, he put the van in gear and pulled back onto the motorway.

One task completed and seven more to go before the morning was out.

At the same time, another van managed to get a lot closer to the NATS centre in Prestwick, Ayrshire. It parked in a bay near the security barrier as the driver pretended to make a phone call, all the time keeping his finger on the button that sent the powerful waves towards the control centre.

The security guard manning the booth was more concerned with his radio suddenly packing up than the van, and he was checking the plug when the Transit reversed and pulled away, its driver heading for his next destination.

Ben Hopper sipped his instant decaf as he scanned the circular image on his screen. Morning was a busy time for Heathrow, and the planes were already beginning to stack up over the four navigation beacons at Bovingdon, Lambourne, Ockham and Biggin. He knew he would have to bring them in around thirty seconds apart, which made for a tense couple of hours ahead.

He was just directing an American Airways flight to start final approach when the Mayday call came through, and he looked out of the window just in time to see the British Airways jumbo clip the ground with its wing before the nose buried itself in the dirt. It somersaulted into the grass, a fireball erupting as aviation fuel met screaming hot engine. Debris was scattered all over the taxiways, slamming into parked planes and rendering half of the airport out of action.

Hopper sat frozen as the scene unfolded, but a switched-on supervisor began barking orders.

'Ben, divert everything low on fuel to Gatwick and send the rest to Birmingham and Manchester.'

Hopper immediately began issuing emergency instructions to the planes hovering above. Sirens howled and telephones rang incessantly, making it difficult for him to concentrate as he tried to explain to dozens of pilots that the airport was closed for an emergency.

The supervisor tapped Hopper on the shoulder.

'Cancel that. I just called Gatwick, and they've got a plane down, too. Birmingham are also asking us to take their arrivals. A few regional airports are still open, so send anything small their way.'

'Christ!' Hopper exclaimed. 'What's happening?'

'I don't know, but we've got to get these planes on the ground.'

Hopper looked at his screen and saw the aircraft transponder markers converging on his screen, and began rescinding his earlier instructions.

'Flight 237, take your—'

The screen flashed, then turned black, and Hopper gave it a bang with the palm of his hand.

'Shit! My screen's down!'

He looked round and saw that the other controllers were facing exactly the same problem. One of the busiest airports in the world was blind, and would have to rely on visuals and radio communications. Thankfully, the latter system was separate from the one that powered the visual displays.

'We're going to have to land them on two-seven right,' the supervisor told his team. 'I need every available person to clear the FOD and open the runway up.'

Any foreign object debris on the ground had the potential to burst tyres, or, more seriously, puncture a fuel tank, which was why the supervisor wanted the other runway swept before any planes attempted a landing. There was no telling how far the debris from the crash had spread, and the last thing he wanted was the whole airport out of commission.

'The CAA will go ballistic,' Hopper pointed out.

'We've got no other choice.'

Chapter 13

15 December 2014

Andrew Harvey was going through the list of rental companies on Martinique when his email signalled an incoming message. Glad of the interruption from the tedium, he checked the content of the message and sat back in his seat, confused.

'Anyone heard of a recent attack anywhere in the country?'

His fellow operatives all shook their heads, and one or two left their desks to see what he was referring to. The email on his screen contained a terse message:

These attacks on Britain are just the start. T

'T?' one asked.

'No idea,' Harvey said. 'Probably another lunatic.'

He forwarded the message and attachment to Gerald Small, adding a note asking the technician to try to trace the sender through the message headers. He'd just hit the Send button when Veronica Ellis exploded out of her office.

'Everyone in the meeting room, now!'

The whole floor sensed the urgency, and they grabbed notepads and tablets before piling into the room. Ellis already had the television tuned to the BBC news channel, and the image on the screen showed an aerial shot of chaos and carnage at Heathrow. The remains of a plane could be seen scattered over a wide area, and the reporter was telling how the plane had been seen to come down on one wing and tumble end over end in a huge fireball.

Sarah Thompson held a hand over her mouth. 'Oh, my God.'

'That's not all,' Ellis said, glancing at her notes. 'There have been multiple crashes on the M25 in the last hour, and the entire motorway is at a standstill. The National Grid is reporting several outages in the area, and TV and phone communications have also been disrupted.'

'Someone's hitting London in a big way,' Harvey said.

'Not just London,' Ellis responded. 'The same thing is happening in every major city in the UK. Manchester and Birmingham have reported crash landings, all air traffic control is down and we're getting news of explosions in over a dozen city centres.'

Harvey took out his phone and called Small's office.

'Gerald, I sent you an email a couple of minutes ago. I need you to scan the attachment and feed it through to the monitor in the meeting room.'

He turned to speak to Ellis, who held up a finger as she prepared to answer her chirping phone.

'Ellis,' she said, before listening with a solemn expression. She saw everyone in the room waiting for her instructions, and covered the mouthpiece as she set things in motion.

'Someone call NHS England and tell them we have major incidents throughout the country. They'll need to get more staff in to cope. I also want all police and fire services informed. They'll probably want to cancel all leave.' She returned to her call. 'No, ma'am. At this point, we have no idea who's behind this. We're just getting up to speed ourselves.'

Ellis listened for another minute before promising to keep the home secretary informed and ending the call. She turned to address the room.

'What do we know, people? What's the chatter been over the last few months?'

'Nothing unusual,' Harvey said, 'but a few minutes ago I received an email with a video attachment. Gerald's cleaning it up and will send it through in a moment.'

'What did the email say?'

Harvey shared the brief message with everyone.

'Any idea who T could be?'

'Takasa?' Farsi offered.

'How many times have we been through this?' Thompson fired at Farsi. 'They're no threat to us.'

Gerald Small entered the room and told Harvey the video was ready to stream, and Harvey grabbed the remote control, setting the monitor to the internal channel.

A hooded figure appeared on the screen, its facial features obscured by shadow.

'We are Da Sunan Annabi,' a deep voice said. The orator was obviously an African national, his English heavily accented. 'By now you will have noticed that something bad is happening to your country. I suggest you get used to it, because this is going to continue for a long time. What you have seen so far is just the beginning, and we will continue to attack your country until every British soldier is removed from foreign soil. You invade our lands, infecting them with your evil Western ways, corrupting our youth. Well, we say enough!'

With that, the video ended.

Harvey couldn't resist the opportunity to bring Thompson down a couple of pegs. 'DSA are toothless, are they? A waste of resources?'

Thompson was still staring at the screen, and Harvey knew she was trying to fashion a way out of the mess she'd created.

He wasn't about to make it easy for her.

'Veronica, we've been trying to work up their new leader for months now, but every time we do, Sarah tells us to let it go. I told you our single-minded focus on Farrar was a mistake.'

'You did,' Ellis said, flicking the monitor back to the news channel, 'but it was ultimately my call. Sarah is still your section lead, don't forget that. Now quit the point-scoring and let's get digging. How did DSA get people over here? How many are there, and who are they? Where did they get their explosives?'

Thompson turned to Harvey. 'Check all entries into the UK from Nigeria in the last month and compare the names and photos with known militants over there. Hamad, bring up CCTV in the areas surrounding Heathrow and see if we can identify what caused the plane crash and the motorway accidents.'

The two men scurried off, and back at his desk Harvey unlocked his PC. He began typing in the search parameters when his monitor went black.

'What the hell?'

'My computer's crashed,' Farsi said, checking the network and power leads to see if they had come loose.

'Mine, too.'

Harvey looked around the office, and saw that everyone was sitting with confused looks as they faced blank screens. He tried his mobile phone, but was unable to wake it up. He rose and addressed everyone in the office around him.

'We've been hit.'

Paul Roberts continued driving down Millbank, his finger on the red button as the microwaves pounded the buildings to his right. Once he passed Thames House, he released the trigger, saving what was left in the batteries for the next major target, which sat on the other side of the river.

He crossed Vauxhall Bridge and found a safe place to park, then climbed quickly into the back to turn the device around so that it was facing in the right direction. He got back into the driver's seat and drove past the SIS building, spraying the offices of MI6 with energy waves.

With Scotland Yard, MI5 and MI6 working on reduced capacity, it was time to visit Canary Wharf. After hitting the financial centre, he would take the next step in the plan.

'Gerald, we need comms as soon as possible!'

Harvey heard Thompson shouting into Small's office as she rushed past, and went to see if he could help.

'How's it looking?' he asked.

'Almost everything's fried,' Small said, looking like he'd lost a loved one.

'What about the old landlines?'

A year earlier, the system had been updated to replace the traditional telephones with VoIP phones, which placed and transmitted telephone calls over an IP network, such as the internet, instead of the usual public switched telephone network. VoIP phones had a number of advantages, but the downside had now become apparent.

'I've got someone working on them, but they were literally ripped out during the upgrade. It could take hours to get them up and running again.'

'What about our data?'

'The servers are housed in another building,' Small said. 'They should be okay, but we have nothing to contact them with. We need new client devices, plus routers, plus—'

'Draw up a list and let me know where to get it from,' Harvey said. He urged Small to get some phone lines in place as soon as possible, then went to Thompson's office.

'Sarah, I want to get down on the street and see what's going on. The whole of London may be blacked out, or it could just be us. If we were targeted, then we should be able to get some new mobile phones locally.'

'Good idea,' she conceded, reluctantly, 'but send someone junior. I need you here.'

'There isn't a hell of a lot I can do here,' Harvey said. 'Without computers or phones, we're back in the Stone Age. Let me go and see what I can source.'

Thompson caved, and he jogged through the building to the main entrance.

Outside, cars were passing the building and joggers bounced their way along the embankment, completely unaware of what was happening to their country.

Harvey ran around the corner and dashed into the coffee house where he bought his daily brew.

'Marco, can I borrow your phone?'

The owner smiled and offered his mobile, happy to oblige one of his regular customers.

Harvey clicked the browser icon and typed *BBC News* into the address bar. He was rewarded seconds later with the latest headlines.

They confirmed that MI5 had been specifically targeted, so their communication problems would only be temporary. All he had to do was source new cell phones and they'd be back in the game. However, getting the servers back online would be an entirely different challenge altogether.

Harvey handed the phone back and thanked Marco before setting off in search of replacement handsets.

It took him fifteen minutes to find a shop that sold mobile phones, and he asked for a dozen pay-as-you-go units and credit for each one. Despite the fact that he was clearly in a hurry, the young salesman tried to get him to register the phones, and offered to sell him insurance and accessories for each one.

'Just the phones,' Harvey insisted.

The sale was rung up, and Harvey handed over his credit card.

'I'm afraid that's been declined,' the store clerk said. 'Have you got another card?'

'No, I haven't. Try it again, please.'

Once more, the transaction was denied, and Harvey realised that the chip in his card must have been affected by whatever had hit Thames House.

'Look, there's a national emergency going on, and I need these phones.'

'Sure. Just as soon as you've paid for them.'

Harvey considered coming clean with the youth, but letting word out that the security services were blind wasn't an option. Trying to steal the phones wouldn't work either: the credit would be cancelled immediately, and he would be left with a set of expensive paperweights.

With no other option, he hurried back to the office, phone-less. When he explained the situation to Thompson, she told him to ask Ellis for access to the cash reserve and get back with the phones as soon as possible.

It took him another thirty minutes to repeat the journey, and by the time he got back to his desk with a couple of bags full of equipment, he saw Ellis in her glass-walled office, talking with three others.

One was Sarah Thompson, and one he recognised as the home secretary's assistant.

While they talked, Harvey prepared phones for Ellis and Thompson, then one for himself. When the meeting broke up, he handed them over, along with the receipt.

'It isn't looking good,' he said, showing them the *BBC News* headlines on his handset.

A train had been derailed in a tunnel near Haywards Heath, blocking the line that linked the southeast coast to the capital. A couple of deaths had been reported, along with numerous injuries, and it was going to be days before anyone could manage the Brighton to London commute. Other rail networks had been similarly affected, and transport across the country had ground to a halt.

An aerial shot showed gridlock in many areas of London, as those who had heard about the attacks tried to flee the city, only to find the major arteries blocked.

The scene shifted to another reporter. He was standing in front of the camera while in the background, rubble covered the streets, the aftermath of an explosion at a shopping complex.

'We need to get to our servers,' Ellis said.

'Gerald's going to let me know what he needs,' Harvey told her. 'Whether or not we can get it here is another matter entirely.'

Chapter 14

15 December 2014

Weighed down by three carrier bags full of Christmas toys, Tom Gray wheeled his daughter through the doors of Inner London Hospital and down the corridor to the assessment clinic.

The nurses' station was unusually empty, and Gray waited around for someone to register him for Melissa's regular appointment. After a few minutes, a doctor rushed past, followed quickly by a nurse, and Gray asked her when he could expect someone to attend to him.

'I'm afraid all non-emergency clinics are suspended for the foreseeable future,' the doctor said. 'We're dealing with a major incident.'

Gray pressed for more information, but the medic was already hurrying away.

The missed appointment was no big deal. Melissa's monthly visits had yet to reveal any communication problems, and his daughter's vocabulary now ran to more than thirty words.

To his regret, none of them was *Mummy*.

'Come on, darling. Let's go home so Daddy can get these presents wrapped.'

He pushed her towards the exit, but stopped short when he saw a room full of people staring at a large, wall-mounted television.

He recognised the BBC news channel, and saw an aerial shot of a motorway accident. Several vehicles appeared to be on fire.

He assumed that was the reason for the major incident the doctor had mentioned, but then the scene changed to show a train wreck, and a caption appeared on the screen:

Britain under attack

Gray pushed his way into the room and asked what was going on.

'Sshhh!'

'Them bastards are at it again,' an old man said.

'Who?'

'Sshhh!'

Gray gave up asking and watched the drama unfold. The images on the screen changed every few seconds, as pictures came in from all over the country. Gray saw train derailments, motorway accidents, downed planes and fires raging in major city centres.

'The emergency services are already stretched to the limit,' the voiceover said, 'with hospitals all over the country calling in extra staff to cope with the influx of trauma cases. So far, we have reports of over three thousand deaths, though that number is expected to rise sharply throughout the day.'

The scene changed once more, this time to a fire at a department store, and Gray recognised it as being only a few hundred yards from the hospital.

'Come on, sweetheart, time to go.'

He reversed the pushchair out of the room and hurried to the exit. Whatever was happening, he was close to it, and his only thought was to get his daughter out of the danger zone.

He was ten yards from the double doors that led to the street when the fire extinguisher in the adjacent waiting room received its deadly signal.

Takasa was watching the latest news reports on his laptop when the phone rang. He snatched it up as the presenter highlighted the chaos in Newcastle following several explosions in the city centre. A view of the city's railway station showed huge crowds of frustrated commuters being turned away from the turnstiles owing to damaged tracks.

'What the hell are you playing at?'

Takasa recognised the person on the other end of the line, and in truth it was a call he'd been expecting.

'Just as you ordered,' he replied. 'I hit Britain hard.'

'Not this damned hard,' the voice said. 'You were supposed to launch a few attacks and outrage the population, not kill them all and destroy the bloody country!'

'Well, I would imagine they're pretty outraged right now.'

'Don't play clever with me, I'm warning you.'

'Look,' Takasa said, 'you wanted the people up in arms, you got it. Don't forget that there have been plenty of attacks in Britain over the years, and they're all forgotten sooner or later. You said you wanted something that would stick in the memory, and I gave that to you. I didn't question your motives, I just delivered what you asked for.'

'You have to make this stop,' the voice said, a hint of anxiety evident.

'Oh, it's too late for that. As of yesterday, all our operatives have gone dark. I couldn't contact them if I tried.'

'Then you have to give me some names. If we can bring one of them in, they could give up the others—'

'Do you really think that's wise?' Takasa interrupted. 'If you give the security services a name, the first thing they're going to ask is where you got the information. How would you explain that? Are you going to tell them you had a cosy chat with the leader of DSA and he decided to turn over a new leaf?'

'No, of course not, but these attacks—'

'Will continue until tomorrow evening. You said two days, and it will be two days. I can't do anything about it now.'

'I'm not going to forget this.'

'I should hope not,' Takasa said. 'One day, you'll be able to thank me personally for my contribution to . . . . What exactly was the overall aim?'

'You'll find out in due course,' the caller told him. 'I just want you to know that you went too far, and that'll be a costly mistake on your part.'

Takasa smiled. He'd known a long time ago that this moment would come, and the precautions he'd taken were now proving invaluable. He reached into his briefcase and pulled out a compact tape recorder.

'If you're thinking of . . . terminating our relationship, I suggest you listen to this.'

He clicked the play button and held the recorder next to the phone for thirty seconds.

'I think you'll recognise that conversation,' he said. 'That was the first time you approached me. Trust me when I say I have every one of our subsequent chats on disk, with the usual precaution of multiple copies dispersed internationally. Anything happens to me . . . . You know the drill.'

Takasa could almost hear the caller panicking. Prior to that meeting, he'd been screened for recording devices to prevent just this situation. What they'd failed to appreciate was that he had considerable knowledge of the systems they used, and that meant being able to easily circumvent their protocols.

'I wasn't suggesting anything of that nature—'

'I'm sure you weren't,' Takasa said, 'but I want you to know that it would benefit both of us if I were to disappear forever once this is over, and that means not having to look over my shoulder.'

'Agreed.'

'Good. I'll cover my tracks at this end. I'm sure I don't need to explain the importance of ensuring I'm never implicated in this. It's in your own best interest to ensure I outlive you.'

Takasa ended the call abruptly and returned to watching the news feed. A mother was explaining that she was so scared that she'd taken her children out of school in case it was the next target.

I wouldn't sink that low, he thought to himself.

But you have every right to be terrified.

Chapter 15

15 December 2014

Prime Minister Andrew Reed entered the COBRA meeting and dumped his jacket over the back of his chair.

'What the hell's going on?' he demanded, taking his seat.

'At this moment, we're not sure,' Juliet Harper, the home secretary, said. 'We lost communication with the security services just after this kicked off, and we're working to get them back online as soon as possible.'

'They took out Five and Six, too?'

'Yes, Prime Minister.'

'Who's behind it?'

'I sent a representative to Thames House, and all they have so far is a video claiming to be from Da Sunan Annabi, or DSA.'

The home secretary gave the room an abridged account of the group's history, beginning with their formation in 2001 and their exploits to date.

'They began as a Muslim organisation, but their ideological roots have been diluted over the years. Previously, they'd never strayed far from their home in northern Nigeria, so that put them pretty far down our threat list.'

'Well, they've strayed now,' the secretary of defence said.

Harper let the remark go. 'The sheer number of incidents is overwhelming the police and fire services. I've issued orders to cancel all leave, but we're going to need more people.'

'Jim,' Reed said, looking at the defence minister, 'we're going to need troops. How many do you have at your disposal?'

'Across the entire armed forces?' James Hanratty asked. 'I can have fifty thousand ready to go within twenty-four hours.'

'Do it.'

The defence secretary pulled out his mobile and made the call, while the Chancellor of the Exchequer added his own thoughts.

'The snow flurries we had in January last year cost the UK economy around half a billion pounds a day, and that was just the result of people not being able to get to work. In December, the software glitch that affected air traffic control caused some flight cancellations and delays, costing millions more. At the beginning of the year, storms and flooding along the southwest coastline caused damage running into the hundreds of millions, and it took the best part of three months to get things back to normal. Multiply that by a hundred, and you've got economic meltdown.'

The projection was greeted with grim faces.

'And it's not just about transport,' he continued. 'Power lines up and down the country have been destroyed, and shopping malls have been targeted, as have office buildings from Carlisle to Brighton. Tomorrow, millions of people will be unable to get to work, and those that can won't want to. Tourism is going to take a big hit, too. This is all happening in the run-up to Christmas, which can make or break many firms.'

'Give me a figure,' the prime minister said.

'As you know, GDP is nudging seven billion a day. I think we can kiss a large chunk of that goodbye for the foreseeable future. On top, there are repairs to infrastructure that are going to make seven billion look like chicken feed. The power companies will be coming to us for help, as will just about every major industry in Britain. The bailout will make the banking crisis look like pocket change. And that doesn't even account for the financial market. I'm afraid this could bankrupt us.'

Harper leaned in close to the prime minister. 'We may need to launch Brigandicuum,' she whispered.

'Brandy-what?' The chancellor looked back and forth between them.

Reed sat back in his chair with a sigh. 'Brigandicuum is a joint intelligence-gathering venture between Britain and the US,' he told the assembled ministers. 'It is designed to infiltrate our enemies' communications at the earliest possible stage, no holds barred. And it doesn't require tens of thousands of man-hours or people on the ground to identify those who would do us harm.'

'It sounds like PRISM,' one of the ministers said. 'We can order internet service providers to hand over details of communications that match specific search terms.'

'It's similar,' the PM agreed, 'but much more proactive. The main difference is, we don't have to wait until a communication is sent between two parties.'

'*Pre*-communication? How is that possible?'

'I don't know the technical details,' Reed said, 'but essentially, it plays on the fact that almost everyone these days has a PC, laptop, tablet or mobile phone. We—or, more specifically, the US—have developed a small program that sits inside the kernel of the operating systems for these devices.'

'Kernel?' the justice minister asked.

'It's the fundamental core of any operating system, the basic functionality that provides interaction between software and hardware. Anyway, this program has been hidden inside the kernels of all major operating systems for a couple of years, and it just requires activation.'

'How does that happen? How is it activated?'

'I've been told it's as simple as placing a text file in a folder on one of the NSA servers. Once the device finds the file, we effectively have complete control over it.'

'I'm amazed the software vendors agreed to go along with it,' the justice minister said. 'If this ever gets out, they can kiss their customers goodbye.'

'Why do you think they turn over six billion a year and pay two million in tax?' Harper asked. 'Think about it. Besides, all of these companies are registered overseas, which means whenever someone uses their software it is essentially an act of external communication and intercepting the data doesn't require a warrant signed by a minister.'

'So who knows about this?'

'Up until this morning, Juliet and me,' Reed said, looking at the home secretary. 'I don't need to tell you how sensitive this is, so it doesn't leave this room. If it goes online, only those I deem necessary will have access to it.'

'What do you mean if?' Justice asked.

'Our legislation doesn't yet allow us to use such surveillance techniques,' the home secretary said. 'Turning it on now would be technically illegal, if morally right.'

'So when were you planning to unleash it? This isn't something you can just put to parliament and expect it to sail onto the statute books.'

'We set this up so that in the event of a major attack, we would have the ability to strike back almost instantly,' the PM told the health secretary. 'In times of crisis, the people will understand the need to be able to react effectively and apprehend those behind such atrocities. An amendment to the Regulation of Investigatory Powers Act will enable us to bring Brigandicuum online instantly, and we should be able to identify whoever is behind this.'

Reed turned to the home secretary. 'Has the amendment been drafted?'

Harper nodded. 'I'll have a copy on your desk in a few minutes. No mention of the how, just the ability to intercept any and all electronic material when it's vital to national security. A bit vague, but I anticipate no objections from anyone, considering the threat we're facing at the moment.'

'Pity this wasn't online a few months ago,' Justice said. 'We might have ended this before it started.'

'Well, it wasn't,' Reed said.

He didn't add that it had been his decision not to implement Brigandicuum at a more opportune moment. Although he recognised it as a powerful tool against terrorism, and potentially organised crime and other evils, the very idea of such invasive surveillance went very much against his grain. It wasn't that he was afraid of losing the privacy-group vote; it was more the betrayal of trust. He'd always tried to be as open with the public as possible—national security matters notwithstanding—and Brigandicuum would destroy any trust he'd managed to build up. Given the political fallout if the public ever learned the details, he would have been staring career suicide in the face.

The health minister's phone chirped, and he took the call. After speaking in a hushed voice for a few moments, he placed the handset on the table, the colour having drained from his face.

'That was NHS England. These bastards are targeting hospitals throughout the country. We've lost A&E capability in the capital, and forty-three other trusts are reporting explosions. We don't know the exact number of casualties as yet, but we've lost a lot of medical staff and vital equipment. There's no way we're going to be able to cope.'

Reed sat back in his chair, wondering again how such devastation could happen without warning.

'Juliet, get Veronica Ellis up to speed on Brigandicuum. I want our people at Haddon Hall as soon as possible.'

He rose, signalling an end to the meeting.

'I'm going to have a word with President Lomax.'

Chapter 16

15 December 2014

Andrew Harvey was on the phone when Veronica Ellis returned to Thames House and made a beeline for his desk.

'Get Sarah and meet me in my office.'

Harvey went to fetch Thompson, and they knocked on Ellis's door a minute later.

'Sit down,' Ellis said, preferring to stand herself. 'Andrew, what's the status of the servers?'

'Gerald says we'll be up and running within the hour. He managed to get some PCs from a local shop and is just installing the necessary software. They'll do until we get proper replacements.'

'Good. Hand over everything to Hamad. You two are being seconded to the NSA.'

Thompson and Harvey exchanged looks.

'Is this just until we're back up and running?' Harvey asked.

Ellis shook her head. 'I would imagine you'll be there for the duration. They've been working on a new program that should help us to identify our attackers, and I need you to liaise with them. Once you've got names and locations, send the details to us and we'll do the take-down.'

'How long have they had this?' Harvey asked.

'And why wait until now to share it?' Thompson added.

'I don't have that information,' Ellis said. 'It seems only the PM and a couple of others knew about its existence, and I only learned about it thirty minutes ago. Needless to say, it's eyes-only, and you speak to no-one about it. Understood?'

Harvey was intrigued, and keen to learn more, though he knew he was unlikely to get anything else out of his boss. 'Understood. We'll head over there right now. I assume it's based in their embassy?'

Ellis handed over a slip of paper. 'Actually, it's a place called Haddon Hall, off the A34, just outside Newbury.'

'That's not going to be easy to get to,' Thompson pointed out. 'The last update said just about every road out of London is clogged, and the M4 is shut, too.'

'I realise that,' Ellis said. 'Do either of you know how to ride a motorcycle?'

'I do,' Harvey told her as Thompson shook her head.

'Good. Sarah, you can ride pillion.'

Ellis went to her desk and pulled a requisition form from her drawer, which she filled in and handed to Harvey. 'Draw that from petty cash and buy one. You'll also want to arm yourselves. There's no telling what's out there today.'

The chit allowed him up to ten thousand in cash, which would be more than enough to buy a decent machine.

'Well, what are you waiting for?'

Harvey and Thompson rose and left the office, walking down to the first floor, where the finance department handed over the bundle of fifty-pound notes without blinking. Normally, Harvey would have had to jump through hoops to sign out enough money to buy a coffee, and he suspected Ellis had called ahead. The same applied to the armoury, where they signed for a brand new Glock 31 GEN4 and three magazines containing fifteen rounds of .357 ammunition each.

Out on the street, the neighbourhood resembled a huge car park. Traffic was at a standstill, with only cyclists and motorbikes managing to navigate their way between the stationary vehicles. A few people were still sitting behind the wheel, unaware of what was happening to the country, but most were on their phones or listening to their radios, catching up with the latest news reports.

Harvey led Thompson along the side of the Thames at a jog, and a few minutes later they crossed Vauxhall Bridge, where a motorcycle dealership sat behind the MI6 building. There were several second-hand machines parked up outside, but Harvey wanted something reliable, and didn't have time to have an older machine checked out by a mechanic.

He picked out a brand new 500CC Honda and handed over six thousand to a young motorcycle salesman with the name 'Jerry' tagged to his chest. The money got him the bike and a couple of helmets.

'We'll need to fill out some paperwork,' Jerry said. 'It should only take twenty minutes.'

'Sorry, but we haven't got time.'

Thompson showed him the police warrant card that was one of her cover identities.

'This about the attacks, then?'

Harvey nodded.

Jerry looked uncertain. At that moment, his manager, a balding, beer-bellied man, came outside and asked if there was a problem.

Thompson explained the situation.

The manager shook his head. 'Sorry, lady, but we gotta do the forms before you take the bike. You of all people should understand.'

'I do,' Thompson said, drawing her weapon. 'Give me the money back and I'll requisition the bike instead. You know I have the power to do that, don't you?'

The manager swallowed at the sight of the grey muzzle pointing at his forehead. His eyes flitted to Harvey.

Harvey shrugged. 'On a day like this, you really want to piss the police off?'

A minute and a half later, they had the keys.

'You ever been on a bike before?' Harvey asked Thompson.

'Never,' Thompson said, holstering her pistol.

'Then just remember to hold on tight and lean when I lean.'

Harvey donned his helmet and secured the strap under his chin before climbing on the machine and starting it up. Thompson climbed on the back and wrapped her arms around him, and he pulled off the pavement and onto the road, heading west for the M4.

Tom Gray woke up to a loud ringing in his ears, and at first he was disorientated. He struggled to focus, and when he put his hand to his face it came away crimson, blood seeping from a gash on his forehead. He tried his limbs, seeking signs of damage, but he was able to move them all, and he pushed himself up onto his knees.

A thin mist of fine powder hung in the air, and the wall three yards away was pockmarked by hundreds of pieces of shrapnel. A hole the size of a car had been punched through the concrete wall, and Gray knew that if he'd been pushing Melissa a little faster, they'd have felt the full force of the blast.

Melissa!

He crawled round to see his daughter, whose little mouth was open in a desperate cry that he couldn't hear. The explosion had damaged his eardrums, and he realised the ringing wasn't the fire alarm but a result of the blast. He checked his daughter over, but saw no sign of blood. Her arms and legs seemed to be functioning normally. He delicately tested them for breaks.

Satisfied that she was clear of physical injury, he gently unstrapped her and lifted her out of the contraption, holding her tight to calm her down.

A nurse stumbled into view, blood pouring from a shoulder wound. She had a large, red stain on the front of her tunic, and she managed a few steps towards him before collapsing to the floor.

Gray carried Melissa over to the fallen woman, and for the first time he saw the damage that had been done to her back. It looked like she'd been blasted with a shotgun at close range, her clothes shredded and bloodied.

Gray knew there was nothing he could do for her, and he walked slowly towards the exit, which intersected with another corridor. The left looked clear, but to the right lay carnage. A couple of bodies lay on the ground. He took a few steps past them and looked into the A&E waiting room.

The scene resembled a horror movie. At least thirty people lay dead, and many more limbs were scattered around, the remains of those closest to the explosion. Three medical staff were already on hand, helping the few survivors. Two of them were frantically applying CPR to a teenage girl, while the other checked the remaining bodies for vital signs.

Gray felt compelled to help, but when he felt and heard another explosion from within the building, he knew it was time to get his daughter to safety. He ran for the door and pushed it open. He knew his hearing must be returning, for his ears were suddenly assaulted by the sound of a hundred desperate motorists leaning on their horns.

He realised that if the news stories were right, driving home was out of the question, as would be any other form of transport. He briefly considered a motorcycle, but there was no way he was going to climb aboard one with Melissa in tow.

He pulled out his phone and checked the distance to his home: slightly more than eleven miles away, a comfortable jog under normal circumstances.

What troubled him was the large number of explosions in the city, which made him reluctant to take Melissa through densely populated areas. The attacks seemed to have been planned with military precision, and if the objective was to get people out in the open, it had worked. All around him, people were beginning to abandon their cars and make their way on foot, the street already teeming with humanity. One well-timed explosion now would be devastating, and Gray chose not to wait around to see if he were right.

He decided that for the time being he would head for somewhere relatively safe, and he set off for Minotaur's offices. As he moved carefully around debris and between panicked citizens, he dialled Len Smart's number.

'Tom, have you seen what's going on? It's crazy!'

'I know,' Gray said. 'I'm caught up in the middle of it.'

He gave a quick playback of the visit to the hospital.

Smart was concerned, mainly for Melissa. 'The streets are scary at the moment. I suggest you get here as soon as you can.'

Gray told him he'd be there within half an hour and hung up before stepping up the pace. He stuck to the side streets, where the chances of being caught in another explosion were drastically reduced, though it added distance to the journey. Up ahead, between the rooftops, he could see a pillar of smoke rising skywards, and as he rounded the corner he saw an insurance building ablaze.

He wasn't surprised to see no emergency services in attendance. Given the number of incidents already reported on the news, the fire service was probably doing all it could. The blocked roads would also add to their headache, preventing the engine crews from reaching the calls.

Gray gave the area a wide berth, and after two more long detours he arrived at the offices of Minotaur Logistics, where Smart and Sonny were watching the chaos unfold on the wall-mounted TV.

'You're late,' Sonny said, without the normal humour in his voice. 'We thought something had happened to you.' He peered at Gray's forehead. 'Are you okay?'

Gray checked his watch and saw that it had taken closer to an hour to cover the three miles.

'Just a scratch. Melissa's fine too. What's the latest?'

'Someone hit us really hard,' Smart said. 'The news said it was DSA, but something this enormous doesn't sound like them. It has to be someone else.'

Gray was looking at the screen, where the BBC news ticker told him that almost thirteen million homes remained without electricity.

'Do we have any information about the roads? I'm anxious to get Melissa home.'

'It looks like they took out the main arteries,' Sonny said. 'Every major route in and out of London is blocked. Even if you do get home, you're unlikely to have electricity. We've got a generator and heating, so you might as well stay here.'

'I'm sure they'll have power back up soon,' Gray told him, but Smart shook his head grimly.

'According to the news, it'll be at least three days before they can make a start on repairs. They need heavy lifting gear to fix the pylons, but they have to wait until the roads are cleared before they can move them into position. Even then, they're reluctant to do the work. A couple of their repair teams have been caught out by booby traps.'

'I'm just surprised they left communications largely untouched,' Sonny said.

'Something on this scale means the attackers have to co-ordinate, and that requires mobile phones or the internet,' Gray said. 'Cutting those lines would hurt them, too. Besides, can you imagine the panic these scenes are causing all over the country? Millions will be glued to the news websites. This is a terrorist's wet dream come true.'

'They're mobilising the armed forces,' Smart said. 'The police are overwhelmed, as you can imagine. They said they want to get the roads clear first so that the emergency services can get to the more serious incidents, but that's not being helped by people abandoning their vehicles. The BBC asked everyone to stay with their cars, but not many people are listening.'

'You can't really blame them,' Sonny said. 'Many have to get home to their kids, and it's unreasonable to ask them to sit in their cars for three days in the hope that traffic starts moving again.'

Sonny was right. Thankfully there hadn't been a course in progress at the training complex; otherwise any potential recruits would have been stuck there for some time.

'Maybe we should offer our services,' Smart said. 'We've got a couple of hundred people on the books, and I'm sure they could be useful.'

'Good idea,' Gray agreed, and he pulled his phone out. He found Andrew Harvey's number in the contact list and pressed the green button.

You have reached the voicemail service for oh-seven . . .

'He's obviously got his hands full at the moment,' Gray said, disconnecting. 'I'll call him back in the evening. In the meantime, contact everyone who's not already on assignment and let them know we might be needing them in the next twenty-four hours.'

'Are you still going to try to make it home?' Smart asked.

'No, we'll stay here tonight,' Gray said. 'I need to pop to the local shops to get a few things in, though.'

'I'll go,' Sonny said. 'You don't want to be taking Melissa out, and I get the feeling you're not going to be leaving her here.'

'Thanks, Sonny,' Gray said. In truth, over the last several months he'd got better at leaving his daughter with others for an hour or two, gradually increasing the amount of time away from her, but the day's events had put any such thoughts out of his mind. Even the thought of leaving her with his two most trusted friends made his skin go clammy.

He prepared a list of items to get, and asked Smart for some money from the petty cash tin.

'Five hundred should do it,' he said. 'There's a camping shop two streets over. If it's still open, get a pop-up tent and some folding camp beds. You can get Melissa's stuff from the chemist.'

'Get some food for us, too,' Smart said. 'I might as well bunk here tonight.'

'Fine, but you come with me. I can't carry all that by myself.'

Smart grabbed his coat from the stand and they left Gray to catch up on the events unfolding on the TV.

Chapter 17

15 December 2014

A light rain began to fall as Smart and Sonny headed towards the parade of shops, the street eerily quiet.

The first store they came to had already pulled down the security shutters, and Sonny didn't hold out much hope of anything remaining open. One by one, they walked past locked-down buildings, but when they reached the chemist they heard raised voices.

He peered through the window and saw three hooded youths shouting and throwing items at the Asian shopkeeper, who was cowering in front of a female assistant.

'Looks like the vultures have smelt blood,' he said to Smart, who was also watching the drama unfold.

'It's people like this who debunk the theory of natural selection.'

'Maybe it's survival of the thickest,' Sonny mused as he pushed the door open.

The boys turned as he walked into the shop, and one of them immediately enlightened Sonny and Smart as to the problem.

'It's these fuckin' Muslims,' he spat. 'They did these bombings.'

'Did they indeed?' Sonny walked over to the counter and looked at the shopkeeper's name tag. 'And who told you that?'

'Me dad.'

'Then your dad's an idiot. Mr Singh here is wearing a Dastar turban, which tells me he's a Sikh.'

Singh nodded fervently, confirming Sonny's guess.

'He's still a Paki,' another youth shouted, before throwing a packet of sanitary towels at the shopkeeper.

Sonny strode over and grabbed the boy by the throat. 'He's from India, you moron, not Pakistan. And even if he was, do you really think he'd set off a load of bombs, then come back here and run a shop?'

'It doesn't matter,' the boy shouted, making sure Singh could hear. 'They're all the same!'

The kid looked barely fourteen, and it saddened Sonny that parents could still preach intolerance. No doubt the boy would grow up a racist, and any children he spawned would follow the same path as generations before him.

'Get the fuck out of this shop and don't come back,' Sonny snarled into the youth's face, and pushed him backwards towards the door.

Hitting children wasn't in his make-up, no matter the transgression, but in this instance, he had no choice.

Instead of retreating, the boy pulled out a knife and lunged at Sonny, who nimbly danced aside and landed a punch to the side of his head. The knife went flying as the kid collapsed to the floor, and Sonny turned to the other two miscreants.

'Anyone else fancy a shot?'

Both shook their heads, and Sonny guessed he'd taken out their leader.

'Grab him and get the fuck out of here!'

A minute later, the dazed youth was helped out by his friends, and Sonny calmly pulled out the shopping list.

The assistant rushed to lock the door before picking up the stock that was scattered all over the floor. Smart helped her while

Sonny found the nappies and baby food and took them to the counter.

'I don't suppose you sell beer and pizza?' he asked, but got a shake of the head from a visibly relieved Mr Singh.

'Didn't think so.'

He instructed Smart to grab some cereal bars and pulled out a twenty, but Singh refused it.

'Take them with my thanks,' he said.

'I didn't do it for a reward,' Sonny said with a smile, putting the money on the counter. 'I'll need a receipt, please.'

Singh reluctantly rang up the sale and bagged the goods, then showed them to the door, locking it after they had left.

'I think we're going to see a lot more of that in the next few days,' Smart said, as they headed towards the camping shop, 'especially with the police preoccupied.'

'You're not wrong,' Sonny agreed. 'Give the scumbags a few hours and they'll realise they can run amok with impunity. No CCTV, no cops, just a load of shops waiting to be relieved of their stock. They'll probably test the waters tonight and tomorrow it'll be full-scale riots.'

'Then we have to get out of the city tomorrow morning. It should be quiet first thing, and we can escort Tom and Gill home.'

Sonny had forgotten about the receptionist, but luckily she lived a short distance from Gray, so they could travel together at first light.

Down the street, the outdoor centre remained open, capitalising on the power shortages by selling camping stoves and bottles of gas at three times the normal price.

'Another sign of the times,' Smart said sadly, as he inspected a portable gas stove that had been marked up from twenty pounds to seventy.

A woman was pleading with a young man in a blue T-shirt about the cost of her items, but the salesman wasn't relenting.

'Sorry,' he said, trying to move on to the next person in the queue. 'The manager sets the price, not me.'

'But I have to feed my kids, and I've got a baby! I have to sterilise her bottles!'

'Next!'

Sonny took the stove and approached the counter, where he asked the woman how much she was being charged.

'He wants two hundred for these, but the real price is only thirty-five,' the woman sobbed.

Sonny pushed his way to the counter and tapped the customer being served on the shoulder.

'Mind if I butt in? I'm trying to get him to lower his prices.'

The man stood aside. 'Be my guest.'

Sonny fixed the shop assistant with a hard stare and read his name tag, but the youngster didn't appear fazed.

'Why are you ripping these people off, Brian? Don't you know what's happened to the country?'

Brian just looked over at an older man who was busy changing prices with a felt-tip pen. 'Go tell him. I just take the money.'

Realising he wasn't going to get anywhere with Brian, Sonny walked over to the manager and grabbed the pen as he was about to mark another item up.

'Hey! What do you think you're doing?'

'I might ask the same question,' Sonny said. 'Why are you ripping people off?'

'Ripping them off? It's called supply and demand.'

'Is that right?'

'Yeah, like when airline prices shoot up during the school holidays. *Supply. And. Demand.* It's not against the law. It's called capitalism.'

Smart had overheard the conversation, and he could see from Sonny's stance that he was ready for action. He quickly walked over to defuse the situation.

'Sonny, leave it. It's not worth it. When we send out the patrols tonight, we'll just tell them to skip this street.'

'What patrols?' the manager asked, suddenly concerned.

'We're in the TA, and they've called us up because they expect rioting here this evening. It's already kicked off in some places.'

The manager looked at them, hoping to see signs of a joke, but both men looked deadly serious.

'Come on,' Smart said, tapping Sonny on the shoulder. 'Let's grab what we need while he's still got some stock.'

'Hang on,' the manager said. 'You're kidding, right?'

'I wish we were,' Sonny said, solemnly. 'It's going to get real ugly tonight.'

'But you have to protect my shop!'

'No can do,' Sonny said. 'Supply and demand, I'm afraid. We have a small supply of troops, and I will demand that they're elsewhere when the mob starts tearing down your shutters.'

He turned and picked up four folding camp beds, leaving Smart to grab the sleeping bags and other items. The manager chased after them, halting Sonny's progress.

'You're just trying to scare me, aren't you? Why would anyone want to start a riot?'

'You'd be surprised,' Sonny said, picking up a sales tag that had been changed from forty pounds to a hundred and twenty. 'I would have expected this to bring everyone together, but some people are just in it for themselves.'

Sonny walked to the counter and dumped the items on top.

'I'll get this,' the manager said, rushing behind the till and pushing Brian out of the way. He quickly rang through the sales and came up with a very reasonable price.

'I've added a twenty percent discount, too,' he said.

'Why, that's mighty neighbourly of you,' Sonny said in his best Texas drawl. 'I assume that goes for everyone else, too?'

The manager nodded, and handed a pen to Brian, telling him to revert all the prices to normal.

'So, you'll be around here tonight?'

'That we will,' Smart said, handing over the cash before heading out of the store. Sonny hung back to make sure the woman got her stove at the correct price, then followed him out into the street.

'Sonny, why are you looking at my arse?'

'Just checking to see if your pants are on fire.'

'It was a little white lie,' Smart said, 'and he asked for it.'

Sonny told him to wait while he checked the area for other open shops, and returned after ten minutes with a bag full of food. Loaded up, they trekked back to the office, where Gray was still glued to the TV.

'Any problems?' Gray asked.

'Nothing we couldn't handle,' Sonny said, looking up at the screen. 'What's the latest?'

'The talking heads say fifty towns and cities have reported attacks. Whoever did this knows enough about our infrastructure to hit us where it hurts. They say the worst is over, but I wouldn't be too sure.'

'Why not?' Sonny asked.

'When you attack your enemy, you have one goal.'

'Hit him hard and fast,' Smart confirmed, 'and make sure he goes down.'

'Or does some bloody stupid things standing up,' Sonny put in.

'Exactly,' Gray said. 'You certainly don't stand back so they can get up and retaliate. They've brought the country to its knees, but the clean-up process has already begun. If that's the end of it, then the roads will soon be cleared, power restored, and people will be back to work in a couple of days.

'If I was behind this, I'd want to dissuade anyone from pitching in and helping out. We've already seen the power workers being targeted, and I don't think that's the end of it. We'll probably see more and more attacks on the emergency services, and the hospital bombings could be just the start. Expect further attacks on the police, fire service and any armed forces brought in to help.'

'To do that would take hundreds, maybe thousands,' Sonny said as Smart began digging through the bag of food and pulled out a loaf of bread and a tin of Spam. 'I can picture one or two slipping past immigration, but not that many. To be honest, Tom, I think we've seen the last of it.'

'I was just hypothesising,' Gray said. 'I hope I'm wrong.'

What should have been a ninety-minute drive turned into three hours on the road, and when Harvey arrived at the gates to the country home, he wondered if he'd made a mistake. The wrought-iron gates were covered with rust, and the large house beyond looked like it hadn't seen an inhabitant in decades. The grounds were overgrown, with weeds and grass standing over a foot high.

He spotted an intercom system on one of the gateposts and pressed the button.

'Remove your helmet,' a tinny voice said.

Harvey complied, as did Thompson, and seconds later the gate clicked open.

'Bring the bike up.'

Thompson pushed the gates open and Harvey started the engine, easing through the gap and waiting for her to climb back on board. He slowly made his way up the weed-infested driveway, and as they neared the front door, it opened. A man dressed in black slacks and white shirt came out to meet them, and instructed Harvey to park the machine at the rear of the house.

Harvey drove slowly around to where a large garage held half a dozen cars and a few more motorcycles. He secured it inside and they walked back round to the front, where the man was still waiting.

'You must be Sarah and Andrew,' he said, holding out a hand. 'I'm Tony Manello. Welcome to Brigandicuum.'

Manello looked to be in his mid-thirties, and the accent reminded Harvey of his trips to New York. The NSA agent led them into what had once been a grand hallway. Years of neglect had taken their toll, and cobwebs hung from the ornate coving. Protective sheets had been thrown over the few pieces of furniture, and a thin layer of dust covered everything, giving the room a deathly, grey feel.

'Housekeeper's week off?' Harvey asked.

'All the action takes place downstairs,' Manello said, leading them into the library, where thousands of books still adorned the shelves that lined three of the walls. The other wall housed a goods elevator, and Manello entered a code on a keypad. The doors whirred open and they walked into the huge compartment.

'You guys don't do things by half measures, do you?'

Manello smiled at Thompson. 'In this case, size *does* matter. We had a lot of large equipment to install, and this was the only way to get it a hundred yards below the ground.'

Manello hit a button and the conveyance dropped at a sedate pace. Within thirty seconds they hit the basement and the doors opened onto a scene straight out of a science fiction movie. The cavern was a lot bigger than either of them had expected. One wall was dominated by a set of eight giant screens that must have been more than a hundred inches wide. On the main floor, at least two hundred personnel were sitting at monitors, working feverishly.

What struck Harvey was the noise—or more precisely, the lack of it. Apart from a few hushed conversations, the only sound was the staccato clicking as a thousand fingers played over keyboards.

'Impressive,' Harvey admitted. 'So what does it do?'

Manello led them over to a control panel beneath the giant monitors. On the screens, a counter ticked over at colossal speed, the number already past the hundred million mark.

'How much have you been told?' he asked.

'Only that you have the means to identify the people behind the attacks.'

'Then allow me to elaborate. There are more than seven billion people on this planet, and anyone worth worrying about is going to have a way of communicating. They might use a computer, or a laptop, or it could be a tablet or smart phone. What this program does is alert us whenever someone types one of our trigger keywords into their device.'

'That's hardly new,' Thompson said. 'We've been able to intercept transmissions for years.'

'Who said anything about transmissions?' Manello smiled. 'The moment someone *types* 'jihad' or 'attack,' we're alerted to it. Our system is notified, and we pull down the entire typing session to see what context it's being used in. If it's innocent, like an author writing his next blockbuster, we filter them out. If it's a genuine threat, we do a full download from the device, including location and registered owner.'

'Are you saying you've hacked every device on the planet?'

'Basically, yes, though 'hacked' would be the wrong word. The software is hidden deep inside the operating systems. It was developed by us, and we just handed the files to the software vendors with the instruction to incorporate it into their systems. All we had to do then was drop a file into the target folder on our server and wait for each device to find it. Once they do, the keyword list is stored in their device's RAM, leaving no footprint.'

'Surely someone is going to stumble across it one day,' Harvey said. 'There are people out there who rip code apart for fun.'

'Not this code,' Manello assured him. 'It is a separate file that can only be opened through a command prompt and requires a sixty-four-digit password. That password is hashed and buried inside the kernel, and when we asked our best people to decrypt it, they came up empty, despite the massive computing power available to them. The chances of anyone stumbling across it and being able to read the file are too small to be of any significance.'

Despite the assurances, Harvey could see trouble looming. The US government had been extremely embarrassed by the Edward Snowden affair, which had come on the back of the WikiLeaks scandal. Compared to those revelations, Brigandicuum would be devastating. Even if it managed to identify and stop the attackers within the next forty-eight hours, privacy groups would have a field day. Still, from a law enforcement perspective, it was undoubtedly a useful tool that would significantly reduce the terror threat to the country. But if word of it ever got out, a lot of careers were going to be cut short.

'When you say you do a full download, how much data are we talking about?'

'Whatever's on the device.'

'But how do you get round the ISPs' download limits? My laptop, for example, has a terabyte hard drive. That's a lot to send. Besides which, my phone account only allows me five hundred megabytes of data per month.'

'That's all taken into account,' Manello assured him. 'The kernel contains a high compression algorithm that cuts the size of the download by ninety percent, which makes most devices manageable. If it is still above a certain size and data limits start to interfere, we have the option to remote onto the device instead. We don't like to do that as it can leave a trail, so that's always the last resort.'

'Are you sure users won't be aware of the downloads?'

Manello shook his head. 'In the case of a really big grab, they might notice Candy Crush Saga freezing for a split second, but that's about it.'

Harvey nodded. 'What happens if an employee takes this to the newspapers?'

'Then we hit a button and make it go away. Unlike other system updates that require the user's permission, we can do a forced upload and remove the Brigandicuum software instantly. The file is opened, overwritten a dozen times with garbage, then sliced apart one bit at a time. I'll leave damage control to the politicians; it's what they're paid for. As an operator, I happen to love it.'

'Yes,' said Thompson, 'but still . . . you have hardware makers involved. Seems like too many parties involved to keep a secret like this.'

Manello shrugged. 'This technology's been in place for a year and we haven't heard a peep. Still, we've only now activated it, so you may be right in the end.'

Manello seemed unconcerned, and for good reason, thought Harvey. If news of the venture reached the public, it would be the government taking the flak, not the analysts dissecting the mountains of data flooding onto their servers.

'So you've had hundreds of people sitting here for twelve months, just waiting for the go signal?'

'No, we've been operating with a skeleton crew,' Manello explained. 'They've been mostly doing maintenance and stress-testing the equipment, but we got orders to ramp things up last week for a full-on demonstration for your prime minister.'

'Why does it have such an obscure name?' Thompson asked.

'It was chosen because it was unlikely that anyone would ever type it into their handset or computer by mistake. If anyone does use it, it is instantly flagged and we know that someone is discussing the program.'

'I take it that the figure on the screen is the number of hits you've had.'

'That's right,' Manello said. 'Unfortunately, everyone and their brother is talking about the attacks, so the number of hits will soon reach the billions.'

'When you say talking, do you mean the software can pick up the keywords in a conversation too?'

'That's right. It also analyses any videos recorded or downloaded.'

The numbers continued to tick over, nearing two hundred million after just a few short minutes. Harvey wondered if the people monitoring the incoming data could ever hope to keep up, given the enormity of the task.

'I read that over a hundred billion emails are sent every day,' Harvey said, 'and many of those are spam. How do you cope with those numbers?'

'Fewer people send emails than receive them,' Manello smiled. 'A spammer will send a single email to maybe a hundred thousand victims, but our only concern is the person *writing* the email, not the people who receive it. Not unless it turns out to be of interest to us.'

'Isn't there a way to filter it out to show only the keywords used *before* the attack?' Thompson asked.

'Only if you have a time machine. It just isn't possible to identify anything typed into a device prior to our program's activation. The exception would be anything saved in a phone's call or SMS logs. We plan to check for videos and files that were saved to disk, too, but the software has to be updated to do that, and then we have to distribute it to every device. We've got developers working on inserting a filtering option, but it could be twenty-four hours before it gets rolled out worldwide. This system was designed to be proactive, not reactive. If we'd gone live last week, this would be another normal December day, and the bad guys would already be locked up.'

'So where do we begin?' Harvey asked. 'Is there any way to narrow down these numbers?' He nodded to the screen, where the digits were already pushing a billion as more and more devices connected to the server to access the keyword list.

'There isn't that much we can do at the moment,' Manello admitted. 'The sheer volume of data makes it impossible to check everything, so we're using local algorithms to check for multiple keywords in each download.'

'How about narrowing it down by IP address? I understand each IP relates to a certain country. Can't you focus on a specific range, such as the UK and Nigeria?'

He told Manello about the DSA video.

'Interesting. Yeah, we have that capability,' Manello said, 'but up until this moment we had no idea where to focus. I'll pass that along and hopefully it'll narrow things down a bit.'

'Have you got anyone else looking at the data, or is this it?' Thompson asked.

'There are a few hundred analysts back home in Fort Meade with access to the feed, but even with them we're going to be snowed under.'

What had promised to be an exciting development in their fight to halt the attacks now looked to have faltered at the first hurdle. Harvey hoped Manello's prediction of better success to come was accurate.

'If you'll excuse me a moment, I have to report in.' Harvey took himself to a private area and gave Ellis a brief account of the situation. 'Do you want us to come in, or remain here?'

'Stay where you are,' Ellis said. 'See if you can get access to a terminal and reach our servers. Co-ordinate with your team from there. As soon as you get anything from the NSA, let me know.'

'Will do,' Harvey assured her. 'What's the latest?'

Her sigh told him it wasn't going to be good news. 'Around seventy percent of homes are without power, six Tube stations have been hit, traffic is at a standstill in almost every town and city centre, and the emergency services are screaming for reinforcements. Up to now, seventy hospitals have reported explosions, and the rest are being evacuated to makeshift units in the car parks. The PM is mobilising the troops, but they won't be effective for at least twenty-four hours. They have the same logistical problems as everyone else: transporting large amounts of equipment is out, so they'll be using helicopters for the more serious incidents until we can get the roads cleared.'

'How did we miss this?' Harvey asked. 'There were no warnings of any kind.'

'Complacency,' Ellis said. 'We've always thought of terrorists as clumsy, disorganised, and few and far between. Today shows us just how wrong we were. That's a mistake that won't be repeated.'

'Now that we have this NSA system activated, it'll be hard for them to catch us napping again,' Harvey said. 'I just wish we'd switched it on last week.'

'I get the feeling the PM was waiting for the next major attack as justification for bringing it online,' Ellis told him, 'though I don't imagine he was expecting anything of this magnitude. It certainly wouldn't have made it onto the statute books in peacetime.'

'Having seen how intrusive it is, I have to agree.'

He promised to call if the Nigeria angle revealed anything, then signed off. He spotted Thompson having her own phone conversation, and went to join her. As he approached, she hurriedly ended the call.

'Who was that?' he asked.

'Just checking in to get the latest updates,' Thompson said, stuffing the mobile in her pocket.

'So what's new?'

'It's a shit storm,' she said. 'What did Veronica say?'

'We're to run the team from here.'

She nodded. 'Manello went to sort out a couple of desks for us. I want you to concentrate your efforts on the UK while I check out northern Nigeria. Someone must be co-ordinating this attack centrally. If we can find that person, we should be able to identify the others.'

Harvey looked up at the counter, knowing that—barring a miracle—the attacks would keep coming.

Chapter 18

15 December 2014

Hamad Farsi knocked on Ellis's door and walked in, catching her in the middle of a phone conversation. He waited until she hung up.

'We've just got word that riots are springing up all over the country,' he said. 'They must realise that the emergency services are stretched to breaking point and are taking advantage.'

The normally unflappable Ellis slammed her palm on the desk. 'It makes you proud to be British,' she growled. 'Barely after five in the evening and the vultures are already out.'

'It gets worse,' Farsi told her. 'Since the news broke that DSA were claiming to be behind this, mosques all over Britain have come under attack.'

Being a British Muslim himself, Farsi could understand how the community must be feeling. Britain was hardly the tolerant society it purported to be, and racial bigotry still thrived in pockets throughout the country. It was bad enough for most Muslims on the best of days, but the recent attacks were going to exacerbate matters.

Ellis rubbed her temples. 'I just got off the phone with the energy minister. A team from the National Grid were sent out to repair a fallen pylon, but the area around it had been mined. Three of them were killed and another four injured.'

'Yeah, I saw that on the news. These are some sick bastards.'

'Sick is right. NG are refusing to make any further repairs unless army bomb-disposal teams clear the sites first.'

Ellis stood and began to pace behind her desk. 'Any chance you could come back with some good news before the day's out?'

'Already got some,' Farsi said. 'Network Rail were checking on a buckled track and found a device that hadn't detonated properly. They managed to recover part of the trigger mechanism, which looks to be phone activated. The phone in question is being analysed as we speak.'

'Then get them analysing faster. Once we have a number, pass it to Andrew and Sarah.'

'Will do,' Farsi said.

'What about the individuals? Are we any closer to identifying any of them?'

Farsi shook his head. 'We've got hundreds of people looking through CCTV coverage, but it's looking pretty hopeless if these devices were planted days ago. Most organisations store their data for just a few days, so we'll be very lucky to get any hits at all. We're concentrating our efforts on the RTAs at the moment, and hopefully we'll discover how those crashes happened.'

Ellis's phone rang, and she snatched it up. After a few seconds of listening, she thanked the caller and carefully replaced the handset in the cradle.

'Oldham is the latest war zone,' she said. 'The local chapter of the English Defence League have torched a mosque and are having running battles with the locals. Greater Manchester Police have pulled everyone off annual leave, but they're still vastly outnumbered.'

Farsi knew Oldham well, having family in the northern town. It boasted a population of a hundred thousand, a quarter of whom were Muslims. The only thing that surprised him was that it had taken so long for things to reach a flashpoint there.

'Apart from CCTV footage, what else have you got the guys working on?'

'We're checking every incoming passenger from Nigeria in the last three months,' Farsi said, 'and cross-checking with those who haven't yet left the country.'

'Expand the search,' Ellis told him. 'Given the scale of this attack, they've clearly been preparing for some time.'

Farsi left to pass on the message, while Ellis fielded yet another phone call.

Takasa ended the short call and placed his phone on the table, unable to take his eyes off it. The news he'd just received was staggering, and he regarded the cell phone as if it was a serpent about to strike.

Lose the smart phone and laptop, the caller had said, before explaining briefly about the new surveillance system's capabilities.

He considered the implications of what he'd just learned. Gone were the days of carefree browsing while hiding behind proxy servers. Instead, he'd have to spend the rest of his life being vigilant every time he used a laptop, PC or phone.

When he thought about it, that didn't seem too much of an inconvenience. This would be his last assignment, ever, so there were no worries about incriminating himself in the future, and it wasn't as if his normal browsing habits would flag him as an international threat. Apart from visiting a few news sites, he rarely went online and never used social media.

He decided that it wasn't a life-changer.

For himself, at least.

For the billions of law-abiding citizens of the world, it would also be business as usual, but for those bent on terror and crime, the game looked to be up. If the information were correct and this new system could analyse conversations, images and video as well as anything typed on the keyboard, criminals would have to go back to the Stone Age if they wanted to continue in their chosen career. Communications would have to be written by hand or on typewriters, then hand-delivered by couriers . . . .

But that would only be if they knew about the weapon being wielded against them . . . .

Takasa was one for quickly recognising an opportunity, and this was a chance to make some serious money. The obvious play was to sell this information to those who would most benefit. But it would also have its limits. News would spread quickly that the West was monitoring every keystroke, and any hope of further sales would disappear.

Another way to profit would be to create software that counteracted their system, blocking all outgoing signals except through one application. Better still, he could have someone create a brand new operating system that wasn't infected with the spyware.

An appealing idea, except the start-up cost and investment would be staggeringly high.

He smiled as he thought of an even better possibility. As news of the government's surveillance software spread, the market-leading hardware manufacturers' stock would take a dive. Billions would be wiped off their share values overnight, giving him yet another opportunity for a dabble in the bear market, selling high and buying low.

The numbers jumping into his head made him dizzy, and he pushed the thoughts aside. He still had a job to finish before he could start planning his future as a stock raider.

Takasa picked up the phone and removed the cover before extracting the battery and SIM card, thinking it was the least he could do to prevent any unwanted snooping. The laptop was already off and packed away, so that wasn't an immediate concern, but getting hold of a sterile phone was.

Using the room's landline, he called his driver and told him to go into the town and purchase another phone, one that wasn't internet-enabled. In such a poor country, there would be plenty of the antique variants to choose from.

While he waited for it to arrive, he plotted his next move. The attacks were well under way, and the next twenty-four hours would see even more devastation as his secondary phase kicked in. He would have liked another couple of days before moving on, but life didn't always run to schedule.

Time to make his exit.

The driver arrived an hour later, and Takasa plugged in the new phone so that it could charge. He turned on the old phone and quickly copied over the few numbers he was going to need later, then deleted the entire call history before once again removing the SIM card.

'Take this to the market and sell it.' He handed the driver the handset and charger. 'You can keep whatever you make.'

Hopefully someone would buy it and keep the focus of any international search here in Kano. Takasa also nodded to a briefcase that was sitting next to the door. 'Take that, too, and put it in the boot of the car. I will need it later.'

The driver left, and Takasa placed a call to London, telling Efram to ensure the special mission was carried out first thing in the morning. He knew that once the first of the cell members was caught, it would only be a matter of time before the rest followed, and he wanted his sole individual target eliminated before that happened.

After passing on the instructions, he called the leader of the council.

'No doubt you will have seen the results of our efforts on the television,' he said.

'Yes, indeed. We could not have hoped for more.'

'Well, that is not the end of it,' Takasa said. 'Today, we brought them to their knees. Tomorrow, we go in for the kill.'

'But I thought—'

'I didn't want to share this part of the plan with anyone until the time was right,' Takasa interrupted. 'If the first phase had failed, there would have been no point, but now that we are so close to victory, I will explain everything in full this evening. Have the council convene at the usual place. I will be there at eight.'

He ended the call and began packing his meagre belongings, ready to move on once his business in Kano was finalised.

As the long winter night began to draw in, Paul Roberts walked through the suburban streets on the outskirts of the capital, exhausted yet exhilarated after the day's events. He'd wondered for months what the result of the attack would be, and here he was, witnessing it first-hand.

The streets were all but deserted, with people in this residential area seemingly afraid to leave their homes. The roads here were clear, but on the way he'd seen hundreds of vehicles abandoned, their occupants having given up any hope of reaching their destination by any means other than on foot. It was what he'd been told to expect, and so far everything had gone to plan, which was remarkable in itself.

There were a multitude of things that could have gone wrong: a cell member getting cold feet and revealing all to the security services; someone blowing themselves up as they laid one of the thousands of devices around the country; or the authorities getting wind of the operation and shutting it down before they'd had a chance to strike.

Thankfully, none of that had happened.

It had been a tense few months, no doubt about that, but he'd stuck to the task, going about life without drawing attention to himself.

Now, he was one day away from completing the main phase of the mission. In the coming hours, he would stoke up resentment whenever possible, using his multitude of Facebook and Twitter accounts. As instructed, he had created them over the last few months, befriending the less-than-desirable elements of society along the way, and it would soon be time to press the right buttons and urge them into action. He knew that the other cell members up and down the country were doing the same thing, which potentially meant tens, even hundreds of thousands hitting the streets in twenty-four hours.

There were already signs that their social media venture was working, with the news channels reporting several attacks against Muslim communities and pockets of rioting up and down the land.

If people think these scenes are abhorrent, he thought, *they're going to find the next few days hell on earth.*

As he neared the flat he'd rented a couple of weeks earlier, a group of youths entered the road from the far end, walking towards him at pace. The implements they were carrying suggested they weren't on their way to choir practice, but Roberts reckoned he could get to the building and be inside before they got close to him.

That notion was quashed when they broke into a sprint, aiming straight for him.

He considered trying for the flat, but they had already closed the gap, and he had no choice but to turn and run. He darted down an alleyway and pumped his legs as fast as they would allow, the physical training he'd received in Nigeria paying dividends. Behind him, he heard shouts as his pursuers tried to close in, but he felt comfortable that he had the legs to outrun them.

He burst out of the alley and into another street, where he turned right and headed towards another dark alley. Feet pounded the concrete behind him, and he heard orders to split up and cut him off, which didn't bode well. He wasn't too familiar with the area, but whoever was chasing him seemed to know exactly where he was heading. Roberts had little choice but to carry on and hope he could emerge in the next street before he was trapped.

The adrenalin was carrying him well ahead of his pursuers when he reached the end of the alley, turned, and found himself in a cul-de-sac. To the right lay houses, so he ran left, towards the end of the street. As he looked for a fence to vault or garden to cut through, Roberts heard the sound of metal hitting the ground, and knew that someone had thrown something at him, probably a crowbar or tyre iron. A half-second later, a baseball bat ricocheted off the ground and became entangled in his legs.

He went down hard, and a couple of seconds later the pursuing feet came to a halt. He looked up to see the four panting youths standing over him.

'Midge, you twat! He ain't a Muslim.'

'He looked like one,' another face said. 'Look at the beard!'

A third had seen the phone sticking out of Roberts's pocket, and immediately took a shine to it. He squatted down and grabbed it, and when Roberts tried to resist he got a kick in the back from the fourth teenager.

Roberts decided to let it go. He could always get another phone.

'Get his wallet, too,' the first kid said, and Roberts played submissive while they rifled his pockets. By this time, the rest of the gang had shown up, and they weren't particularly bothered whether Roberts was a Muslim, Hindu or Christian. All they were concerned with was getting something out of the chase, and they laid into Roberts, giving him a good kicking. One of them had a couple of swings with a baseball bat, but while the pain in his thigh was excruciating, Roberts was glad they hadn't targeted his arms or head.

The kicks continued to come, and Roberts felt a rib crack. He realised they weren't going to let up until he was dead, and the irony hit him hard. It was he who had stoked the flames of hatred, though he'd never expected to be in the firing line.

One of the gang shouted and pointed towards the end of the street, where two Asians were watching the attack, like rabbits caught in a car's headlights. They soon bolted when one of the attackers barked an order.

'Get 'em!'

Roberts remained in the foetal position for a while, wanting to be sure the assault was over. Once the footsteps faded, he rolled over onto his back and took stock.

The rib was definitely broken, hurting with every breath, and his head ached like a bitch, but apart from that, he felt okay. He detected no other broken bones, and when he patted himself down, his hands were clear of blood.

He picked himself up and staggered back to his flat, keeping an ear open for more trouble, but he managed to get through his front door without further problems.

He climbed the stairs and turned on the light, illuminating the living area. One wall was piled high with boxes, and a dozen quad-rotor toy helicopters covered the floor. He'd planned to spend a good part of the evening programming each one with its current location and the GPS co-ordinates of the targets, ready for deployment in the morning, but those details were on the phone that had just been liberated. He had no choice but to go online and do it all over again.

He went into the bathroom and checked himself out in the mirror, glad to see that there was no facial damage: at least he wouldn't attract any unwanted attention when he went out the following day.

He made a sandwich and ate it while surfing the online maps on his laptop, jotting down the co-ordinates he'd need for each of the drones.

In the background, the TV news channel reported an increasing number of riots throughout Britain, and that reminded him to update his Facebook page. He signed in under the name

DJ Maxwell and told his followers that he'd found a Muslim business that was supposed to be run by DSA sympathisers. It was a complete lie, but the way the masses were worked up, they'd believe anything. And orders were orders . . . .

Despite the pain in his chest, Paul Roberts managed a smile as he hit Send and shared the information with a thousand members of the local lowlife.

Mission complete.

But more work lay ahead. The search by authorities for Roberts and his colleagues would be well underway by now, and the hunt would be relentless. That was why the next phase was aimed at reducing the odds of detection by striking at those who sought to bring him to justice.

All he had to do was attach the explosive payloads in the morning, and his beasts would be ready to fly.

Beke Anwo locked the car and walked under the late-afternoon sun to the Kurmi Market, where bamboo awnings offered a little relief from the oppressive heat. The aroma from the spice stall made him hungry, but the driver planned to do Takasa's bidding before he sat down for a meal.

He walked past the dye stalls, where cloth in myriad shades hung from the rafters, and beyond that to a stall where a multitude of electronic goods could be found. On sale he saw VHS players, tape recorders, a vast selection of CRT televisions and the section he was looking for: mobile phones.

He took his master's old handset from a pocket and showed it to the stall owner, a man he'd dealt with before.

'Mustafa, how much will you give me for this fine piece?'

The phone was given a thorough going over, and after a minute Beke was offered five thousand naira, the equivalent of thirty US dollars.

'Are you trying to insult me?' Beke exclaimed. 'That is almost brand new. It has to be worth fifty thousand!'

'Not to me,' Mustafa told him, handing it back. 'Maybe you can sell it back to the person you stole it from.'

'I didn't steal it! My boss told me to sell it for him.' Beke looked at the other handsets on sale and found one of a similar make, though not in such good condition. 'Look, you are selling this one for forty-five thousand and it's older than me!'

'That's called business,' Mustafa deadpanned. 'I buy it at a low price and sell at a high price and then I can feed my family. You want fifty thousand for it, go and open a stall.'

Beke took back the phone and turned away. There was no way he was going to accept such a pitiful offer for such a beautiful machine. In fact, the more he looked at it, the less he felt like parting with it. He took out his own phone and removed the SIM card, placing it inside the smart phone. Once it booted up, he checked that he had a signal and sent a test text message to his brother. The prompt reply told him that the phone was working fine, and he asked Mustafa how much he would offer for his old handset, the most basic of models, capable of making calls and sending SMS text messages, but nothing more.

'Ha! I wouldn't let you kiss my goat for that phone.'

'Come on, give me something.'

Mustafa looked the handset over, then rubbed his chin and said he would take it off Beke's hands for one thousand.

Resigned, Beke accepted the offer. At least he had a new phone to show for it, and the money would be enough to buy himself a decent meal before he picked his boss up.

Chapter 19

15 December 2014

Takasa strolled through the market, doing his best to ignore the vendors as they thrust items into his face in the hope of a sale. They particularly focused on the few tourists who frequented the area, knowing that they could bump the prices by three hundred percent and still make them seem a bargain.

He hated the market with a passion. This was only his second visit, and it was one too many. Unfortunately, living off the beaten track meant taxis passing by his apartment were few and far between, and if he were to plan transport for later in the evening, he had no option but to suffer the throng in order to make the necessary arrangements.

Takasa brushed aside a man trying to sell him a rug and made it to the exit, where a small line of battered taxis waited for fares. He approached the one at the front of the queue and asked to be taken to his apartment. The driver mentioned a sum that Takasa knew would probably be at least double the standard fare, but that still came out to less than ten dollars.

He agreed to the extortionate fee and climbed in, opening the window as soon as it became apparent that air-conditioning wasn't part of the deal. For twenty minutes, the car fought its way through traffic, until eventually it pulled up outside his block.

Takasa handed over a fifty-dollar bill and told the driver to return at seven to take him to the airport.

'If you arrive on time and get me there in one piece, you'll get another hundred dollars.'

The driver's eyes lit up, and he swore to all the gods that he would be there on time, the chance of nearly a week's salary for an evening's work too good to miss.

Inside the apartment, Takasa had a few hours to kill before going to catch his flight, and he called Beke with instructions.

'I will make my own way to the meeting,' he told his driver. 'I have been out making preparations for this evening and I'm running late. I want you to deliver my case to the council before eight. They will need it for a conference call if I can't get there on time.'

The driver acknowledged the instructions, and Takasa hung up. He was tempted to turn on the laptop and see what was happening in the world, but after the warning he'd received, he decided to wait until he got to the airport. There were sure to be televisions showing the latest updates, and failing that, he could just grab a couple of newspapers and spend the flight reading all about his handiwork.

As for the laptop, he decided to take it apart and destroy the inner workings. If the UK and the US could download anything they wanted from his machine, there was little point in leaving it for someone else to take. Once it was turned on, any incriminating evidence would be sucked into the NSA servers and he would instantly become the world's most wanted man. His phone had contained nothing but phone numbers and a few text messages, none of which was incriminating, but the personal files on his laptop would quickly reveal his identity.

He used a small screwdriver to remove the outer casing, then extracted the hard drive. He placed the encapsulated unit on the floor and slammed the foot of the heavy wooden chair onto it again and again. The metal housing eventually split, and he extracted the small disks. At the open window, he rubbed the faces of the disks against the rough stone wall until each one was irreparably scarred, then used the screwdriver to inflict further deep scratches.

He knew it wasn't the most thorough destruction, but if anyone had any interest in the disks, they would already know all about him, making their restoration moot.

Takasa put the disks in his pocket, aiming to lose them in the taxi on his way to the airport, a journey he'd be making only a couple of hours from now.

With little else to do, he set his alarm and got his head down. When he woke an hour later, he took a shower and shaved, knowing it would be a while before he had the chance to do so again.

When the taxi drew up ten minutes early, he grabbed his case and carried it down the flight of stairs, where the driver happily relieved him of it.

Once in the back of the cab, Takasa took the disks from his pocket and slipped them under the backseat carpet, knowing that it would be a long time before they were ever discovered, and that when they were, they would probably be tossed away.

They reached the airport a quarter of an hour before eight, and he had time to check in before calling the elder who would be hosting that evening's meeting.

'Brother, please accept my apologies. I have been out making arrangements for the next phase of the operation so I am unable to join you this evening.'

'That is regrettable,' the elder said. 'I personally wanted to congratulate you on your success.'

'Perhaps next time,' Takasa said. 'My driver should be with you soon. He has my laptop, which you can use to view the next steps of the operation.'

'He is already outside,' the elder said. 'One moment.'

Takasa waited until the laptop was brought into the room and the elder returned to the line.

'Just turn the laptop on and open the file called *Revolution*.'

The council leader asked him to wait, then came back on the line. 'The case is locked.'

'How stupid of me,' Takasa said, staring out of the window at the town in the distance. 'Just a little precaution in case it fell into the wrong hands. The combination is one, three, three, seven.'

A moment later, the phone went dead in his hand. A column of smoke rising from the centre of the city confirmed that the two kilos of plastic explosive hidden inside the locked case had achieved their aim. The building would be obliterated, eradicating the DSA hierarchy and, with it, any connection to him.

Takasa dropped the phone into a trash can and made his way to the departure gate, promising himself a congratulatory gin and tonic during the short hop to Abuja. After that, he would move on to his final destination, where a new life awaited.

Chapter 20

15 December 2014

Tom Gray finished up the lullaby and kissed Melissa gently on the head, then tucked the blanket around her. He stood there for a few moments, staring at the angel on the cot bed, marvelling at the innocence of youth. She looked so peaceful, despite all the horror going on around her, and he hoped she would have no lasting memory of the day's events.

Eventually, he pulled himself away and crept out of the boardroom, leaving the door slightly ajar in case she woke and cried for his attention.

In Smart's office, his three companions sat around silently, sipping coffee. Sonny was checking the news updates on his phone, while Gill had her head in a paperback, the cover of which told Gray that it was one of her favoured romance novels. Smart was also engrossed in a book, though he preferred to read from his Kindle.

'What have you got today?' Gray asked. 'A bit of Hemingway? Some Nabokov, perhaps?'

'*Blood Vengeance* by David Leadbeater,' Smart replied, without looking up. 'It's the proverbial page-turner.'

When Sonny put his phone down, Gray asked how Mackenzie was getting on. The recent recruit had excelled on his first mission abroad, and as requested, Gray had found him a position as a trainer, working alongside Sonny.

'We found a good 'un there, boss,' Sonny said. 'Knows his job inside out and really pushes the applicants to their limits.'

'What about out of work? Any issues there?'

Sonny shook his head. 'I've been out with him a few times. Never drinks more than three pints, always friendly, likes banter but never takes things too far. Can't fault him, really.'

Gray went to the kitchenette to refresh his coffee, glad that his instincts about Mackenzie had proven correct.

He'd just begun to rinse his cup when he heard the sound of an alarm, quickly followed by another. Looking out of the small window, he saw a group of men kicking in the door of a charity shop across the road, adding yet another siren to the mix.

He dashed back to the office, where Sonny and Smart were looking out of the window.

'Here comes trouble,' Gray said.

'Yeah, we heard them.' Sonny grimaced. 'Think we should turn the lights out?'

'Leave them on,' Gray told him. 'If it's dark, they'll think no-one's in. They might think twice if they know the building's occupied.'

Through the open door they could see the main entrance, and they saw a group of youths hurrying past, carrying a selection of tents and other camping equipment.

'Looks like our greedy friend lucked out,' Sonny said to Smart.

More bodies appeared in the street, and it wasn't long before Sonny's Vauxhall saloon caught their eye. One man peered through the car's window, looking for booty, but when he saw nothing he decided to take a closer look. The side window shattered as the thief made a none-too-subtle attempt at entry.

Sonny had seen enough. He made for the door, but Gray grabbed his arm.

'Where do you think you're going?'

'That's my car, Tom.'

'I know. And it's just a car. You can claim it on the insurance.'

'It's not about the car . . . .'

'Pull your neck in,' Smart warned Sonny. 'You're not going out there. Let the police handle them.'

Smart's words made sense as more and more people, some of them obviously armed, gathered around the vehicle. Some were already inside, going through the contents of the glovebox and boot, while others were just happy to inflict as much damage to the exterior as possible.

'You reckon you could have taken all ten of them on?' Smart asked.

'You know I could,' Sonny huffed.

'If you did, they'd come in for us,' Gray pointed out, 'and we've got the girls to consider.'

Sonny was clearly unhappy at standing idle while his car was trashed, but in the end it was only a possession, one that could easily be replaced.

Someone in the crowd began pointing towards the building, and Gray's plan to discourage them by leaving the lights on suddenly lost its appeal. The first of the thugs moved in and began kicking at the glass doors.

He was soon joined by others, and when they began shouting, Gray was unsure if he was hearing them correctly.

'Come out, you Muslim bastards!'

Why they would believe the occupants to be Muslim was beyond Gray, and it wasn't something he had time to dwell on. He knew that the doors were strong enough to withstand a few hits, but they wouldn't hold out forever. When the crowd moved back, he thought they'd given up, but they were just making room for the artillery. A house brick struck the glass in the centre, creating a spider-web-shaped dent, and it was soon followed by another, and another.

Melissa began crying in the boardroom, and Gray ran to get her, dragging Gill along with him.

'Stay here,' he told his secretary. 'The windows are barred, so you'll be safe.'

'What are you going to do?' Gill asked.

Gray could see the fear in her eyes, and he tried his best to calm her.

'We're just going to send them on their way,' he smiled, though he wasn't sure exactly how he was going to achieve that objective. He closed the door behind him as he left, and once in the reception area he could see that the rioters had managed to breach the glass. A man's arm was thrust through a hole near the handle, and Gray could see that he was fumbling for the lock.

The only weapon Gray could see was the fire extinguisher behind the reception desk, so he snatched it up. The arm was still fiddling with the doorknob, but it stopped when Gray slammed the metal cylinder down on the elbow. A scream filled the reception area and the arm quickly retreated, the *crack* telling Gray he'd broken one bone at least.

The man pulled back, but Gray's actions had been far from the deterrent he'd hoped. Others took the injured man's place, kicking furiously at the glass, and Gray knew it wouldn't withstand the abuse much longer.

Gray got a shock as Smart suddenly appeared beside him and clamped a hand on his shoulder.

'We may need to be a bit more persuasive,' Smart said, holding up a bean-bag gun. The weapon had a wide barrel, over three centimetres in diameter. It fired a non-lethal pouch filled with tiny plastic balls, rather than the typical metal round.

'Let them see it first,' Gray warned. 'If they don't take the chance to walk away, they deserve what's coming.'

Smart walked over to the window and found an area that hadn't been damaged. He managed to make eye contact with one of the hooded figures, and held up the weapon so that it was clearly visible.

The man stopped in mid-kick, then straightened up and spoke to one of his friends. Slowly, the crowd began to move back, coming to a stop ten feet from the doors.

'I think they got the message,' Gray said, backing into the office.

'Let's hope so.'

They watched the crowd begin to disperse, but their relief didn't last long. The hoodies were soon back, this time carrying wood and cardboard boxes, which they began throwing at the base of the door.

'This isn't good,' Sonny noted.

More debris was thrown onto the pile, and Gray saw someone move to the rear of Sonny's car and slide underneath. Moments later, fuel began to flow from under the vehicle, and others gathered round to prepare Molotov cocktails.

'I hope that's loaded,' he said, looking at the gun in Smart's hand. 'We've got incoming.'

'Way ahead of you.'

Smart rushed to the door and poked the barrel through the hole the rioters had created. He got his sights on the thug with the first of the petrol bombs and sent the projectile hurtling towards the man's chest. He watched, satisfied, as the bottle flew into the air and crashed to the ground, spilling its contents. Some of the crowd were stunned into inactivity, but a second bomb was readied and sent flying towards Smart seconds later, an arc of flame telegraphing its arrival.

'Len!'

Sonny's warning wasn't needed: Smart was already running, and he leapt over the reception counter, getting to cover just as the incendiary exploded against the pile of fuel. Flames took instantly, and smoke began to pour through the hole in the front door. Gray picked up the fire extinguisher and tried aiming it through the hole, but it was totally ineffective.

'I need to get to the base of the fire!' Gray shouted. 'Sonny, come and open the door!'

Another bottle flew through the air, splashing burning fuel through the hole and onto Gray's shirt. Sonny was there in seconds, whipping off his T-shirt and using it to smother the flames. As soon as the fire was out, he used the shirt to grab the lock and asked Gray if he was ready.

'Go!'

Sonny twisted the knob and pulled one of the doors open, while Gray aimed the extinguisher at the base of the fire, trying to deny the fire oxygen with burst after burst of CO_2.

Gray heard a *crump* behind him, and saw another potential bomber fall to Smart's deadly aim.

The mob finally seemed to get the message. A few more missiles were thrown at the door as they pulled their wounded out of the area, and Gray was finally able to extinguish the flames with the help of Smart, who'd brought another extinguisher from the kitchenette.

'Let's hope that's the last we see of them,' Smart said as the final flame died away. He began kicking the smouldering remains away from the door and next to a brick wall, then went to the kitchen and brought a pitcher of water to soak the embers.

One or two people ran past the office, but they'd already grabbed their booty for the night, and weren't interested in an office building when there were cigarettes and alcohol to be had from the nearby off-licence.

'We need to be prepared,' Gray said, 'just in case you're wrong.'

'The first thing we need to do is barricade the door,' Sonny said. 'Then we need to arm ourselves.'

'We've got three more NLRs,' Smart told him, referring to the non-lethal rounds for his bean-bag gun.

'I was thinking live rounds,' Sonny said. 'They've had their warning, and if they do come back, it won't be to congratulate us on a fine defence.'

Gray and Smart looked at each other. The thought of firing upon civilians didn't immediately sit well with them, but they hadn't started the fight. Sonny noticed their reticence, and he pointed out that the CCTV cameras in and around the building would show that they had acted in self-defence thus far. If they could maintain that stance, there should be no comeback.

'We've got a woman and child in here, don't forget. No court in the land is going to send us down for protecting them from an angry mob.'

'Okay,' Gray agreed. The mention of Melissa had brought things into focus, and there was no way he was going to let anyone get to her. 'Sonny, nip upstairs to the armoury and grab three Glocks and two clips each.'

The armoury was little more than a solid metal cabinet bolted against the wall, and it housed the weapons and ammunition they used at the training complex. Smart handed over the keys, and Sonny returned two minutes later with the weapons and spare magazines.

'Remember,' Gray said, 'we only use these if we have to.'

Shanka Townly was in the middle of rolling a joint when the banging on the front door startled him. His first thought was that the police were popping round for one of their regular visits, something that went hand in hand with being the leader of one of the myriad gangs plaguing London, but when the voice shouted his name, he knew it was one of his own. He looked through the spyhole and saw Connor, along with two others who were propping up a limp figure.

'Ben's been hurt,' Connor said, after Townly undid the three locks and opened the door. Ben was dragged inside and placed on the couch, where he grimaced as a bolt of pain from his broken ribs stabbed at his chest.

'What the fuck happened to him?'

'Someone shot him,' Connor told Shanka.

'I don't see no blood.'

'It was like a shotgun, but they didn't use real bullets,' one of the others said.

Connor explained what had happened when they'd tried to take the office. 'We couldn't kick the door in, so we built a fire to smoke them out, but this huge fucker started blasting away. He hit Ade, then shot Ben.'

'Why the fuck were you robbing an office?' Shanka asked, glaring at his men.

'Someone on Facebook told us there was Muslims there,' Connor told him, opening his phone to show Shanka the post by DJ Maxwell.

Shanka read the timeline, then sat down next to his injured brother. 'How many are there?'

'We only saw three men and a woman,' Connor said, 'but there could be more.'

'Did they look like Muslims to you?'

'I don't know.' Connor shrugged. 'What the fuck's a Muslim look like anyway?'

In truth, Shanka didn't care. Someone had hurt his brother, and they were going to pay.

'Right, well, we're going back, then, and this time we'll be tooled up,' Shanka said. 'Get everyone together. We'll meet at the lock-up in one hour.'

While Connor went to round up the other hundred or so members of the gang, Shanka tried to make his brother comfortable.

'You know we ain't going to the hospital,' he told Ben, as he opened his phone and started up the Maps application. He looked for the Muslim-owned office building, and from the overhead view Shanka could see that it was a detached building, with easy access to the rear. He toggled to the street view, where he saw the bars on the windows. He asked if they were still in place, and Ben confirmed that they were.

An idea crept into Townly's mind, and he let it mature until, twenty minutes later, he had a solid plan.

'I'll be back soon, bruv.'

On his way to the lock-up garage, he called in on a few of his men and instructed them to get some petrol and bring it along to the meeting point.

Just after midnight, the majority of the gang was assembled at the garage. Shanka unlocked the swing-up door and entered, along with Connor. He closed the door and switched on the overhead light, and told Connor to help him move the oily motorcycle engine that was sitting on a piece of plywood in the far corner of the small space. Underneath the wood was a drain cover, and after removing it, Shanka put his arm deep into the hole and grabbed the string that was wrapped around a hook. He slowly lifted out the long plastic bag, then began removing the rubber bands that secured the contents against water damage. Once that was opened, he laid the weapons out on the floor.

There were six Ingram Mac-10 submachine guns along with twice as many magazines, all full and ready to go. He also had four pistols with plenty of ammunition.

'Hand these out,' he told Connor, selecting one of the Mac-10s for himself. Connor swung the door open and began distributing the guns, while Shanka explained the mission ahead. It took ten minutes, but once everyone was sure of their role, they set off to show the world that no-one messed with the Selden Crew.

They kept to the side streets to avoid any patrol cars that might be in the vicinity. A group of hooded youths out at midnight with riots in the area would only mean one thing, and Shanka didn't want to be stopped and searched. Thankfully, they heard no sirens, though there were plenty of car and building alarms going off. Whoever DJ Maxwell was, his Facebook post about there being no police in this part of town seemed to be spot on. In the London riots the previous year, the authorities had been able to call in officers from other regions to break things up, but with every major city facing the same problem, the police had no choice but to prioritise resources. With this being one of the poorer areas affected, it was probably well down their list, the Oxford Street and Mayfair unrests taking precedence.

When they reached a point three hundred yards from the office building, Shanka started positioning lookouts to warn of any trouble, and took sixty men with him to finish the job. He knew it was overkill, but if anyone did turn up to spoil the party, it would be easier to slip away. It was the same reason birds flocked together: safety in numbers meant each had a greater chance of survival.

'Here's how we play this. You three go in and blast the place. If we get a reaction, we know they're still inside.'

'Why don't we just torch it?' one of his men asked.

'Because if there's no-one in the building, I want to get in and find some names. This ain't about burning down an office, it's about my brother. And it doesn't end here, see?'

Shanka got a shrug in response, which was the best he could have hoped for. Few with any brains ever joined a gang, and most of his men were good for nothing more than peddling his drugs and settling scores. That suited him fine, as it meant plenty to take the fall when things went bad.

He ordered three men to kick things off, then stood back to see what happened.

Just after one in the morning, Gray woke from his nap to take over from Sonny, who had been on watch for the past two hours. Before relieving his friend, he checked on the girls. He found Gill fast asleep on her cot, with Melissa lying in the next bed, and he crept out before closing the boardroom door.

'Anything?' he asked Sonny, who was sitting behind the reception desk.

'It seems to have quietened down,' Sonny said. 'A few buildings are on fire down the street, but I haven't heard any sirens yet. The fire service must be at breaking point.'

'Hopefully it will stay quiet,' Gray told him, moving over to the shattered double doors. 'I'd like to be out of here by seven at the latest. Hopefully these thugs will have worn themselves out by then and the streets will be a lot less crowded.'

There hadn't been much they could do to repair the damage, but the desk from Smart's office now lay on its side, and the edge was wedged underneath the door handles. It wasn't foolproof, but if anyone was thinking of rushing the place, it would hold them back for a while.

Certainly long enough for Gray and his team to get them in their sights.

'Go get some sleep,' Gray said, and settled into the warm chair behind the semicircle of polished oak that formed the reception desk.

It puzzled him that the crowd had been shouting racial epithets when there was nothing to suggest a Muslim link to his business, but he eventually settled on the notion that they'd simply mistaken his office for another building.

He began thinking about the safest route home, wondering just how long it would take with Gill and Melissa to worry about. On his own, he could jog it in no time, but the girls would make it rather slow going. Gill's teenage years were a distant memory, so he guessed they would be on their feet for about six hours. It wouldn't be easy going for his receptionist, but at least they would all be out of the city centre, where most of the attacks were taking place.

When he got home, he might have to deal with the lack of power. It was possible that his area had been spared the blackout, but he didn't want to bank on it. Fortunately, he had plenty of candles and a couple of torches, but it was heating for Melissa that he was worried about. His house wasn't that cold, even with the central heating off, but he would make sure she stayed bundled up until power was restored to the area.

With the office lights off, he had a clear view of the outside street, and from under a street lamp he saw someone striding confidently towards the office doors. The approaching figure was suddenly joined by two others, and a crowd began to gather behind the trio as they reached a point five yards from the entrance, where they raised their arms, aiming at the glass.

Gray threw himself to the floor a split second before the bullets from the submachine guns began peppering the reception area. Splinters of wood and glass nipped at his skin as he crawled to the side of the reception desk, and when he glanced into the office he saw both Smart and Sonny taking cover, their weapons gripped tightly.

Outside, the firing stopped. Gray stuck his head out, but his view was obstructed by the table that was wedged against the door, which had given up hope of retaining any glass. Shards littered the reception area, and a chill wind blew through the building as he eased himself up onto his haunches. He looked over at Sonny, hoping his friend could see what was happening, and in response he got a hand signal indicating that one of the shooters was approaching the door.

Gray held his pistol in a two-handed grip and took a deep breath, exhaling slowly, then sprang up from behind the counter. The man before him was barely three yards away, and didn't even have time to register surprise before two rounds entered his skull, one an inch over the right eyebrow and the other through the bridge of the nose.

Gray ducked as more incoming fire shredded the reception area. When it stopped for a second time, he asked Sonny for another update.

It wasn't good.

Sonny indicated that several bodies had gone round the side of the building, obviously hoping to break in through the emergency exit at the rear. It also meant they would be able to shoot through the windows, which would put Gill and Melissa in the firing line.

Gray wanted to get to them, but to do so would mean breaking cover. Sonny and Smart wouldn't be able to offer covering fire as he would be running past them, so would be more likely to take a friendly round than anything else.

He had no choice but to let his friend secure Gill and Melissa.

'Sonny, when I say go, get to the boardroom and grab the girls. Take them upstairs and make sure they keep their heads down.'

Sonny nodded, and on Gray's command he sprang to his feet, covering the short distance to the boardroom and barging through the heavy doors in the time it took Gray to squeeze off three rounds. He found Gill in a foetal position, her body wrapped around the little girl and visibly shaking. Back in the hallway, the firing had stopped, but Sonny knew it was far from over.

He grabbed Gill's arm and dragged her to her feet, the time for niceties well behind them.

'You have to get upstairs,' he told her, pulling her towards the door. The stairs were ten feet away, and after checking to make sure the coast was clear, he put his arm around her and ran, keeping his body between the girls and the front door.

They made it to the foot of the stairs just as shooting erupted once more.

'Hurry, Gill!'

Gill managed a few steps before she stumbled and slid down, rolling her body so as not to hurt Melissa. Sonny caught her at the bottom of the stairs, and was about to urge her upwards once more when the windows on the first floor landing exploded inwards, showering them in glass. Seconds later, a bottle smashed against the outer security bars and flaming petrol poured through the gap. Black smoke immediately started billowing towards the ceiling, and Sonny pulled Gill away from the staircase.

'Stay here!'

He pushed her into a corner and ran to the entrance, where Gray was picking off targets.

'There's a fire upstairs,' he told Gray. 'I'm going to try to put it out.'

Sonny ducked into the tiny kitchen and emerged with the CO_2 extinguisher, then sprinted up the stairs and began tackling the blaze. By this time, it had consumed one entire wall and a large part of the ceiling. Below, he could hear Smart taking pot-shots out of the office window, and he hoped his friends were gaining the upper hand. If any more petrol bombs hit their target, they would soon be overwhelmed. His small extinguisher made hard work of the fire, but eventually he managed to snuff out the last of the flames with the final blasts of CO_2.

Sonny tossed the empty device aside and went into one of the rear-facing upper rooms, pulling out his weapon as he moved. The window here was also destroyed, and through it he saw two more people preparing a Molotov. He waited until the rag was set alight, then shot the man holding it through the chest as his arm raised to throw it. The bottle fell and shattered, flames immolating both men. Sonny trained his weapon on the next target, a man changing the magazine on an automatic weapon. A shot to the throat took him out, and when he dropped his weapon, Sonny got a bead on the man who ran up to retrieve it.

The sound of a siren battled through the shop and car alarms, and the attack stopped as quickly as it had started. Sonny watched the hooded men freeze at the approaching noise, and they quickly dispersed, running in all directions.

All except the one retrieving the Mac-10.

Sonny silently urged him to forget the weapon and leave, but once the man picked up the machine gun, his fate was sealed. His third shot of the skirmish found its mark, and a cry rang out from Sonny's right, followed immediately by a burst of gunfire. Sonny instinctively ducked for cover as the rounds went high and wide of the window, then brought his pistol up and got the target's head in his sights.

Shanka stood with Connor near the side of the building as two of his men prepared their petrol bomb and wondered what the hell he'd walked into. The sign above the door said Minotaur Logistics, and though it claimed to be a security company, he hadn't expected the occupants to be brandishing weapons.

So why the hell were armed men gunning his people down? Was Minotaur some kind of Jihadist code word?

After watching the first of his men go down to a couple of bullets in the head, he should have known something was wrong. Office workers didn't carry guns, and certainly didn't shoot with such accuracy. It had caused his unarmed gang members to scatter, leaving just a handful of them to finish the job.

He watched the petrol bomb being thrown at an upstairs window and saw it smash against the bars, quickly followed by flames licking out of the broken window. With the front breached, he moved to the rear and saw two others stuffing a rag into their bottle while a third man raked the back wall with 9mm rounds. With the bomb finally prepared, the man holding it lit the rag and pulled his arm back to throw it.

That was as far as he got in life.

A bullet tore into his chest and the bottle dropped to the ground, smashing open and covering both of them with burning fuel. The third man tried to open up on the window but his firing pin came down on an empty chamber, and he was in the middle of swapping out his magazine when a bullet ripped through his throat.

Connor started to run over to his dead friend, but Shanka grabbed his arm.

'What the fuck are you doing?'

'I'm out,' Connor said, ejecting the empty magazine from his gun. 'I need his ammo.'

Connor shrugged Shanka off, and the gang leader could only watch as his lieutenant made for the weapon, just as the police sirens broke through the night. Connor froze, obviously undecided, and Shanka guessed he was weighing up the two options: flee, or continue the fight.

He saw Connor choose the latter, a decision that ended his life with a metal slug buried in his forehead.

'No!'

Shanka fired an ill-aimed burst towards the broken window, then ran to Connor's side. His best friend was gone, and the only consolation was that he'd probably been dead before he hit the ground.

Shanka looked up at the window and saw the pistol aimed at his head, the blond man holding it almost expressionless. No anger, no fear, just a determined look that said the next bullet was imminent, and it suddenly struck him that he hadn't seen one person inside who looked even remotely like his idea of a Muslim.

But that wasn't going to affect his decision to act.

At just twenty-one years of age, Shanka Townly's life had barely begun. He was the leader of one of the many London gangs, and one of the few all-white crews. His school education had been brief, the majority of his knowledge gained on the tough streets, so it was inevitable that his reaction to the threat was to swing his Mac-10 up to take out the opposition.

His whole life had been about gaining as much power and notoriety as possible, but when the bullet entered his skull half an inch above the right eye, that dream evaporated.

In the weeks to come, his death barely rated a couple of column inches.

Having dispatched the last of the assailants, Sonny jogged down the stairs to find Gray standing over Gill, checking to make sure she hadn't been hit. Smart walked out of the office and stood by the shattered doors, looking out at the bodies littering the parking area.

'When the police get here, do exactly as they say,' Gray warned. 'They're bound to be trigger happy. We'll leave the weapons in the office, and you two wait outside.'

The others agreed, and when the marked car appeared, blue lights flashing, Sonny and Smart walked slowly out into the car park with their hands in the air. Armed officers leapt out of the vehicle with Heckler & Koch MP5 submachine guns and ordered them to get down on the ground. Both quickly complied, and were immediately cuffed. While they were being searched, another officer entered the building and saw Gray kneeling on the floor with his hands on his head. Behind Gray, Gill sat in the corner, crying.

Once Gray was cuffed, he was forced to his feet and led out to one of the cars, where a senior rank began the interrogation. Sonny and Smart were already being quizzed, and Gray kept it as simple as possible: they were attacked, twice, and used the force they considered necessary to defend themselves. He told them where to find the firearms certificate that allowed him to possess the weapons, as well as the CCTV equipment covering the building. Once both of these had been scrutinised, the police checked his story against those of his friends.

With no major discrepancies, they were told that they would still have to attend the station and give statements, though it was unlikely they'd be held overnight. Given the identities of the slain, the self-defence claim looked solid.

'What about my daughter?' Gray asked. 'I can't leave her, and I know you don't have baby facilities at the station.'

The constable called over a superior, who, after some persuading, agreed to let Gill take Melissa back to Gray's house and report to the station at a later date.

'Normally we'd have Social Services take care of her,' the sergeant said, 'but no-one will be able to get to us this evening.'

Gill and Melissa joined Gray in the back of the car, and they set off for his house. It took some time, and large parts of the journey were spent off-road or in the wrong lane, but after forty minutes they arrived outside his gates. Gray leaned over and kissed his daughter, then asked Gill to make sure nothing happened to her.

One of the cops used Gray's fob to open the gates and escorted the girls inside, making sure they locked up before returning to the car, and Gray was glad to see the lights come on. At least his place hadn't been affected by the power outages, and he'd be able to give Melissa a nice warm bath when he got home.

On the way to the police station, Gray tried to take his mind off his daughter, but it was too hard. He'd been making progress in letting her have time away from Daddy, but under the current circumstances he felt that he needed to be with her.

As that wasn't going to happen, he tried thinking of other issues, such as the office. He would need new premises, that was a given, though he could work from home for the time being. It would also mean having the landline transferred over, but the phone company would have bigger fish to fry at the moment.

One thing was for sure, though: his next office would have a sprinkler system.

Chapter 21

16 December 2014

Andrew Harvey woke to the buzzing of his cell phone, and when the display told him Hamad Farsi was calling, he knew it wouldn't be a social call.

'What's up?' Harvey asked, wearily.

It had been a long day, and he'd finally accepted the offer of a cot in one of the many upstairs rooms to get his head down. That had been just before two in the morning, and his watch told him he'd been asleep for less than an hour.

Across the room, Thompson slept soundly, and he kept his voice down to ensure he didn't wake her.

'We've got a phone number,' Farsi said. 'Ellis said you could do some magic with it.'

Harvey took a pen from his jacket and wrote down the digits.

'Whose number is this?' he asked.

'We don't know. It called one of the devices that had been planted near Clapham Junction, but it failed to go off. Trace that phone, and you should have one of the bombers.'

Harvey was instantly awake. After thanking Hamad, he went over to Thompson's cot. He couldn't help but be struck by how beautiful she looked as she slept, and he felt reluctant to wake her lest the spell be broken.

After a few moments, he dismissed such thoughts and gently shook her shoulder.

'Come on,' he said. 'We finally got a break.'

He waited for her to wipe the sleep from her eyes, smooth out her hair and slip her shoes on, then led her down the stairs and to the elevator.

'What's so urgent?' she asked, as they waited for the contraption to reach their floor.

Harvey gave her a rundown of the short conversation. 'If this new system can identify the phone's owner, we should be able to link it to other devices in their network. Hopefully we can end this within the next forty-eight hours.'

When they reached the basement level, they went in search of Robert Bryant, who had relieved Manello at the shift change a few hours earlier. They found him at the coffee station, topping up his mug with another shot of caffeine.

Bryant looked up at them approaching quickly. 'What have you got?'

Harvey handed over the number. 'Can you identify a phone from this?'

Bryant was already walking towards an operator at a terminal, and he instructed the woman to punch in the details. An entire minute passed before the screen burst into life, with call logs streaming down the page, followed by text messages and a series of images.

'Can you send those numbers to my terminal?' Harvey asked. 'I'll have them analysed by GCHQ.'

'No need,' Bryant told him. 'Susie, network those numbers and see what it brings back.'

The operator's fingers whizzed over the keyboard, and the waiting game began once more. Seconds seemed like minutes as the screen showed a circular symbol underneath the word

Loading. Eventually, something started to happen, but not what they expected.

Line after line appeared on the screen, each one with the same message:

Device not found
Device not found
Device not found

'Looks like all of his calls were to detonate devices,' Harvey said.

'Don't be so sure,' Thompson said, leaning in closer. The display was now buzzing with the details being sucked down from another phone, with yet more numbers to query.

'Can you get a location for these phones?' she asked.

'Sure. Susie, bring up the GPS co-ordinates for all of these numbers.'

Another few clicks and the details were overlaid on a map. Dozens of icons appeared, and a legend at the bottom of the screen explained that more than ninety devices were unavailable. Balloons began appearing next to each symbol, indicating the known details of the number. One was a pizza house, another a hairdresser.

'I'd say these two were of interest,' Bryant said, indicating two mobile numbers.

Harvey pulled out his phone and called Veronica Ellis, knowing that she would be around the office somewhere, her couch likely serving as her bed.

'Looks like we have two suspects,' he said. 'You might want to send SO15 in as soon as possible.'

'Gerald got us access to the servers again. Have the locations sent to my desk,' Ellis said. 'Are we sure these are our guys?'

'That's what the computer says.'

'Okay, get what information you can. I'll start the ball rolling.'

The phone went dead, and Harvey asked Bryant for the information from both devices.

'It's now three,' the American said. 'We got another match a few seconds ago. Susie will send them over to your terminal.'

Harvey jogged over to the hot desk he'd been allocated and logged into the terminal. The first thing he did was ping a message to Ellis with the co-ordinates and phone numbers. Then he began to sift through the information that had been dumped in each folder.

Suspect number one was in north London, another was to the west, and the last sat south of the capital. Harvey thought that they'd probably split the city between them, though how just three people could inflict so much carnage across the country was beyond him.

He went back over to Susie's terminal, where Bryant was overseeing the incoming data.

'Have you found anyone else in their network?' Harvey asked.

'Not yet,' Bryant said. 'Most of these are established companies.'

'Is there any way to filter them out? These guys will probably be using burner cells, so can we just look for numbers that aren't registered to anyone?'

Bryan tapped Susie on the shoulder. 'See what you can do.'

Susie opened a new window and began typing furiously. The code made absolutely no sense to Harvey, but it brought back the results he was looking for.

'These are the only three numbers that don't have a corresponding name and address,' she said.

'There's no way just three people caused nationwide destruction,' Bryant said, echoing Harvey's earlier thoughts. 'They must be organised into cells, acting independently.'

'That's what I was thinking,' Harvey said. 'How easy is it to add a new keyword to the search list?'

'It takes seconds,' Bryant said. 'What do you have in mind?'

'We're likely to find other devices when we bring these guys in, and I want to be able to download everything on them. If we can add an obscure keyword to the list and get our guys to enter it on the device, we can analyse the contents without having to wait for them to be delivered here.'

'No problem. Choose a keyword and I'll upload it now.'

Harvey scribbled down a string of letters and handed it over, then returned to his desk, where he called Ellis again and confirmed the three targets.

'Once you take these guys down,' he said, 'I need SO15 to turn on any devices they find. Tell them to enter *tango alpha elephant*, all one word, no spaces, all lowercase. Once they do that, the data will be downloaded onto our servers and we can start rounding them up.'

Ellis promised to let him know the moment they had the first suspect in custody, and Harvey went back to dissecting the data he had from the phones. He started with the browsing history, working on the basis that there must be a central point where the cell leaders got their instructions, but nothing jumped out at him. He checked them all anyway, clicking each URL to see where they took him, but most were benign. A few news sites, a couple of online stores, and Wikipedia.

He then checked for social media accounts, and found a Facebook profile in the name of DJ Maxwell. Mr Maxwell had more than a thousand friends, and as Harvey flicked through them he could see that most were in London, with almost every single one a wannabe gangster. The older timeline entries were the typical violent, racist banter, but in recent hours the posts had been advocating rioting in one particular area of London.

It was an area he knew quite well, having been there a few times.

The most recent post mentioned Minotaur Logistics, and Harvey felt that it was no coincidence that Gray's business lay directly in their line of fire.

Harvey knew he was paranoid when it came to Gray, the man who'd pulled the wool over his eyes on more than one occasion. And not just his. The government had fallen for Tom's scheming, too, and Harvey knew that when Gray's name came up, nothing was what it seemed. But was Tom likely to incite a riot on his own doorstep? To what end? An insurance scam?

Harvey knew he wouldn't be able to move on until he had an answer, one way or the other, so he began searching the downloaded data for the name Tom Gray.

Nothing came back.

That eased his concern a little, but not entirely.

Despite it still being dark o'clock, he dialled Gray's mobile number.

'Hello?'

Harvey didn't recognise the voice. 'Can I speak to Tom, please?'

'Who's calling?'

'Andrew Harvey.'

'Sorry, Mr Harvey, but Mr Gray is currently being interviewed. This is Duty Sergeant Hamilton at Oak Cross police station.'

Oh, great. Harvey thought. *Tom Gray strikes again.*

'What is he supposed to have done?'

'I'm not at liberty to say,' the sergeant said.

'Fine. Then get the commissioner out of bed and have him call Thames House and ask for me. He'll have the number.'

'Sorry, but I can't do that—'

'Listen, Constable, I am up to my eyeballs countering these attacks, and the last thing I need is to have to come down there. Now either tell me what he's done or put him on the phone.'

'It's Sergeant.'

'Not for long,' Harvey shot back.

It took a few seconds for the custody officer to make up his mind. 'Mr Gray and two friends shot dead six people a few hours ago. His place of business was under attack, and from what I can gather, it looks like self-defence. CCTV backs up their story. They should be released on bail within a few hours.'

Self-defence.

That was the same line Gray had given him a year earlier, and Harvey had serious doubts about that other case. However, if the police had video of this incident and were satisfied, he would have to give his old friend the benefit of the doubt.

'Okay. Please ask him to call this number as soon as he's done there. If things change, I want to know about it.'

Harvey gave the number of his new phone and hung up. On the one hand, he was glad that his friend was safe. On the other, the fact that Gray's office had been the focal point of the rioter attacks couldn't be coincidental. What Gray had been doing there at midnight was anyone's guess, and he couldn't wait to hear his explanation.

Robert Bryant tapped Harvey on the shoulder, rousing him from his ruminations.

'We got a hit on your keyword,' Bryant said. 'I'm having the data pumped to your station.'

Harvey switched screens and saw the download in progress. While he waited for it to finish, he called Ellis.

'I see we picked the first one up. Who was it?'

'Billy Eccles,' Ellis said, 'aged nineteen. Claims he found the phone last night. They entered your code word on his laptop. Does it give you anything?'

'I'm just scanning through the data now,' Harvey told her. Nothing in the browsing history stood out as remarkable, and there were very few text files saved on the hard drive. The majority of disk space had been taken up with pictures of kids doing what kids do.

'I can't see anything that points to him being our man,' Harvey said. 'Did he have any other computers?'

'There's another phone, too. You should be getting that data as well.'

Harvey checked with Bryant, who told him that everything had come down from both devices.

'What you're seeing is an aggregation of all data. The key in the first column of the result designates the device it came from.'

Harvey opened a secure chat window and copied the list of numbers from the phone's call history into it, before sending it off to Ellis.

'I just sent you a private message,' he told her. 'See if the guys back at the office can get anything on those numbers. In the meantime, we'll run them through this system to see if it leads us anywhere.'

'Will do. The other suspects should be picked up shortly, so watch out for the next download.'

Harvey ended the call and turned to Bryant. 'I'm not convinced this is our guy, but the two others will hopefully be in custody within the hour, so expect a few more downloads.'

Harvey returned to the data, though he felt there was little chance of finding a lead from suspect number one.

Hopefully, two and three would prove more fruitful.

Chapter 22

16 December 2014

Erik Houtman was instantly awake at the sound of footsteps on shingle. A lifetime of paranoia had made him a light sleeper, and the slightest noise often shook him from his dreams. Usually it was nothing, but when he heard the sound of shifting gravel again, he knew it could mean only one thing.

He crept out of bed and looked through a gap in the curtain to see several armed figures dressed in black lined up near the front door to the block of flats. With his suspicions confirmed, he grabbed his phone and sent a one-word text message to Conran:

Freedom

He was in the middle of typing the same coded warning to Roberts when the sound of boots on creaky stairs told him the police had gained access to the building. He quickly sent the message, then retrieved his pistol from underneath the pillow.

Only now did he wonder how they'd found him, but it was too late to worry about it. He'd known the time would come. They all had. There had been no suggestion of an exit strategy during the long months of training, just the sure knowledge that one day they would be tracked down, and they could handle that any way they wished.

The tall Dutchman stood in the middle of the bedsit, having long ago decided how he was going to bow out. He held his pistol in a two-handed grip, aiming a couple of feet above the doorknob. It was a tense time, waiting for them to get into position, but when the battering ram sent the door flying inwards, he began emptying the magazine into the hallway. His first shot hit a black-clad figure in the chest, knocking him backwards, while the second and third found empty space.

Before he could get a fourth shot off, a cluster of bullets peppered his chest, and Houtman died knowing that he'd taken at least one of the bastards with him.

His only regret was that he would never get to see the outcome of his revolution, which he knew would be remembered for centuries.

When the text message roused Ed Conran from his sleep, he was tempted to ignore it. It was only as he became more awake that he remembered what he'd taken part in over the previous twenty-four hours, and he knew that it must be urgent if he was being contacted at such an awful hour.

He picked up the phone and saw the caller ID, which immediately set alarm bells ringing. When he opened the message, his fears were confirmed.

How the police had got on to them so quickly was the first question to jump into his head, but he cast it aside as he threw on his clothes. He checked the window and saw nothing in the street below, but he knew it was only a matter of time. The code word meant Houtman was in trouble, and if the Dutchman was already in custody, it wouldn't be long before they got what they needed from him.

The British justice system worked on the presumption of innocence—and that was fine in the vast majority of cases—but with the continuing attacks, Conran knew the gloves would come off. Their handlers in Nigeria had warned them that being caught wouldn't necessarily mean a comfortable cell with three meals a day and satellite television. The chances of the police accepting 'no comment' as answers to their questions were equally remote. Instead, they could expect to be on the receiving end of whatever interrogation tricks the US had kindly shared with the British government.

Conran toyed with the small capsule in his jeans pocket. He'd hoped he would never have to use it, planning instead to slip out of the country in the next few days as transportation slowly got back to normal. That now seemed highly unlikely, especially if Houtman were to name him. His only hope was to get to the port on the south coast and pray the Dutchman held out long enough for him to board a ferry for mainland Europe.

The rest of his devices were set on timers, so they would go off regardless, and with nothing else to hold him back, he checked the window once more. The street was still quiet. He went through to the kitchen to check the back, but again it was all as it should be at four in the morning.

He put his laptop in a backpack, then left the third floor flat, leaving the phone on the bedside table. If Houtman gave them his number, it would be child's play to track him down, and it wasn't as if he had anyone else to call.

His footsteps sounded like cannon fire on the stone steps, the noise echoing throughout the building, but the last thing he cared about was annoying the neighbours. At the front door, he scanned the area through the glass and, satisfied he was clear, walked out into the cold December darkness.

Chapter 23

16 December 2014

Andrew Harvey was mid-way through his third coffee in an hour when Ellis called with updates on the raids.

'We took one down,' she told him, 'but the other was gone before we arrived. It looks like he was warned.'

'Warned?'

'We identified the first one as Erik Houtman, a Dutch national. It seems his last text messages were sent a couple of minutes before SO15 shot him.'

'Did they have to take him down?' Harvey asked. 'He would have been more useful alive.'

'They appreciate that, but when they burst in he opened fire. One officer was hit, but his vest saved him. Houtman wasn't so lucky.'

'Who were the messages sent to?'

'One turned up on the phone the kid claimed to have found. The other was to suspect number three, but he'd skipped by the time SO15 got there.'

Harvey raised his eyebrows at that. 'I'm surprised they weren't synchronised raids. That's pretty standard operating procedure.'

'In normal circumstances, yes, but the second team got caught up in some trouble on the way, and the commander of the first unit decided to go in. Not the best decision he's ever made.'

Bit of an understatement, Harvey thought. 'Okay, what's done is done. Get them to enter the code word and I'll see if it links these guys to the attacks elsewhere.'

Ellis promised to pass the message on, and Harvey went to get a decaf while he waited for the feed to begin. When he returned to his station, the screen was still empty, so he dug into Erik Houtman's file to look for known associates. There weren't very many, but he needed more information to narrow things down. He logged into the Customs and Excise database and checked Houtman's travel logs for the last three years. The only entries were a flight to Nigeria in March and the return journey five months later.

Harvey printed out the passenger lists for both trips, but the only one to have been on both planes was Houtman. He then checked both lists against Houtman's known associates, and came up with two matches on the outbound flight. A quick check of their movements showed that they'd returned from Nigeria within eighteen hours of the Dutchman, each taking a separate flight.

Why would you three spend so much time in DSA country?

He called Ellis with the news. 'I'm sending over photos of the other two suspects. Their names are Paul Roberts and Edward James Conran. Ask Hamad to circulate them to all forces. Also, show them to the kid and see if either is familiar. We need to know where he got that phone so we can narrow down the search area.'

'Will do. By the way, they entered the code word onto Houtman's phone and the data should be coming down soon. Unfortunately, his laptop was password protected.'

'Hang on.' Harvey called Bryant over and asked if the keyword list would pick up something entered as a password to unlock a device.

'Yes, it will. It is one of the first programs to run when you hit the power button.'

Harvey passed that on to Ellis. 'Tell them to try *tango alpha elephant* as the password. It'll fail, but it should trigger the download. That's *tango alpha elephant.* All one word, remember.'

Harvey hung up and toggled screens to see the latest data dump. He ordered the information so that it showed Houtman's records first, then filtered for phone numbers. After checking for overseas numbers and finding none, he copied the forty-plus entries and sent them to Susie's terminal with a request to check them all out. What he was hoping to find were calls to mobile phones outside the London area, but if these men were truly acting as independent cells, then it was unlikely they'd get any leads that way.

With that job delegated, he changed the filter to order by website URLs. He knew the cells must be communicating with someone, somewhere, and through a website would be the obvious choice. He'd seen it before, when he'd helped to take down James Farrar . . . .

The thought of his old nemesis brought Sarah back to mind. Since she'd arrived at Thames House all those months ago, she'd been colder than an Arctic winter, yet in the last twenty-four hours, since the attacks started, she'd thawed somewhat. Perhaps it was the fruitless efforts to locate Farrar that had forged her demeanour, and now that she was able to concentrate on other matters, he was beginning to see the other side of her, the real Sarah Thompson.

When they'd retreated upstairs hours earlier, she'd been polite, chatty even. Harvey would have pressed her for a more in-depth background history, but once she'd begun yawning he'd decided it could wait.

It hadn't stopped him admiring her figure, though. They'd both been offered soap and other toiletries, and he'd watched Thompson brush her teeth over the sink, marvelling at her sleek lines. He guessed she worked out, or at least ran a fair distance each week. Perhaps both, given the shape of her legs under the tight pants.

Harvey realised that he was letting his mind wander. He was already halfway down the list of URLs and hadn't been concentrating on any of them, so he scrolled back to the top and forced himself to focus on something more than his colleague's physique.

He couldn't help looking over at her, though. She was at a desk ten feet away, peering intently at her computer screen. As if sensing his gaze, she caught his eye, locked her terminal and walked over to him.

Harvey's terminal bleeped as she reached him.

'Read that,' Thompson said, and she placed a hand on his shoulder as she stood beside him.

Harvey's heart skipped a half-dozen beats at the surprise contact. He tried to keep his mind on the message, which Thompson explained had come through from Six.

21:34:07 2014-12-15 Kano, Nigeria

Eight senior members of DSA suspected dead after an explosion in Kano, northern Nigeria. Eye-witnesses say the house off Sani Buhari Road belonging to Abdul Al Karam was completely destroyed, along with four neighbouring properties. Vehicle said to belong to their leader, Takasa, found outside the building. Takasa himself assumed to be among the dead.

Further casualties include three children and seven women. Sixteen others still unaccounted for.

End

'Looks like someone did us a favour,' Thompson said. 'No more DSA to distract us, at least for a good while. Now we can focus on rounding up these cells.'

Harvey turned his head to face her. 'Don't you think that's a bit premature? Okay, I agree that the priority is to round up the cells here and put an end to these attacks. But we also need to look into this bombing. What if there was a split inside DSA? What if our attacks were planned by the same faction that just bombed the group's leaders?'

Thompson removed her hand from his shoulder and took a step back. 'That's a matter for the top brass. You just concentrate on the data,' she said coldly, back to her usual austere self.

She strolled back to her own desk, leaving Harvey to wonder what he'd done to upset her this time. Was it that she hated being second-guessed? Maybe she was bipolar.

Whatever it was, it didn't stop him watching her walk away.

Chapter 24

16 December 2014

Ed Conran pulled the collar on his jacket up to protect the back of his neck from the chill breeze. With his hands thrust deep into his pockets, he cut an abject figure as he walked the back streets.

How they'd found out about the cell was anyone's guess. Perhaps it had been a CCTV camera that had been unaffected by the power cuts they'd created, or a vigilant eye-witness. Whatever the reason, he had to get to the south coast as quickly as possible.

In his pocket were three hundred pounds in cash, plus the now-useless pre-paid credit card. If the authorities were on to him, they would be checking for any transactions, and the last thing he wanted to do was leave a trail.

Or did he?

Conran had been walking for more than an hour, distancing himself from the phone as fast as he could. Ahead he saw a convenience store that was just opening. He went inside and found a small roll of masking tape and a cheap ballpoint pen.

'Have the newspapers come in yet?' he asked the shopkeeper.

'Not yet, and I'm not hopeful. Those bombings have closed the streets down. Nothing's getting delivered. I hope they string the bastards up when they catch them.'

'That's if they take any of them alive.'

Conran paid, left, and found a deserted alley where he could work uninterrupted. He tore off a small strip of the tape and stuck it to the back of the credit card, then wrote the pin number on the waxy surface. He then removed the cash from his wallet and put the card back in.

His intention was to leave the wallet lying around in the hope that someone picked it up and used the card, thereby diverting the authorities away from him when the transaction was detected. He knew there was always the chance that the finder might be honest and hand it in to the nearest police station, but in this area he thought it unlikely.

From the alley he could see the shop he'd just visited, and after ten minutes of waiting he saw what he was looking for. A teenager arrived to do his paper round, and when the boy went into the shop, Conran quickly mounted the bicycle that had been left outside. Pedalling ferociously, he rounded a corner and was out of sight by the time the kid came out of the shop, short a day's pay because there was nothing to deliver, and now minus one mountain bike.

Conran quickly put some distance between himself and the shop, then slowed to a more sedate pace to avoid drawing attention to himself.

After stopping to withdraw his maximum daily amount from the credit card, he headed southwest, taking the route he'd planned out weeks ago. Once onto the A3, it was roughly seventy miles to Portsmouth Harbour, where he could catch a ferry to France. Not a particularly gruelling ride, considering the years he'd spent in the saddle, and he reckoned he could make it to the coast within seven hours, barring accidents.

Once on the continent, his first port of call would be Gare de Lyon. In a luggage locker at the Parisian railway station, he had fifteen hundred in cash squirrelled away for just this moment. That should be enough to get him to southern Spain, where it was a short ferry ride across to Morocco. Once on the African continent he could disappear.

As he passed a group of hooded kids who were rummaging around inside a broken shop window, Conran threw his wallet towards them, hoping that one of them would see it and occupy the police for a little while at least. They wouldn't be able to use the card until the following day, but that would keep everyone searching for him in the capital, by which time he should be well on his way to Barcelona at the very least.

It all depended on Houtman holding out against interrogation.

Conran turned onto the A3 twenty minutes later and instantly tensed. Up ahead he saw several uniformed personnel organising the removal of vehicles from the street. Soldiers and police mingled as tow trucks worked to clear the road of abandoned cars.

Conran tried to maintain his cool as he cycled towards them, but when a policeman put a hand out to halt him, he thought the game was up. He stopped, frantically searching his mind for the next move, and was relieved to see the officer wave a hand to a tow truck driver, giving him the go-ahead.

Conran tried to wait patiently, watching a saloon car being dragged up a ramp and onto a flatbed, but he couldn't keep his eyes from darting to the policeman. His behaviour didn't go unnoticed. The officer began to take an interest in him and walked over slowly.

Stay cool, Conran warned himself.

'Morning, sir. Where are you heading today?'

'Wimbledon,' Conran said. 'I couldn't get home last night because of all the trouble on the streets.'

'You don't seem dressed for a bike ride,' the policeman observed.

'No, I borrowed this from the guy I stayed with. I wasn't sure if the Tube was running today, and I have to get home to my wife and kids.'

'It looks a bit small for you.'

'It was all he had,' Conran said with a shrug.

The car had been successfully loaded onto the truck, and the officer's colleague whistled over to him, indicating that it was safe for Conran to continue his journey.

'On you go, then.'

'Thanks, Officer. Hope you catch these scumbags,' Conran said as he pedalled away. He resisted the urge to look back, concentrating solely on burning up the miles between London and the ferry terminal.

The confrontation had him rattled, though. He hadn't factored in police helping to clear the main roads, and he decided that once he reached the outskirts of the capital he would stick to the minor roads. He'd already memorised the three major towns he had to pass through: after hitting Guildford he would follow signs for Godalming and then Petersfield, which lay some seventeen miles from his destination.

Conran looked back but saw no sign of pursuit. If only his luck could hold out a few hours more . . . .

Chapter 25

16 December 2014

Paul Roberts was already awake when he heard the quiet knock.

His first instinct was to reach for his gun, and he carried it to the door, peering out of the spyhole. He'd expected to see swathes of armed police, but standing in the dark corridor was a man he hadn't seen for many months.

Someone he hadn't expected to see again.

He opened the door and let Efram in.

'What are you doing here?'

The visitor adjusted his wool cap, which covered his hair, giving the impression that he was bald. 'I tried calling, but it seems your phone is no longer with you.'

Roberts explained about his altercation the previous evening. 'How did you know I was staying here?'

Efram laughed. 'Paul, do you really think we would just give you the training and a bundle of cash and let you get on with it? I've been watching you, and I like what I've seen so far. I just want to make sure you're ready for the final act.'

'You don't need to worry,' Roberts said. 'I've already scoped out the target. I'll be heading over there soon.'

'You sure? You look a little nervous.'

'I'm fine. I just didn't expect visitors at this hour.'

In truth, Roberts was more than apprehensive. He'd had time to learn a lot about his target over the last five months, and the prospect of taking his man down was daunting, to say the least. Still, it was all part of the master plan, though how his target fitted in only Efram would know.

'I'll be fine,' he repeated, in answer to Efram's quizzical look.

The visitor looked at the quad copters scattered around the living room floor.

'Are these ready to go?'

'In fifteen minutes,' Roberts confirmed. 'Now, if you don't mind, I have to add the final touches before I release them.'

Efram took the hint and made for the door, checking through the spyhole before opening it. He stopped and turned to Roberts. 'This is an integral step in our strategy. I know you won't let me down.'

Efram left, quietly closing the door behind him, and Roberts locked it before going through the rest of the setup process. Once the last of the drones was primed, he carried them all through to the bedroom, where he opened the French windows onto the veranda.

At this hour of the morning, the street below was thankfully quiet. Few would see his toys leave the building, and by the time anyone linked them to the attacks, he would be long gone.

One by one, he took the machines out into the cold morning air, hit the power buttons and watched them lift off. Each one was programmed to soar to a thousand feet then navigate to its target. With a three-hour battery life, they would reach their respective destinations and then hover until the time was right. Being so small, it was unlikely that anyone would see or hear them once they reached their optimum altitude.

The first indication of danger would be when they released their payloads.

When the last of the machines climbed out of view, Roberts scanned the area. He saw nobody taking an interest in his aerial fleet, so he closed the windows, put on his coat and picked up his backpack.

The silenced pistol went into an inside pocket, and he left to face the most challenging part of his mission.

Roberts was soaked when he arrived at the house an hour later, the heavens having opened halfway through his journey. He tried to shrug off the discomfort and focus on the job, the first stage of which was getting over the back garden wall. It was seven feet high and topped with broken glass to deter unwanted guests, but Roberts had come prepared.

He gripped the top of the wall with his fingertips, carefully avoiding the glass, and pulled himself up, peering over the top. The impressive detached red brick house sat in darkness, as did the garden. Roberts dropped to the ground and took a hessian sack from his backpack, wondering how his drones were getting on in the rain. They should be dropping their payloads right about now, but there was nothing he could do to help them except hope they worked as intended.

He threw the heavy sack over the top of the wall and pulled himself up again, this time throwing his right leg up and climbing all the way to the top, the hessian protecting him from the glass shards. He crouched there for a moment, listening for sounds, but none came, so he lowered himself into the garden and pulled the sack down after him. It went back into his pack, and he took the pistol from his jacket before edging towards the house.

A light suddenly came on in one of the upstairs windows.

Roberts froze.

For what seemed an eternity, he wasn't even aware of the rain running down his face, or the chill wind. He was totally focused on the building in front of him, waiting to see if anyone came out to challenge him.

After what turned out to be just three minutes, the light went off again and the area returned to darkness. Roberts gathered himself and kept to the side of the garden as he approached the house. He made it to the back door and peered in through the glass.

He assumed that whoever had woken up had done so to visit the toilet, and so he waited a few minutes for them to fall back to sleep. In the meantime, he checked the door to see how he could force entry. The uPVC frame looked fairly new, as did all the windows. Picking the lock was out of the question: it simply wasn't part of his skillset. His only option was to apply brute force and hope to get upstairs before the element of surprise was lost.

Roberts stepped back, took a couple of deep breaths, and fired two shots at the lock.

Gill was roused from her slumber by the incessant shrill and assumed it was her alarm clock. She fumbled for it on the bedside table, and when her hands hit empty space, she remembered where she was.

Wide awake, she realised the noise was coming from the master bedroom, and assumed it was Gray's alarm going off. She knew Melissa was likely to wake if it continued for much longer, so she got out of bed, turned on the light and went into the hallway.

Gray's bedroom sat at the front of the house, one of four on the upper storey. She went in and saw the bedside clock, but realised the noise wasn't coming from there. Instead, on the opposite wall, a flashing light accompanied the shrill sound. She took a closer look and saw that labels under each bulb related to a part of the house and grounds.

Gill realised that it was a high-tech burglar alarm, and the flashing light told her that the garden was the source of the intrusion.

Panic gripped her, and she struggled to think of what to do next. Call the police? Call Tom?

She settled for hitting the reset switch, which thankfully turned off the alarm. In the sudden silence, she was able to focus a little better.

Could it have been a fox or a cat? Or was it a burglar hoping to make hay while the police were otherwise engaged?

Gill decided to take no chances. She tiptoed through to Melissa's room and gently lifted the sleeping child from her cot. She carried the girl through to one of the spare bedrooms and opened the linen drawer before removing several duvet covers and pillow cases. She placed Melissa in the drawer and closed it slowly, then threw the bedding into the dirty clothes hamper.

Next, she went back to her own room and found her phone. She decided to call Tom first and get his advice. If the phone were answered by one of the police officers at the station, she would let them know what was going on.

Gill was looking for Gray's number in her contact list when she heard the popping sounds coming from downstairs.

Roberts was astonished by the sound that came from the weapon. It was the first time he'd fired a silenced pistol, and he had expected it to be just that: silent. Instead, each round made a very loud popping sound that seemed to carry forever. It was almost as loud as the unsilenced versions he'd trained with.

With all thoughts of surprising his target gone, he kicked the door in and strode into the kitchen. A door led through to the hallway and the stairs, which he mounted two at a time. At the top, he got his bearings and went to the room overlooking the back garden, bursting in with the weapon held in a two-handed grip.

Nothing.

The room was empty, and Roberts felt the first signs of panic clawing at his soul. He swivelled and went back out into the hallway, the gun flicking left and right as he worked out what to do next.

He moved to the next door and kicked it in, only to find a deserted bathroom.

Get a grip, man.

The next door he came to was slightly ajar, and he thought he heard a scraping sound coming from inside. Steeling himself, he kicked it wide open and flattened himself against the outside wall, expecting a volley of fire to blast through the doorway.

Instead, he heard a muffled cry from within the room.

The girl!

Edging his way inside, he scanned the bedroom. The bed hadn't been slept in, and it looked like no-one had been in there for some time. He was about to leave when he heard the sound again, this time a little louder. He got down on one knee and checked under the bed, but apart from a little dust, it was clear.

Roberts straightened and strained his ears, waiting for the sound that would announce the location of his quarry. What he heard was the sound of footsteps running down the stairway, and he set off in pursuit. He reached the top of the stairs in time to see a woman disappearing to the side at the bottom of the stairwell. Not quite what he'd expected. From his research, he knew that Gray lived alone, so why he found no sign of the man and saw only a strange woman running around Gray's house, he had no idea.

He didn't have time to ponder. If the woman got outside and raised the alarm, the police would be sure to come and investigate, especially if she saw his firearm. He pounded down the stairs after her, but found himself in an empty hallway.

He made a snap decision and headed for the kitchen. If he was being chased in his own home, he'd want to arm himself, and that was where the knives were kept. The door was almost closed, not how he'd left it, and he knew he'd guessed right. He ran to the door and kicked it open to find the woman cowering in a corner.

'Please, don't kill me!'

Roberts stood in front of her and pointed the weapon at her forehead. She looked to be in her fifties, and he didn't figure her for Gray's girlfriend. A neighbour, perhaps, or maybe even a family member.

'Where's Gray?'

'He's not here,' the woman sobbed, shaking uncontrollably.

'I gathered that. Where is he?'

'At the police station.'

Roberts knew this would take forever if she kept her answers short and vague.

'What's he doing at the police station?' Roberts snarled, trying to force her into opening up.

'He was arrested. He killed some men tonight.'

Killed some men? That meant Gray was likely to remain behind bars for the foreseeable future, making him untouchable. It wouldn't please Efram, but Roberts could hardly be blamed for something outside of his control. All he could do was finish off the job he'd been given.

He grabbed the woman by the hair and dragged her to her feet, pulling her towards the stairs. 'What's your name?'

'Gill.'

'Tell me where the girl is, Gill.'

'What girl?'

Roberts gave her a knock on the head with the butt of the pistol. 'I heard the baby. *Where is she?*'

The woman sobbed as Roberts dragged her up the stairs and into the bedroom where he'd first heard the sound. He put a finger to his lips, ordering her to shut up, then strained to listen for sounds of the girl.

He didn't have to wait long. A scratching sound came from a chest of drawers, followed by the sound of a young girl's cry as Melissa woke to find herself trapped in unfamiliar surroundings.

Roberts pushed Gill onto the bed and knelt down by the drawers. He pulled the bottom one open and looked down at the tiny, tear-stained face.

'Hello, darling.'

In all her years, Gill Finch hadn't had so much as a school playground fight. She abhorred violence, and had brought up her now-grown children to avoid confrontation whenever they could. The events of the last twelve hours had been like something from another world, one she'd insulated herself from her whole life, but the thought of Melissa coming to harm awoke a primal maternal instinct that had lain dormant for many years.

Two years previously, she had thought she'd been followed home after leaving work, but while no-one had actually approached her, the incident had shaken her. When she'd told Tom Gray about it, he'd assured her that it was probably nothing, but offered her some self-defence tips just in case.

His instructions came flooding back as she watched the intruder kneeling over Melissa, and before she knew it, she was standing over him. She opened her arms as wide as they would go and cupped her hands slightly, just as Gray had shown her. When she brought them together, clapping them hard over the intruder's ears, he screamed in pain as his eardrums burst.

His hands flew to his head and the pistol clattered to the floor. Gill pushed him away from the drawer, grabbing Melissa as he hunched in agony with his hands over his damaged ears. She ran down the stairs and tried to open the front door, but it wouldn't move. She remembered locking it and taking the key out, and realised it was on the living room table.

Footsteps pounded on the stairs above, and with no time to retrieve the key, Gill ran to the kitchen. The back door stood open, but before she could reach it, a bullet whizzed past her head and gouged a hole in the wall.

'I won't miss with the next one.'

Tom Gray was wet and miserable, as were his two companions. He hadn't slept in over a day, and his stomach was demanding food. He promised himself both when he got home.

It had been a long walk from the station, with the duty sergeant refusing to offer them a lift home owing to lack of available officers. He had been told he could call a taxi, but after trying three numbers without answer, he'd given up.

The interrogation hadn't been too strenuous. The investigating officer had watched the CCTV recovered from the office, and when Gray had answered his questions honestly, there was little doubt that his friends and he had been defending themselves. They'd gone through the formalities of fingerprinting and phototaking, then sat in a cell, waiting for a decision to be made. It had taken some time, but eventually they'd been granted police bail and told to report back to the station in two weeks. If no charges were brought at that time, then they could collect the items held as evidence, their weapons included.

Smart and Sonny had said their farewells as the trio parted company, having decided to make their own way home. Gray had offered them a coffee and breakfast, but both wanted to get home and check on their places.

'If my power's out, the freezer will be defrosted and the whole flat will be stinking,' Sonny said as he peeled away. Smart had similar concerns, leaving Gray to face the last twenty minutes alone.

Traffic had started moving as he neared his house, but not the usual rush hour mayhem he'd expect of a typical Tuesday morning. Instead, half a dozen cars passed him, most heading away from the city. Gray guessed they were leaving town until the madness was over.

Not a bad idea.

He arrived at the house looking forward to a hot bath, and decided that took priority over returning Andrew Harvey's call. As he used the fob to activate the gates, he wondered what to prepare for breakfast. Perhaps he could persuade Gill to cook something and then stay and look after Melissa while he had a little kip. It wasn't as if she had an office to go to . . . .

Gray was about to ring the doorbell when a male scream from inside the house made him instantly alert. He lived in a detached property, so it couldn't have been a neighbour that he'd heard. That meant someone was in his house.

Melissa.

Gray ran round the side of the house, where a seldom-used door led into the utility room, and beyond that the kitchen. Sitting next to the door was a planter, which sat within another, larger stone ornament. Gray lifted the planter out and retrieved the utility room key, which he'd placed there in case he ever lost his front door keys. The lock hadn't been used in some time, but he managed to unlock it without making too much noise.

Inside, Gray scanned the room quickly for a weapon but found nothing more lethal than some fabric softener. The kitchen would be more fruitful, so he eased open the door and went over to the cutlery drawer. Just as he reached it, he heard footsteps running towards him, and he grabbed the only thing available—a wooden steak tenderiser—before squeezing himself up against the wall.

Gill ran into the kitchen towards the back door, carrying Melissa. Gray's pulse raced, and it took all his willpower not to rush to her side.

Gray heard the distinct *pop* of a silenced weapon and saw a small hole appear in the far wall. It was enough to make Gill freeze, and he just prayed she didn't turn round for a few seconds.

'I won't miss with the next one.'

Gill was sobbing hysterically, with Melissa following her lead, and Gray strained to hear above the noise. He registered footsteps approaching from the hallway. Only one set.

That would make things easier.

An outstretched hand appeared through the doorway holding a silenced 9mm, followed by a forearm. Gray waited until he saw the upper arm, then moved in.

He grabbed the arm and spun the man round ninety degrees, slamming the pistol into the wall. The gun popped again, but the round went harmlessly into a kitchen cabinet. Gray used the steak mallet on the man's knuckles, delivering two rapid blows, and the gun fell harmlessly to the floor. Gray twisted the arm and delivered an open palm to the intruder's face, crushing his nose and taking all of the fight out of him.

The attack lasted less than five seconds.

Gray retrieved the pistol, pointing it at the prone stranger's head.

'Tom!'

Gill ran over to Gray and threw her arm around him, but for the time being, Gray was all business. He eased her backwards, never taking his eye off the figure bleeding all over his floor.

'How many?' Gray asked Gill, and she told him that this was the only one she'd seen. Gray kicked his prisoner in the thigh and repeated the question.

'I'm alone,' the man moaned, blood from his broken nose splattering the floor tiles as he rose slightly, then fell onto his back.

Tom nodded and motioned for Gill to take Melissa into the living room. 'Ring Len and Sonny. Let them know what happened,' he called after her.

Gray ordered the man to his feet, then told him to ease his jacket open so that he could check for extra weapons. With none apparent, he told the man to strip to his underpants and throw his clothes in the corner.

Gray pulled a wooden chair over from the dining table at the far end of the kitchen, never taking his eye off the prisoner.

'Okay, get dressed again, then sit.'

The man did as instructed, and Gray took a roll of cling film from one of the drawers. He wrapped half the roll around the prisoner's chest a few times, then did the same with his legs, securing him to the chair.

Gray stood in the middle of the kitchen, the pistol hanging loosely by his side. 'I'm not a patient man, so your answers better come quick. What's your name?'

'I want a doctor. That bitch—'

Gray cut him off by raising the pistol and shooting him in the bridge of the right foot.

'Now,' Gray said, clamping a hand over the man's mouth to suppress the screams, 'I don't expect you want me to lose my patience again. What's your name?'

'Paul,' the man gritted out between moans of agony. 'Paul Roberts.'

'Why are you here?'

'I . . . I was trying to rob the place.'

Gray ejected the clip and studied the magazine before inserting it back in the butt of the pistol. 'I have seven more accidents waiting to happen, Paul. Don't make me empty this.'

From the fading light in Roberts's eyes, Gray knew that the message had been received. The man was fresh out of fight.

'Again, who sent you?'

'His name's Efram,' Roberts spat. 'He told me to take care of you and the girl.'

'Efram who?'

'I don't know. He never said.'

Gray raised the gun and aimed at Roberts's right kneecap.

'I swear, I don't know!'

'You're not convincing me,' Gray said, his voice devoid of emotion.

'Tom! What are you doing?'

Gill was standing by the kitchen door, a look of horror on her face.

'I told you to stay in the living room with Melissa,' Gray said. 'This doesn't concern you.'

'I . . . I just wanted to let you know that Len's here.'

'Let him in,' Gray said, moving towards the kitchen door, the gun never wavering from Roberts.

Gill went to the front door and hit the buzzer to open the gates, then waited for Smart to reach the door before she opened it for him. Gray watched her whispering something, and Smart marched down the hallway. He took in the situation, then dragged Gray over to the oven.

'Do you really think this is wise, after what we've just been through?'

'He came here to kill me and Melissa,' Gray said. 'He took a shot at Gill. What am I supposed to do? Give him a packed lunch and send him on his way?'

'You're supposed to call the police and let them deal with it,' Smart said quietly.

'I may be wrong,' Gray told Smart, 'but I don't think this is a random looter who chose my house.'

'Tom's right,' said Gill from the doorway to the dining room, Melissa still cradled in her arms. 'He asked where Tom was, and he was looking for the baby. He knew . . . everything.'

Gray nodded. 'See? Someone sent him here to kill us. If I don't find out who, they'll just send someone else. The police can't make him talk, but I can.'

Smart sighed, and Gray knew he'd made his point. 'Give me five minutes,' Gray murmured, 'then we'll call the police.'

'I've got a better idea,' Smart said. He gave a whispered set of instructions that brought a small smile to Gray's face, then went over to speak to the bound man.

'Listen, buddy, I don't know if you're aware who this man is, but he has a history of not taking kindly to people going after his family.' Smart looked over at Gray, who'd gone into the utility room and could be seen emptying the large chest freezer. 'As far as Tom's concerned, you were never here. The police don't know a thing about it. Only the person who sent you knows. And as far as they're concerned, you failed and disappeared.'

Gray returned to the kitchen with a handful of strong plastic bags and a hand saw and placed them on the table. He then went to the drawer and pulled out a long knife, which he began honing with a whetstone.

'I reckon you've got about two minutes to tell him everything. If you do, I'll try to convince him to call the police so that your injuries can be treated. If not . . . .'

Smart let the words trail off and walked over to Gray to give the man time to think about the proposal.

'Okay!' Roberts said quickly. 'Okay.'

Gray walked over with his smart phone in his hand. After a few taps, he had the voice recorder running, and he placed the phone on the table.

'I want to know who Efram is, how you met him, how much he paid you, everything. Start from the very beginning.'

Smart and Gray watched for signs of deceit, but as Roberts told his story, starting with the meeting with Efram at the beginning of the year, they knew he was telling the truth. As the tale progressed to include the training camp in Nigeria and the skills he'd been taught, they began to realise exactly what they were dealing with.

'You're saying you were behind these attacks?' Smart interrupted.

Roberts lowered his head before offering a slight nod. 'Not just me, though. There—'

Before Smart could stop him, Gray sent a roundhouse to Roberts's face, almost dislocating his jaw.

'You bombed hospitals?' Gray shouted, incredulous. 'I was there when one went off yesterday. Do you realise how many women and children you killed?'

Smart grabbed Gray by the shoulders and dragged him away. 'That's enough, Tom. Go and call Andrew and let him know what we've got.'

Gray was still seething and not in the mood to back off. 'I want to know who's behind this.'

'I don't know!' Roberts said. 'I only met Efram twice, but the orders to kill you came from the colonel at the camp. His name was Mitchell.'

Gray and Smart searched their mental databases, but the name wasn't familiar.

'Describe them both,' Gray said.

'Mitchell was early fifties, buzz-cut hairdo, about your height,' Roberts said. 'Efram was a little shorter, with short, black hair in a side parting. Looks like a government type. He came round this morning to remind me to do this job.'

None of the descriptions rang any specific bells, though Mitchell sounded like seventy percent of the officers they knew.

'Tom,' Smart said quietly. 'Go and call Andrew. Now. He needs to know about this.'

Gray stepped away and let his shoulders slump, consciously draining the deadly tension from his body. He turned, dug in his pocket for Harvey's new number, then dialled.

Chapter 26

16 December 2014

Andrew Harvey almost jumped out of his chair when he came across the tell-tale website URL in amongst the porn and social media dross. Rather than a human-readable series of words, it used the IP address and port number:

http://10.179.161.58:10038

Harvey quickly typed it into a new browser and wasn't disappointed to find only a box ready to accept a password. He knew it would be useless trying to guess the entry code, but then, he didn't need to.

He called Bryant over and shared his discovery.

'I'm not sure how long it will take to crack it,' the NSA man said. 'Our team's not geared up for that kinda thing. I can pass it on to Fort Meade, though.'

'No need,' Harvey told him. 'All we need is a list of everyone who visited that site. Can you empty out the keyword list and just use this URL? That way, we can do away with all the extraneous crap.'

'Consider it done,' Bryant said, 'though there are a few keywords that never leave the list. Don't worry, they won't interfere with your search. Those results get fed elsewhere.'

'I'm intrigued.'

'Don't be,' Bryant told him. 'It's just the name of the project and a couple of things to do with POTUS: Air Force One, The White House, that kinda thing.'

The smile told Harvey that Bryant was lying, but this wasn't the time to push it. He needed an ally right now, not an enemy. Not when they were so close.

Bryant disappeared with the URL, and by the time Harvey had poured another cup of decaf and grabbed some bread and cold meats from the kitchen, the dump had begun. He went over to Susie's desk and asked if she could once again pinpoint each device on the map.

Within minutes, she had a visual representation on her monitor.

'Thanks, Susie. If you could send the IDs and location of each one over to my station, that would be great.'

Harvey was about to leave when the map on Susie's screen expanded. Where before it had displayed just the United Kingdom, it now showed the entire northern hemisphere.

'What's this one?' Harvey asked, pointing to an icon in west-central Africa.

Susie zoomed in, and he could see that the location was marked as Kano, Nigeria. A perfect fit with the DSA angle. He decided to work that himself and pass on the UK-based suspects to Ellis so that she could disseminate the information to local forces.

Back at his desk, he jotted down the African cell phone number, then called Ellis. 'It looks like we got them all.' He explained what they'd found as he copied the details into an internal message, which he pinged to her inbox. 'Any news on Roberts and Conran?'

'No,' Ellis sighed, 'but we can't end this soon enough. We're getting reports of car bombs from Brighton to Durham, with many fatalities. What little CCTV footage we have suggests the vehicles were parked days ago and primed to go off this morning.'

'Jesus.' Harvey rubbed his eyes wearily.

'It gets worse. They used some kind of remote-controlled drones to target police stations during the shift handover. These things dropped napalm-based incendiary devices onto station roofs, and a lot of forces have had to relocate. No injuries as yet, but it slows down their response time even further.'

'Then let's start bringing them in,' Harvey said. 'Sarah is already liaising with the force commanders around the country. Since we have real-time feeds on the devices' locations, it should be relatively easy for the local police to bring all the cell members in.'

'We also got news that someone else called the phone that was found by the boy. We've got police following it up.'

'Send me the number,' Harvey told her. 'We'll run it with all the others.'

Ellis promised to do so and ended the call, and Harvey wondered just how far this would have gone if it hadn't been for Brigandicuum. They might have still picked up the London cell owing to the remnants of the bomb that hadn't detonated properly, but they certainly wouldn't have had the other two hundred or so players dotted around the country.

For all the surveillance technology's good points, though, he still knew it was trouble waiting to happen.

He turned his attention back to the signal in Nigeria, but before he could delve any deeper, his phone rang.

'Andrew, it's Tom.'

'About time, too! What the hell have you been up to? I hear you killed someone.'

'That's the least of your worries,' Gray said. 'Does the name Paul Roberts mean anything to you?'

Hearing the name from Gray stunned him, and he fought to keep his voice under control.

'Yes, it does. Have you seen him?'

'Better than that,' Gray said. 'He's sitting in my kitchen.'

As Andrew Harvey powered the Honda towards the outskirts of London, his mind was awash with questions, not the least of which was *How the hell did Tom Gray get involved in this?*

It wasn't as though Gray went looking for trouble—not in recent years, at least—but it certainly had a way of seeking him out. It now appeared that the rioting that had been concentrated around Gray's office had been more than coincidence. What the link was, though, he didn't yet know. Gray hadn't given too much away on the phone, just the fact that Roberts was being restrained in his home and that Harvey should be the one to collect him.

That idea hadn't sat well with Thompson. She'd wanted to send in a whole team, but Harvey had managed to convince her that going against Gray's request would result in a lack of co-operation. After venting her anger, she'd finally relented, though she had insisted on keeping a team waiting on standby for his word.

He pulled the motorcycle up to the gates of Gray's house and they swung open immediately. Len Smart was waiting at the open front door, and he let Harvey in, leading him through to the kitchen where Gray and Sonny Baines were watching over a man sitting on a wooden chair.

'What happened to his foot?' One shoe was off, and a blood-stained bandage was wrapped around the appendage.

'I'll let him answer that,' Gray said, looking at Roberts. 'Paul, this is Andrew Harvey, MI5.'

Roberts demanded to see ID, and once Harvey flashed his badge, he became suddenly animated. 'He shot me!' Roberts said, pointing at Gray. 'He strapped me to a chair and shot me in the foot! It wasn't an accident!'

Harvey looked at Gray, who offered him a non-committal shrug. Sonny followed suit.

Harvey walked over to stand in front of Roberts. He looked down at the injured foot, then stood on it, putting as much weight on it as he could.

'I'd say you got off lightly,' Harvey said above the screams.

'I demand you take me to the hospital.'

'Not gonna happen,' Harvey said. 'I've got a team waiting to take you to a safe house, where you'll be questioned.'

'I want to go to a police station,' Roberts said, but Harvey ignored him and turned to Gray.

'Has he said anything to you?'

Gray played the recording he'd made, and it tallied with some of the information Harvey already had. There was still a lot more to learn, though, and he called Thompson and had her send in the unit she'd assembled. He also asked her to check on the number Ellis had given him earlier, apologising for not having told her before he left Haddon Hall. 'It slipped my mind when Gray said he had Roberts, and it could be one of the big players.'

While they waited, Roberts made more demands. The recording, he said, had been made while under duress, and was the result of torture.

'If you think that was torture,' Sonny smiled, 'then you'd shrivel at the thought of what I could do in just five minutes with a pair of bolt cutters.'

Further claims came and fell on deaf ears, but when Roberts argued that his human rights were being breached, Harvey thought Gray was going to lose it.

'What about my daughter's right not to be murdered in her own home by a fucking whack-job?' Gray had his hands around Roberts's throat before anyone could react, and it took all three of them to prise him off.

Harvey led Gray out of the kitchen and into the hallway. 'Tom, you need to calm down.'

'Yeah? And what about you? You're always so 'by the book', yet I saw you stomp on his foot.'

'I wasn't the one who put a bullet in it,' Harvey reminded him. 'Now, did he tell you anything else, anything not on the recording?'

'Nothing,' Gray said. 'I asked him who's behind all this, but he says he doesn't know.'

'I believe him,' Harvey said, and explained how the attacks looked to have been carried out by independent cells in each major town and city. 'So far, it all points back to Nigeria, but we just heard that an explosion wiped out DSA's entire leadership last night.'

'Really?'

'Apparently,' Harvey told him. 'The Nigerian government are saying they took themselves out with their own munitions.'

Gray looked confused. 'Then why did this Efram character turn up to make sure Roberts completed the hit on me?'

Harvey thought about it. 'Perhaps he hadn't heard about the explosion, and was carrying out his most recent orders.'

'Possibly,' Gray admitted, 'but I'd like to be kept in the loop, since Melissa and I are the ones being targeted. And when you find this Efram guy, I want to know why.'

Harvey promised to do what he could, and a beep at the door announced the arrival of the escort team. Gray buzzed them in through the gates, and two men in leather jackets climbed out of the black SUV when it pulled up outside the house.

Gray let them in and showed them through to the kitchen, and asked that they carry Roberts out rather than have him trail blood through the house. The men agreed, but the prisoner wasn't going quietly. He called for the police, clearly terrified of the intelligence operatives taking possession of him. He thrashed about as they tried to lift him from the chair, and blood splattered everywhere, crimson droplets covering worktops, cupboards and the floor. Gray intervened and punched Roberts in the sternum, knocking the wind and, ultimately, the fight out of him.

As Roberts was carried out to the vehicle, Smart took the gun from Sonny and handed it to Harvey. One small piece of evidence from a colossal crime.

'I'm concerned about Melissa,' Gray told Harvey as he prepared to leave. 'Are we going to get some sort of protection until this is over?'

'I'll arrange to have a man watch the house,' Harvey said. 'It would also be a good idea to ask Len and Sonny to hang around for a while.'

'How about some weapons? The police have ours.'

Harvey put a hand on Gray's shoulder. 'We're hours away from taking this entire terrorist operation down. Trust me, you won't need any.'

Police Constable Gareth Benson was relieved to finally finish his shift, one that had started at eight the previous evening. Twelve hours later, with aching feet and a hunger to kill for, he walked back to the station to change and clock off.

He'd heard over the radio that there had been a fire on the roof of the building, but thankfully it hadn't caught and had been quickly extinguished by one of the army Green Goddess tenders that had been rolled out to help the city's fire services. As he neared the station, he could see the charred tiles on the corner of the roof, and was glad they'd been able to put it out before it did serious damage. Other forces, he'd heard, hadn't been so lucky.

His radio crackled and he took a forces-wide bulletin announcing the name of one of the suspects still believed to be at large. The name was Edward James Conran, and further details followed.

Benson stopped in his tracks and turned up the volume on his radio, instantly recognising the description. He ran into the station and asked the sergeant on duty if they had pictures of the suspect. A sheet of paper with a black and white image was handed to him, and Benson knew he'd seen the man before.

'I saw this guy on a mountain bike about two hours ago,' Benson said.

'You sure it's him?'

'Positive. I stopped him while we loaded a car onto a transporter, and he told me he was heading towards Wimbledon.'

Benson gave a description of what the suspect was wearing, along with the size and colour of the bike, and the sergeant phoned the control room and passed on the message. Within a minute, every unit in the area had their eyes peeled for Edward James Conran.

Despite the cold wind, Conran was sweating. A glance at his watch as he passed signs for Guildford told him he'd covered around thirty miles in two hours, which was what he'd hoped for. The plan had been to push hard until he was well clear of London, then relax the pace for the rest of the journey.

He decided to stop for a bite to eat, not because he was particularly hungry but because he knew he had to keep up his energy levels. He turned off the dual carriageway and into a small village, where he purchased a pre-packed chicken club and two cans of energy drink from a small store, then ate quickly on a nearby bench.

By the time he climbed back on his bike three minutes later, the clouds overhead were giving up their load, but Conran barely noticed it. What had his attention was the marked police car that cruised slowly past, the occupants taking a keen interest in him.

When the car pulled to a stop ten yards in front of him, Conran began to panic. Had they broken Houtman already? If they had, he suspected it wouldn't have been down to harsh words and threats of prison. That meant that whatever lay in store for him was going to be every bit as bad.

Conran casually spun the bike around and pedalled back the way he'd come, but when he heard the police car execute a three-point turn, his fears were confirmed. All attempts at acting casually evaporated as he pumped the pedals as hard as he could. Trying to outpace the car was futile, so he turned into a side street and jumped off the bike, leaving it lying in the road.

He ran into a garden and began jumping over walls, leaping from garden to garden, knowing that he needed to get clear of the area as soon as possible. All assets would be heading his way, including dogs and police helicopters with infra-red search capabilities. What he really needed was to get to cover, and an opportunity presented itself as he slid over another wall and saw a woman in her sixties, wrapped in a cotton dressing gown and smoking a cigarette, outside the back door. She was clearly shocked to see the bedraggled figure suddenly appear in her garden, and Conran took advantage of her indecision.

He ran towards her, and by the time she managed to shake herself into action and turn to rush back inside, he was on her. He clamped his hand over her mouth and pushed her through the doorway, kicking it shut behind him. Panting, Conran kept his hand over her mouth as he peered through the window, looking for signs of pursuit. He could hear sirens in the distance, and with every passing second they got closer and closer.

Despite the pouring rain, Conran knew the dogs would soon pick up his scent and lead the police to the house, which meant he was going to be in a hostage situation. It wasn't something he'd planned for, so it would take some quick thinking to get himself out of this mess.

Conran put his mouth to the woman's ear. 'Just do as I say and nothing will—'

Pain shot through Conran's skull, and the world went black.

A splitting headache welcomed Conran back into the land of the living, and it felt as if a cow were sitting on his chest. He gingerly opened his eyes and saw that he wasn't far wrong.

The olive-green T-shirt with the Royal Artillery motif covered a thick chest, and tattooed arms stretched the short sleeves. One large hand was around Conran's throat, while the other held a heavy adjustable spanner, which Conran guessed was the cause of his headache.

'What the fuck are you doing in here?'

Before Conran could answer, the elderly woman led two armed police officers into the kitchen.

'This is him,' she said, as if the situation needed any clarification. 'My boy saved me.'

Conran's mind turned to Houtman. The big Dutchman was no coward, and had a deep-seated hatred of authority. He wouldn't have given his colleagues up without a struggle, and Conran expected much of the same. There was little he would be able to tell them, apart from the names of his two associates, which they probably already knew. It was what else they'd want to know that concerned him. Pleading ignorance wasn't going to stop them from giving him an introduction to waterboarding or whatever tactics they used these days, and with such a low pain threshold, he knew that what lay in store in the days ahead wasn't going to be pleasant.

He eased his right hand towards his trouser pocket and retrieved the tiny capsule. When the soldier son was asked to move aside, he had it in his mouth in a flash, and bit down before anyone could move to stop him.

A hand gripped his jaw like a vice, forcing his mouth open while fingers probed inside, but the damage had already been done. The contents of the plastic pill were already making their way towards Conran's stomach. His last memories on the planet were of two leather-clad fingers jabbing at the back of his throat.

Chapter 27

16 December 2014

By the time the SUV returned to Haddon Hall, Harvey had already finished a lunch of tuna pasta bake provided by the onsite cook, his Honda having made better progress on the roads than the bulky people carrier. He stood at the front door of the building as the vehicle pulled up to the steps and a blindfolded Roberts was guided out.

Harvey hit a pre-set number and held the phone to his ear. 'He's here,' he told Ellis.

'Good. Hamad followed up on the number you gave us, but the phone was found in a waste bin in a park. No prints or DNA, and it looks like it was only used once.'

'Too bad,' Harvey said. 'Roberts told us he was recruited by someone called Efram, and that was our only lead to him.'

'Then lean on Roberts—he met the guy. Get everything you can, and by whatever means necessary.'

Before Harvey could clarify, the phone went dead in his hand.

Whatever means necessary.

Personally, he had nothing against that. Once upon a time he would have found the idea of stepping over the moral line abhorrent, but then the last forty-eight hours hadn't been the typical start to the working week. The latest reports suggested more than eight thousand had died as a direct result of the attacks, with many more seriously injured, and if one of his suspects had to feel a little pain to bring it to an end, so be it.

Harvey followed the escorts to an upstairs room, where a metal chair waited. It had been bolted to the floor, and up against the wall stood a similarly fashioned table with a white cloth covering a large plastic box. The rest of the room lay bare, lacking any carpets or wall decoration.

Roberts struggled as he was manhandled to the chair, but once he was secured with handcuffs and chains, the fight petered out. A wooden chair was brought in from another room, and Harvey sat a few feet in front of Roberts, his manner relaxed. He produced his phone and turned the voice recorder on.

'This is how it's going to work. I will ask you questions, and as long as I like the answers, everything remains civil. As soon as I feel you're lying to me, I let these guys take over.'

Harvey was referring to the two NSA operatives standing by the door. Neither looked particularly aggressive, but Harvey guessed that the real fear came from their detached expressions, which suggested that inflicting pain on another human being did not lie outside their comfort zones.

'Let's start with Efram. Describe him.'

'Just a normal face, no scars, short black hair combed in a side parting,' Roberts said.

'Height? Weight?'

'Just a bit shorter than me, about five-ten, and a slim build.'

'You told Gray that he looked like a government type. What did you mean by that?'

'Smarmy,' Roberts said. 'Full of self-importance.'

'Doesn't necessarily mean government,' Harvey said. 'That could be any captain of industry, business owner, supermarket shelf stacker, or just your regular, everyday megalomaniac.'

Roberts shook his head. 'No, there was just . . . something about him. And he . . . well, he had a file on me.'

Harvey knew that any number of private detectives could build a file on a person, but decided to follow it up. He asked one of his chaperones to fetch his laptop from downstairs, and while the errand was being run, enquired about the training in Nigeria.

Roberts told him about the flight over, being met by someone called Dan, who turned out to be a sergeant, their introduction to Colonel Mitchell, which resulted in Tony Eversham getting a bullet to the brain, and then one hundred and fifty days of training in munitions, electronics and explosives.

'How many others were at this camp?' Harvey asked.

'Recruits? About two hundred. I never got the chance to count the exact number. And that's all we were, numbers. We never spoke to anyone outside our little group, not after what they did to Tony.'

'How many were in your cell?'

'Four,' Roberts said. 'Well, three, after Tony . . . .'

'Erik Houtman's dead, too,' Harvey said, looking for a reaction. 'So is Ed Conran.'

'How?'

'They didn't want to answer our questions,' Harvey said.

'I've told you all I know.' Roberts's face had gone ashen. 'Can I please get some medical attention for my foot?'

'How many trainers at the Nigerian camp?' Harvey asked.

'Ah, twelve, I think. Yeah, twelve, including the colonel.'

'I want descriptions.'

Roberts obliged, and a few common elements emerged: all seemed to be British, had a similar, athletic build, wore the same uniforms and had regimental haircuts.

'How often did you see the colonel?'

'Maybe twice a week.'

'Would you recognise him again?'

Harvey received a nod in confirmation.

While waiting for the guard to return, Harvey asked about the explosives they'd used, and where they'd acquired them.

'We were told to visit a warehouse,' Roberts said. 'It was stocked with everything we would need.' He gave Harvey the address.

'And how did you pay for everything?'

Roberts explained how they'd been given cash and pre-paid credit cards before leaving Nigeria, enough to keep them going for the five months of preparation. They hadn't had to pay for the stuff in the warehouse, he said.

The door opened, and Harvey was handed his laptop. He opened it, signed into the secure server and brought up a list of government employees. There were a lot more than he imagined, and he filtered the list to show only males. That cut the number of results somewhat, though thousands remained to go through.

'How old would you say Efram was?'

'Mid to late forties.'

Harvey filtered the results to reflect those over the age of thirty-eight, just to be on the safe side, then further reduced the number of records by showing only those who stood between five-eight and six feet tall. He still had a formidable list to go through, but attributes such as facial hair, spectacles or hairstyle could be easily changed and weren't reliable search criteria.

'What about race?'

'White, British.'

That cut the numbers once more, and Harvey stood, placing the laptop on the chair. He asked one of the guards to release one of Roberts's hands.

'Please stand behind him and make sure he does nothing more than use the left and right arrows to go through that list. I'm going to grab a coffee. Want one?'

Both guards asked for theirs black with one sugar, and Harvey left the room.

Instead of going to the kitchen on the ground level, he made his way to the basement and checked up on the data that had come from the phone in Nigeria. The device's location hadn't changed, but that meant nothing. The owner could have decided to have a day inside, or gone out and left it at home. That would be the more logical explanation, as there had been no activity since seven the previous evening. No calls, no texts, no data usage . . . .

He brought up the map and zoomed in to find the exact location of the phone. A tingle of excitement ran down his spine when he saw that it was a hospital in Kano.

Thompson came over to his station and placed her half-empty coffee cup on his desk.

'What have you got from Roberts?'

Harvey explained what he had so far, and asked her to check out the warehouse Roberts had told him about. He also told her that he was showing the suspect a filtered list of government employees in the hope that he might pick out the mysterious Efram.

'What about the cells?' he asked. 'Has the round-up begun?'

'Not yet. Getting the police to mount simultaneous raids takes some time. If we don't do this nationwide within a one-hour timeframe, the news channels might pick up on what we're doing. Once that story breaks, our suspects will go into hiding, or, worse, make a dramatic last stand.'

'Why not send out a DA-Notice to the producers?' Harvey asked.

'After Levinson? The press aren't exactly our best buddies at the moment.'

Thompson turned her attention to Harvey's screen. 'What's this you're looking at?'

'I was following up on the phone in Nigeria, the one that was used to visit the website,' he said.

'But their leadership was wiped out. So let's not waste time on dead bodies, okay?'

'Actually, the phone's at a hospital. Takasa might just be injured.'

'That blast levelled everything in a thirty-yard radius. What you're seeing are his possessions sitting in a box at the morgue.'

Harvey had to concede the point. It certainly explained why there had been no activity from the phone, but the whole thing still seemed . . . contrived. Still, there was little use in trying to argue the point with Thompson. Once she'd made her mind up, there was no changing it, no matter how strong an argument he presented.

'I'm heading back upstairs,' he said, locking his terminal. After stopping off at the kitchen, he returned to the interrogation room armed with liquid sustenance.

'See anyone you recognise?'

Roberts shook his head. 'Can't you get a doctor to take a look at my foot?'

'Once we're done here,' Harvey said.

Another twenty minutes passed, and Roberts came up empty.

'Sorry, I really thought he was government.'

'I hope you're not trying to waste my time.'

Roberts protested, but Harvey ignored him and picked up the laptop. He logged into the MoD server and did a search for personnel who had left the services in the last ten years, then filtered the list using the same criteria he'd used earlier. He also only wanted to see those who had served in combat units, and that brought the numbers down even further.

He put the laptop back on the chair. 'I want you to find the colonel and the other instructors.'

While Roberts went about the task, Harvey stepped out of the room and called Ellis.

'Nothing on the Efram lead.' He explained that he was now looking at the Nigerian connection. 'The problem is, Sarah isn't happy with me chasing that up.'

'At the moment, I can understand that. We've never mounted such a co-ordinated raid, so we need to focus on that for now. Nigeria can wait.'

One of the guards opened the door and indicated for Harvey to come back in. He told Ellis he'd call her back and joined Roberts in the interrogation room.

'What is it?'

'I found one of them,' Roberts said. Harvey picked up the laptop and studied the face on the screen. There was nothing particularly striking about it, no obvious features that would make the man instantly recognisable.

'You sure?'

'That's Sergeant Dan,' Roberts assured him. 'He was our main explosives tutor.'

Harvey read the man's service record and felt the thrill of the hunt fill him with a burst of new energy. Just as quickly, though, he slumped back in his chair. Here he had his best lead to date, but neither Ellis nor Thompson would let him pursue it.

Well . . . if *he* couldn't spend time on it, he knew someone who could.

He opened the email app on his phone and fired off a message to Tom Gray.

Chapter 28

16 December 2014

'Len, ever heard of a Michael West?'

Gray handed his phone to Smart, who studied the image on the screen. 'Can't say the face rings a bell. Name's not familiar, either.'

Sonny had a look, too, but came away shaking his head. 'Why are we interested in him?'

'Andrew emailed it to me. Wants to know if we've come across him.'

Gray took the phone back and tapped the screen a couple of times. 'According to the bio Andrew sent, West was regiment. Served two years before he got dishonourably discharged over an incident in Afghanistan in 2010. Last seen in Kano, Nigeria five months ago.'

'Which is home to DSA,' Smart said. 'Is he linked to these bombings?'

'Looks like it,' Gray said. 'Andrew thinks that he's one of a dozen ex-soldiers who might have been recruited through an agency like ours, and wants me to put the feelers out.'

'Then let's get started,' Smart said.

Gray powered up his laptop, and once the desktop appeared, he went to the online storage folder where the company documents were kept and entered his user details. Within minutes, the list of high-end security companies had been divided up, and all three of them were on the phone, trying to track West down. Gray took the kitchen, while Sonny had the living room and Smart sat in the dining room.

'Hi,' Gray said, when the first of his calls was answered, 'my name's Kevin McDonald and I'm calling from Haslo International.' He explained that the company specialised in advanced mineral extraction and was sending a team out to central Africa to work up a potentially lucrative deposit that had been recently discovered. He needed a security detail, and a partner firm had recommended the services of Michael West.

'Is he available for a one-year contract?'

'Sorry, we don't have anyone on our books with that name.'

'Oh, I must have been given the wrong information. Sorry to trouble you.'

The next call went much the same way, but he hit the jackpot on the third.

'I'm afraid Michael is currently on assignment,' the security company's representative said. 'He won't be available until March next year.'

'That's fine. The job won't begin until the end of April. I'll need a dozen men altogether, preferably people Michael has worked with before. Initially it will be a one-year contract.'

Gray knew that such a deal would cost almost two million if Minotaur performed it, a figure that was not to be sniffed at. 'I'm also going to need the names and addresses of everyone he's contracted for over the last eighteen months, for reference purposes.'

'I'm afraid we don't normally divulge that information.'

It wasn't what Gray had been expecting. His company required customers to evaluate his contractors both during and after every job, and a clause in the agreement allowed Minotaur to pass on their details to other prospective clients for just such purposes. This kind of transparency helped him stand out from the less respectable operations that cared more about money than reputation.

'I understand,' Gray gambled, 'but we've been burnt by previous agencies sending us substandard people, which is why we insist on doing our own checks. I'll try another firm. Have you had any dealings with Minotaur Logistics?'

He could almost hear the sales rep's panic at the thought of such a big catch slipping the net. 'Bear with me a moment.'

Gray knew he'd hit the mark. He was ready with a pen and paper to take down the information, but it wasn't forthcoming.

'The best I can do is to contact Michael and ask if he agrees to me sharing this information.'

'No need,' Gray said. 'From our brief conversation, I'd say your company has something to hide, and that's not the kind of relationship we like to engage in. I'll take my business elsewhere.'

He ended the call before there were any further objections. The last thing he needed was West being warned about someone delving into his previous work, even if it were a prospective client.

Gray left the kitchen and informed the others of his find, and then sent a reply to Harvey's email.

Harvey uploaded the latest sets of mugshot images and sent them to the chief constable of West Midlands Police. Using the same technique he'd applied to identify Roberts and the other passengers on the flight to Nigeria, he'd found just short of two hundred people who'd made similar journeys at around the same time.

Now that the forces had names and faces to go along with the locations of the devices, there was less chance of any cell members slipping through the net—a net that was closing rapidly.

His phone beeped, and he saw the incoming email from Gray. After scanning through it, he placed a call to Veronica Ellis.

'I've got a lead on one of the people who provided the training in Nigeria,' he told her. 'I'd like to follow it up.'

'What have you got?'

'A name. Michael West, ex-SAS. He contracts through an agency called Bicknell Security, but we don't have a current location for him.'

'Good work. We'll deal with him later, but for now we're two hours away from launching our operation. Focus on that for now.'

The line went dead, leaving Harvey frustrated that he would have to wait a little longer to chase up the overseas connection. Nevertheless, they had a good starting place, and by the end of the day he would be visiting Bicknell Security to find out exactly which client West had been working for.

His phone rang again. It was Lancashire Police, wanting to notify him that they were set to go at seven in the evening, the time that had been agreed. Over the next ninety minutes, more and more confirmations were received, until the last force in the country gave the thumbs-up.

He decided to grab some food while he had the chance, and he went to the kitchen where he loaded a plate with cold cuts, cheese and buttered bread before returning to his station. Thompson saw him, and two minutes later appeared next to him, similarly stocked up, but with two ice-cold sodas as well.

She handed one to Harvey. 'I'm glad it's nearly over,' she said, taking a sip of her drink. A thin film of moisture clung to her lips, and as she slowly licked them dry, Harvey began to suffer an acute case of localised high blood pressure. He tried to cast such thoughts aside, but her proximity meant he could smell the perfume she favoured, a heady scent he found intoxicating.

'You've done some good work over the last few days,' Thompson said.

Harvey nodded coolly, not trusting his voice under the circumstances. He took a few mouthfuls of food before clearing his throat. 'So what's the plan when this is over?' he asked. 'Resume the search for James Farrar?'

'I guess so,' she said. 'I think it should be a lot easier with Brigandicuum to help us. He'll be ours in no time.'

'And after that, for you? Back to Six?'

'I guess so,' she said again.

She rested her chin in one hand and looked at Harvey. 'I mean it—you did some really good work. I'm sorry about my behaviour since I arrived at Five, but there was a lot of pressure to bring Farrar in, and I guess it got to me. I'm not normally such a pompous bitch.'

Harvey couldn't help but laugh, and Thompson's face lit up, too. She was truly captivating, and he was so caught up in the moment that he didn't notice his phone ringing until Thompson pointed down to it with raised eyebrows.

He answered it, and Thompson stood, placing a hand on his shoulder for just a second before walking back to her desk.

His eyes followed her all the way.

Chapter 29

16 December 2014

Tom Gray placed the bowl of spaghetti Bolognese and two serving spoons in the middle of the table and told Gill and Smart to dig in.

An anxious Gill had accepted his offer to stay for a couple of days, grateful not to have to spend the rest of the week alone in her flat. Although trouble seemed to follow Gray around, being next to him was usually the safest option in a crisis, and when Harvey's armed guard rang the bell and introduced himself, she clearly felt safer still. A couple of large vodkas and tonic had completed the transformation, and the earlier events were forgotten as Gill tucked into the offering on the table.

Gray headed back to the kitchen to fetch the garlic bread, then spooned some food into Melissa's bowl, using a pair of kitchen scissors to cut her pasta into manageable pieces.

'I checked through everyone on our books to see if any of them was in Afghanistan at the same time as Michael West,' Smart said. 'It looks like three of our guys might know him.'

'Give me their details after dinner. I'll have a word with them.'

Once the plates were cleared away and Melissa was tucked up in bed, Gray joined Smart at the laptop. The three names were highlighted on the personnel spreadsheet in yellow.

'Mackenzie knows him?'

'Looks like it.'

Gray dialled Mackenzie's number.

'Paul, it's Tom Gray. How's things?'

'Good, boss. What can I do for you?'

'Ever heard of Michael West?' Gray asked.

'Westy? Don't get me started on that prick. He's not applying for work, is he?'

'No, but someone recommended him to me,' Gray lied.

'Avoid him like the plague, boss. The guy's a psycho.'

Mackenzie went on to explain that both men had taken part in Operation Moshtarak, a joint offensive against the Afghan town of Marja, Helmand Province. They'd been tasked alongside US Navy SEALs with capturing Taliban leaders, and after a couple of raids yielded no results, their patrol had come across an Afghan in his forties.

'This guy was shitting himself, and Westy thought it would be fun to wind him up. He kept screaming that the guy was Taliban, making like he was gonna shoot him. The guy suddenly started getting angry when he saw Westy laughing at him, and he spat in Westy's face. The next thing you know, guy's got a round through his head.'

'That sounds bad,' Gray admitted, 'but I always like to hear both sides of the tale. Have you got a contact number for him, or know anyone that has?'

'Personally, I don't care if I never hear from him again, but I'll ask around.'

Gray thanked him and hung up. He tried the other two numbers, but neither man had any contact details for West, both taking the same view as Mackenzie.

'Not a popular guy, Michael West,' Gray told Smart. 'I guess all we can do is pass what we know to Andrew and let him crack on with it.'

An hour and a half after the nationwide operation started, almost two-thirds of the suspects had been arrested and another sixty had been killed or had taken their own lives. Seven suspects remained at large, having abandoned their phones and laptops once their part of the mission had been completed, but armed with names and photos, the police were confident of catching them in the next few hours. If they didn't, the images would be given to the news outlets.

That left two—one in Bristol and the other in Leicester—who were currently involved in armed standoffs. The situation in the Midlands was the one that caused Harvey most concern: the suspect had taken refuge in a youth club and was holding thirty kids hostage.

Thompson came over to his desk to inform him that three more of the fugitives had been apprehended, leaving only six. 'Any news from Bristol?'

'Still trying to talk him out,' Harvey said. 'The SAS are on standby, but hopefully we won't need them. What did you find at the warehouse?'

'Deserted,' Thompson said. 'It was rented out at the start of the year, cash up front, but the name they gave turns out to be an eight-day-old who died back in the sixties. We'll need Roberts to meet the Etch-a-Sketch people and come up with E-FITs of the people he met there.'

'I've been thinking,' Harvey said. 'Roberts said he was given a bundle of cash and some pre-paid credit cards. If all two hundred of them got the same, that works out at a hell of a lot of money. You'd then have to pay for the training, explosives and all the other equipment they needed, which means someone put some serious funding into this.'

'We suspect DSA had financial backing from AQIM,' she said.

Harvey didn't buy that. Algerian terror group AQIM, or Al-Qaeda in the Islamic Maghreb, had reportedly earned around fifty million dollars through kidnapping and extortion in the last decade, which probably wasn't even half the money DSA would have needed to pull off an operation of this magnitude and complexity. The research he'd done on the group while trying to identify their new leader, Takasa, didn't indicate that they had access to any other major funding. So exactly who had financed it?

'We're talking about forty or fifty million sterling,' he said. 'That's far more than AQIM made in ten years, and they wouldn't have given DSA every single penny.'

'I agree, that needs to be looked into, but for the moment we need to sort out the men on the ground. Let's get them locked up, and then we can go after the people who organised this.'

Thompson rose and walked back to her own station, but this time Harvey's eyes didn't follow: he was more concerned with who was ultimately behind this, and the more he thought about it, the more the explosion in Kano seemed a little too coincidental.

It was just after one in the morning when word came in that the last of the suspects had been rounded up, and if Harvey hadn't been so tired he would have joined in the celebrations. High-fives abounded, along with whooping and cheering as the staff in the control centre were finally able to vent the tension that had consumed them all for the previous two days.

Thompson sidled up to him armed with another couple of sodas, but he declined the offer. 'I just want to hit the sack. I need a few hours before we follow up on Nigeria.'

'Sounds like a plan,' she said, stifling a yawn. 'Sadly, I've got a couple of things I need to finish up. No rest for the wicked.'

Harvey left her to it and made his way upstairs to the room they'd been allocated. The folding camp bed felt like a majestic four-poster when he climbed in, but when he closed his eyes he found that sleep wouldn't come. His mind wouldn't let go of the idea that DSA's leadership were gone.

The Nigerian government's official stance, as reported on the news, was that the leadership had been building a device when it went off by accident. That struck Harvey as highly unlikely, as that kind of thing was normally left to foot soldiers, not generals. Which meant the only real alternative was that the entire DSA council had been killed by a hostile party that didn't want to claim responsibility. That in itself seemed improbable, because acts of terror were designed to heighten fear of a particular group, and he couldn't recall a single incident where the terrorists hadn't demanded recognition, especially when one group struck a blow against a rival outfit.

Despite the quandary, he drifted off, the long day finally catching up with him. His dreams were filled with visions of explosions, at first from afar, but then closer and closer. He found himself standing outside a building when the façade began to bubble outwards, the blast happening in ultra-slow motion. He was lifted from his feet and thrown backwards to the ground, where he lay helpless as masonry flew at him. A chunk the size of a suitcase arced towards his chest, and a crushing sensation enveloped him.

Harvey jolted awake but was unable to move, the weight still pressing down on him. As his eyes adjusted to the darkness he saw Sarah straddling him, her mouth inches from his. Before he could say anything, their lips met, and she moaned as her tongue sought his. Harvey's hands played down her back to her bare buttocks, and she writhed deliciously on top of him, stirring him upwards. Thompson slid down him and pulled down his boxer shorts, revealing his arousal. It was Harvey's turn to moan as she gently kissed him, before sliding onto him like a velvet glove. She rode him, gently at first, her firm breasts heaving as she gained intensity, and he met her pace, their breath coming as one until both were spent.

Thompson collapsed next to him, her head on his chest as she stroked his stomach.

'Not that I'm complaining, but—'

Thompson turned to look at him and put a finger over his mouth. 'Shh.'

She lowered her head again, and within a minute Harvey heard her purring as she fell into a deep sleep. He joined her soon after, and this time he found his dreams to be significantly more pleasant.

When Harvey woke, he found himself alone. He stretched, recalling the dream he'd had about Thompson, then caught the scent of her perfume on the bed sheet. Realising it hadn't been a dream, he looked over to her bunk, but saw nothing except for a pile of clothes. His watch told him he'd slept for eight hours, more than he'd had for a long time, and he decided to walk down the hallway to take a shower before heading downstairs for breakfast. He wrapped himself in a towel and was about to open the door when Thompson walked in, similarly attired.

'Morning,' she smiled, walking past him. He watched her stop at the bed and remove the towel, wrapping it around her head. When she turned to face him, completely unabashed, he felt the stirrings of the previous night return with a vengeance.

It didn't go unnoticed.

Thirty minutes later, Thompson headed back to the shower, leaving Harvey to wonder what had brought about such a change in her. It was probably the relief of wrapping up such a massive operation so quickly, he decided. Victory as an aphrodisiac and all that. Whatever the reason, he wanted more of the same.

Thompson had awoken something in him that had lain dormant for a long time. In the past there had only been one special lady, but his work patterns soon put an end to any hopes of that relationship blossoming. Since then, he'd had a couple of flings, but none had left him feeling like a schoolboy experiencing his first crush.

He wondered absently if this could ever turn into something more serious, or if it were merely a celebratory round of sex, releasing the stress of the last few days. Sarah was, after all, a beautiful woman, and he imagined she must have a string of suitors, men with a lot more to offer than a middle-grade operative.

Harvey realised that he was already feeling the first pangs of jealousy, even though he had no idea where Thompson wanted to take this. *Grow up*, he told himself. *Go with the flow, and enjoy it while it lasts.*

Thompson returned from the shower, the smile still in place, and he gave her a peck on the cheek before going to complete his own ablutions. On his return, he found her dressed and running a comb through her hair.

'I just spoke to my boss,' she said. 'I've been called back to Six.'

'So soon? But we haven't even started working on the people behind all this.'

'That's why I'm being recalled,' Thompson said. 'Five deal with domestic issues, whereas we have international reach.'

'I don't understand,' Harvey told her. 'Are you saying Six are taking over from here?'

Thompson walked over and caressed his face. 'Don't pout, Andrew. It doesn't suit you.'

'I'm not pouting. I just feel it would be better if we worked together on this.'

'I agree,' Thompson said, 'but this comes from the home secretary herself. You've done a fantastic job over the last few days, and I think you'd be a real asset in taking this forward, but we have our orders.'

Harvey couldn't help feeling used, in more than one sense. 'What about us?'

The words felt childish, even desperate, as they left his mouth, though Thompson didn't seem to notice.

'I took the liberty of checking your work calendar, and you're due a couple of weeks off. Why not take some leave and come and stay at my place for a while? I'll probably be working late most days, but it would be nice to have someone to come home to.'

Thompson rubbed her hand against his groin in an effort to get the point across, and Harvey instantly warmed to the idea. The feeling was temporary, however. 'I just hate the thought of getting this far and abandoning the case.'

'You won't be,' Thompson assured him. 'I'm going to need someone to bounce ideas off, and you're just the man. Although you're not officially on the project, that doesn't mean I can't use that brain of yours. Now, hurry up. I need you to get me back to London.'

Harvey dressed quickly, energised by the thought that he wouldn't be completely cut out of the loop. He told Thompson he would be heading downstairs to collect some belongings and would meet her at the front door.

In the basement, Harvey found Tony Manello running the early shift. The NSA operative was staring up at the big screen, sipping at a black coffee.

'She's an impressive beast,' Manello said. 'Fifty-nine cells taken out in less than two days. I tell ya, I'd hate to be a bad guy right about now.'

'Amen to that,' Harvey agreed. 'Tell me, though. How do you feel personally about having every single word you type monitored?'

'As long as you've got nothing to hide, what's the problem?'

'No problem for you, maybe. But what about someone abusing the system? Imagine an NSA analyst trips across a congressman's downloads and finds he's been having an affair or is involved in less than legitimate dealings. Isn't there the temptation to sell that information on? Or, worse, blackmail them directly?'

'Nah.' Manello laughed. 'Everyone with access to this system knows the penalty for using it for extracurricular purposes. Trust me, no-one wants to contravene our information security policy. Besides, all of our devices are monitored by a separate team, and we undergo random surveillance. We all understand the scrutiny we're under.'

'What about your president? How does he feel, knowing every spoken and written word is going into this database?'

'Actually, he's exempt, so it's not a problem for him,' Manello explained. 'We can block the output so POTUS, senior military and intelligence personnel, your cabinet members, anyone of any political importance gets to continue without fear of revealing anything detrimental to the national security of our nations.'

It made sense that certain interests would be protected, but the more Harvey thought about it, the scarier it got. Every word he typed at the office would be under scrutiny, and in his line of work he was bound to enter more than his fair share of keywords likely to trigger downloads. It was Big Brother taken to a whole new level, and he wasn't sure he was comfortable with it, especially as he'd likely have to face the same scrutiny as the NSA staffers.

'I'd better get going,' Harvey said. 'I just want to grab some data from my terminal, then Sarah and I will be out of here.'

He took a flash drive from his pocket, but Manello put out a hand to stop him. 'Sorry, Andrew, but nothing leaves here, and certainly not on a memory stick.'

'Can I copy it across to our secure server?' Harvey asked.

He got a shake of the head from Manello. 'The access you've enjoyed so far was a one-off owing to the size and nature of the events. Going forward, all information will be processed by us and fed through to the relevant government departments as and when necessary. That keeps the loop as small as possible.'

'So when does my access expire?'

'Twenty minutes ago,' Manello said. 'I got a call locking it down. Any requests to use the system will now have to go up to your boss and she'll pass it to your home secretary.'

Harvey was frustrated, but Manello clearly didn't have the power to change NSA policy. Well, if he couldn't get direct access, then Thompson's offer was the next best thing. 'Is it okay if I log into my terminal and close down the link to the office?'

'Have at it.'

Harvey entered his password to unlock the PC and scribbled down a phone number before going through the process of closing down his connection to the company servers. Once finished, he closed down the terminal and stood, pocketing the small pad of Post-it notes in the process. He shook hands with Manello and made to leave, but a firm hand gripped his biceps.

'The pad, please.'

Harvey sheepishly took it from his pocket, tore off the top slip, and handed it over to Manello.

'Had to try.' He shrugged, pocketing the rest of the pad. As he rode the elevator back up to the ground floor, he used a pencil to take a light rubbing of the top of the pad, revealing the imprinted number of the African cell phone. The door pinged to announce his arrival on the ground floor, and he found Thompson waiting by the front door.

'So, are you going to book some time off and spice up my winter evenings?'

'I couldn't think of a better way to spend Christmas,' Harvey said with a smile.

They walked round to the back of the building, where the Honda was waiting. Harvey climbed on and Thompson once again took the pillion position, squeezing him tightly. Once he reached the main road, he opened the throttle and the powerful machine effortlessly ate up the miles. When he got to the motorway, he saw that traffic was once again moving, though not in the volumes he would have seen a week before. It was still enough to make him check his speed, and an hour and a half later he pulled into the car park for Thames House. The journey through the capital had seen a steady flow of vehicles, suggesting the worst of the blockages had been cleared up.

They rode the elevator to the office, where Thompson collected her belongings before heading over the bridge to the Six building. Before she left, she dropped a slip of paper into Harvey's shirt pocket. As she disappeared, he took a quick look at the note. It contained an address in Pimlico and a succinct message:

9PM. Bring wine.

The prospect of the evening ahead was tempered by his desire to see their operation through to its conclusion. He decided to visit his boss to see if she could shine any light on the decision to cut Five out of the picture.

'Believe me, Andrew, I'm as angry about this as you are.'

Ellis stood behind her desk with her arms folded tightly across her chest, a sure sign that she was ready to explode. He'd only seen it a couple of times, neither of which had been particularly pretty.

'We don't even get access to this new system,' she continued, 'which really pisses me off.'

'I was told the orders came down from on high.'

Ellis nodded. 'The home secretary herself ordered us to drop it and let Six take over. We're to co-ordinate the interrogations, but anything we glean has to be passed on to Vauxhall for action.'

'It makes no sense,' Harvey said. 'You'd think they'd want every possible resource working this. Something doesn't smell right.'

Ellis gave him a familiar look, a raised-chin posture that suggested she felt great pride about her work and her people. 'Exactly how I feel. The question is, what do we do about it?'

'I may have a way in,' Harvey told her. He explained about Thompson's invitation to bounce ideas off him, carefully leaving out the physical aspect of their new-found relationship.

'I always found her manner to be . . . acerbic,' Ellis said. 'Especially towards you. Why would she suddenly warm to you overnight?'

'Perhaps it's just my raw, animal magnetism.' Harvey winked suggestively, drawing a raised eyebrow from Ellis.

'Whatever it is, I want you to keep on pressing the same buttons.'

Harvey nodded. 'I'll get what I can from her. Does this mean we're going to be launching our own investigation?'

'No,' Ellis said, 'we're just going to follow up on a lead, one that we wanted to verify before passing it over to Six.'

Harvey knew Ellis was playing a dangerous game, one that could end her career. When you answered to a major political figure, you had very little leeway for interpreting instructions. Fortunately, Ellis could make black and white orders look as grey as a Moscow winter.

'So how exactly do you want to play this?' he asked.

'From what you've told me, the trail leads to Nigeria. If, as you suggest, the bombing in Kano was no accident, it would be prudent to investigate the phone at the hospital. Obviously you can't be in two places at once, so we'll send Hamad. Meanwhile, you pump Thompson for all you're worth and Hamad can follow up any leads.'

The double entendre told Harvey that his attempts to play down his new bond with Thompson as purely platonic hadn't fooled Ellis. That aside, he had reservations about including Farsi in the operation.

'If we ask Hamad to go to Nigeria, he would have to communicate with us constantly, either by phone or by email. Both of those can be tracked.' He told Ellis what he'd learned from Manello, about intel staffers living under increased surveillance. 'Bearing in mind the scrutiny I'll be under from now on, it wouldn't take long for them to know what we're up to.'

'Then get yourselves clean phones and new laptops,' Ellis said.

'I'm not sure that'll be enough,' Harvey said, thinking of Manello's underground operation. 'The best option may be to make it look like business as usual here, and send someone else in Hamad's place.'

'Something tells me you already have someone in mind, and I hesitate to ask who it is because I'm not sure I'm going to like the answer.'

'Tom Gray. He'd be perfect,' Harvey said quickly, before Ellis could protest. 'Travelling to places like Kano is part of his job, so he wouldn't arouse suspicion. Plus he has the skills to look after himself.'

'But no tradecraft,' Ellis pointed out. 'Besides, you told me he refuses to leave his daughter's side. How will you convince him to abandon her here while he trots off to Nigeria?'

'I'll think of something.'

Ellis fixed him with a stern glare. 'You know how I feel about Gray. He's unreliable, possibly even unstable. In fact, I heard just today that he killed a few people during this crisis.'

'That wasn't his fault,' Harvey said. 'It was self-defence.'

'Perhaps, but you can't deny that trouble has a way of finding him, and the last thing we need is Gray starting an international incident. What about Kyle Ackerman? He's already in the region.'

Kyle Ackerman, an ex-marine now working for the UK Trade & Investment department in South Africa, had run similar missions in the past, but to say he was close to the target location was a little wide of the mark.

'I think you'll find that Kano is roughly the same distance from Pretoria as it is from Heathrow,' Harvey said. 'I did consider him, but there's no real advantage of using Kyle over Tom.'

'Apart from the number of bodies they leave behind,' Ellis said.

'Which is why Tom is the best choice. We now have a leaderless DSA and no-one knows how they're going to react to their new situation. Things could go quiet for a while, or the whole area could explode into violence. We need to send in people who are prepared for the worst-case scenario, and that means Gray and his team.'

'Oh, so it's a whole team now? Were you thinking fifty? A hundred?'

'Just Gray, Smart and Baines,' Harvey said, ignoring the jibe. 'Perhaps one more.'

Ellis sat at her desk and fiddled with a pen. 'Okay, send his team in.'

Harvey turned to leave, but Ellis wasn't finished. 'But Gray stays here, and the rest go in purely as support for Kyle, who'll lead the investigation. Gray's men can provide security, under strict rules of engagement.'

'Understood.'

Harvey went back to his desk and began plotting the mission in his head. Avoiding electronic communications was going to be paramount, which meant it wouldn't be easy to give Ackerman the big picture over the phone or by email.

The second, and much less difficult, task would be convincing Gray to provide a team to run the mission.

Chapter 30

17 December 2014

Tom Gray was enjoying his second peacefully domestic night in a row when the buzzer for the gates tore him away from helping Melissa with her dinner. When he reached the monitor, he instantly recognised the car waiting for entry.

'Come on up,' he said, and went to the front door to welcome his guest.

Harvey pulled up to the steps and sprinted from the car, his jacket covering his head to protect him from the driving rain.

'What have you got?' Gray asked, taking Harvey's coat and hanging it up in the utility room. He put a fresh pot of coffee on to brew and swapped his daughter's empty dinner plate for a cartoon-themed yoghurt.

'It hasn't been officially announced, yet, but it looks like we got them all.'

'Why not? I'd have thought they'd want that all over the news, to bring a little calm to the country.'

'It should be done some time this afternoon,' Harvey said. 'They just wanted to confirm that everyone had been rounded up and that no-one had slipped through the net.'

'So that's the end of it?' Gray asked. 'How did the information on West pan out?'

'I'm meeting someone tonight who might be able to shed some light on him.'

'At least tell me you managed to take down Efram and the guys who trained them.'

'Not quite,' Harvey said, motioning for Gray to take a seat. 'That's the reason I'm here. What do you think of the DSA leadership dying all at once in that explosion?'

'On the face of it, I'm chuffed to bits,' Gray said. 'However, you told me they'd been messing around with munitions. Normally they'd leave that to the grunts.'

'My thoughts entirely, though it looks like Whitehall are going to use that as the official line.'

'So investigate further,' Gray told him.

Harvey explained how MI5 had been instrumental in bringing the cells down but had subsequently been taken off the investigation.

'Something tells me that doesn't sit well with you,' Gray said. 'I can't imagine you nursing a bruised ego, so you must be curious as to why you've been shut out. Am I right in thinking you're not going to let this lie?'

'Perceptive, as always,' Harvey said. 'For reasons I can't go into, I'm unable to follow it up myself, but I've been given the go-ahead to assemble a small team to act as security for Kyle Ackerman.'

The name was familiar to Gray. He'd met Ackerman twice, both times memorable for the wrong reasons. 'I take it you want me to provide that team?'

'If these are the people behind Paul Roberts, it means they're the ones who issued the kill order against you. I thought that would be a good enough reason to send Sonny and Len in.'

Gray rose and paced the kitchen, his hands thrust deep into his pockets. 'Why them in particular?'

'I know them and I trust them. It's imperative that the people who go in know how to follow orders.'

Gray was sure that if he tossed the proposition their way, both Baines and Smart would jump at the chance, but he felt he had a duty to keep them out of harm's way. They were his closest friends, men who had saved his life, and putting them back on the front line didn't sit right with him.

On the flip side, if he was forced to pick his two most capable employees, they would be top of the list.

He went over to his daughter and stroked her short hair. 'What's the full brief? Is this going to turn into a wet op?'

'Far from it,' Harvey said. 'All we want is information.'

'And once you get it?'

'They come home. We just want to gather our own intel and compare it with the news coming from Six.'

'What if you find huge discrepancies?' Gray asked.

'Your team comes home, job done.'

Silence ensued as Gray mulled things over. In the many hours since his encounter with Paul Roberts, he'd got together with Len and Sonny to discuss who could possibly have a motive to kill him. He'd been specifically targeted, of that there was no doubt, though why the new leader of DSA—an organisation thousands of miles way—would want him dead was beyond him. None of his employees had ever come into contact with the Nigerian outfit, let alone engaged them in battle, so that ruled out the revenge angle.

Unless, they'd deduced, it was an individual with a grievance within their ranks. Gray knew of several people who would like to do him harm, not least Stuart Boyle, the teenager who had killed his son Daniel and whom Gray had subsequently kidnapped and held for ransom. Gray dismissed him as an option, simply because he didn't have the resources or intellect to launch such an audacious attack.

Sese Obi, the wannabe-African warlord he'd helped defeat a year earlier, was a more realistic proposition. However, the last they'd heard, Obi had been embroiled in local skirmishes hundreds of miles away from Kano, and wouldn't have had the time or funds to be the driving force behind the bombings.

That really left only one person. A man with connections to—and a motive to hate—the UK government, as well as the wherewithal to mastermind the attacks. He also had more than enough reason to want Gray wiped off the face of the planet.

'Tell me about James Farrar,' Gray said.

Harvey looked confused. 'You know all about him.'

'I mean, tell me what progress you've made in finding him. You told me he skipped bail ages ago. Where is he now?'

Harvey gave him a condensed version of their search efforts over the previous months, and voiced his frustration at not being able to follow up on certain leads.

'So this Thompson woman is brought in to lead the search, but she concentrates her efforts on places you know Farrar would avoid like the plague. That's like looking for a polar bear in the Amazon rainforest.'

'That pretty much sums it up,' Harvey admitted, and Gray could see realisation dawn.

'You just told me the home secretary only wants Six to continue the investigation, and one of the people involved is Thompson, who did her best to make sure the search for Farrar failed.'

Harvey nodded slowly. 'Usually when you start talking like this, I take it with a pinch of salt.'

'But it smells right, doesn't it?'

Harvey nodded again. 'I'll float the idea past Ellis and see what she thinks,' he said, grabbing his coat from the utility room. 'In the meantime, you think about lending us Sonny, Len and one other for a few days.'

'Consider them yours,' Gray said, 'and I'm coming along, too.'

'That was what I originally asked Ellis for, but she wants you to stay out of it. Besides, what about Melissa?'

'Ken and Mina can take her for a few days.' His in-laws had taken the insurance money from the house fire that killed Vick and bought a place in southern Italy. 'They live far away from here now. She'll be safe with them.'

'The boss won't like it,' Harvey said.

'Then she doesn't have to know,' Gray said, a determined look in his eye. 'I believe I'm still free to travel when and where I want, so Melissa and I are going abroad for Christmas. What I do from there is no-one's business.'

'I can't talk you out of this, can I?'

Gray ignored the rhetorical question and pulled out his phone. 'Sonny,' he told it, letting the auto-dial feature do its work.

Harvey waved his hands like a madman, causing Gray to ask what the hell the problem was.

'Just ask him to come over,' Harvey whispered. 'Give him no further details.'

Gray thought it strange, but did as he was told. After hanging up, he asked the MI5 operative to explain.

'One of the key parts about this operation is that electronic communications are out. Your team will rendezvous with Kyle in Abuja and fill him in on the details.'

'Are you saying I'm under surveillance?'

'I can't go into specifics, but I can tell you the parameters under which you'll have to operate. Don't ask me to elaborate, because I can't and I won't.'

Gray nodded for him to continue.

All communications had to be face to face, Harvey said, with telephone and email out of the question. Dead drop emails were also out, so Gray's team couldn't even create a message, save it as a draft and wait for Harvey to read it. That method was usually successful at circumventing any eavesdropping techniques, but Harvey warned Gray not to try it.

'I'm serious, Tom. Don't even type out a draft text message. In fact, just leave anything electronic here at home.'

The idea that anything he said or typed into a phone or computer sent a chill through Gray. 'How long has this kind of surveillance been going on?'

Harvey looked uncomfortable but answered after a moment's pause. 'Not long. Only since the attacks.'

Gray's forehead furrowed at the news. 'This doesn't sound like something you just cobble together in response to a major incident,' he said. 'They must have been working on this for months, if not years.'

'As I said, I can't go into that.'

'Well, you should certainly question it,' Gray nearly shouted. 'You can see how angry I am about this, and I bet others will be too when they find out.'

'They won't, Tom. What I've already told you is in strict confidence, and it goes no further.'

Gray was about to reply, but Harvey wasn't finished. He looked over at Melissa, who was holding up her empty dessert carton. 'For both your sakes, forget I ever mentioned this.'

Gray took a swift step forward. 'Don't you dare threaten my daughter.'

'I'm not,' Harvey said, his hands raised in submission. 'I'm just warning you that it isn't just the British government who have a stake in this.'

Gray stopped and considered the implications for a moment. 'How big?'

'You don't want to know.'

The discussion was interrupted as Sonny buzzed to announce his arrival. Smart arrived a few minutes later, and Gray let

Harvey explain what was required of them. Both Smart and Sonny were happy to take on the mission, until Gray dropped the bombshell.

'Tell them about the restrictions they'll be under.'

Harvey reluctantly gave them a rundown of the rules regarding communications, and their reaction was the same as Gray's.

'Our government actually signed this off?' Smart asked. 'When?'

'Yesterday,' Harvey said. 'Look, if they hadn't, a couple of hundred bombers would still be out there, killing thousands of innocent people. We managed to take them all down in twenty-four hours.'

'So the end justifies the means?' Sonny said. 'I didn't recall seeing an announcement about it on the news.'

'And hopefully you never will,' Harvey told him. 'Look, I can't say I'm thrilled about having my privacy stripped from me, but if it manages to prevent another attack like this, they can happily read my emails.'

'What about long-term?' Smart asked. 'I mean, three years down the line and every lunatic and extremist is locked away. Then what? Does it get mothballed, or will they turn their attention to more mundane activities like rooting out internet trolls?'

'I have no idea, Len, but before it got that far I expect they'd target drug dealers, criminal gangs, paedophiles and a host of others from the arse end of society. All I really know is, it can make a big difference.'

Gray had to admit to himself that there were positives to take from it, and as he wasn't involved in any illegal activities it shouldn't affect his life too much. But still . . . . Well, the time for hand-wringing was over. 'All right, everyone, let's concentrate on the mission.'

Harvey told them to focus on committing the information he was about to give them to memory. 'Because of these surveillance restrictions, once you meet Kyle, you'll have to fill him in—in person. I'll come up with a reason to get him to Abuja and you'll have to handle it from there.'

It took twenty minutes for Harvey to explain what was required, and once they were able to recite it all back he prepared to leave.

'What about weapons?' Sonny asked.

'You'll have to pick some up when you get there.' Harvey checked his watch. 'I'm afraid I have to leave right now.' He nodded at the group and made for the front door, but as he reached it, he stopped and turned to the three men.

'Seriously, do not breathe a word of this to anyone. I'm probably under special surveillance because of what I know, which means they'll know I've met you and they'll be looking through your browsing habits for anything out of the ordinary. Just keep using your electronic devices as normal until the mission starts, but once you set off, leave them here.'

And with that, Harvey dashed out into the rain, leaving Gray and his men to make their final preparations.

Chapter 31

17 December 2014

Andrew Harvey's cab pulled up outside the address in Pimlico and he gave the driver a reasonable tip before climbing out and taking in the surroundings. The row of white terraced buildings stretched down the street, each one fronted by black metal railings, and he knew it was an area out of his reach, given his meagre salary. How Thompson could afford it wasn't his business, but he suspected it wasn't down to diligent savings and shrewd investments.

He rang the bell and the door was answered a minute later by Thompson dressed in a white towelling robe. As he entered the hallway, he smiled and held up the bottle of red wine he'd brought along. Thompson ignored it and pushed him up against the wall, her mouth latching onto his.

The kiss was fleeting, and as Thompson pulled away she let her hand brush over his crotch.

'I was just about to take a shower,' she smiled. 'Join me.'

Thirty minutes later, a naked Harvey nursed a glass of Simone Rouge on the double bed while Thompson combed her silky, blonde hair at the vanity table.

'Nice place you've got,' he said. 'Six must pay a lot better than our mob.'

'Hardly,' she laughed. 'It belongs to a relative and I get to rent it at a huge discount.'

That explained a lot, but Harvey wondered who exactly could afford to rent out such a property at knockdown prices. He made a mental note to follow up on it.

'So, what progress have you made with Michael West?' he asked.

'He disappeared off the face of the earth two weeks ago. I sent someone round to Bicknell Security and got the name of his client, but they said West and his team just upped sticks and left them high and dry.'

'I'm sure Brigandicuum will be able to locate him,' Harvey said, but Thompson shook her head.

'I asked, but Manello isn't hopeful. We've found little in the way of social media activity on West, so we can't add his Facebook or Twitter accounts as keywords and wait for a hit. Tony uploaded West's last known email address as one of the search parameters, but so far all we've got are hits from marketing firms and the usual spammers.'

'What about the old-fashioned way? Have you checked for passport usage, credit card transactions, all the usual stuff we had to make do with a week ago?'

'We tried all that and came up empty,' Thompson said.

'Okay, so West aside, what have you found in Nigeria?'

'We hit a dead end. The chief wanted to send a team over there, but the foreign secretary ruled it out. Apparently, the Nigerian president wasn't happy with the thought of us trampling all over their own investigation into the Kano bombing as it would make them look incompetent in the eyes of the world. President Habbas said his armed forces—such as they are—had found no suggestion of DSA involvement in the UK attacks apart from the video claiming responsibility, and that could have been made by anyone.'

'I'd have thought he'd have welcomed international help,' Harvey said. 'He'd have had the opportunity to mount a large multinational operation against DSA and rid his country of them.'

'Frankly, he seems a bit pissed off that his country is caught up in this at all.'

'Then send a covert team in,' Harvey suggested, but again Thompson shook her head.

'The foreign secretary was adamant that we not go against their wishes. We do have one man on the ground, but so far he hasn't come up with anything to contradict the official reports. And with DSA's leaders all dead now . . . .' She shrugged. 'I don't expect much to come of it.'

'So that's it? Investigation over?'

'Temporarily,' Thompson said, moving over to join him on the bed. 'And that's enough about work.'

Her hand started at his ankle and slowly climbed up past his knee and to his groin, where she found him ready and waiting.

When Harvey arrived at the office the next morning he went straight to Hamad Farsi's desk and asked him what he'd found on Michael West.

'Considering the nature of the business, Bicknell Security isn't that secure.' Farsi handed over a handwritten sheet of A4. As instructed the previous day, he'd recorded his findings using only pen and paper. 'I managed to get into their office late last night and locate the file on West. The meat of it's on there.'

Harvey scanned the document and noted the name Harcourt Industries Limited. 'It says this is his current employer. Have you spoken to them yet?'

'Not easy,' Farsi said. 'They don't exist. No record of them at Companies House, and the address turned out to be a dairy distribution centre in Swindon.'

Despite what had gone on between them over the last couple of days, Harvey had suspected that Thompson wouldn't be as forthcoming as she'd promised, which was why he'd sent Farsi on the nocturnal mission. It was obvious that his suspicions were correct: Thompson was shutting him out.

Harvey thanked Farsi and went to report to Ellis. He found her pacing behind her desk, and he could see that she wasn't in the best of moods.

'Thompson's holding out on us,' he said, explaining what he'd been told the previous evening and the information Farsi had uncovered.

'She's the least of my worries right now.' Ellis snatched a document from her desk and waved it at Harvey. 'Brigandicuum has been online for less than a week and they're already shaping policy around it. According to the home secretary's office, the number of staff we need going forward is going to be greatly reduced thanks to the amount of accurate information the new system will provide. Budget cuts of thirty percent are being considered, with a consultation process beginning in two weeks' time.'

'They're cutting our numbers?'

'So they say,' Ellis said, holding up the paper. 'A new rapid-reaction force is being set up to deal with the operational side of things, and our role will be to co-ordinate arrests based on the information we get from Haddon Hall.'

'That's it?' Harvey asked. 'We don't even get to analyse the data ourselves?'

'Apparently that function is no longer a required step in proceedings. With Brigandicuum being foolproof, we just arrange to take them down.'

'Who handles the interviews?'

'It doesn't say, but don't expect it to be us.'

Harvey was shocked at how quickly things were moving. 'I find it amazing that they can come up with a completely new structure for the security services overnight,' he said. 'It usually takes the government years to plan a change this big.'

'They'll have been working on this since day one,' Ellis said. 'I guess they had everything worked out and were just waiting for it to go live.'

'It's a pity it didn't go live last week,' he said. 'We'd have saved a lot of lives.'

'Perhaps they weren't ready.'

'Oh, they were ready enough. The place was buzzing, and there was no sign of anything still being worked on. It was like they were just . . . .'

'Waiting for the right moment?' Ellis finished his sentence, and her words left them both deep in thought.

It was Harvey who broke the silence. 'Did you get the note I left you? Gray thinks James Farrar might be involved in the attacks.'

Ellis nodded. 'I got it, and I decided Gray was seeing ghosts. At least, that's what I thought yesterday.'

'And now?'

Ellis hit a number on her phone and asked Gerald Small to come to her office. While she waited for him to arrive, she asked Harvey for Thompson's mobile number, which he jotted down for her.

'Gerald,' Ellis said, when Small knocked on the door and entered, 'I need you to hack a phone for me.'

Harvey handed over the slip of paper and Small asked what in particular she was interested in.

'All conversations from this moment on.'

'And the reason we can't just route this through GCHQ . . . ?'

'It's sensitive,' she said. 'How long until you'll be ready to go?'

Small assured her that he could be in within ten minutes, and rushed back to his office to get things in motion. Ellis took a seat and asked Harvey what he thought about Gray's theory.

'Like you, I was sceptical,' he said, 'but having thought about it, who else would have a motive to specifically target Gray?'

'He works in the security business, so he must have pissed someone off along the way.'

'Bad enough to make them launch an attack on Britain?'

'Fair point,' Ellis conceded.

They were interrupted as her desk phone rang. It was Small, confirming that he was ready with a trace. Ellis hung up and hit a pre-set number on her mobile. When it connected, she asked for Manello.

'Hi, Tony. This is Veronica Ellis. I have a request for you.'

Harvey waited while his boss went through authentication measures and explained what she wanted from Brigandicuum.

'I need you to add James Farrar as a search parameter.'

Harvey waved his hands at her before making a cut-throat sign, but Ellis held up a finger to silence him. Eventually, she thanked Manello and hung up.

'I thought we were doing this on the quiet,' Harvey said. 'Why did you tip our hand?'

'I'm shaking the tree,' Ellis told him. 'Now we just have to wait and see what falls out.'

'So how was your first assignment?'

Despite Paul Mackenzie having been with Minotaur Logistics for over nine months, this was the first time Gray had managed to sit down and have a proper chat with him. The drive to the airport was the perfect opportunity for Gray to find out a bit more about his star recruit. He, Melissa and Mackenzie sat in the back of the car, while Smart drove and Sonny rode shotgun.

'Not bad. My principal liked to do things his own way, which meant some hairy moments, but mostly it was same old, same old.'

'That's why we get paid the big bucks,' Gray smiled. 'So tell me about yourself.'

Mackenzie explained that he'd joined the army at eighteen and served in the Parachute Regiment for five years before trying his arm at SAS selection. After making it through the gruelling six-month process he'd had a couple of stints in Iraq, making sergeant on his return. His most recent deployment had been to Afghanistan as part of Operation Moshtarak, where he'd led a patrol that included Michael West. It turned out that Mackenzie had actually testified at the subsequent court martial, but due to a lack of any other corroborating evidence, West had been found not guilty of murdering the civilian. The regiment, however, didn't like having its name sullied, and West had been returned to unit within a couple of weeks of the verdict.

'After he was RTU'd, I never heard from him again,' Mackenzie told Gray, 'though a mate told me he'd bought himself out of the army and gone contracting.'

'What about you?' Gray asked. 'Why did you leave? Your file said you'd just made E squadron.'

'It's a long story,' Mackenzie said, looking at the backs of his hands.

Gray looked too, and wondered if the problem had been down to the colour of Mackenzie's skin. One thing he'd rarely tripped across was racism within the regiment. On the rare occasions when it had reared its ugly head, it had never been aimed at one of their own.

Gray shrugged. 'Well, we've got a long journey ahead of us.'

Mackenzie still seemed hesitant, but after a few moments of silence he began to open up.

'I did it for a girl,' he said. 'We met just after I joined E squadron, and we soon hit it off. I spent most of my free time at her place and we rarely got out of bed. The problem is, she likes the little luxuries in life, and I couldn't afford them on what the army pays. So, I decided to quit and go contracting in the hope that I could make some decent money.'

'You'll certainly do that,' Gray assured him. 'I just can't believe you gave it all up for a woman.'

'She's kinda special.'

'They all are,' Gray agreed, 'and E squadron's loss is our gain. A man with your talents will be in high demand. I'm just glad we found you first.'

'That was a no-brainer,' Mackenzie said. 'I asked around for the best agency and your name came up every time. I plan to make myself indispensable for the next few years, and then once I've got a little tucked away I'll go into business for myself. I haven't decided what I'll do yet, but I like the thought of being my own boss.'

'There's nothing better,' Gray agreed.

'So what's this mission all about?'

'A simple security detail,' Gray told him. 'We're heading into DSA country, and as tensions are quite high, we'll need to be on our toes.'

Smart pulled off the A4 and onto the approach road for Heathrow Airport. Flights had resumed thirty-six hours earlier, though there was still a backlog of passengers trying to get away for the Christmas period. Thankfully, Abuja wasn't high on the destination list and Gray's three companions had been able to secure seats. As for Gray and Melissa, flights to southern Italy were at a premium, and he had no choice but to show up at the desk and try to get standby tickets.

Gray had booked them rooms at a hotel in Abuja for the next couple of days, which should be plenty of time for him to get to San Giovanni in Fiore, drop Melissa off and join up with his men.

'I need to hit the toilet,' Mackenzie said. 'See you in-country, boss.'

He walked off in the direction of the gents, and Gray gave Smart and Sonny some final instructions.

'When you see Kyle, bring him up to speed on what Andrew's looking for. Hopefully he can get things arranged by the time I get there.'

They parted company at the departure area, and Gray took Melissa to the desk of one of the budget airlines that flew to Rome and other points in southern Italy. He explained to the middle-aged woman behind the counter that his parents had been involved in a serious car crash and that he had to get to Lamezia Terme International Airport in Italy as soon as possible. His story was met with the requisite amount of sympathy and the news that everything was booked solid for the next few days.

'Could you at least put out an announcement that I'm willing to offer five hundred pounds for two seats?' Gray asked, desperation in his voice. 'I need to get there before they . . . .'

He let the words tail off.

The woman considered his dilemma, then relented, calling a supervisor and explaining Gray's situation. The moustached manager offered to do what he could, and returned fifteen minutes later with an elderly couple who had agreed to the offer of waiting for the next flight. Gray thanked them profusely and handed over the money, which they grasped as if it were Solomon's treasure.

With tickets arranged, Gray took his daughter to the check-in desk and handed over the single suitcase. Everything Gray needed for his onward journey was in his backpack, which he carried through to the departure gates.

The flight took off forty minutes later, the fully laden Boeing 737 climbing into a rain-soaked sky.

Veronica Ellis gripped the phone, wondering just what the hell was going on.

'I'm sorry, Juliet, but are you telling me I'm no longer allowed to decide which investigations I can touch?'

Ellis rarely used Home Secretary Harper's first name when conversing with her, but after being told to drop the Farrar case, she wasn't concerned about the breach in protocol.

'Not at all. I just think Sarah Thompson is best equipped to take this particular enquiry forward.'

'I don't understand how,' Ellis argued. 'From what I've heard, she's been tasked with following up on the Nigerian aspect of the bombings. I would have thought she'd appreciate us taking Farrar off her hands.'

'Sarah's team may be overloaded at the moment, but you will soon find yourself in the same position. I'm looking at more than thirty terror threats on my screen right now, all picked up by Haddon Hall. They'll be routed through to you shortly.'

'Okay,' Ellis said, trying her best to sound contrite. 'I'll let my team know.'

'You do that,' Harper said. 'And one last thing. Any further requests for access to the new system have to go through me.'

The phone went dead in her hand, and Ellis slowly replaced it in the cradle. She didn't like to admit it, but Gray might have been on to something when he suspected Farrar of being involved in the bombings.

And her shaking of the tree had yielded fruit. Manello had clearly contacted Thompson to report Ellis's interest in Farrar.

Ellis knew this because Gerald Small's eavesdropping on Thompson's mobile phone had already proved successful. The second call placed by Thompson had been to the home secretary's own mobile phone. The message had been brief and to the point.

Ellis is looking into Farrar.

Now, having spoken to the home secretary, Ellis knew why nothing about Farrar had been forwarded to her by Manello, and that it never would be.

Ellis stuck her head out of the door and asked Harvey to join her. When he arrived, she told him to shut the door.

'It's official. We're not to go looking for James Farrar.' She relayed the conversation she'd just had with the home secretary, and how Manello had told Thompson about her request to find information on Farrar.

'So we suspect that Farrar might have had something to do with the bombings,' Harvey said with disbelief, 'but the minister doesn't want us poking our noses in?'

Ellis nodded.

'You know, I came up with a crazy take on this, and that just about seals it for me.'

'This whole thing has crazy written all over it,' Ellis said. 'What's on your mind?'

'Well, I was wondering about the timing of it all.'

'Go on.'

'See, Farrar was suddenly released on bail late last year, just a couple of months before Paul Roberts and his crew were recruited. Now I know the home secretary can't decide which judge gets to hear a particular case because that's the Lord Chief Justice's job. However, Harper might have been able to influence him enough to have someone sympathetic hear Farrar's appeal.'

'Clutching at straws,' Ellis said, 'but carry on.'

'According to Manello, Brigandicuum had been sitting idle for a year, just waiting to be activated, and suddenly they get orders to fully staff it a week before the attacks begin. Quite why it wasn't already operational, I don't know, but the PM has been spouting transparency like he means it. Maybe he wasn't comfortable with the idea of snooping on a global scale, and needed a massive jolt to convince him to unleash it.'

Ellis's eyebrows narrowed. 'Are you suggesting the bombings were staged—by us—as an excuse to turn Brigandicuum on?'

'The home secretary seems to be treating it like her own pet project. She decides what information we see and, from what you've told me, which investigations we can undertake. I also got news that the SAMs that took out the planes were ours. Old stock that had been taken away to be decommissioned. Looks like someone had different plans for them.'

Ellis sat down at her desk, considering Harvey's theory. Eventually, she shook her head.

'No, that can't be right. Juliet Harper is as ambitious as they come, but she would never condone an attack on British soil, aimed at her own people. More to the point, she knows what would happen if it ever got out.'

'Who would ever know?' Harvey asked. 'The DSA leadership blew themselves up, and the person assigned to search for James Farrar had us looking everywhere but central Africa. And when we try to launch our own investigation, we're told to drop it.'

'I think you've been hanging around Tom Gray for too long,' Ellis said, but she still mulled over the possibility that Harvey was right. 'Say I believe you. We'd need *irrefutable* proof before we started making accusations.'

'That's where it gets tricky,' Harvey said. 'The person controlling the information we need is our number one suspect.'

'Then we'll have to hope Kyle manages to unearth something useful.'

They were interrupted as Gerald Small knocked on the door and walked in, his laptop open and ready for use.

'I just got a couple of interesting text messages from the phone you asked me to monitor.'

He set the laptop down and turned it towards Ellis.

Gray and 3 others on their way to Kano via Abuja.

Reason?

Not yet known.

Stay close.

'Someone knows Gray is on his way,' Harvey said. 'They must have been watching him.'

'I thought I told you not to send Gray,' Ellis said sharply.

'There was little I could do. When he made a connection to Farrar, there was no stopping him. He isn't under any travel restrictions, and I could hardly have him arrested for leaving the country.'

'Of course you could!' Ellis said. 'I could think of a dozen reasons for taking his passport, not least hampering our investigation.'

'Which we're not officially undertaking,' Harvey pointed out.

Ellis slumped in her chair and rubbed her temples. She'd met Gray only a couple of times, but knew how hard-headed the ex-soldier could be. He exuded a steely determination and was fiercely loyal to his close friends, though he could be as slippery as a Teflon eel when it suited him.

'If this goes pear-shaped, it's on your head.'

Harvey nodded, her words clearly hitting home.

'Judging by those texts,' he said, 'pear-shaped would be a great outcome. I'll have to warn Kyle to expect trouble.'

'Do it, but be careful,' Ellis warned.

'I'll send someone out to get me an unregistered cell and give him a call.'

Ellis stood, walking to the door and opening it. 'I also want you to ask Hamad to speak to Paul Roberts. If Farrar really is involved, then this Efram character might be a friend or former colleague. You said Roberts couldn't identify him from current staff, so we might as well check those who left in the last couple of years. And anyone associated with Farrar.'

'Will do.'

'Gerald, any luck getting into Harper's phone?'

'Locked down tighter than the PM's since the hacking scandal,' Small told her.

Ellis had expected as much. 'I'd like you to keep trying,' she said. 'And find out all you can about the phone that texted Thompson.'

As she watched Harvey and Small walk back to their stations, Ellis collapsed in her chair, knowing that she must now contemplate the ultimate in worst-case scenarios.

Chapter 32

18 December 2014

'Melissa!'

Mina Hatcher plucked her granddaughter from Gray's arms and squeezed, planting a big kiss on the girl's head. 'You're getting so big!'

Gray was glad to let someone else take control of his daughter while he dealt with the suitcase and hand luggage. Ken Hatcher helped out, taking one of the lighter bags while he led Gray to the airport car park.

'How long are you staying for?' Mina asked. 'At least until Boxing Day, I hope. We want to see this gorgeous creature open her presents.'

Gray looked sheepish. 'Sorry to spring this on you, but something big came up. Can you please take care of Melissa while I go and do a job?'

The Hatchers looked concerned. 'What kind of job?' Mina asked, and Ken wanted to know how long they were talking about. Months? A year?

'Only a week,' Gray assured them. 'A Saudi prince personally requested that I lead his security team while he's visiting Britain, and I can hardly turn down one of my biggest customers.'

Gray felt uncomfortable with the lie, but he didn't want to worry his in-laws unnecessarily. The gig he'd mentioned sounded a lot less ominous than travelling into DSA territory.

'Of course we'll look after her,' Mina said. 'I just wish you'd let us know when you called.'

'I'm sorry, but the prince is paranoid when it comes to phone conversations. His representative insisted I not mention the visit to anyone, not even close relatives.'

His explanation seemed to satisfy them, and Ken asked when he planned to leave.

'My flight's in an hour,' Gray said, loading the suitcase into the boot of Ken's car. 'Everything Melissa needs is in there. She likes her vegetables, but I can't get her to eat red peppers.'

They spent a few minutes discussing Melissa's other needs, including the nappy rash that had started to develop over the last couple of days. Mina assured Gray that his daughter would be fine with them, and he took his time saying goodbye to her, promising to be back as soon as possible.

After a final kiss, Gray tore himself away from his daughter and walked back to the terminal, the ticket to Abuja tucked in his top pocket.

Hamad Farsi pulled up at the gates to Haddon Hall and found himself confronted by two guards, the bulges in their jackets clearly concealing side arms. One of them approached the car and Farsi wound down the window to show his ID. The guard checked the name against a clipboard and gave a nod. A moment later, the gates swung open.

'Park it round the back.'

Farsi thanked him and drove to the rear of the building, where the once-manicured lawn had been transformed into a car park.

Two helicopters sat off to one side, their pilots sitting in the cockpits, ready to leave at a moment's notice.

More security guards patrolled the area, and one of them checked Farsi's credentials again before indicating where to leave his saloon. The MI5 operative parked up and climbed out, laptop bag in hand. An escort took him into the building, where Tony Manello was waiting.

'Hamad, welcome.'

Farsi shook hands and asked where Roberts was being held.

'This way,' Manello said, leading him up the wide staircase.

Farsi knew that, apart from Roberts, thirteen other suspects from neighbouring regions were being held here. Ideally, all of the bombers would have been transferred to Haddon Hall, but with limited space, they were being rotated in and out as often as possible. Roberts himself had been scheduled to move to a recently re-commissioned maximum security facility that had been closed down a year earlier, so Farsi's request for access had come just in time. An hour later, and he'd have faced a five-hour drive to the north of England to interview his man.

He found Roberts sitting in a room not much bigger than a closet. Farsi thought it implausible that the sad figure before him could have caused such devastation. The slumped figure looked nearly inert, the bruises on his arms and face recent. He sat in a wheelchair and had a cast covering his lower leg and foot.

Roberts briefly looked up as Farsi entered the room, then let his head droop once more, looking every inch a beaten man.

'Have you got another room available?' Farsi asked. 'I need to go through some mugshots with him.'

Manello guided Farsi and the handcuffed, chair-bound Roberts down the hall and into the interrogation suite. Farsi declined the offer of a guard inside the room, and Manello closed the door on his way out.

After setting up the laptop on the metal table, Farsi brought up the list of ex-government employees and asked Roberts to take a close look at each one. While the prisoner skipped from one profile to the next, Farsi stood behind him.

Prior to leaving Thames House, Farsi had checked each record to see if any of the men had a connection to James Farrar. There was one hit, an intern who'd worked for him for a couple of years before moving to the Home Office. Farsi had placed the prime suspect at number nineteen on the list, hoping to avoid any chance of a false-positive identification.

When Roberts reached number nineteen, he skipped past the picture, then paused and went back.

'I think that's him.'

'You sure?' Farsi asked. 'You said he had black hair. This guy's blond.'

'It's him,' Roberts insisted. 'The hair's different, but I know the face. I saw him just a couple of days ago.'

Satisfied that they had the right man, Farsi took the laptop, closed it down and knocked on the door.

'Am I going to get anything in return for my help?' Roberts asked, unable to conceal his desperation.

As the door opened, Farsi turned and locked eyes. 'Sure. I'll see to it that you get to share a cell with the most vicious sodomist in the system.'

Farsi left the room, Roberts's pleas for mercy falling on deaf ears. He thanked Manello for his help, and once back in his car he pulled out his phone and dialled a pre-set number.

'We have confirmation,' he said, heeding Harvey's warning not to share anything specific over the phone. 'Have you made progress?'

'Plenty. I'll fill you in when you get back.'

'Okay. On my way.'

Once he reached the main road, Farsi turned on the radio and tuned it to a news channel, where the reporter brought him up to date on the clean-up process. Traffic was just about back to normal throughout the country, and airports indicated that the backlog of flights would be clear in the next three days. The power companies were still taking things cautiously, though they believed they could have ninety-five percent of the electricity supply restored within a week.

On the down side, the official death toll had risen to more than nine thousand and was expected to reach five figures in the coming days. The economic cost was also mounting, with clean-up estimates ranging from six billion to thirty billion, and that was before the knock-on effect was factored in. Businesses were suffering as investors fled the country, while the stock market was at its lowest in more than twenty years.

The home secretary's announcement of 'enhanced surveillance methods' had made the headlines, though the opposition parties claimed she'd done too little too late, and that the worst atrocity in Britain's history had happened on her watch. Despite calls for her resignation, Juliet Harper remained defiant, highlighting the fact that the attacks had been neutralised within forty-eight hours, thanks to the skill and dedication of the security services.

Farsi knew it was a bullshit statement meant to pacify her detractors. If it hadn't been for the new system, they'd still be sifting through what little CCTV coverage was available while the attacks continued around them.

He arrived back at Thames House just over an hour later, the light traffic having been kind to him. Once he reached the office, he went straight to Harvey's desk.

'What do we have?'

'Our friend Joel Haskins—AKA Efram—disappeared yesterday. As you know, he quit his post at the Home Office a couple of days before the attacks, and the last sighting was by Roberts. Since then, no credit- or debit-card transactions, his mobile phone is off, and the lease on his flat expires in three days' time, all paid up.'

'Looks like he wasn't planning to hang around,' Farsi said. 'Any record of him leaving the country?'

'Not on his own passport, and facial recognition at the major airports hasn't found any matches.'

'If he's involved, he'll have planned an escape that can't be tracked,' Farsi mused. 'I'll get someone to dig up a list of private airfields and see if any flights left for the continent in the last seven days.'

'There's another possibility,' Harvey said. 'I did a check on Farrar's assets and he had a boat moored at Brighton Marina. It's nothing special, but could easily make it across the Channel. I called the harbour master an hour ago and he told me it left last night.'

'Destination unknown, I'm guessing.'

'You guess correctly, but I've alerted the French, Belgian and Dutch authorities to be on the lookout for it.'

'And what have you asked them to do if he turns up?' Farsi asked. 'Take him in?'

'No,' Harvey said. 'I'll bet a month's salary that he's going to join up with the others behind this. I want to put a tail on him and see who he leads us to.'

'Who are you going to send?' Farsi asked.

Harvey's smile said it all.

'Go get yourself a new legend and be ready to move.'

Chapter 33

19 December 2014

A weary Tom Gray reached the Hilton in Abuja just after seven in the morning. He hadn't managed any sleep on the two flights from Italy, and he wanted nothing more than to crash in a comfortable hotel bed for the next twenty-four hours.

As he entered the expansive reception, that dream was dashed as Sonny crept up behind him and slapped him on the shoulder.

'Morning, Tom! Ready to go?'

Gray turned, and over Sonny's shoulder he saw Smart, Mackenzie and Kyle Ackerman walking down the stairs, their luggage in tow.

'You have to be kidding.'

'Sorry, mate. The plane's booked for nine thirty. Kyle checked the arrival time of your flight and got us on the first one available.'

Ackerman approached and ran a hand through his short brown hair before shaking hands with Gray.

'Good to see you again, Tom.'

They stood the same height, though Ackerman was a good twenty pounds leaner than Gray.

'Likewise. I hear we're heading out now.'

'Harvey's orders,' Ackerman said, then dropped his voice to a conspiratorial whisper. 'Once we leave the hotel, keep your eyes peeled. It seems someone knows we're here and where we're going.'

Gray was instantly alert, and his first thoughts were for Melissa. If someone knew about their travel arrangements, they must surely know where she was, which meant she was in danger.

'My daughter . . . .'

'Andrew didn't mention that,' Ackerman said, pulling out a mobile phone. 'I'll let him know, and—'

Gray stopped him with a hand on his arm, glaring over at Sonny. 'Didn't the guys warn you not to use one of those?'

'They did, but it's for emergencies only. Andrew told me to get a clean cell in case we had urgent news. I'd say this was critical.'

Gray removed his hand and let Ackerman dial. 'Just keep it brief and to the point.'

'There's an issue with our friend's youngest,' Ackerman said when the call connected, and Gray leaned in closer to hear the conversation from both ends. 'We might need child protective services to pay her a visit. Just precautionary.'

'I'll need details,' the tinny voice said, and Ackerman looked to Gray for inspiration.

'Just tell him the lawyer knows where the relatives live,' Gray whispered, and Ackerman passed on the message.

'I'm on it,' said Harvey's distant voice, and the call ended.

'That good enough for you?' Ackerman asked, and Gray nodded, though he knew he wouldn't be able to shake this new feeling of dread.

'She'll be fine,' Sonny said. 'Let's get this done so we can go and pick her up.'

'Speaking of which,' Ackerman said, 'what's the mission? Andrew was vague, to say the least.'

'I'll fill you in when we get to Kano,' Gray said, looking round for signs of anyone taking an interest in the group.

They filed out of the hotel and into a waiting taxi, and Mackenzie climbed into the back next to Gray.

'What's the problem with your daughter?'

'It's probably nothing,' Gray told him. 'I just worry about her too much.'

'Sonny told me you've had an incident-packed few days,' Mackenzie said. 'Doesn't sound like nothing to me.'

'Well, she's safe for now, and this will soon be over.'

'Sonny said you don't like leaving her with others. It must be a wrench being away from her.'

'Sonny talks too much,' Gray snapped, then instantly regretted it. Mackenzie wasn't the focus of his anger at the moment, and it wasn't fair to take it out on him. 'Sorry. She . . . she's with her grandparents in Italy. It's only for a few days, just until this mission's over.'

'Still, it must be hard, for both of you.'

You have no idea, Gray thought.

No idea at all.

When they finally arrived at the airport, Mackenzie was the first out of the taxi. He hauled his bag from the boot and stood with a pained expression while the others grabbed their belongings and paid the driver.

'What's up?' Gray asked.

'I really need a dump,' Mackenzie said, as they set off in a rush towards the check-in gates. They arrived with a couple of minutes to spare, and after exchanging their tickets for boarding passes, Mackenzie asked them to hang around while he went to the toilet.

'Sorry, but I hate shitting on planes.'

'Be quick,' Gray warned. 'We've only got a few minutes before boarding closes.'

Mackenzie dropped his bag at Gray's feet and jogged to the toilet, which gave off an unwelcoming odour as he opened the door. Inside he found a row of cubicles, two of which were unoccupied, and after dismissing the first with its overflowing bowl, he entered the second and locked the door.

He pulled down his trousers and retrieved the mobile phone that was strapped to his inner thigh, then quickly typed out a message and hit the Send button. Once the text had been sent, he quickly removed the battery and SIM card from the phone and dropped them into the cistern. He opened the cubicle door, and after checking that none of his party was around, he stepped out and dumped the rest of the phone in the waste paper bin. Ideally he would have taken it onto the plane, but there was always the chance it would be detected as he went through security, and he'd have a hard time explaining it away to the others.

As he made his way back, he felt just the slightest trace of guilt at the thought of betraying Gray. He was a fine man, according to Smart and Baines, and in the little time he'd spent with the man, he'd found nothing to contradict those sentiments.

Getting close to Gray hadn't been that hard, given his training. He knew he stood out among the other Minotaur contractors, so securing a training position with Gray's company had been a doddle. The only uncertain part had been getting into Gray's inner circle, but spending his days working as an instructor alongside Sonny, as well as the socialising, had done the trick.

While he hadn't had a real chance to get to know Gray personally, he knew plenty about him. He'd used the internet to glean most of the information he'd needed, with his bosses and Gray's friends providing the rest.

Gray was indeed a remarkable man, who'd been through a hell of a lot in the last few years, but business was business, and

Mackenzie was being paid handsomely to stick close to him. To what end, he didn't yet know, but he felt the moment was drawing closer.

Back at the check-in gates, he joined up with the others and they made their way through security and to the boarding gates. His little diversion meant they were the last to board, and he once again took a seat next to Gray in order to find out even more about his boss's past.

Andrew Harvey knocked on Ellis's door and walked in, dragging Small after him.

'Sorry, Veronica, but Gerald's got something.'

The technician placed his open laptop on her table and showed her some text on the screen.

'This was intercepted from Thompson's phone a few minutes ago,' he explained.

Ellis read the short message and the colour began to drain from her cheeks.

Gray's kid in Italy with grandparents.

'When did this come in?' she asked.

'A couple of minutes ago,' Small said. 'I tried to track the sender, but the phone is off.'

Ellis stood and paced the room. 'Did you warn Gray that someone was following them?'

Harvey nodded. 'I was told that his daughter was with relatives, and Gray's accountant confirmed that Melissa's grandparents have a place in southern Italy. Someone must have overheard my conversation with Kyle.'

'Or they're monitoring all of your calls,' Small suggested.

'Unlikely. I used a burner cell and didn't even buy it myself. No-one could possibly know about it.'

'Well, from what Veronica's told me about Brigandicuum, it's possible that they have voice-matching capabilities, too. Once you speak to someone over the phone, your voice could trigger a download.'

There were so many possibilities, yet none of them struck Harvey as the obvious choice. Could someone with a directional microphone have overheard Ackerman's side of the conversation? Or was Brigandicuum more powerful than Manello had let on?

'However they did it, our priority is to make sure Gray's daughter is safe,' Ellis said. 'God knows what he'll do if anything happens to her.'

'I've already got two assets watching the place,' Harvey said.

'Something tells me that's not going to be enough. Ask them to collect the grandparents and the girl and take them to a safe house until this is over. They may or may not be targets, but I'm taking no chances. I don't have to remind you that we wouldn't have to do this if Gray was still at home.'

Harvey took the jibe on the chin, his mind suddenly focused on the message on the screen. There was something about it that cried out to him, but he couldn't quite make the connection. He leaned in and read it again, but frustratingly nothing jumped out at him.

'What is it?' Ellis asked.

'I'm not sure,' Harvey said, and explained the feeling he had about the text. 'I'm sure it'll come to me.'

'If it does, let me know. Now, go and get those assets moving.'

'I'm guessing you don't want me to tell Gray about this latest message,' Harvey said, as he walked to the door.

'No, just let him focus on the mission. You can explain when he's on his way back.'

Harvey and Small left Ellis's office, with the technician heading back to his own little kingdom. Harvey picked a brand new cell phone from his drawer and dialled the number of the operative who was keeping a watch over the Hatcher place.

'I need you to move in, identify yourself to the three occupants and take them somewhere safe. Tell them I ordered this on behalf of a friend.'

With the instructions relayed, he tried to concentrate on the message on Gerald's laptop, but the answer remained tantalisingly out of reach.

Chapter 34

19 December 2014

Tom Gray had to be shaken awake as the plane made its final approach to Mallam Aminu Kano International Airport. His watch told him he'd managed just over an hour, and he felt worse for having had the short nap.

A headache threatened to add to his misery as he trudged off the plane with the others, and he was pleased to discover that their first port of call was the hotel Ackerman had booked.

After a thirty-minute taxi ride they pulled up outside the building, and Gray didn't care that it looked two-star at best; he just wanted to get his head down for a while.

'What's the plan?' Ackerman asked, as they waited for the receptionist to book them in.

'I'll tell you once we get into the rooms,' Gray said quietly, conscious of two strangers in the lobby.

The party walked up the stairs and piled into the small room assigned to Gray and Ackerman. Smart opened a window to let out the musty smell while the others took a seat on the two wooden-framed single beds. The room was functional at best, with a side table and chair, and an en-suite with toilet and shower.

'Andrew identified a phone signal believed to have been used by the leaders of the attack,' Gray said. 'It's coming from a hospital, so he's assuming someone managed to escape the blast that killed their hierarchy. He wants us to go and speak to the survivor, if there is one.'

'What if he's already been discharged?' Ackerman asked.

'Assuming it's a male, Sonny will use his charms on a nurse and find out where he lives.'

Sonny folded his arms, acting humble but clearly flattered at being chosen for the role.

'He could also be dead,' Mackenzie pointed out.

'Andrew realises that, but he wants us to at least try. If we can get someone to give us a description of their leader Takasa, it will help in tracking him down.'

'So what else do you have in mind?' Ackerman asked.

'We go through the passenger lists for the three days either side of the explosion. Hamad Farsi tried, but the data is held on a closed network at the airline.'

'All right,' said Ackerman. 'I already know about that. Sonny told me while we were waiting for you to arrive from Italy. I've already called ahead and made arrangements. It could be tens of thousands of names to go through, though.'

'According to Andrew, the airport has seen record-low numbers of passengers this year, apparently due to DSA's presence in the area. Hopefully it won't be that big a job.'

'I suggest we hit the hospital first,' Smart said. 'If we can get a description, it'll be easier to filter the passenger records.'

'Sounds like a plan,' Ackerman said. 'Let's get going.'

Gray yawned and fell backwards onto the bed.

'Do you guys need me to be there?' he asked.

'Not at all,' Smart said. 'Grab a couple of hours. We'll be back soon.'

Ackerman led the way through the bustling market towards the hospital, ignoring the vendors as they clamoured for a sale. It was heavy going, as each stall owner wanted to offload something on the tourists, and by the time they managed to battle their way to the far end, the journey had taken longer than expected. They'd assumed they could manage the one-kilometre walk in less than twenty minutes but had already spent that long fighting off spice salesmen. They also drew stares from a few of their fellow shoppers, making the team wary and alert.

When they eventually arrived at the hospital, Ackerman found the reception desk and introduced himself.

'Hi. My name's Kyle and I'm from the British High Commission in Pretoria.'

The nurse looked distinctly unimpressed and waited for him to continue.

'We are looking for a white male, aged twenty-seven, who went missing at around the time of an explosion just off Kufar Mata Road near the old city. Did you hear about it?'

The nurse nodded but clearly wasn't about to offer up any further information.

'The man I'm looking for is called Michael Andrews. Has anyone by that name been brought here in the last few days?'

The nurse rifled through a pile of papers, then shook her head. 'Perhaps he was taken to City Hospital.'

'We've already tried there,' Ackerman lied. 'They said he was most likely here. Was anyone involved in the explosion admitted to this hospital?'

'Yes, but he wasn't a white male.'

'It would really help if I could speak to him, to ask if he saw Michael in the area just before the blast.'

The nurse picked up a phone and spoke in her native language, then pointed to some chairs and asked the group to wait.

'What do you think?' Sonny asked the others as they took their seats.

'She called a doctor and asked him to come and deal with us,' Mackenzie said.

'You speak Hausa?' Ackerman asked.

Mackenzie nodded. 'My father spoke it when I was growing up.'

Ackerman rose as a doctor wearing a stereotypical white gown approached them, the mandatory stethoscope around the neck completing the ensemble.

'I'm Doctor Akulna,' he said, shaking Ackerman's hand. 'I understand you were enquiring about one of my patients.'

Ackerman once again went through the cover story, glad to find the doctor slightly more receptive to his request.

'Beke Anwo was seriously injured in the blast, though we have managed to stabilise him. I'm not sure he would be up to any questioning, though.'

'I'd like to at least try,' Ackerman said. 'Michael's family are most concerned, and if we can establish that he wasn't in the area, it would be a great comfort to them.'

'Very well, but I can't allow you all into his room. Two of you can remain here.'

'Okay, I'll take Len,' Ackerman said.

'You'd be better off taking Mack,' Smart said. 'His Hausa might come in handy.'

Ackerman agreed, and the pair followed the doctor up the stairs and along the corridor to Anwo's room. Inside, they found him lying in the bed, both legs and his left arm encased in plaster. An oxygen tube was taped under his nose, and a drip fed clear liquid into his right arm.

A nurse was spoon-feeding him a clear broth, and she looked up when they entered.

'How's our patient doing?' the doctor asked.

'Very hungry,' the nurse told him, as she emptied the last morsel from the bowl. 'I'll go and get some more.'

She left the room, and Akulna pulled down the bed covers and examined the bandages wrapped tightly around Anwo's chest. His hands then moved up to the swollen face.

'You're a very lucky man,' the doctor told him, but got no response. Anwo appeared to be focused on the other two men in the room. The doctor made way for them, and Ackerman was the first to approach the bed.

'Hello, Beke. My name is Kyle. I'd like to ask you a few questions about the explosion, if that's okay.'

Anwo gave him a puzzled look, and the doctor explained why. 'The explosion perforated his eardrums, so you'll have to speak slowly and clearly.'

Ackerman repeated his request, and Anwo nodded his head.

'Thank you,' Ackerman said, pulling a chair up to the bed and sitting down. 'First of all, what were you doing in the area when the bomb went off?'

'I was just walking past,' Anwo replied, his voice hoarse, and Ackerman could see broken teeth as he spoke. 'Luckily there was a big car between me and the building. It must have saved me.'

Ackerman nodded and began describing the fictional Michael Andrews. 'Did you see anyone in the area who looked like that?'

The doctor excused himself, and once he'd left the room, Ackerman's manner changed instantly. 'Where's your phone?' he asked, leaning over Anwo.

Mackenzie was already at work, rummaging through a plastic bag containing shredded, bloodied clothes. When he stumbled across the handset, he pulled it out and held it up.

'Explain to me how you came to own a phone that was used to plan the recent attacks on Britain,' Ackerman said.

'I don't know anything.'

But Anwo's face betrayed him, as did the machine monitoring his heart rate.

'Let me try,' Mackenzie said. He placed the phone on the bed stand and stood over Anwo, pressing down on his bandaged chest just hard enough to cause discomfort. '*Kake jin Hausa?*' Do you speak Hausa?

Anwo nodded slightly, and Mackenzie continued. '*Kada ka damu, ni a nan ya taimake ka.*' Do not worry, I am here to help you.

The injured man looked confused, but Mackenzie continued in Hausa. 'I was sent by your master. This man wants to track him down and kill him, but I will not let that happen. You must refuse to answer any more of his questions. Do you understand?'

Anwo nodded again.

'Good. Now, talk to me as if you were angry. Do it quickly.'

The bed-ridden man began shouting in Hausa, all the time glaring into Mackenzie's eyes.

'Excellent. Now, I want you to start screaming for the nurse, as loud as you can. When she comes, just tell her you need to go to the toilet.'

Anwo tried to shout, but the bandages restricted his diaphragm, and it came out more of a yelp.

'Louder,' Mackenzie urged, 'and once we leave, phone someone to pick you up and take you to a safe house. They'll be back for you.'

He gestured for the man to be quiet, solely for Ackerman's benefit, then moved quickly towards the door as Anwo released a more powerful cry.

'He refuses to talk,' Mackenzie said to Ackerman. 'He's calling for the police. We'd better leave.'

They walked quickly away from the room and hurried back down the stairs, whispering a quick 'Time to go' when they passed

Smart and Sonny in the reception area. Once out of the building, they jogged along for half a kilometre before slowing to a walk.

'What did you get out of him?' Sonny asked, as they made their way back to the hotel.

'Nothing,' Mackenzie said. 'We tried to question him, but he started screaming for the police. We couldn't hang around after that.'

'Do you think he was involved?'

'Definitely,' Ackerman said.

'So what now?'

'We'll have to rely on the airport records,' Ackerman told Sonny. 'Unless you've got any better ideas?'

'How about paying him a late-night visit?'

'Risky,' Ackerman said, 'and we're not here to draw attention to ourselves.'

'It shouldn't be too difficult,' Sonny pressed. 'Up the drain-pipe, pop the window and have a quick, aggressive chat.'

'Let's call that plan B, shall we?'

Five minutes into the slog through the market, Mackenzie spotted a stall offering a vast selection of mobile phones and, knowing that he'd need one to pass on the latest developments, he formed a quick and simple plan.

He waited until they'd managed to cover another fifty yards, then tapped Ackerman on the shoulder.

'I saw a shawl back there that my girl would love. You guys go ahead. I'll catch you up.'

Ackerman was about to protest, but Mackenzie offered a quick smile and a pat on the shoulder, then jogged into the crowd.

Tom Gray woke to a growling stomach, and his watch told him he'd been sleeping for barely forty minutes. The headache that had been threatening for the last half day had finally abated, but he still felt dehydrated. He climbed out of bed and went into the en-suite toilet, where he ran the cold tap for a few moments, hoping for the water to change from a dull rust colour to something more palatable.

He gave up after a couple of minutes, though he used a mouthful of it while brushing his teeth and a splash more to sort out his hair. Looking slightly more respectable, he walked down to the lobby and popped his head into what appeared to be the restaurant, but the place was deserted. With no other choice, he asked the receptionist for directions to the hospital before strolling out into the heat of the afternoon, the plan being to try to join up with his men and grab some sustenance on the way.

In the distance he could see the building his friends had gone to, and he walked towards it, keeping an eye out for a shop that would provide him with food and drink. The first place he came to sorted out his thirst problem, and he followed his nose in search of something more substantial than the airline meals that had seen him through the last couple of days.

The aroma of spices drew him towards Kurmi Market. Alas, the first stalls he encountered offered only the uncooked versions of local cuisine. He continued onwards through the maze, trying his best to explain to the locals that he didn't want a wooden crocodile statue, just something to fill his stomach.

He eventually came across a rickety wooden stand that had cooked chicken hanging from metal hooks, and he took a chance on a bowl of what looked like curry. It was served with unleavened bread, and, despite looking rather unpleasant, tasted delicious.

Gray emptied the bowl in double-quick time and was contemplating another helping when he looked through the back of the stall and saw someone familiar in the adjacent aisle. He watched as Paul Mackenzie thrust a handful of the local currency into the hands of a cloth salesman in exchange for a multi-coloured wrap, but the tall recruit's real focus was clearly on the next stall, which offered a wide selection of mobile devices. Scarf in hand, Mackenzie slid to the next stall and pointed to a flip-up handset. He didn't bother to dicker over the price, but simply handed over a fistful of naira, then disappeared back in the direction he'd come from.

Gray's face heated as he watched in disbelief. The one thing he'd hammered home to everyone was that phones were strictly off limits, yet here was Mackenzie buying a new handset. Why he'd need one, Gray wasn't sure, but he suspected it was so that he could stay in contact with his girlfriend, who certainly sounded high-maintenance.

Gray set off in pursuit, but something popped into his head and he checked his pace.

What if Mackenzie weren't going to use it to call his girlfriend? What if he wanted it to stay in touch with someone else?

He thought hard about what he knew about the man, and there wasn't that much. He remembered his CV mentioning that he'd left the army shortly after joining E squadron, which had struck Gray as odd at the time. Every member of the SAS wanted to be chosen for that particular unit, so to be given the opportunity only to walk away a few months later didn't add up. Even the recent revelation that there was a beautiful woman influencing his decision didn't feel right. Gray himself had been besotted with his first wife Dina but had made it clear from the start that he was SAS through and through. It was the birth of their son Daniel that finally prompted him to consider a different, safer line of work.

Gray let Mackenzie get a lead on him, then took a circuitous route back to the hotel, all the time considering his options. Confronting Mackenzie head-on was unlikely to be productive, so he thought up a couple of ways to find out exactly what Mackenzie's intentions were.

By the time he got back to his room, he had the basic plan in his head.

'I thought you were sleeping,' Smart said, as he walked into the room. 'We got worried when we came back and you were gone.'

'I needed something to drink,' Gray told him. 'How did it go?'

Ackerman told him about the brief meeting. 'Going back for a second interview is out of the question.'

'What about his phone? Is there anything useful on it?'

Ackerman looked over at Mackenzie, whose head dropped. 'I left it on the nightstand. When he started screaming, it completely slipped my mind.'

'There's always plan B,' Sonny reminded him, and before Ackerman could object, he explained what he had in mind.

'I like it,' Gray said after a moment's thought. 'Len, you and I will go with Kyle to get the airline passenger lists. Sonny, I want you and Mackenzie to scope out the hospital from the exterior and let me know if you're going to need anything to make this happen.'

'Are you sure about this, Tom? It's incredibly risky.'

'Relax,' Gray smiled. 'It's what we do best. Let's get moving.'

Ackerman pulled a plastic bag from his hand luggage and followed Smart and Gray down the stairs and out into the street, where they flagged down a taxi. Once they had climbed in and pulled away, Gray told them that he had something entirely different on his mind.

'We're not going after the guy in the hospital,' he said, and got confused looks in return.

'Then why send Sonny and Mack to check it out?'

'I don't think we can trust Mackenzie,' Gray said.

'Because he forgot the phone?'

'That's part of it, but when I was in the market I saw him buy a new mobile.'

'Why the hell would he buy a phone?' Smart asked. 'We went over that.'

'Exactly my point,' Gray said. 'Leaving the guy's phone at the hospital is one thing, and it could be excused in a rookie, but this guy was in the top one percent of the regiment. To go on and disobey a clear order says there's more to Mackenzie than we thought.'

'So what do we do about it?' Ackerman asked.

'I need you to call Andrew.'

Gray gave Ackerman a set of instructions and listened in as they were relayed back to England.

'If you're right about this,' Ackerman said, as he ended the call, 'how do you want to handle it?'

'Sonny's plan B,' Gray said. 'A quick, aggressive chat.'

Chapter 35

19 December 2014

Andrew Harvey stood in the small kitchenette, stirring his coffee absently as he stared at nothing in particular. The revelation that Gray's man Mackenzie could be tied up in the whole mess had come as a shock, though it finally explained the source of the text messages to Thompson, the most recent one of which had read:

Gray's kid in Italy with grandparents.

He knew for a fact that Ackerman hadn't mentioned grandparents during their conversation, strengthening the argument against Mackenzie. All he had to do now was get irrefutable proof, and Gray's idea might just work, with a little tweaking.

He picked up the drink and walked back to his desk.

'Any news from the continent?' he asked Farsi.

'No sign of Farrar's yacht yet. I think he may have tried farther afield, so I've alerted the Spanish, Portuguese and Moroccan authorities in the south, along with Germany and the Scandinavians to the north. I can't imagine he'd go too much farther in that vessel.'

'Hopefully we can trick Mackenzie into giving us a heads-up on Farrar.'

'What do you have in mind?'

'When I get a pre-arranged text from Kyle, I'll call him ten minutes later and tell him we've found Farrar and that they can come home. If Mackenzie's the one passing info to Thompson, we'll know about it.'

'And if he's not the one?'

'Then we're back to square one, and we'd better hope they have a plan B.'

'You really think Farrar is behind all this?'

Harvey sat back in his chair and clasped his hands behind his head. 'To be honest, I still can't believe Juliet Harper is involved.'

'She's a politician.' Farsi shrugged, his statement needing no clarification. 'What should concern you more is Brigandicuum. I've been thinking about it, and there's no way this can be kept under wraps.'

'They have that covered,' Harvey told him. 'It's totally deniable. A press of a button and it's history. All traces will be wiped.'

'You really think it'll be that simple?'

'They've been planning this for years. I think they'll have all bases covered.'

'Then how do we make a conviction stick? We're working on the premise that Harper set the attacks in motion in order to get this thing online. If we have no proof that Brigandicuum exists, what case do we have?'

'That's exactly what I was thinking,' Harvey said. 'And if we do get proof, we can kiss the world's greatest anti-terrorist system goodbye.'

'So it's a trade-off. Either we let Harper get away with it, or we lose Brigandicuum.'

Harvey had come to the same conclusion a few hours earlier, and he still wasn't sure which was the best outcome. Brigandicuum was undoubtedly the best tool they had, and it would help immensely in the war against terror, but at what price? Was it worth the lives of almost ten thousand British citizens, not to mention those visitors from other countries caught up in the carnage? Could he consciونably allow Harper to get away with mass murder in order to prevent further atrocities? His heart said no, but the thought of throwing away their greatest asset meant making a decision was almost impossible.

Still, he knew, he had to get the proof first; deciding what to do with it would come later.

He got up and went to Gerald Small's office, knocking before walking in.

'Did you manage to get into Harper's phone?'

'Not yet,' Small said. 'None of the usual methods worked, which is no real surprise. I'm still trying, though.'

'When you get a second, could you look into something else for me?'

'Sure. What is it?'

'When I was at Haddon Hall, I logged into my MI5 profile. Will our logs have a record of that?'

Small nodded. 'Of course. We'll have all the details, including the IP address you logged in from, date and time, and the files you accessed.'

'Do you think you could use that to get onto the machine I used there? The one at Haddon Hall?'

'I'll certainly be able to identify it,' Small said. 'Whether or not I can get access is another matter completely.'

'I'd like you to try,' Harvey said.

Small turned to his computer and his fingers danced over the keys. 'It'll take some time,' he said over his shoulder. 'I'll come and get you if I strike gold.'

The taxi dropped the trio off outside the British Consulate on Emir Palace Road, and Ackerman showed the armed guard his credentials. The plastic bag was inspected, the soldier eyeing the bottle suspiciously, but when Ackerman explained that it was for one of the senior staff, he was allowed to take it in. Ackerman led Smart and Gray into the foyer, and all three were pleased to discover that the place was air-conditioned.

'Kyle Ackerman to see Dennis Engle,' he told the woman behind the Perspex shield at the reception booth. 'He's expecting me.'

She asked him to take a seat and picked up the phone.

'So who's this Engle guy?' Smart asked. 'Another spook?'

'I don't think so,' Ackerman said. 'All I got from the Pretoria office was that he likes his bourbon, hence the token of appreciation.'

He held up the plastic bag just as a portly man appeared in front of them, sweating despite the near-frigid air. His face was almost beetroot-red, and Ackerman wondered if it was just hypertension or something alcohol-related.

Probably the latter.

'Dennis Engle,' he said, holding out his hand, though his eyes were fixed on the duty-free bag.

'Kyle Ackerman. Is that for me?'

'Oh, sorry,' Engle said, handing over a bulging manila envelope before wiping his face with a handkerchief. 'I had to pull a lot of strings to get this from the airport authorities. You mentioned . . . .'

Ackerman took the hint and handed Engle the bag, watching his eyes light up at the sight of the sour mash.

'We just can't get this over here,' Engle said. 'Yet another reason to hate this shit-hole. That, and the bloody heat. And don't even get me started on the sodding terrorists . . . .'

As the rant continued, Ackerman opened the folder and checked the first few pages. Each entry had a passport photo, which was a lot more than he'd expected. It would certainly make their job a lot easier.

He shook Engle's hand again and thanked him for his help, then made a beeline for the exit, closely followed by his companions. When they looked back, Engle was already heading back to an office, and Ackerman guessed he would be unavailable for the remainder of the day.

'We need somewhere quiet to go through these,' Gray said. 'Let's get back to the hotel before Sonny and Mack turn up. I want to try to find Farrar before they get back.'

Smart flagged down a taxi, and once inside Ackerman handed them both a few sheets, which they studied on the short journey. By the time they reached the hotel they'd managed to get through a dozen each, but that still left a couple of hundred pages to trawl through.

Once back in Gray's room, they locked the door and Gray dug out a photo of James Farrar that he'd printed out prior to leaving England.

'This is who we're looking for,' he said to Ackerman.

They divided up the papers, which contained ten passport records apiece. It helped that the majority of profiles were for African nationals, meaning they were able to skim through until they came to a Caucasian face.

Fifteen minutes into the exercise, Smart held up the piece of paper he'd been scanning.

'Got 'im!'

Gray took the printout and ran his finger down the list until he came to a very familiar face. The smug expression he remembered even adorned Farrar's new passport photograph, although the name—Harold Ericson—was obviously new.

He checked the flight details, and saw that Farrar had left the country on the fifteenth, four days earlier. His EgyptAir flight to Cairo appeared to have been the final destination, but Gray suspected Farrar wasn't stupid enough to telegraph his final destination by buying a through-ticket.

'Now that we've identified your man, what do we do?' Ackerman asked.

'Get Andrew on the phone,' Gray said. 'Ask him to follow the trail, and tell him the original plan remains in place.'

Ackerman made a quick call, giving Harvey the flight and passport details, and told him to expect a text message in the next hour, per their earlier plan regarding Mackenzie. He listened for a moment, then hung up.

'Andrew says Hamad can get into the Egyptian airline database, so we should have news soon.'

'Great,' Gray said, gathering up the sheets of paper. He stuffed them back into the envelope and handed it to Smart. 'Take this somewhere and lose it. Kyle, when Sonny and Mack get back, make your excuses and send that text to Andrew. I'll tell Sonny and Mack that we couldn't get the list and that the guy in the hospital is our only lead. Andrew should get back in touch while we're developing a plan, and then we just have to wait for Mack to squirrel away and make his move.'

Smart took the envelope and left, returning ten minutes later. The trio had to wait another hour before Sonny walked through the door, Mackenzie in tow.

'How does it look?' Gray asked.

'Shouldn't be a problem,' Sonny said. 'His room is at the back of the building and there's plenty of tree cover.'

'Good. Then we go in tonight. Kyle, can you see if you can rustle up some food?'

Ackerman took his cue and left the room, and Gray asked Sonny for details of the layout and any equipment they'd need. Sonny told him that there was access via a drainpipe, so no need for a rope. All he really required was something to force the window with.

'I saw a stall in the market that sells knives,' Smart said. 'Sonny and I can go and get a couple.'

'Do it after lunch,' Gray told them. 'We might need to add more to the list before you go.'

Ackerman returned a few minutes later and dropped a large paper bag on the table. 'I got bread, cheese and what could either be lamb, goat or horse, though the man assured me it was beef.'

The men tucked in, most of them enjoying their first bite of the day. Gray pressed Sonny on the layout of the hospital and Ackerman about the number of staff he'd seen during his visit.

When Ackerman's phone beeped twice, all eyes turned to him. He unlocked the handset and checked the message before handing it to Gray.

Gray studied the phone with all the dramatic flair he could muster. Then he clicked off and faced the team.

'Harvey says he's found Farrar. We're to head home.'

'Where is he?' Smart asked.

'He didn't say. He just told us to grab the next flight home, job done.'

'Sounds good to me,' Smart said, throwing his piece of dried meat into the bin.

'Okay, guys, pack your gear and meet back here in fifteen minutes. Kyle, book us some tickets.'

Sonny and Smart retreated to their room, Mackenzie to his.

'I guess we'll find out soon enough if Mack's playing us,' Ackerman said to Gray once they were alone. 'Have you decided what to do if he is?'

'We're going to leave him here, but first, I want you to go shopping again.'

Andrew Harvey stood over Gerald Small as the technician's fingers flew over the keyboard. While it was great news that Gray had confirmed Farrar's involvement, it didn't leave much time for him to get access to the home secretary's phone. The only concrete proof he could envision would be capturing a conversation between Harper and Farrar, and he expected it to happen soon.

That's because Mackenzie and Sarah Thompson had engaged in a rapid-fire text conversation moments ago:

Harvey has found Farrar

Are you sure?

Certain. He just told Gray. Ordered team to come home

Thompson had since been in touch with Harper, though only to pass on the message, and what the home secretary had done from that point was anyone's guess.

Hamad Farsi stuck his head into the room and handed Harvey a piece of paper.

'We have a flight to Cuba, but the trail ends there.'

Harvey took the single sheet and read the brief details. It seemed a strange destination for Farrar, whose profile suggested he hadn't exactly enjoyed his other stints in hot climates. In most of the reports Farrar had submitted from his assignments in Belize and the Philippines, the humidity had been mentioned at some point. It was this knowledge that had helped him shape his original search for the man, but it appeared that decision had been flawed.

On the flip side, the Cubans were known to offer political asylum to wanted men, especially those with a background in intelligence.

'Good work so far, Gerald. Keep trying.'

Harvey followed Farsi back to their bank of desks. He unlocked his computer and opened up the Maps application. He saw that Cuba was roughly six hundred kilometres long, though it was a relatively thin island. The capital, Havana, was located in the northwest, near a major town whose name caught his eye.

'Wouldn't it be ironic if he was staying here?' he asked Farsi, pointing to a town called Moron.

'Yeah, I saw that, but knowing the man as I do, he'd more likely be here.' Farsi moved his cursor over a place named Colon, and they both had a chuckle.

'Time to get serious,' Ellis said as she strode over to them. 'I just got off the phone with Harper.'

'What did she say?'

'She wants everything we have on Farrar with a view to sending a team in.'

'I'm guessing that team won't involve us,' Harvey said.

'Correct. At least, it won't involve me. I've been relieved of duty, effective immediately.'

'She can't do that!'

'No, but she can have a quiet word with the person who can. My counterpart at Six, Martin Evans, will run both units until my replacement can be found. He'll be here in the next fifteen minutes.'

'So that's it? She wins?'

'Perhaps not, Hamad. You still have a quarter of an hour, maybe twenty minutes, to get what you need before you head out.'

'Where are we going?' Harvey asked.

'Cuba. I suggest you start by checking their real estate websites for recent rentals and purchases, notably high-end properties. Farrar likes his comfort, so forget about the poorer areas of the island. Andrew, get on to Doug Wallis at the CIA and see if he can help. They should have people in-country who can call in a few favours.'

'Is all this really necessary? I mean, if Harper and Farrar are working together, one phone call from her and he'll be long gone by the time we get there.'

Ellis offered a grim smile. 'Not if she thinks we're looking in the wrong place. I told her we'd tracked him to Cairo, then on to a place in Indonesia. I think her priority is to get me out of the picture so that the investigation stalls, so I need you to create some evidence pointing to Farrar landing in Jakarta with no onward travel.'

'She must realise you weren't doing this alone,' Harvey pointed out. 'Thompson, for one, knows that Hamad and I were looking for him, too. Add the fact that my workstation is probably being monitored and she'll probably know everything we do.'

'I thought we agreed that Hamad would handle the searches. What digging have you done?'

'Nothing, really, but I did just search for Cuba online.'

'Then I suggest you book a package holiday to Havana in the next five minutes to throw them off the scent. A week in April should do it. Once you've done that, arrange to meet Agent Wallis for a late lunch. Hamad, you were looking to see who owns the flat Thompson is living in. What did you find?'

'It's owned by one of a dozen firms run by a holding company that has its headquarters in the Cayman Islands. That's as far as I could get.'

'Then after you've tried the real estate websites, look into each company and see if any have property in Cuba.'

'That'll take a lot longer than fifteen minutes,' Farsi said.

'You can do it remotely. As of now, you are both on leave. Good luck, gentlemen.'

Ellis returned to her office and began clearing out her drawers, and Harvey went back to Small's station to pass on the news.

'You're just in time. I managed to get into your terminal at Haddon Hall.'

'That's great. The only trouble is, I have to clear the building in the next ten minutes. I'll be working remotely for the next few days at least.'

Small turned to his keyboard and tapped out a series of commands, and Harvey soon recognised his own desktop profile on the screen. 'I'm putting a shortcut to the Haddon Hall server on your laptop. You'll be able to access it from anywhere, just as long as you log into our network first. The username and password are already configured.'

Harvey gave a long, low whistle at the hacking job his colleague had performed. 'That's remarkable. Nice work. But I've got a feeling my account is going to be locked out pretty soon. I'll need a way to get back in if that happens.'

Small scribbled something on a slip of paper and handed it to Harvey. 'I'll create a new profile with that username and password. If you get locked out of your normal account, try that one. I'll put the shortcut on there, too.'

'Thanks, Gerald. I need you to buy a burner cell and text me on this number.' Harvey jotted down the number for his own anonymous phone. 'Just in case I need your help again.' He smiled. 'And you know I will.'

He left Small to finish up and went to Ellis's office.

'I've been thinking,' he said as he walked in. 'If we do go to Cuba and find Farrar, then what? We're not exactly equipped to bring him home. I mean, it's not as if we can just knock on his door and ask him to come with us.'

Ellis put a silver pen in her cardboard box, followed by a photograph of her Alsatian puppy. 'I thought about that, too, but there's nothing I can do. You'll have to go with what's already available.'

'You mean Gray and his team?'

'You're the one who wanted your friend on board. Now it's up to you to make it work. Go and give him the good news.'

She sat down heavily in her chair, surveying the empty desk. 'Keep me in the loop,' she told him. 'I'm not sure I can help much, but . . . .'

Harvey looked at the dejected figure before him. Only now that she was being forced out did he realise what a special person she was. They'd had their share of disagreements, but she'd always been fair and had the team's best interests at heart. To be dismissed for wanting to see justice done was an absolute travesty, and he was determined to make it right.

'We'll get him, Veronica. I'll see to it personally.'

Chapter 36

19 December 2014

Tom Gray looked up as Ackerman entered the hotel room. He'd been gone for fifteen minutes, and had a serious look on his face as he walked through the door.

'Well?' Gray asked.

Ackerman handed over his phone and Gray looked at the screen. 'The tickets are booked. We leave here at seven this evening.'

Gray scratched the side of his head, and Smart took his cue to walk over to the window, directly behind Mackenzie.

'So what do we do until then?' Sonny asked.

'Maybe Mack can tell us a bit more about himself,' Gray suggested. 'For starters, who's this girl you told me about? What's her name?'

'Helen,' Mackenzie said. 'Why do you ask?'

Gray cocked his head. 'It's funny. I just don't picture you with a Helen. Now a Sarah . . . .'

Mackenzie's expression didn't change. 'Trust me, she's unlike any Helen you've ever known.'

Gray hit a couple of buttons on the phone and kept his eyes on Mackenzie as he waited for it to ring. He noticed a slight twitch as the call connected, but otherwise Mackenzie remained calm.

'Aren't you going to answer that?' Gray asked as Smart wrapped a powerful arm around Mackenzie's neck.

'What the hell's going on?' Sonny asked.

'If you feel inside his trousers you'll find a phone on vibrate,' Gray told him. 'It was the one used to notify MI6 that we were here and looking for Farrar.'

Sonny did as instructed and soon came across the mobile. 'And you were going to tell me about this . . . when?'

'I didn't have the chance,' Gray said, 'but now you know. Mack here is also the one who told Six where to find my daughter. Isn't that right?'

Mackenzie simply stared straight ahead, and Gray knew he wouldn't get anything out of him, even with the threat of torture. Everyone in the room, with the exception of Ackerman, had been through interrogation training in the regiment, and Gray knew Mackenzie could hold out for at least a couple of days.

Time they couldn't afford.

'So now what?' Sonny asked.

'We tie him up and go. Kyle has paid for the room for two more days and asked that we not be disturbed. That should give us enough time.'

Ackerman opened the door and brought in a large paper bag. He rummaged inside and handed one knife to Gray, another to Sonny. Next, out came an ancient petrol lamp, its glass housing blackened and cracked. Gray took it and removed the glass, leaving just the copper base, with a full reservoir and singed flat spirit wick. In the bag was a disposable lighter, and Gray used it to test out the lamp, which produced a decent flame the first time of asking. Thankfully there were no smoke detectors in the room, as a column of black wound its way towards the ceiling.

Gray set the lamp aside and walked over to Mackenzie, placing the tip of his knife under the man's eye.

'We're going to get up nice and slowly, and you're going to lie on the bed. No need to tell you what'll happen if you make any sudden movements.'

Smart dragged Mackenzie to his feet and walked him over to the nearest bed.

'Lie down, arms outstretched.'

Ackerman walked over with a handful of rope and tossed some to Sonny. They both began tying Mackenzie to the top corners of the bed, then moved down to work on his feet.

Once he was secure, Gray took his knife from Mackenzie's face and slit his T-shirt open from waist to neck, the two sides flopping down onto the sheet.

'Anything to say before we go?' Gray asked.

Mackenzie offered only silence in return.

'Fair enough.'

He instructed Sonny to gag the prisoner, then fetched the lamp and extended the wick to a couple of inches before placing the apparatus on Mackenzie's chest. Ackerman came over with the bag containing the finishing touch.

'This is fine thread cotton,' Ackerman said. 'I took the liberty of dousing it beforehand, so it should take a flame nicely.' He demonstrated by slicing off a strip and holding it over the lamp, and the fabric caught immediately.

Ackerman threw that piece into the metal bin and used his knife to slice the remainder of the cloth into thin strips, which he placed either side of Mackenzie's torso.

'That flame should keep going for a couple of days,' Gray said, 'so I wouldn't try to struggle if I were you. If that falls, you'll be toast before anyone finds you. Meanwhile, I'd try real hard to stay awake for the next forty-eight hours. Shouldn't be hard once the place starts to stink of your shit and piss.'

Ackerman left the room and returned a moment later, holding Mackenzie's passport. 'Ready to go?'

'Where are we heading?' Sonny asked.

'Jakarta,' Ackerman told him. 'That's where the trail ends.'

Andrew Harvey sat in Armando's, nursing a half of lager, checking his watch every thirty seconds. It was unusual for Doug Wallis to be late, even to these impromptu meetings, and he couldn't help but feel nervous.

It wasn't often that he called upon his American friend, but it was times like this that made him glad they had the informal arrangement. They got together roughly once a month to share the latest scuttlebutt, though there were times when one of them would call an emergency liquid lunch in order to get intel that the bosses didn't want to share with each other.

When Wallis finally arrived he was full of apologies. 'I got dragged into an emergency meeting. What's so urgent?'

He motioned to the barman for his usual pint of bitter while Harvey told him what he needed.

'You want access to our people in Havana?'

'I don't need to meet them, just some help with . . . logistics.'

'Such as?' Wallis asked, sipping from the brown drink that had been placed in front of him.

Harvey handed over a handwritten list of the items Gray had requested, having also added a couple of his own.

'Looks like you're planning an invasion.'

'We're just after one man,' Harvey assured him. 'One of ours.'

'I'm going to need a lot more details before I sign off on this. Give me names, for a start.'

Harvey rubbed his temples. 'I can't, Doug. I need you to trust me on this one.'

'Then I'm afraid I can't help,' Wallis said, standing up and straightening his coat.

Harvey grabbed his sleeve and pulled him back into the booth. 'Okay, but this can't go through official channels.'

'I'm listening.'

'His name is Harold Ericson. I need to send an ex-fil team in to bring him home.'

'What's Ericson done?'

'We believe he's behind the recent attacks,' Harvey said.

Wallis sat back in his chair. 'So tell me why this doesn't go beyond the two of us. One call from your prime minister and our guys would pick him up for you.'

'Because the PM doesn't know. We think a senior cabinet member was in on it, and this is big enough to bring down the entire government.' Harvey waited for Wallis to absorb the implications of his statement. 'See? This is why I'm saying you can't tell a soul.'

Wallis allowed himself a chuckle at Harvey's predicament. 'Christ, Andy. You Brits don't do things in half measures.'

'From what I've heard, your government's not exactly squeaky clean.'

'Touché,' Wallis conceded.

Harvey leaned in close. 'Look, if you don't help me, the people ultimately behind these atrocities will walk, and God knows where they plan to attack next. It could well be Stateside . . . .'

Harvey locked eyes with his CIA counterpart, and the silence seemed to drag on for what seemed like minutes. Eventually, Wallis relented.

'I know one of the people in Havana. I'll make a call.'

Harvey exhaled, not realising that he'd held his breath while awaiting the answer. 'Thanks, Doug. I owe you.'

‘Oh, don’t you worry. I plan to collect big time.’

Harvey assured him he would repay him any way he could, and explained that in addition to the armaments, he would need help locating Ericson. ‘Our men are already on their way, and Hamad and I will be setting off tonight. If you could have an address by the time we get there, that would be great.’

Wallis nodded. ‘How many did you send?’

‘There’ll be five of us in total.’

‘All your own people?’

‘We had to go external, but they’re good men. The best.’

‘Okay, I’ll go and make the call. Give me a ring later when you have further details.’

‘It’s best if we meet in person,’ Harvey said.

They agreed to join up again at six that evening, and Harvey left, grabbing the first available taxi. He gave the driver Farsi’s address and hoped his colleague would have everything they’d need for the trip by the time he got there.

Chapter 37

19 December 2014

'So tell me why Farrar is in Cuba, we tell Mackenzie we're heading to Jakarta, but we're actually going to Pretoria.'

'Because we need new passports if we're going to stay off the radar,' Gray told Sonny as they queued at the departure desk. 'Harvey wants everyone to believe that Farrar is in Indonesia. Once we get to Pretoria, Kyle's colleagues will meet us with new ID papers and tickets to Havana.'

'So that's why you let Mackenzie keep his phone,' Sonny said. 'I thought you'd gone soft.'

'No, I wanted him to be able to call his people once he's rescued. I told the hotel manager to send someone up to the room at six in the morning the day after tomorrow to check on our friend who isn't feeling too well. Once they find him, we'll know if our ruse worked.'

'Mackenzie will have had plenty of time to think this through,' Sonny pointed out. 'He's bound to know his phone was traced.'

'That's possible,' Gray said, 'but Harvey's also tracking the recipient, so he'll know if Mackenzie gets in touch, even if he uses another phone.'

Ackerman joined them, dumping his overnight bag at their feet and handing Gray the phone. 'Andrew said he'll meet you in Havana. He'll sort out accommodation and get back to you with the details.'

'Did he mention the items we requested?'

'His contact is working on that. He might even have an address by the time you land.'

'That'll certainly save us some time,' Gray said, as he reached the head of the queue. He handed over his passport and ticket, then collected his boarding pass and waited for the others to check in.

The flight to South Africa required a stopover in Abuja, and by the time they arrived in Pretoria, darkness had descended. Once they'd cleared immigration, they made their way to the arrivals hall, where a man in his thirties held up a board with Ackerman's name on it. They followed the driver out to a waiting SUV, and Ackerman ushered the trio inside.

'Got the documents?' he asked.

The driver opened the glove compartment and handed him a thick envelope. Inside were three passports, and Gray could see that they weren't British.

'You're Australians,' Ackerman said, handing them out. 'You should all have a two-week holiday visa, staying at the National Hotel in Havana. Here are your tickets, and there are three suitcases in the back. It would look strange if you turned up for a two-week holiday with just hand luggage.'

'Did you arrange the other surprise for Mackenzie?' Gray asked.

'It's all in place.'

Gray shook hands with Ackerman. 'As always, I really appreciate the help.'

'Don't mention it, Tom. Just go and sort that bastard out.'

Andrew Harvey sat at his laptop in Farsi's front room and wondered just what search criteria he should use to filter out the results from Haddon Hall. He wasn't sure how long he'd have, once connected to their system, so he needed to plan his strategy in advance.

His second meeting with Wallis hadn't gone to his liking, though the American had managed to arrange the weapons he'd asked for. The downside was that the CIA had no record of Harold Ericson beyond his entry at Jose Marti International Airport. Ericson was registered at the Hotel Habana Libre for visa purposes, but he'd never turned up, which meant he must have had other accommodation arranged in advance. Harvey knew it was likely that wherever he was staying, it was under yet another name, making the search almost impossible.

Harvey hit the remote icon on his desktop and was soon presented with the familiar Brigandicuum search screen. He entered the home secretary's mobile number and watched as the web of related numbers stretched out from London to Europe and then farther afield. Harper was one of the high-level officials whose phone was blocked from the Brigandicuum system, but everyone who had had phone contact with Harper was shown. The only drawback was that the results were limited to data that had already been downloaded by Brigandicuum. Doing an up-to-date worldwide scan would mean adding the phone number to the keyword file, which was something Harvey couldn't do. His eyes were on the long, thin island in the Caribbean, and it wasn't long before a green line snaked from England's capital to a waterfront property to the north of the capital, Havana.

He zoomed in and saw a detached house with what looked to be a swimming pool on the roof. The plot was surrounded by a white wall, with the nearest neighbours over five hundred yards away.

'Got you,' he breathed.

He still needed proof that Farrar was there, though. It could well be the residence of the British Ambassador, or another dignitary whom the home secretary had called. Harvey checked the time of the contact, and saw that it had occurred only twenty hours earlier. It still wasn't conclusive, but as the seconds ticked by, it remained the only connection to the minister's phone.

Harvey entered the Cuban phone's number into the Brigandicuum search screen and hit the Download button. Immediately, data began scrolling down the screen, and Harvey selected the link to filter it to text messages. There were only thirteen in total, and it didn't take him long to find what he was looking for.

'Bingo!'

Farsi walked in from the kitchen with two cups of coffee. 'What did you find?'

Harvey turned the laptop towards him. 'A text conversation between Harper and someone in Cuba. It was routed through a crude attempt at a relay in the Philippines.'

Progress report?

They think you're in Indonesia.

Not even warm.

Okay, I'll keep you informed.

'Looks like she swallowed the Jakarta story,' Farsi said.

'Let's hope so,' Harvey said. He made a note of the location of the house and took a screenshot of the satellite view, which he sent to his phone.

'Do you think Farrar will come quietly?' Farsi asked.

'I hope so,' Harvey said. 'If he doesn't . . . well, that's why we have Tom Gray.'

Paul Mackenzie was running out of ways to keep his eyes open as the hours wore on. He couldn't see a clock, but guessed that over twenty-four hours had passed since Gray had tied him to the bed and set his little booby-trap.

As soon as Gray and his team had left the room, Mackenzie had tried blowing the flame out, but the gag over his mouth made it impossible. He'd also had a couple of near misses, not least when he'd sneezed twice in succession. The lamp had wobbled on his sternum, and it was a miracle that it hadn't fallen off and set fire to the bed.

A faint knock on the door stirred him to full alertness. He immediately began making as much noise as possible without upsetting the lamp. The gag muffled the sound, but he continued nonetheless. Another knock, and he was relieved to hear the sound of a key entering the lock.

The hotel manager stuck his head inside the door, and pushed it fully open when he saw his guest strapped to the bed. He ran in and removed the lamp, then pulled the gag down, asking what had happened.

'I was robbed,' Mackenzie said, sounding almost as desperate as he felt.

The manager helped to untie him, asking if he'd suffered any torture, but Mackenzie waved him off. 'I'm fine, I just need to get dressed and get to the airport. Unless you'd like me to involve the police and the media . . . ?'

The manager was only too happy to avoid the negative publicity, and he promised to do all he could, starting with a limousine to the airport. The hotel bill had already been paid, so he offered Mackenzie a few dollars to help with sundry expenses.

Mackenzie checked his jacket and found that his wallet and phone were still there, but Ackerman had taken his passport. 'Thanks, but what I really need is to get to the British embassy.'

'We have a British consulate,' the manager told him. 'I'll let them know to expect you and have a car waiting to take you there.'

He left the room in a hurry, and Mackenzie went to his own room and grabbed his belongings before going down to reception.

'I called ahead,' the manager told him. 'They will be expecting you.'

Mackenzie was shown to a waiting car, and after a short drive he was dropped off outside the consulate. A portly man was waiting at the steps, and he ushered Mackenzie into the building.

'The name's Dennis Engle. I understand you had some bother with your passport.'

Mackenzie noted the smell of alcohol on the man's breath, but as long as he got his paperwork, he wasn't concerned. He repeated the lie about being robbed, and Engle led him into a side office, seating himself at a desk before making a quick call.

'If you could fill this in, that would be great.'

Mackenzie took the passport replacement form and entered his details. He was almost finished when a young woman knocked on the door and let herself in.

'Go with Karina,' Engle said. 'She'll take your passport photograph. I'll begin processing this.'

Mackenzie picked up his holdall and followed her.

'You can leave that here. It's no problem. I won't be going anywhere.'

Mackenzie dropped the bag by the door and followed the girl down the hallway and into another small room. He fixed his hair as best he could, then posed in front of an instamatic for his picture. It took a few minutes for the prints to be developed, and then Karina escorted him back to Engle's room.

'Almost done,' Engle said, tapping away on his keyboard. He looked at Mackenzie, then back to the screen, and, satisfied that the image on file matched the man in front of him, he hit the Submit button.

'Your papers will be delivered in a few minutes,' Engle said. 'In the meantime, do you wish to file a police report?'

'No need,' Mackenzie said. 'I'd just like to get home.'

'I understand. Do you have a flight booked?'

'I'll do that once I get to the airport.'

'Nonsense, I'll get Karina to do it for you. I assume you have the money . . . ?'

Mackenzie handed over a credit card, and Engle asked Karina to pop back in. She returned five minutes later with a printout of the flight details.

'Thanks for everything,' Mackenzie said, shaking Engle's hand.

'It's what we do.' The red-faced attaché smiled.

The car that had brought Mackenzie was still waiting, and he told the driver to take him to the airport. On the way, he sent a text message to Sarah Thompson, updating her on developments.

When he arrived at Mallam Aminu International, he checked in at the EgyptAir desk, then made his way through security, placing his holdall on the conveyor belt and depositing his metal items in the tray provided. He stepped through the detector as his luggage passed through the x-ray machine, then went to collect his coins and phone.

'Excuse me, sir. Please take your bag and come with me.'

A confused Mackenzie did as requested, and followed the man to a room where three uniformed officers were waiting.

'What's this about?'

'Did you pack this bag yourself?'

Mackenzie nodded, and the security officer opened it, pulling the contents out carefully. He got to a pair of rolled-up socks and weighed them in his hands.

'What's in here?'

'I . . . nothing, there's nothing . . . '

The officer unravelled the socks to reveal a transparent bag containing a white powder.

'Nothing?'

'That's not mine!'

Two of the three policemen already had their weapons drawn, while the third approached with a pair of handcuffs.

'You can explain that at the police station.'

Mackenzie knew he'd been set up, but explaining it to these people would be a waste of breath. It had to have been Gray, probably working in partnership with the attaché, Engle.

Whoever it was, they had royally screwed him.

The Air France flight climbed into the dark sky, with France's Charles de Gaulle Airport their first port of call. After a brief stopover, they would take to the skies again, scheduled to touch down in Havana ten hours later.

When the Fasten Seatbelt sign was extinguished, Harvey got up and went to the toilet, stopping at the galley on the way back to get some water. When he returned to his seat, he found Farsi engrossed in a file he'd printed out before leaving London.

'According to this, blackouts are a regular occurrence in Cuba. Maybe that's something Gray can take advantage of.'

'We'll mention it to him, but I'm hoping it won't come down to a full-on assault. Farrar is bound to have some form of security, and I don't relish a firefight on foreign soil.'

Given Gray's track record, Harvey felt certain that violence lay ahead. The ideal scenario was to walk up to Farrar's front door, grab him and take him to Guantánamo Bay, which was officially US soil. From there he could be flown back to the UK for interrogation.

The likelihood of that happening with Tom's team on the scene was minimal, though. Gray had seen his nemesis Farrar put behind bars once before, only to be released and apparently given the opportunity to mastermind the recent attacks.

Harvey seriously doubted that Gray would let Farrar walk again, especially as his daughter had recently been targeted. By taking Farrar into custody, the chance of him absconding again—no matter how remote—was there. He'd have to drill Gray on the rules of engagement once they met up in Havana, and it wasn't a conversation he was looking forward to. Thankfully, he'd have the calming influence of Len Smart to counter Gray's maverick persona, and he hoped that between them they could convince Gray to do it by the book.

'So what did Sarah say when you blew her off?' Farsi asked, breaking into his thoughts. 'How's she gonna cope without her stud popping round each night?'

'Hamad, you really are crude. Besides, that was all in the line of duty.'

'Oh, my heart bleeds. Don't tell me you didn't enjoy it.'

A smile made its way onto Harvey's face. 'It sure beat a night in front of the television with a microwave meal, but it was the only way to get information out of her. That said, it was getting too uncomfortable. She was pressing me on Farrar's whereabouts and wouldn't believe that I didn't know anything.'

'Which fortunately was true at the time. One flash of her thighs and you'd have caved.'

'Oh, ye of little faith.'

Farsi got up and went to the toilet, navigating the narrow aisle carefully as turbulence juddered the plane from side to side. His eyes were focused on the leggy flight attendant in the galley, and he paid little attention to the female passenger seated six rows behind him.

Sarah Thompson saw Hamad Farsi rise from his seat and she lowered her head, pretending to be engrossed in the *Hello!* magazine on her lap.

She had little fear of being recognised, but didn't want to risk making eye contact. The patchwork leather hat over the short, black wig and glasses perched halfway down her nose had transformed her into a frumpy, middle-aged nobody. The ensemble was completed by the baggy, brown woollen jumper and beige cargo pants, which disguised her figure. Her cheeks were padded out with rolls of cotton wool pressed against her lower gum, altering her jawline. The overall effect added at least twenty pounds, and she felt sure her own aunt wouldn't recognise her. Especially not in these god-awful Ugg boots.

Ever since Harvey had cried off from their nightly get-togethers, she'd been suspicious, and it hadn't taken long to discover that he and Farsi had been given leave. Having two senior operatives out of the office at the same time had pointed to something out of the ordinary, especially under current circumstances, so she'd done a little digging.

All operatives had a series of legends—fake identities that they'd use when working undercover—and a quick search of those issued to Harvey and Farsi showed new papers issued earlier that day. From there it was simply a matter of querying the airlines for tickets booked in those names, leading to the discovery that both of them were booked on through-flights to Havana.

There was nothing on any of the threat boards to suggest Cuba was plotting anything against the UK and, knowing Harvey as she did, she could only imagine one reason for the trip.

James Farrar.

It had been a mad dash arranging her own legend and getting tickets on the same flights, but she was determined to foil whatever Andrew Harvey had in mind.

Chapter 38

20 December 2014

It was after seven in the evening by the time Gray and his colleagues made it to the arrivals hall at Jose Marti International, the twenty-eight hour journey having been spent in sheer boredom. Gray had at least managed a few hours of sleep this time, but his body clock was misfiring badly and it felt more like morning than early evening.

With no-one to meet them, they exited the airport in search of a taxi. A line of vehicles straight out of a black and white movie sat to their left, and they climbed into the first one, a 1950 Series 62 Cadillac sedan. It looked in surprisingly good shape on first inspection, but once the driver hit the ignition, the car showed its true colours.

With a belch of grey smoke, it pulled into traffic, and they were soon on the Avenida de La Independencia, the three-lane highway leading into the centre of Havana. The driver set a leisurely pace, and Gray suspected it was more down to the car's age than an attempt to let them take in the sights.

Traffic was relatively light, and they made the twenty-kilometre journey in a little over forty minutes. They pulled up outside a huge, seven-storey white building overlooking Havana Harbour, and Gray paid the driver before leading the men into the gargantuan reception area.

'Kyle came up trumps,' Sonny said, obviously impressed with the new surroundings.

'We're not here on holiday,' Smart reminded him.

Gray sorted out the reservations in the name of Tim Green, and the concierge handed over two keys for rooms on the second floor.

'You also have a message, Mr Green.'

Gray took the envelope and moved towards the elevator before opening it.

'Andrew's already here,' he told his companions. 'Let's dump our things and go see him.'

Gray had a single room, while Smart and Sonny had been booked into a double. As he walked in, Gray was confronted with a large double bed, a mahogany table with two chairs, and little else apart from a dressing table. The CRT television set looked like it had survived the revolution, though the en-suite appeared modern enough.

He locked up and caught up with the others in the adjoining room, where Sonny was testing out the bed.

'Once this is over, I might just hang around for a few days,' he said, relaxing on top of the bed sheets.

'I've got a feeling we'll be leaving in a hurry,' Gray said. 'Stow your gear so we can go and meet Andrew. He's on the next floor up.'

They took the stairs to Harvey's room, and as they entered the hallway they saw him about to enter his room.

'You finally made it,' Harvey said, opening his door and letting them in.

Farsi was sitting at a small table, tapping away on his keyboard. He got up and shook hands with the new arrivals.

'My CIA contact managed to arrange the weapons you asked for,' Harvey said. 'We have to go and pick them up tomorrow morning. In the meantime, I thought we'd scope out the target tonight. I've got a hire car and thought we'd leave at around eleven.'

'That gives us a couple of hours. What's the food like here?'

'They do a wonderful steak in the restaurant,' Farsi said. 'Argentinian beef, the best there is.'

'You had me at steak,' Gray said. 'So what's the plan?'

'Ideally, we pick Farrar up without any shots fired and take an eight-hour drive southeast to US soil. Think you can manage that?'

Gray looked Harvey in the eye. 'If it goes like that, sure.'

'And if it doesn't?' Harvey asked.

'Then I suggest you keep your head down and fire only when you have a clear target.'

'Tom, I know you guys have history, but my brief is to bring him home.'

'History is a bit of an understatement.' Gray laughed, but the grave look on Harvey's face told him it was no joke.

'I'm serious. If there are any . . . accidents, it'll come back on me. So we follow the plan: take him to Guantánamo, fly him back home and get to the bottom of this.'

'Handing him over to the authorities didn't work out too well last time, did it?'

'No,' Harvey conceded, 'but this isn't just about revenge, no matter how much you want it to be. I know he targeted you—'

'—and my daughter,' Gray reminded him.

'Yes, and Melissa, but he isn't the last link in the chain. We believe someone in the cabinet ordered this, but if you kill Farrar we'll never be able to prove it.'

It wasn't what Gray wanted to hear, but as always Harvey made a good point. Over the last forty-eight hours he'd pictured himself standing before Farrar many times, and each encounter had ended with his enemy departing for the next world. At no point had he envisaged sharing a plane home with him.

'Okay, we take him with us,' Gray said, 'but if he manages to wriggle out of this, all bets are off.'

'Deal.'

'Erm, I think someone mentioned steak?' Sonny said, trying to break the tension.

'He's right,' Smart said. 'It's gonna be a long night. Let's eat and get ready.'

They trooped down to the restaurant, and Farsi's claims about the food were right on the money. Gray had the juiciest sirloin he'd ever tasted, and they washed it down with an overpriced bottle of Bolivian red wine.

Afterwards, they retired to their rooms. Gray opened the suitcase Ackerman had arranged for him, and was pleased to find black pants and a dark blue jumper, ideal attire for that evening.

They met up outside the main entrance an hour later, and Harvey handed the valet the ticket for his car. The three-year-old Ford was brought around a minute later, and they piled in, Harvey pointing the nose east.

Despite the hour, the streets were still packed, with both locals and tourists flocking to the many night spots in search of music and more. They passed through the Tunel de La Habana, which took them under the Canal de Entrada, then along Via Monumental until it branched off onto Via Blanca.

'We're getting close,' Harvey said. 'How far away do you want to park?'

'Drive past the place and carry on at least half a click,' Gray said. Five hundred metres wouldn't take them long to walk, and he wanted to get a feel of the area. It looked quite affluent, so he had no concerns about the group being accosted while on foot.

Harvey pulled off the four-lane highway and kept the speed down to twenty-five as he drove past the target, a white, two-storey building surrounded by a six-foot wall topped with broken bottle glass. Two lights glowed on the upper floor, and a silhouette walked past one of the illuminated windows.

A minute later, Harvey found a grove of trees to park under, and they poured out of the vehicle.

'We just need eyes-on tonight,' Gray reminded them. 'Andrew, you and Hamad wait by the car. Sonny, you take the beach side. Len and I will check the back.'

Gray set off with Smart a yard behind him, and they stuck to the trees until they reached a point adjacent to the corner of the white-washed wall. From across the road, they could see very little, and Gray used hand signals to explain that he wanted to get in closer.

A large wooden gate was built into the middle of the wall, and after making sure he couldn't be seen from the upper windows, Gray crouched down and dashed across the road. He was hoping to find a gap between the boards so that he could see into the court-yard, but the gate was sturdily built. A small door was built into it to allow pedestrian access, but he couldn't find a handle to open it. In fact, the whole gate looked like it could only be opened from the inside, suggesting the compound would always be manned, even when the main occupant was out.

He listened intently, and eventually he heard a sound above the hiss of the waves slapping against the nearby beach.

Footsteps.

Convinced that Farrar had security inside, Gray retreated across the road and told Smart what he'd found.

'We'll need to know their strength before we go in,' Smart said. 'That means we either stick our heads over the wall, or we find another way to get a bird's-eye view.'

Gray looked around, and his gaze drifted upwards. 'We'll have to get into one of these trees.'

'Up you go, then,' Smart said. 'I'm not exactly built for it these days.'

Avoiding the ones nearest the road, Gray found a specimen that had some solid-looking branches, and he got Smart to give him a helping hand to the lowest one. Foliage from the neighbours prevented him seeing into the compound, so he edged higher, taking his time to prevent the rustling leaves from giving away his location.

Once he was ten feet above the ground, he found a gap in the branches that afforded a limited view of the enclosed garden, and his fears were confirmed. Two men were chatting by the corner of the house, M4 carbines held across their chests.

Gray motioned to Smart that he had eyes-on and planned to stay in position. With luck, he'd spot a pattern to their movements, or at least see how many people were working the night shift. So far he'd seen just this pair, and they didn't look like locals.

Two large SUVs were parked at the side of the house, and an ornamental fountain took centre stage in the front garden, encircled by a pebbled road. A couple of small bushes were the only other features in the garden, meaning Gray and his men wouldn't find much cover once they were inside the walls.

Ten minutes later, another figure appeared from the side of the house. Like the others, he was carrying a rifle, and they talked for a minute before one of the original pair disappeared towards the back of the building. Gray looked for CCTV cameras but saw none, though they could easily be hidden out of sight, so he couldn't assume the grounds weren't being covered.

After another thirty minutes, Gray had seen one other shift change, yet another new face coming to relieve the original guard, which made at least four people securing the premises. He decided he'd seen enough for one night, and it was time to get back to the car and see what intel Sonny had managed to gather.

He climbed down slowly and the pair retraced their steps to the Ford, where they found the others waiting.

'I wasn't able to get too close,' Sonny told them, 'but I saw two guards out back and they were relieved by a third.'

He gave a rundown of timings, and they coincided with the ones Gray had observed.

'It looks like they rotate around the perimeter every thirty minutes, perhaps with one other inside to cover breaks,' Gray said. 'That means six that we know of, and possibly more.'

'Let's get home and work on a plan while it's still fresh in your minds,' Smart said.

They climbed back into the Ford and Harvey took them the circuitous way home, eager to avoid driving back past the target building. When they arrived back at the hotel it was nearly two in the morning, yet there were still plenty of people in the lobby owing to the in-house entertainment.

They climbed the stairs to Gray's room and ordered room service. While they waited for it to arrive, Gray took a couple of pages of hotel paper and began sketching out a plan of the compound.

'This is where I saw the guards,' he said, marking two crosses on the drawing. He handed the pen to Sonny, who indicated the location of the men he'd seen.

'Looks like the best way in is over the wall here,' Smart said, indicating the side of the house where the SUVs were parked. 'The vehicles will offer us some cover when the fight kicks off.'

'*If* it kicks off,' Harvey reminded him. 'The prime objective is to complete the mission with zero shots fired.'

'That's not up to us,' Gray said. 'We need to get to Farrar. If anyone tries to stop us, it's their funeral.'

'Tom, you said—'

'I said you can have Farrar alive. Everyone else makes their own choice.'

'I think Len's right,' Sonny said, changing the subject. 'Approaching from the beach would be suicide.'

'And we still don't know if he's even in there,' Smart added.

'We can sort that out tomorrow with a quick phone call,' Harvey said, and explained what he had in mind.

They considered other entry points for an hour while they tucked into the sandwiches that had been delivered, but couldn't find an alternative to Smart's suggestion. It was after three in the morning when Gray called it a night and told them all to get plenty of sleep.

He had a feeling they were going to need it.

It had been an hour since Sarah Thompson watched Harvey pull up to the entrance to his hotel, and she forced herself to accept the fact that they'd be settling in for the night. There was little point in hanging around, so she set off for her own hotel, which lay a mile to the west.

What had surprised her most was seeing Harvey leave the hotel a couple of hours earlier in the company of Tom Gray. She'd followed them and seen them park up near the beachfront home, and had watched as Gray and his friends went to check it out.

It had been during that stakeout that Mackenzie had sent the message to say his cover had been blown, and that someone must have been tapping her mobile.

Harvey.

He seemed a pretty straight guy, despite what the home secretary had told her almost a year earlier when she'd been tasked with taking the lead in finding James Farrar. It was Juliet Harper's assertion that Harvey, Farsi and Veronica Ellis were complicit in Farrar's disappearance, and at first Thompson had believed it. Harvey was obstreperous at the best of times, always insisting on looking in places she knew Farrar would never have visited. She'd been through the fugitive's file a dozen times, and instinct told her that Farrar wouldn't be caught dead in some of the third-world countries Harvey insisted on checking out. No, Farrar liked his luxuries and hated equatorial climates, so it would be somewhere with moderate temperatures, not too many bugs, and plenty of civilised company. That meant most of the places Harvey had suggested were way off the mark. Even when he'd recommended looking at more viable locations, she'd passed his suggestions on to the home secretary, who'd insisted on being the sole and final point of contact before any resources were allocated.

In the last few days, though, Harvey had seemed to go out of his way to get to Farrar, which wasn't something he'd do if he'd helped him disappear in the first place. He'd almost certainly sent Gray to Nigeria to look for him, based on the reports Mackenzie had sent her, and now Gray and Harvey had joined forces in Cuba.

Could Farrar really be here? If he were, then Gray had mentioned Jakarta in front of Mackenzie deliberately to put him off the scent.

Mackenzie had been one of the best in E squadron, which was why the home secretary had chosen him to work for Gray. She'd thought it odd at the time, assigning someone with such skill to a man who had nothing to do with the search for Farrar, but once Harper had explained how Harvey, Farrar and Gray had a common past, it made some kind of sense. The part about Gray wanting to help the man who'd tried to kill him didn't, however. As Harper had explained, it was the connection between Harvey and Gray that Thompson would be covering. There was no way to get Mackenzie close to Harvey without it seeming suspicious, but he was a natural fit into Gray's outfit.

And in that respect, the home secretary had been proven right.

But it still didn't explain why they were both searching for Farrar if they were the ones who'd helped him escape.

She thought about calling it in now and getting Harper's perspective, but with a tainted phone, it would be too risky. At the very least, it would alert Harvey to her presence on the island. She would have to wait until the morning to find another way to get the message to Harper.

If that was the right course of action . . . .

Conflicting ideas bounced around her head as she pulled up to her hotel, and when she reached her room she realised that she hadn't slept in over twenty-four hours. She set the alarm for eight in the morning and collapsed onto the bed, praying that a few hours of sleep would leave her with a clear enough head to make sense of this madness.

Chapter 39

21 December 2014

Harvey's Ford looked distinctly out of place as they cruised down the potholed road towards the meeting point. Graffiti covered just about every inch of the walls lining the street, the stores long since empty.

The meeting point was a warehouse that on first glance looked abandoned, but the man brandishing an automatic weapon as he stood by the wrought-iron gate told them they'd reached their destination.

'Tom, you come with me. Hamad, take the wheel. Any sign of trouble, take off and call Doug.'

Harvey and Gray climbed out of the car and Farsi shuffled into the driver's seat.

'You expecting trouble?' Gray asked as they walked towards the gate.

'We're dealing with locals,' Harvey told him. 'Who knows how this is going to go down. Just try not to piss them off, okay?'

'I'll be good, I promise.'

The armed guard nudged the nose of the weapon towards them as they approached.

'I'm here to see José. The name's Black.'

They were ushered inside, where two men stood next to a black SUV. The tailgate was down, and an array of weapons sat on display. The elder of the pair blew a cloud of cigar smoke towards the ceiling and gestured for them to come forward.

'Please.' He smiled, showing two rows of yellowing teeth. 'Select what you need.'

Gray looked over the selection, please to see that the Heckler & Koch weapons looked to be in decent condition. He quickly stripped one down and checked for dirt. It had been well maintained.

'Who's paying for this?' he asked.

'My boss,' Harvey said, 'so don't get greedy.'

'In that case, I'll take three of these,' Gray said, moving on to the handguns. He chose a Glock 17 and gave it a similar inspection, declaring it fit for purpose. Five of them were added to the growing pile.

'What are these for?' Gray pointed to items in the pile.

'Tasers,' Harvey said. 'I wanted an option other than killing everyone we come across.'

Gray shrugged, and continued to sort through the items on display. He chose some comm units and three sets of night-vision goggles. He checked the battery indicators and saw that the NVGs were fully charged, but the two-ways could do with a little more juice. He began loading everything into a holdall that was sitting on the floor. He included two Tasers to placate Harvey, then began cramming as much ammunition into the bag as possible.

'Do we get a receipt?' Harvey asked. 'I just want to make sure we get billed correctly.'

His request drew another smile from their host. 'This isn't Walmart, my friend. If you don't trust me . . . .'

'That won't be necessary,' Gray said, hoisting the bag onto his shoulder. 'I'm sure you'll come to the right figure.'

He started walking towards the exit, Harvey trotting to catch up.

Once outside, they saw the car waiting, the engine still running.

'And you told *me* not to piss them off,' Gray said, shaking his head.

'What if they decide to add a couple of attack helicopters to the list? Ellis is going to have kittens.'

'From what you told me, Ellis is out of a job unless we get this done right. And if we do, she'll be the last to complain about how much it cost to do it.' Gray dumped the bag in the trunk and they climbed into the car.

'I don't like the idea of leaving the weapons in the car for the next twelve hours,' Harvey said. 'I suggest we drive over to Farrar's place and stash them nearby.'

'Nice idea,' Gray said, 'but not too close to his house. There's a chance he might be out and about, and we can't risk bumping into him.'

He pulled out his phone and checked the local area on the map, then showed it to Farsi. 'Hamad, if you can drop us off here, Andrew and I'll take a walk into the woods and find somewhere to dump the bag.'

Farsi was looking at a satellite photo of a tight clump of trees roughly a kilometre wide and four hundred yards long. Via Blanca ran directly alongside it.

'No problem.'

It took half an hour to get to the location, and Farsi pulled over to the side of the road to let Harvey and Gray out. Traffic was thankfully light, and they crossed the highway and disappeared into the trees, the canopy blocking out the sun as they ventured deeper into the undergrowth. Gray checked for signs of human tracks and was glad to see none, meaning their stash was likely to go undiscovered for the remainder of the day.

'This will do,' he said, as they reached a tree trunk that looked to have fallen years earlier. Harvey kept watch as Gray carefully bent back some ferns and scraped out a shallow hole. He opened the bag and extracted the comm units and charger, then placed the holdall in the hole and eased the foliage back into place. He stood back a few paces and, satisfied that the weapons were sufficiently hidden, he marked their current location on his phone's GPS app.

They retraced their steps and emerged back into sunlight, darting across the road and back into the car.

'Where to next?' Farsi asked.

'Back to the hotel,' Gray said. 'Let's get something to eat and a few hours' sleep. I need everyone wide awake when we hit them tonight.'

Sarah Thompson saw the car carrying Harvey and his team pull over to the side of the road and wondered for a split second if they'd noticed her tailing them. She'd been following them since they left the hotel just before lunch time, and it hadn't been easy to keep them in sight as they entered one of the seedier areas of Havana. It was obvious from the bag Gray had been carrying that they'd acquired something—most likely weapons—during their brief stopover.

The previous evening had been the typical stakeout, so she knew that they planned to storm the house at some point. It was unlikely that they'd do it during the day, but she knew she couldn't afford to let them out of her sight. She tried to control her breathing as she maintained her speed, and she kept her eyes on the road while cruising past them as two figures emerged from the vehicle.

She watched in her rear-view mirror as Gray and Harvey crossed the road and headed into the trees, and once she was round the bend and out of sight, she made a U-turn and parked up facing the way she'd come. She got out of the car and walked back along the treeline until she could make out the front of Harvey's car, then made her way in amongst the trees. Down on her hands and knees, she edged closer to the car, moving slowly so as not to give her location away.

After ten minutes, Harvey and Gray reappeared, minus the bag. She watched them climb in, and then the car pulled off the grass verge and turned back towards Havana.

Torn between running back to the car to follow them and her curiosity about the bag Gray had ditched, she elected to let them go and walked to the area where Harvey and Gray had entered the trees. She easily picked up the trail and followed until it abruptly stopped near a fallen tree trunk. It didn't take her long to find the holdall, and a quick glance inside revealed the small armoury.

Thompson pulled out her phone, a new burner cell she'd purchased that morning. She'd had plenty of time to call Harper to update her on developments, but even now, she was unsure what to report.

How would the home secretary react to the news that Harvey and Gray had found out about Mackenzie, and that they were now here in Cuba and possibly on Farrar's trail? It certainly didn't make sense to her yet, and if she called it in she'd most likely sound like a babbling fool.

Still, she entered the familiar number . . . but something made her pause before hitting the button to connect the call.

She'd been wondering about Harvey's motives ever since she got on the plane, and nothing seemed to add up. If he were helping Farrar, then why come to visit him and leave such an easy trail to follow? On the flip side, he and Gray had just scoped out the house and looked ready to launch a full assault.

Could she have been wrong about Harvey? Was he really here to bring Farrar home? If he were, then it meant Harper's intel had been way off the mark.

Harper's intel.

It couldn't have come from within MI5, or Harvey, Farsi and Ellis would surely have known about it, and she'd certainly seen nothing about it over at Six before being assigned to the case. In fact, now that she thought about it, she hadn't been offered any evidence that the trio were involved in Farrar's disappearance.

So who had actually briefed Harper?

She cast her mind back a couple of years to the time when Harper's predecessor had been brought down after it emerged he'd been running a covert team led by James Farrar. Black-ops teams were part and parcel of every government, but this one had sought to kill Tom Gray and his close colleagues in order to preserve the lie that Gray had died during his siege. When news broke that the government were targeting their own citizens, the unit was shut down and several high-profile heads had rolled.

Had Harper revived it? Was that who had fed her the info?

It couldn't be. That whole episode was still under scrutiny, and it would be career suicide. Even if Harper had reformed the unit, she would have used them to investigate Ellis and company rather than adding Six to the mix.

And why assign Harvey to the search in the first place? If the home secretary thought MI5 were involved in Farrar's disappearance, the prudent thing would have been to cut them out of the loop. Instead, Harvey had been tasked with leading the investigation. On top of that, they were only allowed to allocate resources in the search for Farrar on the home secretary's authorisation. Harper had let Thompson have people to search in countries far from Farrar's actual location, but blocked her requests when they got too close.

With no other credible source, Thompson could only reach one conclusion: there'd never been any evidence implicating Harvey.

Harper had made the whole thing up.

Thompson shook her head. This was nonsense! It would have to mean Harper knew who had set Farrar free, and was using Harvey as a scapegoat.

Implausible as it sounded, nothing else came close to making sense.

She put her phone away and sat on the tree trunk, trying to think of a way to get a definitive answer. Confronting Harvey would tip her hand, but if she let Harper know what she'd seen over the last thirty-six hours, there was a chance that she might warn Farrar. If they were indeed working together, then Farrar would either flee or have time to prepare a welcoming committee for Harvey's assault.

She finally made up her mind, and opened her Text Later app. She composed a new message and keyed in the time to send it. Calculating how long it would take to reach Harvey's hotel, then have an in-depth chat with him, she added on an extra hour for good measure.

If her plan to get the truth from Harvey didn't work, the text message would reach Harper in the next three hours.

Chapter 40

21 December 2014

Gray knocked on the door and walked in, just as Andrew Harvey emerged from the en-suite bathroom. Farsi turned from his computer to look at them both with a broad smile on his face.

'Did you just get laid while I was in having a shower?'

'I wish,' Farsi said. 'No, I did some more digging on the Cayman Islands holding company that owns Sarah's house. She told you she was renting it from a relative, right?'

Harvey nodded.

'I think I know who.' Farsi turned the laptop screen towards Harvey, who saw a familiar picture.

'Juliet Harper?'

'She's Thompson's great-aunt. Harper's the youngest of five daughters, and one of her sisters is Thompson's grandmother.'

'It would explain why Harper put her in charge of the search,' Gray said.

Harvey stroked his chin. 'Yeah, and why she'd trust Harper, even if she was being fed a line of crap.'

'Also,' Farsi said, 'I've been checking Thompson's phone for new traffic, but she hasn't used it since last night. I think she may know it's being tapped.'

'That was to be expected. Once Mackenzie got free, it was only a matter of time before she figured it out. What about Harper's phone?'

Gerald Small had finally managed to get limited access to the home secretary's handset. He could intercept her newly written messages but was still working on getting into the text library, which Harvey would need as evidence.

'Tried that, but there are no incoming messages relating to Farrar.'

Harvey knew that when things went quiet, it was seldom a good sign.

'Hang on,' Farsi said, tapping away at the keyboard. 'Looks like we have another phone that's had Harper's number typed into it.'

'There'll be a lot of those, I imagine.'

'I know, but this one is eight clicks from us, and closing fast.'

Harvey was immediately alert, bending closer to watch the dot's progress on the screen. 'Download everything you can from that phone. Tom, let the others know to expect company.'

Gray dialled Smart's room on the hotel phone and asked him to come up as soon as he could. By the time he returned to the laptop, Farsi had the new phone's contents on the screen.

'Bring up that one,' Harvey said. Farsi double-clicked the file and a text message appeared on the screen.

Harvey located Farrar at 4 Avenida de La Mar, Havana, Cuba. He's planning an assault on the house.

Smart knocked on the door and walked in, closely followed by Sonny.

'What's the emergency?'

'Someone's tracking us,' Gray said, pointing to the laptop.

'Who?'

'We've no idea, but they appear to be heading this way,' Farsi said. He switched the screens to show the pulsing red dot, now only two kilometres away from their hotel.

'Let's get out of here,' Gray said. 'Grab your stuff and be in reception in one minute.'

He disappeared along with Sonny and Smart, leaving Harvey to throw some clothes on and grab his jacket. Farsi pocketed his wallet and passport, then closed down the laptop and joined him at the door.

Gray was already waiting in the reception area by the time they made it downstairs, and Smart and Sonny were only a few seconds behind them.

'What's the plan?' Harvey asked.

'I want eyes-on,' Gray said. 'We need to know who we're dealing with. Hamad, let's get you set up in the restaurant so we know when they reach the hotel.'

They found an empty table in the restaurant and Farsi opened the laptop. The red dot on the screen had moved closer, but was now stationary.

'Could be stopped, or just stuck in traffic,' Smart said.

'Sonny, come with me. We'll hide up near the entrance.'

Gray handed out the comm units and they did a quick check to make sure they were all working.

'If that dot starts moving again, let me know,' Gray said.

He led Sonny to the gift shop where they both bought baseball caps and sunglasses, then they walked out of the front door and through the large arch into the sunshine. Palm trees lining the approach road swayed gently, waving a welcome to a family of new arrivals that pulled up outside the building in an ancient cab.

'Over here,' Gray said, leading Sonny to the left, where a row of tables sat under a portico. Gray took a seat facing the hotel entrance while Sonny sat opposite him, and Gray used their comms to ask Farsi for an update.

'They're about twelve hundred yards out.'

'Roger that.'

A waiter appeared and asked for their order, and Gray requested two coffees, more to keep up the pretence than anything.

'Can you also bring me a newspaper?'

The waiter nodded and disappeared, returning two minutes later with a tray. He placed the drinks in front of them and offered Gray a selection of American broadsheets. Gray took the *New York Times* and paid the bill, adding a generous tip.

'*Now within five hundred yards.*'

Gray donned his sunglasses and held up the newspaper, peering over the top of it. He could just make out the entrance to the hotel grounds, and he saw a taxi turn onto the approach road, ferrying more guests to the hotel.

The countdown continued, until Farsi reported the target vehicle a hundred yards out.

'*Fifty . . . twenty . . . turning in now.*'

'Shit,' Gray murmured. 'There are two cars. Which one is it?'

'*I can't tell.*'

Gray watched both vehicles approach the front of the hotel.

'We'll have to wait until they get out and pick the most likely.'

Both cars came to a stop outside the main entrance, and the valet opened the door to what looked like a middle-aged hippy. He climbed in and drove the vehicle away as the woman made her way into the hotel.

'Not her,' Gray said, focusing on the other vehicle. The passengers were already decamping, and the three men looked more promising. He gave quick descriptions to the team, and once the trio had disappeared inside, he got up to follow them.

'Regret leaving the weapons in the woods?' Sonny asked.

'They're not going to pull guns in such a public place. Not with so much CCTV, and certainly not in Cuba,' Gray said. 'Let's try to find out which room they take and plan a little visit.'

As they entered the lobby, they saw the three men standing at the reception desk. Gray told Sonny to wait by the door and walked over to stand a few feet away from them, pretending to be engrossed in the selection of tourist leaflets. He chose one and scanned through it, all the while listening to the conversation between the trio and the receptionist.

The men seemed keen to book a scuba diving excursion, and spent five minutes arranging one affiliated to the hotel, then enquired about the local nightlife.

One of the men turned and caught Gray's eye, but there was no sign of recognition, and he began to doubt that these people were here for anything other than a few days of sun and fun. He went to join Harvey, who waited in the restaurant with Farsi and Smart.

'These aren't our people,' Gray said.

'You sure?'

'Positive. I eyeballed one of them and he didn't blink. Did you see the woman who came in before them?' he asked Smart.

'The frumpy-looking one? Yeah, she stopped at the desk for a moment, then went upstairs.'

'Then we wait for her to come down.'

After getting Harvey's room number from the receptionist, Sarah Thompson took the stairs to the third floor and knocked on his door. When she got no reply, she tried again, placing her ear to the door.

Harvey obviously wasn't in, which meant they probably hadn't returned to the hotel yet. Realising her best bet was to take a seat in the lobby and wait for them to return, and as she descended the stairs she decided to grab a sandwich for the stakeout.

On the ground floor, she headed to the restaurant, but before she got inside a man appeared at her side.

'Looking for someone?'

Thompson turned and found herself staring into Tom Gray's eyes.

'I see you recognise me,' Gray said.

Thompson cursed herself for being caught by surprise, but she quickly regained her composure. 'I'm looking for Andrew Harvey. I know he's with you.'

'And who might you be?'

'Sarah Thompson. We worked together.'

Gray gripped her elbow and escorted her into the restaurant to the table the team were occupying.

Harvey looked up, his face a mask of confusion.

'Hello, Andrew.'

It took a moment for Harvey to put a face to the voice.

'Sarah?'

Thompson offered a weak smile. 'I think we should take this somewhere private.'

James Farrar closed his eyes and reached down to run his fingers through Joel Haskins' hair. It had been almost a year since he'd seen his lover, and they'd been making up for it over the last forty-eight hours.

'You know, I think I prefer you as Efram. Why don't you dye your hair?'

Joel's head continued to bob up and down, but he found time to pinch Farrar's inner thigh. 'I hate it when you call me that,' he said.

'Don't you know it's rude to talk with your mouth full?'

Their bout of pleasure was interrupted by the telephone. It was the handset set up for the relay service in Manila, which forwarded his calls but looked for all intents and purposes to be the end point. Knowing that only one person had the relay's number, he pushed his boyfriend's head away from his crotch and snatched up the mobile.

'Your timing's impeccable,' he said.

'I see you're in Cuba,' Harper replied, ignoring his insolence.

'What the . . . ? I warned you what would happen if you tried to find me.'

'I wasn't looking for you, James. Every time someone enters any of my details into a device, the contents are downloaded and I receive a warning. Two hours ago, someone prepared a text message saying that Andrew Harvey has your address and is planning an assault. If you live on Avenida de La Mar, then this threat is real.'

Farrar sat bolt upright. 'That's impossible. I covered my tracks when I left Africa. It must be someone at your end.'

'Preposterous! I've had a tight rein on things from the very start. For the first six months I had MI5 searching for you on the quiet, with no external agencies involved. You, more than anyone, should appreciate how hopeless that made their task.'

'Well, they seem to be back up to speed now, don't they?'

'I put my own great-niece, Sarah Thompson, in charge of the operation and she kept me updated every day. Whenever they got close to you in Africa, I blocked their efforts. I fail to see what else I could have done. Needless to say, we probably wouldn't be having this conversation if you hadn't taken things too far.'

Farrar ignored the jibe. 'You should have taken Harvey off the case once the bombings started.'

'I did, James. I warned Ellis to drop the case, and when she didn't, I had her removed. I thought that would be the end of it, but Harvey appears more tenacious than I anticipated.'

Farrar cursed and reached for a glass of water. 'Who sent you the message?'

'I haven't got proof, but Sarah isn't answering her phone and hasn't been seen for two days. I think she may have tailed Harvey to Cuba. That message was typed into a phone but was never sent, which means she could have been trying to warn me but was interrupted.'

'Does she know your part in this?'

'Of course not.'

'You do understand what you're saying, don't you? If she knows my address, she'll want to bring me in. That would be disastrous for both of us.'

He waited while the home secretary mulled over the options, though he knew there was only one. He would have to move to a new country—that was certain. It also meant anyone on his tail would have to be eliminated, including Thompson. Would Harper condone terminating her own blood, no matter how distant the relationship?

He didn't have to wait long for the answer.

'Do whatever you feel necessary, James.'

'Understood. Tell me exactly what capabilities this system of yours has.'

'We can track the phone's location via GPS, download the contents and activate and view the camera.'

'Just what I need,' Farrar said. 'How do I access it?'

'That's out of the question.'

'If I'm to find Thompson and Harvey, I'll need real-time information. By the time they report to you and you find the time to contact me, Harvey could be ten yards away and I wouldn't know it. I needn't remind you what happens if I'm not able to intercept them and put a stop to their plan.'

Again the phone went quiet, but Farrar knew Harper had no option but to comply with his demands.

'Okay,' the home secretary eventually said, 'I'll get the NSA to create a new account, but you'll only have access for the next twelve hours, and it'll be heavily monitored. Deviate from the current mission in any way and you lose access immediately.'

'Understood,' Farrar said. 'Do you know how many are coming? You mentioned Harvey and Thompson, but are they alone?'

'I checked with Five and Harvey's colleague, Hamad Farsi, is also on leave. You'll have to assume he's with them.'

'Okay. Send me the login details as soon as you can.'

He cut the connection and looked over at Joel. 'We're moving. Send West in here and then start packing.'

'Where do we start?' Gray asked.

Thompson was sitting on the bed in Gray's hotel room, while the rest stood around her.

'How about Sarah here tells us what brought her to Havana,' Harvey suggested.

'I was following you, of course. I know you're planning an assault on Farrar's house.'

'Yes, we saw that,' Farsi said. 'We intercepted the message meant for your great-aunt.'

Thompson barely flinched. 'How could you possibly have got that? I was using a clean phone. Unless . . . .'

' . . . unless we had access to Brigandicuum,' Harvey finished for her. 'Yes, we do.'

'How? Your access was shut down.'

'It seems the NSA were so busy worrying about every other computer on the planet that they forgot to secure their own. Let's just say we found a way in.'

'What's important,' said Farsi, 'is that we know you're working with Juliet Harper to keep Farrar's location a secret.'

'I'm doing no such thing!'

Farsi opened the laptop and turned it towards her. 'Then explain this message.'

'I came here because I thought *you* were helping Farrar,' she said. 'Harper told me that you were suspected of helping him to escape, which was why you'd done such a miserable job of finding him for six months. When I followed you to his house last night, I thought it strange that you didn't just knock on the door, and when I saw you dump your bag of weapons in the woods this morning, I realised things weren't as they seemed. I wrote that message with the intention of coming here to talk. If I was wrong about you and anything happened to me, it would have gone to Harper after three hours.'

Harvey looked over to Gray. 'What do you think?'

'I think bringing that phone in here was a big mistake,' he said to Thompson. 'If we killed you, we'd be checking your phone, right?'

Harvey sighed and shook his head. 'That's not what I mean.' He paused for a moment, gathering his thoughts. 'Okay, Sarah, let's say I believe you. Why did you hamper my search efforts? I told you months ago that we had a lead in North Africa, but you denied me any assets to check it out.'

'That wasn't me—it was Harper. All requests for resources had to go through her, and she obviously knew that you were too close to finding him. She granted my requests for searches in South America and East Asia, probably because she knew Farrar wasn't there. Kept me busy and on what I thought was the right track.' She shrugged. 'Clearly, she played us both.'

Harvey stared at her for a moment, trying again to decide if she could be trusted. 'What about Bicknell Security? You told me you'd spoken to Michael West's client, but you couldn't have, because they never existed.'

'I only repeated what my operative told me,' Thompson said. 'I had someone call Harcourt and that was the answer he was given.'

It was just possible that she was telling the truth. Someone could have been manning a phone. One of Harper's people, perhaps, or even Farrar's. Efram?

Suddenly Farsi's laptop beeped. He hit a couple of keys, then turned up the volume.

'A call was just downloaded from Farrar's phone,' he said.

The message began playing, and nobody dared to speak as the conversation between the home secretary and Farrar filled the room.

'So much for blood being thicker than water,' Gray said, when the call ended. He looked at Thompson, whose face had turned ashen.

'I can't believe she'd do that,' Thompson murmured.

'I can,' Harvey said. He sat down next to her and put an arm around her shoulder, then looked up at Gray. 'We need a plan. Over to you.'

'Well, they know we're coming,' Gray said, 'but they don't know that *we* know. There's our advantage.'

'You still want to go in?' Harvey asked.

'If we don't, we tip our hand. Advantage lost. Hamad, see if you can trace the numbers Farrar's called with that phone. One of them could be his security detail.'

Farsi started typing away, and in a couple of minutes he had a tight web showing on the screen.

'All of these records are a couple of weeks old,' he said. 'There's no recent activity.'

'That's to be expected. They'll be using proper comm units while they're on duty, not phones, but as long as they're carrying them, it makes our job easier.'

'Easier, maybe,' Harvey said, 'but a full-on assault is still risky.'

'That's not what I was thinking,' Gray told the group. 'I say we lure his forces into a trap and take them out.'

'Sounds good to me,' Sonny said, looking down at Thompson. 'All we need is some bait.'

Chapter 41

21 December 2014

'I've got tickets booked on the first flight to Grand Cayman tomorrow afternoon,' Joel Haskins said, as he continued to pile clothes into his suitcase.

'You couldn't get anything this evening?'

'Everything's booked solid. Well, there was a flight to Moscow, but I didn't think you'd want to go there.'

'Damn right I don't. What time tomorrow?'

'Three twenty-five. Once I've finished packing I'll plan our onward travel.'

Michael West burst into the bedroom. The big soldier ignored Farrar's glare and addressed the pair matter-of-factly. 'Your system's online and we've got movement on the woman's phone. It left the hotel twenty minutes ago.'

'Heading here, I assume.'

West nodded. 'ETA fifteen minutes. My men are in position.'

Farrar looked at his watch and saw that it was barely seven in the evening. 'You don't find it unusual that they'd turn up before dark?'

'Not particularly,' West shrugged. 'I expect them to stop about a kilometre away and walk the rest of the way. They're probably planning to set up close to the house and wait until the early hours before attacking. Once they dig in, we'll surround them and take them out.'

'Let's hope you're right. I want you to leave two men here, though, just in case.'

'That's not necessary. We're talking about three people, one of whom's a woman. They're not likely to get past us.'

'Then you won't need eight men to deal with them,' Farrar smiled. 'Humour me.'

West tried to hide his frustration, but Farrar could see he didn't like the order. He didn't want to have to play the 'don't forget who pays your wages' card, because he knew full well that if he were to piss West off, there was a chance he'd simply leave and find another lucrative contract. Farrar paid West well above the going rate, but even a mercenary had his pride. And West was a bit of a loose cannon.

Thankfully, West nodded, got onto his comms and instructed one of the team members to pull back and protect the building. 'I'll be co-ordinating the mission from here anyway, so you've got your two. Is there anything else, or can I go and do my job now?'

Farrar let the impertinence slide. 'If you can do it without waking the neighbours, that would be good. We won't be leaving the island for another twenty hours, and the last thing we need is the local police turning up on our doorstep.'

'That was always the plan,' West said. He turned and marched out of the room, leaving Farrar to finish his packing.

'They're still holding their positions,' Farsi said over the net. 'Two are inside the building, two more at the rear of the house, by the beach, and the remaining four covering the approach road, one pair to the north and the other to the south.'

'Roger that,' Gray whispered. 'What about Sarah?'

'Right on schedule. She'll be here in ten minutes.'

'Copy. Out.'

Gray felt the damp earth soaking into his clothes, but there was nothing he could do about it now. At least no insects had decided to explore his face yet, which was always a danger when one was buried under three inches of turf.

It had taken two hours to get the three of them into position in a fifty-foot triangle around the fallen trunk where they'd stored the weapons. First, they'd marked out a plot twice the size of each man near the foot of a tree, then dug them out carefully. It had taken a lot of skill to get the grass out in one piece, and once the top cover was removed, a hole had been excavated underneath. The dirt was carried out of the area so as not to leave any tell-tale signs, and finally the men lay in the holes while their comrades gently covered them over again. Gray had been the last to be buried, so he'd had to recruit Harvey and explain what was required. He only hoped his friend had done a good job, otherwise his plan to make it home for Christmas was going to turn to shit pretty quickly.

Each of them had nose and ear plugs, and the NVGs covered their eyes, but there remained the chance that a beetle, or worse, might decide to investigate their mouths. It had happened to Gray before, and he'd once had to resort to eating a large centipede rather than giving his location away.

Cramp was another problem to overcome. To accommodate the night-vision goggles, the three men were forced to lie on their sides. The alternative was to leave the glasses off until they emerged, but as the purpose of the exercise was to gain the element of surprise, there simply wasn't time to jump up from their hiding places and start fiddling with the headsets.

If Sarah were minutes out, Gray knew he'd be in the hole for another three hours at the very least. Farrar's men would wait until dark to tackle them, he was sure of that. His main concern was that Farsi's laptop not run out of battery by then.

'Hamad,' he whispered, more to stop earth flowing into his mouth than anxiety over anyone hearing him.

'Go ahead.'

'Watch the juice on that laptop. We can't have it dying on us.'

'Already in power-saving mode,' Hamad assured him.

With that fear allayed, Gray tried to relax his mind. The plan was simple enough, and it was too late to second-guess it. Having intercepted the call from Harper to Farrar, they knew Thompson's phone would soon be tracked, so Sarah would meet up with Harvey at the side of the road, and it was Andrew who would walk into the woods and place the phone in the clearing. After that, he would retreat and the three of them would drive Sarah's car a mile to the east. Farsi would stay with it to provide updates, while Thompson and Harvey would walk north to the beach and lie up a few hundred yards from the house.

After that, it was simply a waiting game.

'They're here,' West said over the comms. 'Looks like they parked on Via Blanca. I've got movement north, through the trees.'

He received a series of double-clicks in his headset, confirming that his team had heard the broadcast. Each two-man team had a designation, and he began moving his pieces into position, like a grandmaster engaging in a deadly game of chess.

'Alpha, move west half a click and then south towards the road. If anyone's in the car, take them out.'

Click-click.

'Tango, move east two hundred yards, then south three hundred yards.'

Click-click.

With the two teams that had been covering the road moving to their new positions, he was left with the pair guarding the back of the house. It was highly unlikely that Harvey would have the skill or resources for a beach assault, so he ordered them around the building and told them to lie up ten yards inside the treeline.

'Now what?' Farrar asked. He'd been standing behind West, looking over his shoulder.

'We wait until they're settled into position. They're unlikely to strike until at least one in the morning, when they think we're at our weakest. While they count down the minutes, we move in closer. At eleven, we take them out.'

Chapter 42

21 December 2014

'We've got one vehicle, and it's empty,' the southernmost team reported.

'Roger, Alpha One. Target is two-five-zero yards north. Move in one-five-zero yards and hold your position.'

Click-click.

'No surprises yet?' Farrar asked. He'd left West three hours earlier and sought to reassure Joel, who'd become increasingly anxious at the thought of being caught in a shootout, but as the action began to unfold, he couldn't help but oversee it.

'Going like clockwork,' West said. 'My men are moving in now. They'll be on top of them in twenty minutes.'

'Why so long? Can't you hurry this up?'

'If they move any faster,' West said, as if explaining to a small child why they shouldn't eat from the cat tray, 'they'll give their location away. That would be bad.'

'There's no need to take the piss,' Farrar said. 'I just want this over and done with.'

'It will be. Just leave it to the professionals, okay?'

Farrar bit his lip and concentrated on the screen, though there was little to see. The red dot hadn't moved in hours, and West's men weren't highlighted on the map.

'How do you know where your men are?' Farrar asked.

'Practice,' West said. 'Besides which, I have the GPS location of the target, and my men have the same GPS app on their phones. They'll know when they're within range.'

It sounded like West had everything in hand, so Farrar told him he was going downstairs to get coffee.

'Black with two sugars,' West said over his shoulder.

'Movement your way,' Gray heard in his earpiece. 'Three hundred yards east, two-fifty west and two hundred south. Closing slowly.'

He gave two clicks in response, and felt his pulse quicken as the moment neared. After what seemed like an hour, Farsi updated the team to let them know the closest targets were at one hundred yards.

'Coming in pairs. Should be with you in ten minutes.'

Click-click.

Once the targets were inside the kill zone, Gray and his team would spring up from their hiding places and cut them down. It would then be a sprint down the main road to the house. Harvey and Thompson would lay down covering fire against the front windows, while Gray and the others went round the back and made their way inside. With Farsi calling out the enemy locations, it should be easy enough to eliminate the remaining threats.

'Len, you set?'

'Set.'

'Sonny?'

Gray waited, but got no reply.

'Sonny, you there?'

'Sorry, boss, I fell asleep.'

Much as he loved Sonny Baines, Gray found his sense of humour exasperating at times.

'Cut the crap,' Len broke in. 'It's grown-up time.'

'Roger that.'

'When they're inside the perimeter,' Gray whispered, 'we go on my mark.'

Farrar returned to the spare bedroom and put the cup down next to West.

'Almost there,' the soldier told him. 'Another five minutes and you can head to bed.'

Farrar took a sip of his own brew. 'Don't forget to hide the bodies afterwards. We don't want a dog walker to trip over them in the morning.'

West turned to say something, but Farrar's phone cut him off. It was Juliet Harper on the line.

'What is it now?' he asked.

'I was looking for confirmation that Sarah is there, so I had her phone downloaded. I can confirm that she's in Havana, but it seems she got a message from Paul Mackenzie to say that Tom Gray is with Harvey. You might have more company than you expected.'

'Gray's here?' Farrar glanced over to West, who glared at him with narrowed eyes.

'We're not certain,' Harper said, 'but he was with Harvey two days ago, in Kano. They know Mackenzie was working for us.'

Farrar covered the handset and turned to West. 'Tell your men to stop. There may be more than we thought.'

'How many more?'

'My guess is at least three. Tom Gray, Len Smart and Simon Baines.'

West got onto the comms. 'Wait one. I repeat, wait one.' He ignored the clicks coming through the headset and turned back to Farrar. 'I know Gray. At least, I know of him. He was decent enough back in the day, but he's been out for a long time now.'

'So have the other two, but they're like cockroaches: they refuse to die.' He told Harper he'd ring her back, then ended the call. 'So what's the plan now?' he asked West. 'Your men could be walking into a trap.'

'I'll send two in while the rest hang back. If it is a trap, we'll know shortly.'

'Something's wrong, Tom. The teams to your east and west are moving north towards the house.'

'What about the others?'

'Still approaching your position.'

Shit! Something had them spooked, and if the remaining four made it back to the house, it would be almost impossible to get to Farrar.

'Tell Andrew and Sarah to get between them and the house, and if necessary, stall them long enough for us to catch up.'

He hated the thought of pitting the pair against four seasoned soldiers, but he had no other option. Hopefully he and Sonny could take their targets out and reach the remaining threats before that became necessary.

'Roger. Your two targets are within thirty yards.'

'Tell me when they get inside the triangle.'

Sweat began to trickle down Gray's face as Farsi counted down the distance.

'Twenty yards . . . inside the kill zone, ten yards from the phone. Five yards.'

'On three,' Gray whispered into his mic. 'One, two, three.'

He threw back the turf covering him and sat upright, his silenced weapon coming up as he identified the first of the targets. The night-vision goggles outlined the figure in front of him beautifully; two silenced shots to the chest took him down. The second fell at the same time to a popping double-tap from Sonny's gun.

With the immediate threat eliminated, Gray rose to his feet and stretched his legs to get some movement back into them. As he walked over to the bodies, he called Hamad. 'Where are they now?'

'Seventy yards north, still moving slowly.'

Gray gave each of the corpses a head shot to be certain that they were out of the game. 'Let's go.'

He led the way at walking pace, doing all he could to keep the sound of boots on undergrowth to a minimum. It wasn't long before he spotted the next target, a man with his hand to his ear as he listened to an incoming message. Whatever it was, he never got to hear it. Gray brought him down with two rounds to the head, and his weapon was seeking its next mark before the corpse hit the ground.

Sonny's rifle spoke twice, and a fourth player was taken out of the game. Now muzzle flashes lit the trees like lightning as the enemy finally realised what was happening.

'Alpha One, report!'

'I hear gunfire,' Farrar said, standing to the side of the window that overlooked the woods.

'Someone, tell me what the fuck is happening out there!'

West was becoming increasingly anxious at the lack of response, and the fact that his men were shooting meant he'd underestimated his opponent. He went over to the window just as the first member of Tango team emerged from the trees and ran across the road. He made it to the other side before collapsing as if he'd been kicked in the back.

'Tango Two, what the hell's going on? Where's Echo team?'

The silence in his headset matched that from the forest, as the gunfire suddenly stopped.

Six men down.

There wasn't time to reflect on the losses. West knew the house would be their next objective, and he had to make sure no-one got close enough. It wouldn't be easy, as the enemy had the numerical advantage, but he could even that up a little.

'Charlie, get down to the basement and bring me two M4s and all the ammo you can carry.'

A minute later, the last remaining member of West's team entered the room with two rifles, two boxes of ammunition and a half-dozen magazines. He started filling them as West handed Farrar one of the weapons.

'You know how to use one of these?'

Farrar looked for the safety and switched it to three-round burst, then took one of the clips from Charlie and rammed it home. He racked the slide, putting a round in the chamber, and looked at West. 'Yeah.'

'Good. Give that to your boyfriend, show him how to use it and then come back for yours.'

Farrar ran to the master bedroom and handed the rifle to Joel. 'Ever fired one of these?'

Joel shook his head, so Farrar gave him a fifteen-second crash course before leading him back to West, who handed him another assault rifle.

'Where do you want us?'

'One of you cover the left side of the building, the other the right. Charlie and I'll take the front.'

Farrar grabbed four spare magazines and gave two to Joel before heading off to the window on the first floor landing. He opened it fully and stood to the side, only an inch of his profile visible from the outside. Looking down the hallway, he saw Joel copying him at the opposite window, and he gave his lover a reassuring smile before turning back to scan the night for Gray and his team.

'I've got movement at the side window,' Sonny said into his mic.

'Farrar?' Gray asked.

'Negative.'

'On my mark, take him out. Len, are you in position?'

'Roger that. Twenty yards inside the trees. I can see the first-floor windows but no-one near them.'

'Okay. On three, lay down suppressing fire while I get round the back.'

Gray was crouching two hundred yards to the east of the house, and he readied himself for the dash across the road. He started the countdown and waited until he heard the tinkling of glass as Smart took out the windows before running at full speed across the tarmac.

Two bullets pinged off the road in front of him, but he kept going, throwing himself behind one of the trees that lined the street. Two more rounds thumped into the side of the trunk, sending splinters of wood past his head.

With his colleagues otherwise occupied, Gray knew cover fire would be out of the question. He took a deep breath, then stood and sent a three-round burst towards the open window on the first floor, moving for the beach as he fired. He found cover behind another tree before more rounds were hurled his way.

'Target down,' Sonny said. 'Moving towards the rear.'

As Gray swivelled to let off another burst, he heard an animal cry from the direction of the house, and a silhouette ran away from the window. He took the opportunity to crab his way towards the sand, his rifle aimed towards the building, until he found Sonny waiting by the other end of the wall.

'You've been begging me to get you back in the action. Now's your chance. You go first,' Gray whispered. 'I'll cover you.'

Sonny smiled and vaulted the three-foot wall that ran parallel to the beach, then sprinted for the glass doors. Once in position, he motioned for Gray to follow him.

The first-floor balcony hung above them, and Sonny cradled his hands so that Gray could climb up. Once in position, Gray leaned over and grabbed Sonny's outstretched arm, pulling him up. They discarded the NVGs and found themselves staring into a huge bedroom, where four suitcases sat at the foot of a double-king bed. Using hand signals, Gray indicated that once through the door to the landing, Gray would go right and Sonny would head towards the front of the house.

On Gray's signal, they burst through the doorway. Sonny headed off to the open door opposite and his sights found a man's broad back. Three bullets dropped him to the floor, and after a quick scan for other hostiles, he moved on to the next room.

Back on the landing, Gray saw James Farrar weeping as he cradled a man in his arms, crimson running from a hole just above the corpse's right eye. Gray reached to his waist, drew his sidearm, and aimed it at Farrar's head.

'Farrar.'

Farrar's head jerked up and Gray found himself looking into the teary eyes of his nemesis.

'You might as well kill me now, Gray.'

'That's all I've ever wanted.'

Gray moved the sights down to Farrar's chest and pulled the trigger.

Chapter 43

21 December 2014

Harvey ran up the stairs and found Gray standing over Farrar's bloody body.

'What the hell have you done? I told you we need him alive!'

'Relax, Andrew. I just zapped him with the Taser. That's someone else's blood.'

Harvey approached Farrar's prone form, knelt and found a pulse on the man's neck.

'Hamad, bring the car round. We need to get going,' he said, turning to Gray. 'Have you identified any of them?'

'The one in the front room looks to be Michael West, the guy you asked me about a few days ago. I don't recognise the others.'

'Front's clear,' said Sonny, arriving at the landing and pausing to take in the scene.

Harvey pulled out his phone to take pictures. If any of the bombers could identify them, it would help to cement the case against them.

'Go and see if you can find any evidence of Farrar's involvement,' he told Thompson, who'd joined them on the landing. 'I know this guy. He'll have something. Flash drives, phones, laptops, bring it all.'

Harvey photographed the corpse lying next to Farrar. Clearly it was Efram, aka Joel Haskins. In the front rooms, they had West, who was a known player, and another soldier who wasn't. He checked the rear bedrooms, and found Thompson and Gray going through Farrar's luggage. Two USB drives had already been separated, as had a few CDs.

He walked back in the hallway, where Farrar was coming to, Sonny standing over him.

'Hello, James. Some people back home would like to have a word with you.'

'I want my solicitor.'

Harvey laughed. 'You think you're going back to a nice comfy cell to await trial? Fat chance. You'd be on to the home secretary asking her to pull some strings.'

Farrar glanced over to where Joel lay, the blood already coagulated around the head wound, his eyes staring up, unseeing. He turned back to Harvey. 'So where are you taking me?'

'South, to a little chunk of American soil.'

'Guantánamo?'

'Right first time. Come on, up you get.'

Harvey dragged Farrar to his feet as Gray emerged from the bedroom with a small bag.

'I think that's everything,' he said. 'Is there anything you'd like us to bring along, James? Anything that might incriminate the home secretary and save your own skin?'

'I don't know what you're talking about.'

'Save it for your waterboarding sessions,' Gray said. 'Sonny, get something to secure his hands.'

Sonny disappeared downstairs and returned a minute later with some electrical tape. He bound Farrar's wrists behind him and led him down the stairs. Outside, Farsi was waiting with the car; Sonny opened the rear door and pushed Farrar in, climbing in beside him.

Thompson took the front seat, while Harvey gave Gray the keys to the other car before taking the last seat in the vehicle.

'We'll wait for you on the top road,' Harvey said, and told Farsi to go.

Gray and Smart set off into the trees at a jog, their ride four hundred yards through the trees, but they'd barely broken sweat by the time they reached the car. Gray had just pulled onto the highway when flashing blue lights appeared in the rear-view mirror and turned off towards Farrar's residence.

Chapter 44

23 December 2014

Andrew Reed sat behind his ornate desk, hands folded in front of him and a grim countenance under his greying hair. He felt like he'd aged a decade in the last few hours, and the file that had been delivered to him that morning was the reason. He considered thumbing through it again, but the contents were already etched deep into his mind.

A knock on the door to his private office roused him from his thoughts.

'Come.'

Juliet Harper walked slowly into the room and stood before him.

'Prime Minister.'

'Take a seat, Juliet.'

Harper sat opposite him and straightened out her skirt.

'I received this file relating to the interrogation of James Farrar a few hours ago,' the PM said. 'So, where do we begin?'

'Andrew, you must understand that everything I did was for the benefit—'

Reed slammed his hand down on the desk. 'Don't you dare pretend this was about the good of the people! You killed thousands of them!'

'That was never the intention,' Harper said, her composure never waning. 'I envisaged only a handful of casualties. Farrar took my brief and manipulated it for his own purposes.'

'Ah, so it's all his fault.'

'It is. We need Brigandicuum, and without last week's attacks, you would have left it in mothballs indefinitely. Yes, people died, and I sincerely regret that, but we now have a defence mechanism greater than any nuclear arsenal. We can stop terror attacks while they're still in the embryonic phase.'

'So it was just a means to an end, is that what you're saying?'

Harper nodded, and the prime minister rose from his desk and began pacing, his hands in his pockets.

'When I came to power,' he said, 'we'd been sitting on the opposition bench for over a decade. We watched from the sidelines as the country spiralled into debt, education standards slipped and welfare accounted for the biggest percentage of our budget for more than thirty years.

'To inherit all that was already a major challenge, but when my predecessor told me about Brigandicuum, I made my feelings clear to you. The country was still reeling from the PRISM revelation, so there was no way I was going to activate something that made that look like amateur hour at the junior detective society.'

'If you had, none of this would have been necessary,' Harper said.

'Necessary? Are you mad? I made the executive decision not to bring it online, and that should have been good enough for you. If you didn't like it, you should have resigned, not planned a terror attack to have it activated.'

Juliet sat very still and spoke softly. 'My job is to protect the people of Britain from terror attacks. You were denying me the best possible tool to carry out that task. We're now safeguarded against anything our enemies can throw at us, and yes, people died in the thousands, and they'll be appropriately remembered, but what we did this week will guarantee our country's safety for years to come.'

Reed returned to his seat. 'That's where you're wrong. I'm taking Brigandicuum offline.'

Harper leant forward in her seat, her face colouring. 'You can't do that!'

'I can, and I am. What's more, I've a good mind to reveal its existence. No-one should have this tool. Not us, not the Americans.'

'You wouldn't be so foolish. That would damage this country more than the attacks. The Americans would simply find another way to implement it, and our relationship with them would be over. That's just for starters. Once people find out that the five major phone manufacturers and the dominant search-engine provider were complicit, those companies will be finished, resulting in the loss of hundreds of thousands of jobs in the UK alone. Never mind the effect on their investors and suppliers. With people thinking twice about using their phones and computers, commerce across every sector will be affected. This could knock the country back thirty years!'

Reed knew she was right. He'd already considered the implications of revealing the details contained within the file, and it didn't bode well for an already struggling economy. He would have to step down, of that there was no doubt, but that was a small sacrifice compared to what the people had endured.

Those facts aside, someone had to pay for the heinous crimes committed in the name of national security.

'Okay, so I don't make an announcement, but I still need to decide what to do with you.'

The faintest of smiles appeared on Harper's face. 'As you just said, this can't reach the public domain. You appointed me to protect the people of Britain, and I intend to do that for some time to come.'

Reed was stunned by her brazen attitude. 'You expect to walk away from this unscathed?'

'The official line is that Takasa died in an explosion last week, along with the rest of the DSA hierarchy. No-one knows that Takasa was actually James Farrar, and they don't need to. The smaller players are either dead or in custody. If you make me take the fall for this, I guarantee the details of this operation will reach the media.'

'Are you blackmailing me?'

'I'm just saying the loose ends are tied up, so there's no need to dwell on it.'

'You seem to be forgetting that Joel Haskins, along with Michael West and his men, were massacred in Cuba at the weekend. Then there's James Farrar to consider.'

'I already spoke to the Cubans,' Harper said. 'They believe a local drug lord was eliminating a new player. As for Farrar, he's no longer a problem.'

'Explain.'

'As you probably already know, he has a set of recordings that could expose our role in the attacks. As long as he contacts a Swiss solicitor every ninety days with a new password, those details remain buried.'

'Yes, I read about his leverage in the file,' the prime minister said, not liking the way the conversation was going.

'A close contact in the CIA tipped me off that Farrar had been taken to Guantánamo Bay. He's since been moved out of the country, safely under lock and key. I took the liberty of sending someone to explain to him that he will stay there until we need him again. It could be months, it could be years, but he'll remain incarcerated until that day arrives. Just as long as he plays ball.'

'You're seriously thinking of letting that madman loose again?'

Harper shook her head. 'Hardly, but it's the only hope he has left.'

Reed rose and began pacing again. 'That isn't the end of it, Juliet. What about the people who brought him in? There are several names in that file, and one of them is Tom Gray. Given that he knows your role in this, history tells me he won't let this go.'

'Then you'll have to take care of him. Offer him money, anything, just keep him quiet.'

'And if I can't?'

'Then you'll be known as the PM who brought his country to its knees.'

Reed sat back and stared at her, disgusted by the smug look on her face. What was particularly chilling was that Harper was considered by many to be his natural successor when his stint as party leader was at an end. He was looking at the woman who would one day lead the nation, and he had only a few moments to decide if he could let that happen. Could he allow such an extremist to take over the reins? If he didn't, the alternative had already been spelt out in plain terms.

'You make a very convincing case,' he said at last. 'Send David in on your way out. I have some arrangements to make.'

Harper smiled as she rose. 'You know it's the right decision, Andrew.'

Reed nodded, then turned to face the bulletproof window as she made her way out. A minute later, his personal assistant knocked and entered.

'Take a seat, David. We've got a lot to do.'

Epilogue

24 December 2014

Tom Gray handed his daughter another strand of tinsel and lifted her up so that she could hang it on the Christmas tree.

'Wow! Looks like we've got an interior designer in the family,' he said, even though the tree looked like it had survived an explosion at a bauble factory.

The decorations were put on hold as the intercom announced a visitor at the gates, and Gray carried Melissa over to the control panel, where he saw Andrew Harvey sitting in his car.

'Come on up,' Gray said, pressing the gate release.

Two minutes later, Harvey knocked on the door and Gray let him in.

'This is for you,' Harvey said, handing Melissa a large, colourfully wrapped present. She immediately began tearing at the paper, and Gray put her down on the floor while she ripped it apart to reveal a fluffy bunny rabbit toy.

'Thanks,' Gray said. 'I was just about to make coffee.'

'Just one sugar for me. I'm cutting down.'

Harvey sat in a chair and watched Melissa getting acquainted with her new friend while Gray disappeared into the kitchen. He was back two minutes later with a couple of steaming mugs.

'I trust you saw the PM's announcement,' Harvey said.

'You could hardly miss it,' Gray told him. Every channel had interrupted regularly scheduled programming to show the live news conference in which Reed had revealed the real people behind the recent atrocities. 'Do you think he'll survive this?'

'Probably not,' Harvey said. 'I think he was telling the truth when he said he had no idea it was going on, but will the public really buy it? And if he didn't know, then he seems incompetent, right?'

Gray nodded.

'Also,' Harvey said, 'he'll have zero American support after revealing Brigandicuum. It took them years to set that up, not to mention tens of billions of dollars, and now it's worthless—and a horrible embarrassment. I can't see them wanting to deal with Britain while Reed's still in command.'

'He must have known that was coming.'

'I'm sure he did,' Harvey agreed. 'Ironic, really. We get an honest prime minister, and it costs him his job.'

'At least Harper's going down with him,' Gray said.

'And I don't think she'll ever be released,' Harvey said. 'There are even calls on Facebook for the death penalty to be reintroduced in time for her trial.'

'That's hardly new,' Gray said. 'People are always asking for that, and we both know it'll never happen.'

'No, it won't.'

They sat in silence for a while, before Gray asked about James Farrar.

'He's on his way back from Incirlik air base in Turkey.'

'Do you think they'll be able to keep him inside this time?'

'Definitely,' Harvey said. 'They're recommissioning an old prison to hold everyone involved. They'll all be held in solitary until the trial, which is expected to take place late next year.'

'Why so long?'

'There are more than one hundred and fifty defendants. It'll take a long time to organise their defence teams, and the decision has yet to be made about whether they'll all be tried together, or in smaller groups.'

That made sense to Gray, but he didn't like the idea of having to wait almost a year to see justice done. And he was sure he wasn't the only one. Just about everyone in the country either had been a victim or knew someone who had. The news he'd watched that morning said it would still be months before the country fully recovered from what they were now calling Twelve-Fifteen, and for many it would live with them forever.

'Veronica wanted me to pass on her thanks,' Harvey said.

'It wasn't just me,' Gray reminded him. 'You and Hamad did most of the leg work.'

'I think specifically she wanted to thank you for not shooting Farrar when you had the chance.'

Gray smiled. 'In that case, she owes me big time.'

Melissa abandoned her new toy and began rummaging in the box of decorations. Quickly, she found a long red and silver garland and began towing it around the room.

'Have you got plans for tomorrow?' Gray asked. 'You're welcome to come over. It's just going to be me and Melissa, and we can't finish a whole roast between us.'

'I'd love to, but Sarah already invited me over to her place.'

'Really? Let bygones be bygones, eh? Despite her running Mackenzie?'

'Turns out he was Farrar's idea. He figured that once his disappearance made the papers, you'd get involved somehow. Mackenzie was supposed to be his insurance.'

'If he was Farrar's man, why go to the trouble of having Roberts take me out? Why not Mackenzie? Not that I'm complaining, but he would have done a better job.'

'Farrar wanted your death to look like just one of many during the attacks. If Mackenzie took you out, the trail would lead back to Harper, and ultimately to him.'

Andrew nodded, his coffee mug hiding his smile.

'Well, I hope you two make a go of it,' Gray said. 'Think you can keep hold of this one?'

'She already knows what I do for a living, so my long hours aren't going to be a strain on this relationship. I'm surprised you didn't spend Christmas with the in-laws, though.'

'I think they were less than happy at being dragged out of their home,' Gray said. 'I'll give them a few months to calm down, then pop over nearer Melissa's birthday.'

Harvey's phone beeped, and he checked to find a new text message.

'Still using a smart phone?' Gray asked. 'After all we've been through?'

'Brigandicuum is officially offline,' Harvey told him. 'This morning I spoke to Tony Manello, the guy heading it up, and he confirmed that the auto-kill function was activated. No more data will be collected from anyone's devices again.'

'You sound like you'll miss it.'

Harvey shrugged. 'On the one hand, we're still combing through the data we downloaded over the last week, and it was tremendous. We've identified over three hundred new potential threats from it already. On the flip side, once those threats are neutralised, there'll be another thousand to replace them, and we won't know about them until it's too late.'

'Sobering thought,' said Gray.

'Yeah . . . . From a security point of view, it's irreplaceable, but personally, I never liked the idea of everything I typed or said being scrutinised.'

'Then we're on the same page,' Gray said.

Harvey finished up his drink and placed the cup on the table, then removed an envelope from his pocket and handed it to Gray.

'It's from the PM. He wanted to make sure you were properly compensated for your services.'

Gray opened the letter and found a handwritten note and a cheque.

'That's very generous of him,' Gray said, noting the amount. 'I'll make sure Len and Sonny get their share.'

'That's yours,' Harvey said, tapping his pocket. 'I'll be going to see the others when I leave here. And keep that note for when HMRC comes calling. Reed stipulated that the payment is tax free.'

'I'll use it as a deposit for my new place,' Gray said. 'After what Melissa's been through, I've decided the time is right to move away. Besides, this place is too big for just the two of us.'

'Any idea where you'll go?'

'Just away.' Gray paused for a moment. 'I was going to speak to you about something after the holidays, but as you're here, I need a favour.'

'Name it.'

'New identities. For me and Melissa.'

'That's a bit extreme, isn't it?'

'Two weeks ago I would have agreed, but I haven't exactly been making any friends recently. I just want Melissa to have a normal upbringing, and that can't happen unless Tom Gray disappears.'

'What about your business?'

'It's in good hands. Len and Sonny are taking it in the right direction. I've already told them about my plans, and they're very supportive. They'll continue to pay me a consultant salary, so finding work won't be an issue. I'll share my new identity with them, but apart from us four, I don't want this going any further.'

'I'll have to get Veronica's approval,' Harvey said. 'That makes five of us in all.'

'Okay, but that's it. Not even Hamad, understood?'

Harvey nodded. 'Any idea where you'll go?'

'It has to be a place where Melissa can get a decent education. Perhaps Europe, maybe even Stateside. If you could organise a green card, I'd appreciate it.'

'I'll have a word with a friend, Doug Wallis at the CIA.'

'Okay, but no names.'

'No names.' Harvey rose and offered his hand to Gray. 'Best of luck with everything.'

'Thanks. I'm sure our paths will cross again one day.'

As Andrew Harvey walked out through the front door, he didn't doubt it for a second.

THE END

If you enjoyed this series and want to know when Alan McDermott will release his next book, just send an email to alanmac@ntlworld.com with Next Book in the subject line.

About the Author

Photo © 2013 Darlene McDermott

Alan McDermott is a husband and a father to beautiful twin girls, and currently lives in the south of England.

Born in West Germany to Scottish parents, Alan spent his early years moving from town to town as his father was posted to different army units around the United Kingdom. Alan has had a number of jobs since leaving school, including working on a cruise ship in Hong Kong and Singapore, where he met his wife, and as a software developer creating clinical applications for the National Health Service. Alan gave up his day job in December 2014 to become a full-time author.

Alan's writing career began in 2011 with the action thriller *Gray Justice*, his first full-length novel.